the wattle island book club

Sandie Docker grew up in Coffs Harbour, and fell in love with reading when her father encouraged her to take up his passion for books. Sandie first decided to put pen to paper (yes, she writes everything the old-fashioned way before hitting a keyboard) while living in London. Now back in Sydney with her husband and daughter, she writes every day.

www.sandiedocker.com
@SandieDockerwriter

sandie docker

the wattle island book club

MICHAEL JOSEPH

an imprint of

PENGUIN BOOKS

This book contains references to suicide. If this raises any issues for you,
help is available from Lifeline on 13 11 14.

MICHAEL JOSEPH

UK | USA | Canada | Ireland | Australia
India | New Zealand | South Africa | China

Michael Joseph is part of the Penguin Random House group of companies whose
addresses can be found at global.penguinrandomhouse.com

First published by Michael Joseph in 2021

Cover design by Laura Thomas © Penguin Random House Australia Pty Ltd
Cover illustrations: (background) Anastasia Lembrick/Shutterstock; (lighthouse) Eisfrei/
Shutterstock; (seagulls) asya_su/Shutterstock; (wattle) AlexGreenArt/Shutterstock
Typeset in 11/17.5 Sabon by Midland Typesetters, Australia

Printed and bound in Australia by Griffin Press, part of Ovato, an accredited
ISO AS/NZS 14001 Environmental Management Systems printer

 A catalogue record for this
book is available from the
National Library of Australia

ISBN 978 1 76089 037 7

penguin.com.au

For Mishell

One

Standing on the edge of the cliff, Grace Elliott turned her face to the sky. Her heart beat hard against her chest. Sweat dripped down her brow. She closed her eyes and drew in a deep breath. The air was cool; salt teased her tastebuds. Far beneath her the water flowed silently, at least from this far up. All she had to do was let go. Release the grip of pain and heartache that had smothered her for so long.

Opening her eyes, she looked down to the blue-black river that cut a deep scar from the Pacific Ocean in the east into the nearby mountains at the edge of the Great Dividing Range, then across to the grey rocks on the other side of the valley.

Grace knew the jagged stones and boulders below were far away, yet they seemed too close. Her hands began to tremble as she stepped further out on the metal platform. It swayed ever so slightly as she adjusted her weight, the clang of her boots on the perforated steel ringing in her ears.

'Just breathe,' the instructor said. Breathing was something Grace had mastered these past few years. She drew in the crisp, fresh air, the faint taste of eucalyptus catching at the back of her throat.

Despite what people said, she wasn't brave. She simply hid her fear well, buried it under false smiles and fake words that others needed to hear. She wasn't sure false smiles would help her current predicament, though. A predicament she'd willingly got herself into. But today was it: her last stand. Pain and fear had taken so much from her. Until now. This was Grace Elliott's definitive line in the sand.

The soft voice of the instructor whispered in her ear. 'Are you ready?'

With a slight tilt of her head, she nodded. Then she threw her arms out to the side and flung herself into the autumn air's cool embrace.

Wind whooshed past her ears, ever so fast, blocking out all other sound. A kaleidoscope of tumbling colour rushed around her, a blur of green and brown and blue, speeding in and out of her vision. She tried to swallow but her mouth was dry. Bracing cold water kissed the top of her head just as she jolted up, her body flinging back in the other direction. Up, up, she flew. And back down.

The river red gums that liked to hug the waterways in this part of New South Wales came into focus first as her body slowed, though they were the wrong way up. Up then down.

Then the silver platform from which she'd hurled herself sharpened in her vision, the blue sky bright and clear above. Autumn skies were Grace's favourite.

The thick elastic rope biting into her ankles steadied and cheers reached her ears as she swung back and forth, water dripping from her close-cropped hair as she hung upside down above the river.

'Woo hoo!'

'Way to go!'

Blood charged through her veins and she screamed, joy rushing through her every pore.

For the first time in ever so long she felt alive.

Sitting on the riverbank, Grace ran her hands through the sun-warmed grass as she watched and cheered on the rest of the group as they bungee-jumped from the platform one at a time. As each jumper made it back to ground safely, they also sat along the bank, in twos or threes, chatting to each other in between jumps.

Other than Linh, who'd come with her, Grace didn't know any of their names, but she shouted for them anyway. As a newcomer to the group, they knew nothing about Grace and she hoped she could keep it that way. That was at least, she supposed, within her control, unlike so many other things. She could tell them what she wanted, should anyone bother to ask, and leave out anything she liked.

An old lady with short lilac curls was last on the rope and a cry of 'Cowabunga!' echoed down the valley as the woman threw herself off the platform, a streak of bright orange and navy velour hurtling towards the river, arms flailing in joyful abandon.

'How awesome is she?' Linh plonked herself down beside Grace, her jump now complete. She shook her long hair, spraying Grace with drops of river water. Lucky she was Grace's best friend.

'And what do you reckon her story is?' Linh's dark eyes glinted.

This was a game they often played, making up life stories of strangers they observed.

Grace rubbed her chin. 'Hmm. Ex-French Foreign Legion, for sure. Or maybe a Cold War spy?'

Linh pulled her knees up to her chest and hugged them. 'Oh, yes. That's better. Her code name is Olga Romanov. She's retired now, of course.'

'Of course.'

'But she needs the occasional adrenaline fix after a life of excitement. So now she does crazy adventure sports. Her fake husband back on the farm has no idea.'

Grace smiled. 'She'd still be in the spy game today if it weren't for an accident on her last job that robbed her of hearing in her left ear. Pesky gramophone exploding at the ball of a mafia boss.'

Linh hit Grace on the leg.

'Have you ever thought about writing books?' Grace asked.

'Linh Tran.' Linh spread her hands through the air as if her name were up in lights. 'First Vietnamese-Australian to win the Booker Prize.' She collapsed in laughter, falling into Grace.

Grace put her arm around her. She didn't know how she'd have got through the past few years without her. Linh always managed to bring a smile to Grace's face, or keep her calm when she was nervous. Even this morning, on the bus trip from Port Maddison to the river location of their bungee jump, Linh's reassuring hand on Grace's shaking leg had been the only thing keeping her calm as she had stared out of the bus window at the Federation homes and Californian bungalows of her hometown melting into the green and brown shadows of the bush.

A cool breeze rippled over the water, reflecting fractured shards of soft light along the riverbank. From somewhere hidden in the tall gums, kookaburras laughed.

'So, what did you think?' Linh sat back up. 'Are you glad I talked you into coming today?'

'Ah, the other way around. I talked you into coming, remember?'

'Tomaytoes, tomahtoes.' Linh waved her hand in dismissal now. 'What's important is, did you enjoy the jump?'

Grace looked up to the clear blue sky. 'It was amazing. Without doubt the single most amazing thing I've done in a very long time.'

But then, that wasn't hard.

'Brilliant.' Linh put her arm around Grace's shoulder. 'You deserve to suck the marrow out of life.' She looked at Grace as she quoted the poem stuck to Grace's computer screen at work, a slight glistening in her eyes. 'Let's hurry up.' She cleared her throat and indicated towards the rest of the group, who were heading back to the minibus. She stood and held her hand out to help Grace up.

'Thank you.'

Arm in arm they joined the others.

A little way down the road from the bungee site, the bus pulled up outside the River Gum, a tiny pub in one of the forgotten towns dotted around the countryside. Located too far north of Sydney for a daytrip, many of these old colonial settlements had languished over the years. Only a few establishments, like the River Gum, had managed to adapt and survive, albeit as shadows of their former heyday selves.

Pristine baskets of yellow, pink, white and purple flowers hung from rusted iron beams that held a corrugated roof over a faded wooden veranda. Grace's mum would know the name of the pretty little flowers that looked out of place against their rustic backdrop. Impatiens? Pansies? Grace had never been interested in learning about her mother's favourite hobby. Perhaps she should add it to her current bucket list. Grace made a mental note to ask her mum about maybe starting a small garden in her front yard. What was one more task on Grace's ever-increasing list of dreams and wishes and activities?

She'd made her first bucket list when she was seven. Her Uncle Craig had put her up to it.

'Grace, it's good to have dreams. Big ones to chase your whole life. Little ones you can easily conquer. And if you write them down, it's more likely you'll catch them before you kick the bucket.'

Back then, Grace hadn't understood why anyone would want to kick a bucket and why you had to chase your dreams before you did. But she worshipped her Uncle Craig, and with yellow crayon on a piece of blue paper she took from her mum's craft stash, she wrote her very first bucket list.

Grace Elliott's Bucket List, age seven and one half:
- *Eat cupcakes for breakfast*
- *Join the Babysitters Club*
- *Paint hair pink*
- *Solve a mystery like Nancy Drew would*

On the morning of her eighth birthday, she'd sneaked into the kitchen and opened the Tupperware container full of chocolate cupcakes decorated with hundreds and thousands her mum had baked the night before, and scoffed five of them for breakfast. She'd been pleased with herself that she'd got so many down before her mum padded into the room in her blue fluffy dressing gown. Her self-satisfied grin had soon turned green, though, as the cupcakes churned and then ejected themselves from her stomach.

After a lie-down and some dry toast for lunch, little Grace had felt better, so she'd stomped into the laundry and kicked the red plastic bucket that lived there. Hard.

Stupid bucket and its stupid list.

But what if Uncle Craig was right? What if, once you kicked the bucket, the list of dreams disappeared? She'd raced back into her room and crawled under her bed where she'd kept her crayon list. Uncle Craig had said it was bad luck to show anyone your list and she'd hidden it there between the slats of her bed and the mattress.

She'd rested her head on the bed. Her list was still there. With a purple crayon she'd put a tick beside *eat cupcakes for breakfast*. Just like the one she had put next to *paint hair pink*, grimacing at the memory of her mum's loud screams when she'd found Grace in the bathroom a few months before the cupcake incident, the tube of pink paint in her hand, pink drips falling down her shoulders.

Studying her list, then eight years old, she'd realised she wasn't all that interested anymore in joining the Babysitters Club, but she still very much wanted to solve a mystery. The problem with that one was she couldn't find any. Not in Port Maddison. Maybe she'd need to move to River Heights and befriend Nancy to make that happen. Maybe that was one of those chase-your-whole-life dreams Uncle Craig had always spoken about.

Having swapped her purple crayon for orange, Grace had made some changes.

Grace Elliott's Bucket List, age eight:
- *Eat pancakes on the roof* (only one or two pancakes – she'd learned her lesson)
- *Meet Cory from* Boy Meets World
- *Play netball for Australia*
- *Feed a panda*
- *Study how Nancy Drew solves mysteries and move to River Heights*

The memory of her early bucket lists brought a smile to Grace's lips as she got off the bus. Every couple of years since then she tweaked the list; changed it, added new items. Well, *nearly* every couple of years. Bungee jumping had been added two years ago and it had taken this long to build up the courage. Among other things.

As the rest of the group piled out of the bus, laughing, trying to outdo each other with tales of how hard their hearts had been beating as they had flung themselves from the platform, Grace held back and took out her phone. She snapped a photo of the pub's exterior, the bright mixed with the broken, and filed it in her album named 'life's little moments'. The album she never showed anyone. Her own private record of how beautiful and fragile life was.

Inside, the pub was in much better condition than the rusted exterior would lead passers-by to believe. The booths, with wooden tables and brown leather bench seats, were clean and appeared to have been refurbished recently. And the woodwork of the sash windows was well varnished. In the back corner was a wide bar wrapped in a patchwork of corrugated iron in various shades of distress that appeared to be deliberate. This was where the bungee group gathered, around a pop-up banner.

The MAW logo was emblazoned across the top in blue and white and aqua, its motto, 'Get MAW out of life', splashed across the left corner. Uncle Craig would have approved of that, if he were still around. And he would have approved of this revitalised go-getter Grace too. A list of MAW's activities spilled down the banner like a movie credit roll. Skydiving, rock climbing, kite surfing, spelunking – Grace would have to look that one up – and friendship.

Friendship. Well, she wasn't sure there was room for that in her new action-packed plan for life. She was here for the adrenaline. The surge of life that ran through her as she jumped off a metal platform tied to a rope. She was here for the chance to feel alive again. And besides, she had Linh.

She looked around the group. It was unlikely she'd find any new kindred spirits among the motley band of adventurers anyway. Romanov, her lilac-tinted hair standing on end in all directions was at the bar holding a champagne flute, her sun-spotted pinkie finger delicately poised mid-air. She was talking to a thick-set man perhaps in his seventies – the guy who'd jumped first – and Grace was fairly certain Romanov was flirting with him.

There were others there around Grace's age, talking loudly and taking selfies in a tight group close to the bar. A couple – maybe they were a couple, Grace wasn't sure; they could have been siblings, as they did look quite a bit alike – were arguing quietly at the edge of the group. No one else seemed to notice the tiff, but one thing life had taught Grace recently was the power of observation.

It helped pass time during the endless waits and uncertainty, and kept her amused when little else did.

One of the group leaders was handing out beers to anyone who didn't have one yet, his head bobbing happily. He handed one to Grace, but Linh intercepted it, passing Grace a sparkling water.

'Thanks.' Grace knew Linh always had her back.

In time gone by Grace would have loved nothing more than a glass of cold beer after an exciting day out like this. But she hadn't had a taste for beer, or any alcohol since . . . well, since long enough that she didn't want to think about it. That was the old Grace. The new Grace found other joys in life now.

The rest of the group splintered into pairs and trios, sitting in booths, on stools, some ordering potato wedges, some talking about future adventures planned, some reminiscing about previous exploits. Grace sunk onto a stool at the bar, Linh beside her.

'So what about that guy?' Linh asked, pointing to a bald man in his sixties. 'What's his story?'

'A post-break-up refugee, desperately seeking something of the man that existed before his ex took his soul from him.'

'For sure.'

'And him?' Grace asked, indicating towards the man enthralled in Romanov's presence – broad shoulders, chiselled jaw, serious face.

'His name's Billy, but don't call him that. It's William. He hates Billy.' Linh's eyes narrowed. 'He's an ex-SAS from England. Those two have a lot in common.' She winked.

Grace nearly spat out her water, trying not to laugh. They continued imagining the lives of the MAW members, including one count of being fired from a job, one count of adultery, and one count of a gambling debt leading to financial ruin.

The whole time, though, Grace couldn't take her eyes off Romanov. 'Can you imagine us doing this sort of thing at her age?' Grace asked.

'How old do you reckon she is?'

If she had to guess, Grace would say the old duck was in her eighties. Not that her guess could be trusted. She was painfully aware of how life could sometimes swindle the years away from someone. 'I don't know.'

'Maybe we should ask her.'

'What? Go up and ask straight out? We couldn't. We're not that rude.'

There was a twinkle in Linh's eye. 'We can be anyone we like here. Even busybodies.'

Oh no she wouldn't.

'Excuse me?' Linh waved to Romanov to get her attention. 'My friend and I would like to ask you something.'

Oh yes she did!

'No, we wouldn't.' Grace slapped Linh's arm down.

'It's okay, dearie,' Romanov said. 'I'm an open book. Not too many secrets this lot have from one another.'

Grace really hoped that wasn't true. She didn't want this group knowing her secrets. She wanted to be normal. Plain old boring Grace, as normal as anyone else going. No baggage. No history. Simply living life.

As false a bravado as that might have been.

'Out with it.' Romanov raised her gnarled fingers, beckoning a response.

Oh to hell with it. Linh was right. Today Grace could be anyone she wanted. Even a busybody.

'Um, well, you were amazing today, and I was, well, wondering how old you are?'

She couldn't believe she'd come out and asked like that.

A look of serenity passed over Romanov's face. 'Dearie, I'm two husbands, three major wars, five great-grandchildren, three trips to England and one naked sunrise on a Hawaiian beach old. What about you?'

Grace had no response. None. She felt as small and useless as she ever had. And that was saying something.

Linh laughed and raised her glass in salute. 'Definitely a spy,' she whispered.

Grace shook her head. 'It puts life into perspective, doesn't it?'

Stark perspective.

Could Grace ever measure her life the way Romanov did? Of course not. She hadn't even had a first husband, let alone a second. She had no children and she'd never been overseas and had certainly never, ever, had a naked sunrise. Anywhere.

She'd measured the last few years of her life in specialist appointments and work commitments, not interesting destinations and exotic experiences. But wasn't that why she was here? Why she'd resurrected her bucket list after a few years of letting it slide? To fully experience life, like Uncle Craig had always encouraged her to. To put her past behind her, to close that chapter. To start counting moments instead of minutes. Long, wasted, painful minutes that stole her days and weeks. Her years.

The Maddison Adventure Warriors was Grace putting a little Romanov back into her life.

She sat up straighter.

'Cheers.' Linh clinked her glass with Grace.

'Cheers.'

Grace made a mental addition to her bucket list.

- *Naked sunrise on a beach*

Two

The next morning, Grace emptied the last few mouthfuls of muesli from her breakfast bowl into the bin beneath her yellow laminate benchtop. She didn't have time to finish them. Or the stomach, really. Another one of the side effects of her life recently. But instead of dwelling on that, she thought about the thrill of yesterday's bungee jump.

It had taken her ages to wind down last night and then, of course, she'd slept in. Her habit of spending way too long in the kitchen each morning hadn't helped keep her on time today either. A year ago, she'd painted the original white subway tiles that had come with her tiny Californian bungalow sky blue in an attempt to brighten her world. And it had worked. The morning sun beamed in through the sash windows, bathing the whole room, and Grace, in warmth and light. This morning, basking in the glow of her favourite room and the memory of yesterday's adventure, she'd sat at the small dining table a little too long. And now she would be late to work.

Not that anyone would mind. They always cut her slack. But she was only happy to accept it when she genuinely deserved it – if she was sick, or had an appointment. It never sat right with her if they excused her tardiness out of pity. A bungee jumping hangover wasn't exactly a valid excuse.

In the hallway she pulled on her comfortable black flats that lived, when not worn, under the white table below the unadorned picture rails. Grace had had so many plans for her 1930s home when she'd bought it five years ago – her twenty-five-year-old self had been full of excitement for the place's potential. Some of those plans she'd realised, like stripping out the horrendous 1970s brown carpet, and having someone render and paint the original red-brown brick facade. Most she hadn't.

She smoothed her hands over her black linen trousers. They were only a month old but the waistband was already loose. She didn't like wearing belts, though, the way they dug into her skin, and she didn't want to waste time shopping for new clothes, time she could spend on far more important things, so she would make do.

Above the hallstand was the only mirror in her house, hung at exactly head height so she could check her hair. Her auburn pixie cut was perfectly in place, the tinge of red still new to her. If there was an upside to the physical trauma she'd been through over the past few years, it was her stylish new do. And every morning she took a moment to bask in the joy it gave her, reminding her she was still here.

Her other physical changes she was less inclined to be reminded of.

She trailed her fingers through her collection of book-themed pins in the glass bowl on the hallstand, choosing the red bookworm, pinning it to her white cotton top. Red was her favourite colour, but she couldn't risk wearing it.

There was a familiar beat to the knock on the front door.

'Are you home, love?' June called.

'Right here, Mum. Just about to head to work.' Grace rushed to the front door, hoping to head her mother off before she could get inside. Curse the day she ever gave June a key. Not that she'd had much choice.

'Ah, there you are.' Her mum stepped inside, unwrapping her crocheted cotton scarf from around her neck and laying it on the side table, right next to the official photo taken yesterday of Grace hanging upside down. Everyone had come away with a 6-by-8-inch print of their jump.

'What's this?' June tried to cover her frown, but she wasn't as skilled as Grace at hiding her feelings.

'Nothing.' Grace reached for the picture, but her mum was fast. Especially when her my-daughter-is-trying-to-hide-something-from-me sense was tingling.

'So this is what you haven't been telling me.' June raised her gaze over the edge of her blue-rimmed spectacles. 'I knew you were hiding something.'

'Sorry, Mum.' Grace nodded. It wasn't the only thing she was keeping from her mother, but she knew it was better that June believed it was. 'I didn't want you to worry.'

'I'm your mother. It's my job to be concerned about you.' June flicked her long straggly grey hair behind her shoulder. She had aged so much in the past few years, and looked much older than her fifty-three years.

'I know, Mum. But maybe we both need a break from the worry.' Grace certainly did. And she'd been the cause of far too much of it for June lately.

June reached out her hand and brushed Grace's cheek, just like she used to when Grace was a kid and she fell off her bike or grazed her knee sliding down a hill or collected any number of bumps and bruises. A touch from her childhood she still so desperately needed. A touch that used to take all the pain away.

'I have to get to work, Mum. Can I tell you about it later?' Grace picked up her handbag, hoping her mother would take her not-so-subtle hint.

'Of course, dear. I didn't mean to get in the way. I thought you'd be gone already.'

Every second Monday June came over to weed the garden. That was the arrangement in theory, one they had put in place when Grace first got sick. It had been something for June to focus on, distract herself with – an excuse for her to hover close to Grace during treatment. Of course, June did more than that in her fortnightly visits, especially with Grace now back at work. She cleaned the bungalow from top to bottom, cooked and froze meals, did a load of washing. Not that either one of them acknowledged it, both needing to feel they were doing the other a favour.

'Go, go.' June shooed her away. 'Don't let me hold you up.' She cast her eyes back down to the photo. A familiar look of fear flashed in her eyes.

'Mum, relax. It was perfectly safe.'

'Of course. I just . . . ever since the . . .' She left her unspoken word hanging in the air. She never said it.

Cancer.

'Mum.' Grace took her mother's hand and squeezed it gently.

'I only want to make sure you're looking after yourself, love.' June's eyes dropped. 'Not pushing yourself too hard.'

'I'm not. I promise.'

Guilt wrapped its tentacles around Grace's heart. The past few years had been so hard on June. Grace didn't like keeping things from her. But sometimes – this time – it was for the best.

If Grace had learned anything since her diagnosis, it was that hope was what kept you going. And if she could give that to those around her, then she would. Especially her mum. It had been just the two of them since Grace was ten, when her father died. But June had stayed strong. When Uncle Craig, June's twin, had passed away when Grace was twenty-one, June had remained strong. But when Grace got sick, June had begun to crumble. Ever so subtly, but Grace noticed – fewer trips to the hairdresser until she stopped going altogether, a blouse not ironed, a scratch not seen to, a hole in her normally pristine jacket.

The least Grace could do now was protect her.

'Mum, you really don't need to worry so much. Look at me.' Grace smiled. 'Honestly, do I look like I'm taking care of myself, or like I'm not?'

June shrugged. 'Actually, you look great.' She stepped closer and scrutinised Grace, the way only a mother can, her pale eyes narrowing. 'A little thin in the waist, but your cheeks are full. And those beautiful baby blues of yours . . .' she stopped, smiled. 'A hint of your old spark, perhaps.'

Grace knew she was looking the best she had in a long time. It was a common misconception that people who had cancer *looked* sick. Other than when she'd lost her hair to chemo, though, no one would have ever looked at Grace and questioned her health. Misconceptions weren't always a bad thing.

'Yep. Best I've felt in ages.' She looked at her watch. 'Now I really have to go.'

'Don't work too hard. They expect too much of you, you know.'

Grace kissed her mum on the cheek as she headed out the door.

'Why don't I stop by and cook dinner tonight?' June called. 'See if we can't get some meat back on those bones.'

Grace's heart swelled with love as she walked down her front path and the tentacles of guilt tightened ever so slightly.

Standing outside the Port Maddison Regional Library, Grace paused, as she always did, before entering the sliding glass doors, a smile spreading across her face. Throughout her recent ordeal this place had been her one constant. Working between treatments had been a warm and familiar retreat, a safe beacon that life was still normal, when it was anything but. And on the days and weeks she was too ill to leave her home, her library family had organised a rotation of books to be delivered, so Grace could escape between the pages into worlds far brighter and happier than her own.

'Good morning, Gladys.' Grace waved to the old lady sitting on the concrete bench outside the library. Shaped like an open book, the royal-blue bench had been part of the library's renovation five years ago. And five years ago Gladys had taken up dawn-to-dusk residency on it, feeding the seagulls that came in from the harbour two hundred metres down the gentle green hill.

'Morning, Grace.' Gladys nodded, putting down her book – the latest in the No. 1 Ladies' Detective Agency series. She'd read almost all of them now. Grace would have to put her thinking cap on to pick a new title for her before sunset.

Stepping through the glass doors as they separated to grant her entry, Grace drew in a deep breath and held the woody vanilla aroma in as long as she could before letting out her breath slowly. She loved the fact that no matter how modern a library might be, the smell was still the same.

Inside, white shelves snaked around the open space, downlights overhead following their tracks. In the back corner the kids' section was an explosion of primary colours, and the eastern wall of windows overlooking the harbour led to a covered outdoor deck.

At the borrowing desk, Linh greeted Grace with a wink, as she checked out Mr Bartlett's weekly haul of ten books – five hard-hitting crime novels, five bodice-ripping romances. He was always their first patron on a Monday morning.

Grace made her way to the back of the library where the offices and storage rooms were hidden behind white woodgrain-panelled walls. Her first job of the day was to add the new book club tubs to the catalogue and box them up in sets of ten, complete with discussion questions printed out and slipped into the accompanying folder. As much as she loved interacting with the patrons, the quiet seclusion of her tiny sorting office was exactly the peaceful start to each week that helped ground Grace in her work world.

She hummed to herself as she started boxing up the new additions to the library collection, sticking the laminated cover sheets to the lids. When she had taken over running the library's book clubs six years ago, there had only been eight of them, and management had been ready to get rid of the program entirely. But Grace had fought hard to keep the book clubs and worked to build their numbers. Now, the tiny Port Maddison Regional Library serviced fifty-three book clubs with names like Wordy Women, Read Between the Wines and Words and Nerds. They were Grace's pride and joy.

The air-conditioning was turned up and goosebumps danced across Grace's arms. Linh always liked to set it to 'arctic' when she opened in the mornings, which Grace didn't mind at all. Layers had been her best friend since her diagnosis and she wrapped the shawl she kept in her room around her shoulders and settled back to work.

Right before lunch, Grace's skin burst into a heat so intense that not even the air-conditioning could help her. She tore off the shawl and grabbed one of the tub lids to fan herself with. And she counted in French. *Un, deux, trois* . . . Numbers were about all she remembered from her high school language classes, and somehow it helped to pass through the hot flushes – a lasting side effect of her surgery – to imagine she was sitting under the Eiffel Tower, so very far away from her reality.

Sweat dripped down her face and along the curve of her neck. She fanned the white cotton shirt, pushing cold air onto her burning skin. At least the cotton would dry quickly and the colour wouldn't stain.

Soixante-trois, soixante-quatre, soixante-cinq.

A little over a minute. A quick one. She took a long sip of water from her ever-present bottle. She wouldn't be sorry to see the back of these flushes now she was finished with her treatment, that was for sure.

'Hey, Grace.' Linh walked in and stopped when she saw her. 'Oh. Are you okay?' She handed her the roll of paper towel that was kept on the top shelf just inside the door.

'Yep. Just give me a minute.' Grace dabbed her face dry.

The temperature of Grace's skin started to drop almost as quickly as it had risen and she smiled at her friend.

'So,' she said. 'Next adventure is skydiving. Are you in?'

The colour drained from Linh's face. 'Bungee jumping is one thing.' She put her hand up in protest. 'But skydiving? Are you mad?'

'Quite possibly. You do remember the promise you made to me in the hospital? To do anything to make me feel better . . .'

Linh's eyes flared but there was kindness behind her false ire. 'I meant bring you soup and chocolate. Not throw myself out of a plane.' Her eyes narrowed. 'How long are you going to hold that over me?'

'As long as I can, Linh Tran.' Grace grinned. 'A pact is a pact.'

Linh pursed her lips and said something under her breath in Vietnamese that Grace was fairly certain was a swearword.

Despite her protestations, Grace was sure Linh would enjoy MAW's next adventure. Besides, it was Grace's duty as her best friend to help her expand her friendship horizon. If the past few years had taught Grace anything, it was that not a soul on this earth had any idea what was coming next.

Linh had mostly kept to herself since arriving in Port Maddison. A small town at heart masquerading as a regional hub, the thirty-odd thousand locals tended to be cautious of newcomers, and Linh was terribly shy, preferring the company of books to people most of the time. The bold Linh that Grace had seen at the bungee jump just needed a little more encouragement.

Linh had been a trusted friend whenever Grace had had chemo. Now Grace was finally done with treatment, it was time for her to repay her for all her kindness and, most importantly, drag her into a wider social circle.

'So you'll come?'

'Do I have a choice?'

'Not really.' Grace batted her eyelids.

'Sometimes I hate you, Grace Elliott.'

'No you don't.'

'Yes, I do,' Linh said, turning to walk out, a broad grin on her face.

Just then, the phone in Grace's office rang. It was a call being forwarded from the front desk.

'Hello?' The voice of an older woman sang out. 'Is that Miss Elliott?'

'Yes.'

'The lovely man who answered said you are the lady in charge of the book clubs at Port Maddison Regional Library.'

'That's right. How can I help you?'

'Excellent. I have decided to resurrect the Wattle Island Book Club, and I'd like to talk to you about the possibility of availing ourselves of your services.'

'I'd be happy to help you Mrs . . .'

'Sato. Anne Sato. The thing is, it's been some time since we were active, seven years in fact, and to be perfectly frank, I need some help getting it off the ground again, and sourcing some decent material to read.'

Grace smiled. 'Then you've come to the right place.'

'Thank you. I love my old group and I miss our meetings terribly, but none of us are spring chickens anymore and I dream of the Wattle Island Book Club lasting long after I'm gone. And this is where I need your help, Miss Elliott.'

'Please, call me Grace.'

'Grace. Our selection of novels on the island is rather limited since our bookshop closed.'

'Oh, I'm sorry to hear that.'

'Yes, well, that's another story. Would you be interested in helping me start up our book club again? Perhaps suggest a few titles? No subject matter is off limits. And perhaps we can discuss the logistics of our partnering in this venture.'

Grace drew in a breath, hoping Anne might do the same – the woman could apparently talk without pause. She took some information from Anne and promised to figure out the details. Helping Anne choose titles would be easy enough. Matching people with books was a skill Grace prided herself on. How she'd get the books to Wattle Island was another matter entirely.

'Thank you, Grace. You've made an old woman very happy.'

Grace smiled. 'I look forward to speaking with you again, Mrs Sato.'

'If I'm to call you Grace, you can call me Anne.'

'Goodbye, Anne.'

'Goodbye, pet.'

As Grace reached over to hang up the telephone, she heard distant, muffled words from the receiver that sounded something like, 'This might actually work.'

'Anne? Are you still there?'

'Sorry, pet.' Anne's voice called out. 'I can never figure out if I've hung up this new smarty-pants phone.'

Grace stifled a laugh. 'Is there a red button?'

'Oh yes. Here it is.' The phone went dead.

Grace sat back in her chair. Well, well, well. An island book club. That was a new one. The magic of books lay in their ability to transport readers to another time and place. The idea that the library's book club sets could head off on an adventure of their own across the seas was a reversal of that magic that Grace found poetic.

How would she get tubs of library books to a tiny little speck of land 500 kilometres out in the Pacific with only irregular direct flights from here, though? This would take some planning.

She paced her tiny office. Grace had never been to Wattle Island, though everyone in town knew of its natural beauty and its remoteness, a combination Grace thought rather mysterious. Port Maddison was the only town that serviced the island, with a supply boat sailing—

Yes. The supply boat.

She opened the library database and called Captain Jeremiah Allen of the *Seafarer*. He'd been running the service for as long as anyone in town could remember and was a regular at the library. He'd surely be willing to help her out.

In a gravelly voice, the old sea dog told her what she'd need to know about schedules and logistics and Grace took notes.

'So, they're starting up again.' He clicked his tongue. 'After all these years. I never thought, not after . . .'

'After what?' Grace leaned in closer to her desk.

He cleared his throat. 'Huh?'

'You didn't think they'd start up again after what?'

'Ah, nothing. Nothing you need to concern yourself with. Let me know when you want to kick this off.'

He hung up before Grace could ask any more questions and she was left with a tinge of curiosity that made the hairs on the back of her neck dance.

Three

Anne Sato sat in the old wicker chair on her tiny veranda, looking out to the vast sea. Her cottage was perched so high on the cliff that she could hardly hear the waves crashing below. Only a few days had passed since her first call to the Port Maddison library, yet already her book club was taking shape. Adjusting her red-rimmed glasses, she double-checked her phone, ensuring she'd hung up properly this time. Miss Elliott – Grace – had been ever so helpful once again. It was only their second call and she'd already figured out the logistics, and this afternoon, as the sun bathed Anne's little corner of the island in a soft yellow glow, they'd settled on their first title.

Anne had thought something a little risqué, exciting, might be a good way to drum up interest. But Grace had suggested she go with something safer – and something well-known if Anne wanted to attract some younger members.

So *Bridget Jones's Diary* it was.

Anne hadn't actually heard of it, but Grace had assured her

anyone under fifty would have. Grace would also send along some questions to help them get started.

Anne hauled herself up, pulling herself away from her view, and stepped inside her cottage. To the side of the door was a hallstand and from within the drawer she took out her favourite Japanese silk scarf of teal and green blossoms and wrapped it around her head, tying a thick knot over her left ear. She slipped on her gold brocade flats, adjusted the emerald green folds of her loose silk maxi dress, lifted her patchwork tote bag onto her shoulder and headed out the door.

The day had been bright and clear, far too bright for her to bring out her inks and start moving them across a canvas; too light for anything moody. Perhaps this evening the clouds would come over and create an atmosphere she could work with.

It was a lovely afternoon for a walk, though.

She passed the row of wooden white-washed cottages that lined the headland down the hill to the beach. They all looked the same: square, squat, two windows in the front, and gabled roofs of corrugated iron. The houses were former army residences from way back when the island served as a training outpost during the Second World War. Now, only a few were occupied by those who wanted a simple existence with a view of the sea. The rest were rented out as holiday homes, mostly in the summer. The only feature to distinguish the houses on Soldiers' Way from each other were their coloured doors. Hers, of course, was dark blue, the colour of the inky sea on a broody day, and her neighbours took it in turns to reflect the rainbow with red and yellow and green running down the street. The last house in the row, before the slope levelled out, was Hamish's. Of course he had to upset the status quo and have a boring old black door, which looked most out of place, if you asked Anne.

Ever since he retired to the island twenty years ago, she'd tried to encourage him to splash out with a bright orange, or pale purple, but he always refused. 'Black is classic,' was his standard response. Anne never understood how a man of music – if you could call bagpipes music; she still hadn't made her mind up about that – was unable to embrace the charm of the rest of Soldiers' Way. But she never pushed. She owed him so much, she could forgive him this one character flaw. Well, two character flaws, if you counted those infernal bagpipes.

Anne turned towards the town, which was tucked in under the hills that folded on top of each other to form the headland. In summer it would be throbbing with tourists. Well, relatively speaking, anyway. But now, as the first hints of winter began to push the remnants of autumn aside, it was only the locals in residence, plus a few scientists who seemed to flit in and out at various times of the year to study the flora and the Wattle Island gull, and a small handful of adventure tourists who liked the bush tracks and diving and didn't mind the unpredictable weather the season brought with it.

The shops had begun to close and there weren't too many people about. The bakery was dark, the hairdresser was pulling down her blind and waved to Anne. The lights in the pub were on and it wouldn't be long before the locals trickled in for their after-work refreshment. Maybe she could put a flyer up on the pub's noticeboard about book club – an open invitation to anyone who wanted to join in. Not that it was the new readers she was worried about.

Perhaps it was foolish of her to try to restart the book club. Would the memories of the last time they'd gathered be too strong? Would people want to come again after all this time and all that had happened? Despite her doubts, Anne knew she had to try. They'd been languishing for too long, all of them. Not that they didn't have reasons, but languishing at her age was a certain precursor to death. And she'd have none of that. Besides, they needed something to bring them back together.

Most of the scars of that wretched night had faded, and on the surface, Wattle Island was the idyllic haven it had always been. But there had been a shadow hanging over them for seven years and she knew she had to set things right before it was too late.

If her stroke last month had taught Anne one thing, it was the stark realisation of her own mortality. And simply waiting and hoping the shadow would lift wasn't working. How could it? Waiting and hoping were poor substitutes for action. Of course they'd never be the same, none of them. But that didn't mean she couldn't try to breathe life back into her friends and family.

She would need to continue her ruse that she was fully recovered and capable of taking on the task of running the book club, but she'd learned in the last month to mask the slight paralysis and weakness she still had in her left hand. As far as any of them were concerned, she was back to her normal self.

But, of all the hurdles in front of her that she would have to overcome to start up the book club again, her physical limitations would be the easiest. Maybe she should start a choir instead. That would be perhaps better received. Except she couldn't sing. Or a toastmasters group. She could definitely hold an argument. Or a knitting circle, maybe? Except she hated knitting, and that would hardly help her hide the issues with her hand. And besides, book club had brought this town together so long ago and held them together for all those years. Perhaps now it could help them move on from that tragic night.

Anne stopped in the middle of the main street as Maree came out of the general store, just as Anne knew she would at this time of day. Maree was predictable in her Friday shop, so much so that

Anne could probably guess what was in the hessian tote bag she was carrying: Earl Grey tea, pre-sliced cheese, a half-loaf of wholemeal bread, a cucumber (always a cucumber), and a packet of Tim Tams.

This would be Anne's first test. She drew in a deep breath. Maree was one of the original members of book club. And she had been there that awful night seven years gone – one of the first on the scene, in fact. If Anne could get her on side, there was hope.

Maree waved at Anne and stopped right in front of her, her face so close Anne could see the fine wrinkles in her brow, despite not wearing her glasses.

She stepped back. 'How are you this afternoon, Maree?'

'Excellent. You? You look well.'

'Chipper as always,' Anne said, moving the soft bulk of the bag on her shoulder to cover her left hand. 'I'm glad I bumped into you. I wanted to run something past you.'

This was it. Anne's mouth was dry and she swallowed quickly, hoping to find her words. She needed word to get around, and if you wanted word to get around on Wattle Island, Maree was your woman.

'Oh, I know that expression, Anne Sato.' Maree looked down her diamond-studded nose – her seventieth birthday present to herself. 'What are you cooking up in that devious brain of yours?'

'I'm glad you asked.' Anne put her arm around Maree and guided her towards the fountain in the middle of the park behind the shops. It had been part of the townscape for as long as anyone could remember. This is where they'd sat so many years ago as young women when book club first began, on one of the four wooden benches that surrounded the fountain. It was fitting they should discuss this here now.

Anne lowered herself onto one of the benches and Maree followed.

'Anne?'

'I was thinking, maybe it's time . . .' She paused. Despite having rehearsed what she would say a hundred times over, the words were harder to get out than she'd anticipated.

'Time . . .?'

'To bring book club back.'

The words hung between them.

'Oh.' Maree blinked and went very still.

'Hear me out. I know it seems like everyone has moved on, but we haven't. I know I'm still haunted. I know you are too.'

Maree shifted beside her.

'And I think the only way for us to truly move forward is to bring back book club.' Bring back the very thing that was bound to cause buried pain to surface. 'Face our demons, so to speak.'

Maree coughed.

'Okay. I know it isn't that simple, but I'm thinking maybe bringing book club back and stuffing it full of good memories again, somehow it will help us deal with . . .' She didn't say it. No one ever did. '. . . what happened.' Not that anyone truly knew what had happened that night.

Maree sat perfectly still. Anne took that as a good sign. Maree could have protested, could have got up and walked away. But she stayed.

'I've been talking to a lovely librarian from the mainland . . .' Perhaps if she kept talking, she could convince them both that this was a good idea. When she finished, Maree turned and looked at her with kind eyes.

'Well, that does sound like a good plan.' She furrowed her brow. 'Does Sam know?'

Anne looked at the grass beneath her feet and shook her head. 'I'm headed there next.'

Maree nodded. 'And Ruth?'

'You're the first person I've told.' Anne forced a smile. 'I was going to leave Ruth till last.'

'Probably a good idea. Maybe I can talk to Shellie and get her on board. And then we tell Ruth. Safety in numbers.'

Anne let relief wash over her.

'How do you think Sam will take it?' Maree asked.

Anne shrugged. 'I don't know. I know he still misses her. But surely it's been long enough.'

'I don't envy you that conversation.' With a gentle touch of Anne's arm and a look of sadness, Maree bade farewell and Anne turned her thoughts to the mission at hand.

Perhaps that was overstating it a little. Visiting her grandson was hardly a mission. But broaching the subject with Sam of restarting the book club – well, that wasn't going to be easy. She'd not slept properly in days from thinking about it. And without his okay, she wouldn't be able to bring herself to do it. Of course she should have spoken to him first. Even before approaching Grace. But, truth be told, she was scared. And it was much easier to beg forgiveness than ask permission. She'd heard that somewhere.

Anne rose and continued on her way to her grandson's place on the other side of the island. As she left the town behind her she could smell the salt air of the sea that lay behind the row of wattle trees that marked the edge of the township. Weaving through the branches of silver-green leaves, she stepped onto the beach and removed her shoes.

The waves rolled into the shore, depositing tiny shreds of seaweed on the soft yellow-white sand. It was unusual for seaweed to wash up this time of year. Maybe there was a storm coming. Goosebumps rose on her skin as she imagined the melancholy colours the sky and sea would turn if the heavens became angry, and how her dark blue and black inks would dance across the canvas as she tried to capture the mood of the storm.

She collected some of the seaweed, in case the urge to create a collage came over her later, and put the damp blades in the patchwork bag that hung over her shoulder. She continued up the beach, sand squeaking beneath her bare feet, until she reached the dock, a sturdy wooden structure sitting on barnacle-covered pilings. A lone figure sat on its edge, fishing pole hanging out over the water. A perfect picture of serenity. Too perfect. Off towards the horizon, dark clouds gathered.

Anne knew all too well how the dock's mood could switch from serene to wild with a trick of nature. She'd seen it happen many times before.

Wattle Island, 1947

Waves pitched then fell as the wind picked up, whipping Anne's long brown hair around her face. She pulled her woollen jacket tighter around her, but it did no good. Sharp pellets of rain drove into her face and through her clothes, soaking her skin.

'Get inside, lassie,' the captain of the *Seafarer* called, and Anne stumbled towards the small wheelhouse. Her stomach churned as the boat lurched.

Above, the black clouds tumbled over each other, wrestling for position in the darkening sky. Lightening slashed the air. Thunder boomed.

A wave crashed over the boat, sweeping her off her feet as she reached the door of the cabin. She slid across the deck and slammed into the wooden crates of supplies that butted into the side of the vessel with every rise and drop.

A hand reached down to help her up. The captain's son.

'We're nearly there.' His dark brown eyes were steady. He was only a few years older than her, maybe sixteen, but he was clearly much braver. He helped her inside and she pushed herself up tight against the wall. She couldn't see where they were going through the sleeting rain but she hoped he was right.

Closing her eyes only made her feel more nauseous, so she tried fixing them on the helm of the boat. But she could see the captain struggling and that wasn't reassuring at all.

Instead she looked out of the salt-encrusted window behind her – towards Sydney, towards home. What used to be home, anyway. So far away now, three hundred-odd miles of water and twenty-odd hours of sailing now separating her from the last thirteen years of her life. Her parents were gone, she was all alone in the world, being shipped off to live with an aunt she'd never met.

She counted to ten, hoping to hold back the tears that threatened to escape. Not that anyone would have noticed. The captain and his son were far too busy ensuring they didn't end up at the bottom of the Pacific, and there was no one else on board. Still, she wouldn't let herself cry out of fear she might not stop. She had to be strong and brave, just like her parents would have wanted.

Almost as quickly as it had started, the squall surrounding them eased – only a little, but it was enough to offer a small amount of relief. The rain continued to pelt down, but the wind had lost some of its fury.

'We'll be right now, love,' the captain said. 'There, can you see it?'

Anne looked in the direction the captain was pointing and squinted. All she could see were waves and rain. She moved back outside and stepped carefully towards the front of the boat. Ever so slightly her focus changed and she caught sight of the island. A cliff looming out of the rain. As they inched closer she could make out a dock jutting into the heaving sea. Then a shoreline emerged through the haze. Wattle Island.

Her new home. A new life, one she didn't want at all.

As the boat pulled up beside the dock, the captain's son leapt onto the wooden structure and secured the *Seafarer*'s lines to the piling.

'Let Jeremiah help you,' the captain called. 'She'll be slippery up there.'

Jeremiah held out his hand and Anne took it. With one strong pull, he hauled her off the boat and suddenly she was standing on the dock, her legs shaking.

'Give it a second,' he whispered in her ear. 'It always takes a moment to shake off your sea legs.'

As Anne waited to regain her balance, she looked around. In the early morning light, the dock was as pale as the sky and the sea. The beach was leached of any colour. All around her grey. She gulped back tears.

Jeremiah and the captain unloaded the crates from the boat just as a man strode towards them.

'Shocking day for it.' He shook the captain's hand. 'But we're mighty glad you came. We were getting a bit low on the good stuff.' He nodded to the top crate and Anne followed his gaze. Beer.

As the rain continued to fall, the men finished loading the supplies onto a truck waiting at the end of the dock, then drove off, leaving Anne standing there.

Jeremiah leapt back to her in three long strides. 'Come along, miss. No shelter out here. Can I take your bag for you?'

Anne shook her head and followed him, holding a small leather suitcase in one hand, clutching her most prized possession with the other, tucked away beneath her coat. She hoped the well-read copy of *Anne of Green Gables* had survived the voyage. Her mother used to read it to her when she was younger, and it was her favourite of all the books her mother had on her shelf in the living room, not least because she was named after Anne Shirley. After her parents' accident, once it was decided by the Child Welfare Department that Anne would go and live with her father's sister on Wattle Island, everything happened so quickly she'd had no time to grab her things properly. The moment the landlord of their rented terrace house had learned what had happened he'd wanted Anne out. She'd thrown a few clothes into a suitcase, and as she was being led out of the only home she'd ever known, she'd snatched the book off the shelf and had clung to it ever since. For the first few meandering hours of the trip she'd sat at the back of the vessel and tried to read.

As hour after hour had dragged by and all she could see around her was water, she'd given up and wandered the deck of the supply boat, the book held loosely by her side. As night fell, she'd stowed it under her coat, which she'd used as a makeshift pillow. Not that she'd got much sleep. The night had been too black. The sound of the engine too loud. The worry in her growing.

Then, as the sun rose, the storm had hit. So fast. So violent. No warning. The captain and Jeremiah had scrambled to stay in control and Anne had no time to stash her book anywhere safe, except beneath the coat she'd donned to try to keep the weather at bay.

Trudging along now behind Jeremiah, Anne kept her eyes down, hugging the book to herself tightly, imagining she was floating on the Lake of Shining Waters and Gilbert would row by any moment and take her back to Avonlea.

In the corner of the dimly lit pub, Anne sat, soaked, her suitcase at her feet. There was a fire going on the other side of the room and she could just feel its heat radiating across the empty space. The captain sat at the bar, a beer in his hand. Jeremiah was laying out their coats in front of the fire, and the man who'd met them at the dock was talking to the publican, his gaze flicking to Anne every few seconds. She tried to sink further into the leather bench she was sitting on, but there was nowhere to hide.

'Let me take your coat.' Jeremiah came over to her and held out his hand. 'See if we can't get it dry with the others.'

Anne grabbed her collar and closed it around her neck.

'It's all right. You'll get it back.' Jeremiah smiled. 'You must be freezing under there.'

She was. Desperately so.

Placing the copy of *Anne of Green Gables* on the table, she peeled the coat off and handed it to Jeremiah.

'What's that?'

'Something from home.' She cast her eyes down.

He reached for the book but she snatched it back.

'It looks wet,' he said.

The edges of the pages were warping. Anne held back tears. No. She wouldn't cry.

'Maybe we can do something about that too.' He pointed to the book and beckoned her over to the fire. 'Let me show you.'

She hesitated and then handed him the book, following him to the fireplace. As warmth radiated from the fire, he flicked through the pages.

'Keep them moving so they don't stick.' He returned it to her and she copied his movement.

For the next hour, as the rain raged outside and the captain drank another beer and another, Anne sat in front of the fire, drying her book, drying herself. Other than Jeremiah bringing her some water and a dry scone, and telling her they would take her to Aunt Bess once the storm had passed, they left her alone.

A crack of thunder rattled the leadlight windows on the far side of the pub and Anne jumped. Jeremiah looked over to her and smiled, pointing to the soft light now pushing through them. She stood up and looked outside. Through the clouds thin rays of sunshine cracked the grey and the rain was now just a drizzle. She stared out the window as the tiny town before her was bathed in increasing brightness. There was a fountain in the middle of a park, a few shops. Not much else.

'Shall we go?' Jeremiah was standing behind her. 'These two have had too much to drink – they'll probably get lost. I know the way to Aunt Bess's. Everyone round here does.'

Anne collected her suitcase and followed Jeremiah out of the pub. The paths around town were slippery and she stepped beside him carefully. With the town behind them they trudged up a muddy hill. The row of identical houses they passed hugged the slippery slope as if one more inch of rain would release their grip and send them sliding into one another as they tumbled down.

At the top of the hill they came to a stop. The cottage was the same as all the others: greyish-white, nondescript, a little run-down. They climbed the two steps of the veranda to get to the front door and before they could knock, it swung open.

'You must be Anne.' Bess put her hands on her substantial hips.

Her lips were turned up at the edges but there was no warmth in her expression. Anne couldn't tell if she was smiling or scowling.

'I'm your Aunt Bess. But you probably figured that. You must be tired, a whole day at sea, and that wretched storm. Come in and get settled.' She moved to the side to let Anne in. 'Thank you for bringing her, Jeremiah.' She dismissed him with a turn of her back.

Anne watched him walk back down the hill, a hint of an ache

pulling at her heart. Jeremiah had been kind to her on the boat, the only warmth in a very cold day.

'Come along. Out of those damp clothes and have a cup of tea.' Bess stomped across the stone floor to the kitchenette and put the kettle on the wood stove.

The cottage was as uninspiring inside as it was out. In the living area a small wooden table and chairs sat in the middle of the room, a brown sofa on the back wall next to a side table with only a wireless on top. There was one photo on the wall in a simple frame – Bess, Anne assumed, in a wedding dress next to a handsome soldier, the smile-scowl on the bride's face a haunting echo of the one that had greeted her.

No book shelves. Not even a single book on the side table.

'The outhouse is through the back door. My room is to the right.' She pointed down the short, narrow corridor. 'And yours will be to the left. Get yourself settled, then, and come back for your tea.'

Anne tiptoed to her room. There was a single bed against one wall, a small wardrobe that had clearly seen better days against another, a tiny window in the third. Bedside the bed was a nightstand, a lamp, and the Bible.

She pushed images of her bedroom back in Sydney out of her mind – the soft pink broderie anglaise curtains over the bay window, the pastel-coloured bed quilt her grandmother had made, the white bookshelf in the corner full of the titles that made up her childhood. All gone now, sold with all her parents' things to provide Bess with Anne's upkeep.

She pressed her lips together and swallowed the lump in her throat. No matter how hard she tried, the happy memory forced itself through – lying under her fluffy quilt, warm in her mother's embrace, reading *Anne of Green Gables* together.

Perhaps, like her namesake, being sent to live on an island as an orphan would turn out just fine.

'Hurry along.' Bess's voice cut through the cold air. 'I won't abide dawdling. Unpack and come out for tea.' Bess turned on her heel and clip-clopped away.

Perhaps not.

Be brave, she told herself over and over. Yet she felt anything but. She felt hollow. Lowering herself onto the hard, creaky bed, Anne took off her jacket and hugged her book against her chest. She'd read the beautiful words within the pages again and again, yet she never really knew what being in 'the depths of despair' meant. Until now.

———

Anne shook the ancient memory of her arrival on Wattle Island from her mind. There was never any point dwelling in the past. One could get lost there in its twists and turns and tunnels buried deep.

Besides, there was enough in the here and now to keep her busy. She had a book club to restart, after all. And a grandson to convince.

She sucked in a deep breath as she turned into Sam's dirt road and saw the light on in the garage. No surprise there. He'd justified his move to the remote side of the island six years ago by saying it would give him the space to work in peace. And while he did spend almost every waking hour hidden away in his garage studio, there was more to the move than that, Anne knew.

He seemed settled here, though. More settled than he had been on Soldiers' Way, anyway. Still, Anne worried about Addie. She was only nine and Anne didn't like her great-granddaughter living such a detached life. She knew what that was like. Though nothing on the island was that far away, she supposed. And Addie seemed content, having no real memory of their life in town. Anne worried too much, she knew. But her worries weren't unfounded. Sam had taken the events of their last book club much harder than Anne had realised at the time and this isolation wasn't good for him.

She checked the time. Sam would finish up soon; she could wait. She walked to the side of the old barn Sam had converted into a house, careful not to make too much noise, and greeted Emmeline Harris, Addie's pet cow, who was happily chewing on some grass in her pen.

The property had once been part of Hadley Follett's sprawling dairy farm, but over the years, with no one to take over, Hadley had slowly divided up his land – a piece here, a section there – until the original farmhouse was surrounded by smaller plots like Sam's.

Some people had turned theirs into hobby farms. Sam had made a new home for himself and Addie out of the barn – all rustic wooden cladding on the outside, exposed beams and large rooms inside – and a studio out of the garage that sat in the wild grass across from the main house.

'Hello, lovely.' Anne patted the beast's caramel-coloured cheek. She was the most docile and content bovine Anne had ever known. Not that she'd known many. She'd got Emmeline Harris as a pet for Addie a few years back, from Hadley, saving the cow, which was no longer viable for milking, from a terrible fate. Emmeline Harris had been Addie's favourite cow on the farm and Anne couldn't bear her great-granddaughter having to suffer another loss.

With a deep low, Emmeline moved her heavy frame to the back of the field and Anne took that as her cue to go inside and put the kettle on.

It wasn't long before Anne heard the garage door open and she walked to the front entrance to greet her grandson.

He walked up the path to the big barn doors, hands pushed deep into the pockets of his faded jeans, his broad shoulders slumped ever so slightly. The loose T-shirt he had on was covered in clay and he still hadn't shaved. It had been so long she'd almost forgotten what he looked like under the bedraggled black mess cascading from his chin. It made him look much older than his actual thirty years. His thin face lifted when he saw her waiting in the doorway. Such a handsome face behind those wild whiskers. Even a trim would make a difference. In fact he'd look quite dashing with a *short* beard.

She was biased, of course, but even with her bias, she could see the lines around his haunted brown eyes deepening with every year, his once dazzling smile a forgotten echo.

'Obaachan.' His eyes softened. Anne loved it when he used the Japanese word for grandmother.

'Sam-kun.' She held out her arms and he wrapped her in a strong embrace. 'Is Addie out exploring?' she asked when she untangled herself from him.

He nodded. 'Collecting wildflowers. You're early today. To what do I owe this pleasure?'

'Well, I have a favour to ask.'

Sam's left eye crinkled at the edge. 'Ah, and here I was thinking you'd simply come by earlier than usual so you could tell me how much you love me.'

'Always. But also a favour.' She turned and headed inside, not waiting for an invitation.

Anne sat at the sturdy wooden dining table in the centre of the open-plan kitchen–living area, while Sam prepared a pot of green tea on the bench that ran the length of the barn wall. He'd done a good job with the conversion, turning the once cavernous space into a comfortable home. The long kitchen behind Anne was fitted with salvaged item – an old farm hob for cooking sat next to a trough-turned-sink, and at the far end of the room, a piece of an old wrought iron gate, repainted, hung from the ceiling and was used as a pot rack.

In front of Anne was a soft blue sofa covered in Addie debris – a teddy, a cardigan, one old shoe.

'Thank you.' Anne took her tea from him. 'I'm glad Addie isn't home yet.' She reached across the table and patted his hand. 'I wanted to talk to you without her here, actually.'

He titled his head to the right. Always to the right, even as a boy. 'This is more than just a favour, isn't it?'

Anne swallowed hard. She didn't know if she had the strength to do this. But she had to summon it from somewhere. Sam had always appreciated directness, and she was usually so good at it herself.

'Obaachan?' he asked gently.

She drew in a deep breath and as she let it out the simple words, terrifying words, came.

'I want to start book club up again.'

Sam stiffened.

'I know . . .'

He turned his head away from her.

'I realise this might be a shock to you, but I think it may help. Bring us all back together. Help us move . . .'

After all her rehearsing she still couldn't say it. Not to him. How could he move on from that night when he lost so much?

His voice was low when he finally spoke. 'You're serious?'

'I think it will do us all good. And more to the point, I miss it. So very much.' Her voice cracked. 'I know it's hard for you—'

Sam stood and turned his back to her, resting his hands on the sink. 'You don't know. You don't know anything about . . .' He stopped.

Anne held her breath. All these years she suspected Sam had been hiding something from her about that night. All these years she'd asked and he'd never said. Perhaps bringing book club back would be the key to unlocking whatever it was he held deep inside him.

His shoulders slumped. 'I can't stop you.'

'But will you—'

He turned to face her. 'You cannot ask me to join.' His eyes flared.

'Not join, per se, simply . . . be there for me. Strictly in a helping manage the books capacity.' She stood and stroked his straggly beard.

Sam slammed his hand into the kitchen bench and Anne stepped back. The dark cloud, so heartbreakingly familiar to her, shadowed his face. His usually calm eyes were a storm of emotion. She'd pushed too far.

'Sam-kun,' she said softly. 'You wouldn't have to say anything, or answer questions. Not even sit with us. Just be there to help me, if I need it. Collect the books. Ever since the stroke . . .'

It was a low blow, she knew, to use her health to manipulate him, and she hated herself for it. But she was desperate. Time was running out. He needed this book club as much as she did. He just didn't know it yet.

He ran his hands through his thick black curly hair that was now sprinkled with grey. He was too young to be going grey. Too young for the burdens he carried.

With a frown, Sam sat back down. 'I'll help you with the books. Of course. But you can't ask me to be part of the book club.'

Anne nodded. It was a start. And she wouldn't exactly *ask* him to be part of it.

A lilting voice on the afternoon breeze floated in through

the open kitchen window, and Sam's frown lifted at the sound, the only time his smile reached his eyes these days.

The front door flung open.

'Obaachan,' Addie called, and wrapped her arms around Anne's neck, the wildflowers she was carrying tickling Anne's skin.

Every Friday Anne came over for dinner. Every Friday Addie greeted Anne as if her presence was a happy surprise.

'Did you bring it?' Addie kept her eyes on Anne as she kissed her father on the cheek, brushing dirt from her pink cord trousers.

From inside her patchwork bag, Anne pulled out the book she'd promised Addie. 'But, Miss Adrienne Sato, no reading till after dinner.'

Addie pouted, but the joy didn't leave her expression. Unlike Sam, who looked very much like his grandfather, leaving no doubt about his Japanese heritage, Addie had none of her great-grandfather in her. She was a cross between Anne – pale skin with freckles dotted across high cheekbones – and her mother – blonde curls that fell down her back, bright blue eyes.

Anne's heart caught. 'Shall we start cooking, then?' Distraction.

Addie got out the pots and pans and Anne put Addie's little posy of wildflowers in a vase on the window sill. Through the window over the sink, the last of the day's light faded, casting long shadows across the fields that covered this part of the island. The sky turned orange and the distant drone of bagpipes filled the air.

With those first few notes, Sam got up from the table and headed back out to the garage. Anne watched him out the window as he shut the wooden door and she waited. No light came on.

The monotonous bass of the bag droned against the high-pitched melody of the chanter, as Hamish, standing on the highest point of Soldiers' Way, played his monthly sunset serenade. It was the only sound that washed over the island, bringing familiar peace to all its residents.

Peace to all except Sam.

Beside her, Addie hummed along to the tune, her memories untainted. Blessedly so.

'Where did Daddy go?' Addie asked. She added salted butter to the pan as Anne began to cut up the meat.

'He'll be back in a minute.' Anne ran her thin, gnarled fingers thought Addie's silky hair.

She knew the mention of restarting the book club would unsettle Sam, but she also knew she was doing the right thing.

At least, she hoped she was.

Four

Grace sat in the waiting room surrounded by huge abstract paintings of marbled blues and greens. She was sure they were hanging on the crisp white walls in an attempt to evoke a feeling of calm, to distract patients from the fact that behind the heavy white doors, Dr Puddy sat waiting to deliver news that could change lives. The first few times Grace had sat there, she'd studied the paintings so intently, in a futile effort to ignore why she was there, that she knew every stroke, every stipple, each change of hue intimately. These days she simply kept her eyes closed, imagining she was somewhere else. Anywhere else.

Usually her mind took her to a serene nondescript forest, or a quiet beach, where she stood among the leaves or in the sand and breathed deeply. All alone. Sometimes she visited Paris, and imagined what it would be like to stand under the Eiffel Tower. Ah, Paris. A destination that had been on her bucket list since she was twelve.

Grace Elliott's Bucket List, age twelve:
- *Eat crepes in a Paris cafe*
- *Climb the Eiffel Tower*
- *Learn archery or fencing*
- *Solve a mystery à la Sherlock Holmes*

Admittedly, learning archery and fencing was a fascination that only lasted one month after Grace had read *Robin Hood* and *The Three Musketeers* back to back, and the amended bucket list shortly after saw it replaced with *eat 100 different flavours of ice cream*. She'd kept a list and to date she was up to fifty-three flavours.

The desire to visit Paris, though, stayed. Always.

Today when she closed her eyes, she was jumping off a bridge into a river. A smile crept across her face. At least it was something different.

'Ms Elliott?' The nurse called, pulling Grace out of her daydream. Her stomach flipped.

That was always the worst part. The moment right before your life may or may not change, when it was too late to turn around and flee the surgery and continue on in ignorant bliss, and your nerves were completely on fire with dreaded anticipation as you took your seat.

'How are you today, Grace?' Dr Puddy stood up and shook her hand. She always did that and it always made Grace feel better. Like they were equals. They weren't though. In this situation they were anything but. Still, it was nice to pretend.

'How have you been feeling lately?' she asked.

Grace had learned early on that Dr Puddy didn't mean emotionally. All she wanted was a quick checklist of physical markers – fatigue, nausea, pain, swelling – and if Grace was eating properly and getting enough sleep.

They'd been doing this dance for three years now, a well-practised two-step. Not that Grace had ever learned to actually dance and somehow, of all the things she'd wanted to learn over the years – *age thirteen: learn how to play the piano* (never attempted); *age twenty-two: learn how to knit* (accomplished, though badly); *age nineteen: learn how to speak Russian in order to read* War and Peace *in its original language* (oh, how she wished she'd known how impossible that would be!) – dancing had never ended up on one of her bucket lists.

Perhaps she should add *learn to dance* to her latest bucket list. Or perhaps she should be paying better attention to her doctor.

Doctor Puddy made notes, as usual, and then referred to her file. 'Your CA 125 is a little up, but your scans show no significant change. We'll keep watching that.'

Grace nodded.

'Are you still comfortable with your decision from our last appointment about how you'd like to proceed?'

'Yes.'

'Very well. Keep looking after yourself, listen to your body, and we'll see you in three months. Unless there are any changes.'

When she arrived home, June was waiting for her, as Grace knew she would be.

Three appointments ago Grace had insisted it was no longer necessary for June to accompany her to see the doctor.

'I . . . I can't abandon my baby girl,' June had spluttered at the suggestion.

Grace had taken her hand. 'Mum, I appreciate all you do. Really. But they're so routine now it seems silly to waste your time. Besides, you need a rest. If you're exhausted, who's going to pick me up if things go pear-shaped?'

She'd known that appealing to June's need to save her daughter any way she could would do the trick; June conceded on the condition that she cook Grace dinner after every appointment moving forward.

It wasn't really a manipulation. Grace would need June fighting fit if things took a turn. But more than that, Grace needed a break from her mother's constant scrutiny. Grace had a plan on how she wanted to move forward from this pivotal junction in her treatment, her life. Well, the beginnings of a plan. She was still figuring out the details. But she did know that she couldn't do it with June looking over her shoulder all the time, fussing if she sneezed, fretting if a headache hit. And she couldn't do it if she was worrying about June worrying about her.

Did that make her selfish? Maybe. Definitely.

But sometimes all the love and care and good intentions in the world could be smothering.

A delicious aroma of tomato, basil and parmesan floated on the evening breeze as Grace approached her front door. Lasagne. Her favourite.

'Is that you, love?' June called from the kitchen, as Grace stepped into the hallway.

'Yep,' she called, smiling to herself. June always asked this, as if it could ever be anyone else.

'I'm in here. Dinner's nearly ready.'

Grace put her handbag down and took off her yellow book pin.

'There you are.' June stepped towards her and gave her a hug, not quite committing to the embrace. It was rare these days for June to hold Grace tightly. Perhaps she was afraid she'd break her. 'So, how'd it go?'

Grace smiled warmly at her mum. 'Everything's looking good.' There was no point mentioning the CA 125. June would only panic.

'Really?'

'Yep. Dr Puddy couldn't be happier.' It wasn't really a lie.

'I'll get the champagne flutes.' June's shoulders relaxed and she grabbed a bottle of Perrier out of the fridge. 'I had a feeling we'd be celebrating tonight. I knew you could beat this,' she called over her shoulder as she poured them each a drink. 'Strong genes you've got.'

Grace swallowed hard then hugged her mum from behind. 'The strongest.' She buried her head in her mum's neck, just for a moment, the comforting scent of lavender and talc unchanged since her childhood.

Mineral water bubbled in the glasses as Grace and her mum clinked the fake crystal.

'Dinner smells divine, Mum. Thank you.'

Sweat began to bead across her brow. Oh, no, not now. Not tonight. June always panicked when Grace had a hot flush. She excused herself and shuffled to the bathroom, hoping her mother hadn't noticed.

Un, deux, trois . . . she let the trickle of cold water from the tap run over her wrists and transported herself to the Palace of Versailles, into the middle of the Queen's Library. There were far grander libraries in palaces and museums around the world, but there was something about Marie Antoinette's private little room of gold and sage that had always appealed to Grace.

Visit the Queen's Library, Versailles – bucket list, age eighteen.
Breathe in. Out.

'You okay, love?' June called from the hallway. 'Dinner's ready.'

'I'll be right there.' The heat started to dissipate. *Deux cent.* Over three minutes. That one was too long.

She let out a breath and patted the last of her sweat away with the ruby-coloured handtowel then opened the bathroom door and jumped back. June was standing right there.

'I was worried you'd fallen in.'

Grace gripped the handtowel behind her back but June's eyes narrowed. She'd already seen it. She said nothing, though.

'Let's eat.' Grace smiled and turned her mother around, pushing her towards the kitchen, letting the handtowel fall to the floor. She'd deal with that later.

Sitting opposite her mum, Grace pushed the lasagne around her plate.

June raised her glass of Perrier and waited for Grace to do likewise. 'To being cancer free.'

Grace clinked her glass with June and forced a smile. She wasn't free. She'd never be free. But she'd allow June this moment of joy.

'So, what's been happening in your circle, Mum?' Grace asked, escaping into the ordinary.

June started with the patchwork circle she was part of and how they simply couldn't agree on the background fabric of the charity quilt they were sewing and bossy old Frances was being a right tyrant about the whole issue. And how the guy who cleans the pool next door keeps flicking leaves into her back yard and she's told him a hundred times to stop but he won't listen and now she thinks he's doing it deliberately. And can Grace believe the bridge club were changing their Saturday start time to nine-thirty? It had been nine on the dot for as long as anyone could remember. And wasn't the reporting in the local paper about that homeless man being hit by a car terrible, and ever since Port Maddison became a mecca for Sydneysiders seeking a sea change, their tiny community was changing and not always for the better.

'You've hardly touched your dinner. Is there something wrong with it?' June looked at her closely. 'Something else going on?'

'No, Mum. It's great. I'm just not that hungry.'

'Hmm.'

And there it was. *The Look.* The left eyebrow raised just so, the lips pursed ever so slightly. A look Grace was all too familiar with. Like the time Grace tried to lie her way out of being caught smoking when she was fifteen. That was one bucket list item she always regretted. One month's grounding and a taste in her mouth that still made her feel sick when she thought about it all these years later.

She put on her Disney face, the beaming smile that she'd perfected over the past few years when people asked how she was but had no interest in the actual answer, especially if they knew she was – cue whispers – sick.

'It's just the drugs. You know sometimes I don't do well on them.'

The Look again. 'But we're nearly through it, right?' June's faded eyes bore into Grace.

'Yes.' Grace held her gaze steady, reassuring. 'We're nearly done. So . . .' it was a long shot, Grace knew, but she had to try. '. . . I was thinking maybe it was time for you to look at going to stay with Aunty Kay for a while.'

June dropped her fork. 'But I couldn't leave you.' She stared at her daughter.

'Yes. You could.' She reached across the table and took her mum's hands. 'You deserve a holiday. And now is as good a time as we've had in ages.'

June wasn't convinced. 'Maybe. Let me think about it.'

Grace knew that meant no.

'Now, tell me more about this crazy adventure group of yours. The Maddison Adventure Weirdos.'

Grace laughed. Her mum didn't often make jokes and it was nice to see her try.

*

A week later Gladys greeted Grace as she arrived at work. 'Morning, Grace.'

Grace stepped towards her and lifted the tattered knitted blanket that had fallen to the ground back over Gladys's legs.

'Thank you, dear.'

There was a cool bite to the air that morning and Gladys, always dressed in a lime green cardigan, even in the middle of summer, would certainly be feeling the cold.

'Are you sure I can't convince you to come inside?' Grace asked.

'Happy as Larry right here.' Gladys shook her head as Grace mouthed the familiar response with her.

Inside the library, Mr Bartlett was at the round table past the borrowing desk, his five romances and five crime books tucked safely away inside his trolley bag. Spread out over the table in front of him were 1000 pieces of a puzzle. Soon he would be joined by the Port Puzzle Pals for their fortnightly session and by the end of the day they would complete the picture of Venetian canals and gondolas, breaking only for lunch at the fish and chip shop down the hill.

Mr Bartlett nodded at Grace as she walked past, heading to the staff room at the back of the library to off-load her coat and bag.

Before she had a chance to head back out to the main part of the library, Linh came bursting in.

'Are you still buzzing from yesterday? I am. I can't believe you talked me into that!' Linh's words came fast. 'Wait. You don't seem as hyped as me.' She grabbed Grace by the shoulders. 'We jumped out of a plane, Grace. *Out of a plane.*'

Grace laughed. 'Yes, I know. I was there.'

'Wasn't it the best?'

This, thought Grace, from someone who'd been reluctant to join Grace on her MAW outings.

'Oh, the rush!'

If Linh didn't take a long slow breath soon, Grace was worried her friend would start hyperventilating. Not that she could blame her. While Grace wasn't still feeling the exhilaration like Linh, the memory of yesterday's jump was clear.

The rush of air was unlike anything Grace could have imagined. Free falling, far from being scary, was exhilarating. Freeing. It was strange how letting go, relinquishing control, could be so liberating.

Skydiving had been on Grace's bucket list since she was eighteen and had gone through an adrenaline stage. On paper at least:

Grace Elliott's Bucket List, age eighteen:
- *Sky dive*
- *Swim with sharks*
- *Drive in a racing car, preferably with Lewis Hamilton*
- *Become a trapeze artist*

And while she did go to circus school the summer after finishing the HSC, and wasn't too bad on the trapeze, sharks she'd ruled out pretty quickly after watching a documentary that scared the life out of her, and she certainly didn't have the money back then to go skydiving.

Linh leaned over and hugged her. 'I can't wait for the next outing.'

Grace smiled, wondering if Linh would come back down to earth at any point soon. For Grace, that feeling of drifting on the currents after the parachute had deployed, the sense that she could have floated far, far away from her reality, was now less of a rush and more of a longing.

And she felt restless.

The restlessness had been sneaking up on her lately, teasing the edges of her consciousness. Never rearing up to overwhelm her, but never quite disappearing.

Over the past few years she'd experienced nearly every emotion there was – fear – an awful lot of that; bravery – nowhere near enough of that; joy; sadness; excitement; despair; hope; resignation and defiance. Through it all, though, even the last few months, she'd always felt a sense of purpose. Whether that was simply moving from one appointment to the next, or more recently ticking off bucket list items, even in her darkest of moments two years ago, when the struggle was too much, there was structure to her black thoughts. When. Where. How. Her terms, not cancer's. A plan made, though she didn't execute it.

She wasn't sure when the solid lines of her life had started to shift and shimmer and the restlessness had begun. Her future, now more certain than it had been in years, should have seen the lines of life more solid, not less.

Even her beloved job hadn't been holding her attention the way it usually did.

'Grace?' Linh brought her out of her thoughts. 'Are you ready?'

Grace blinked. It was Monday, ten-fifteen. Her favourite part of the week.

'Yes. Sorry. Of course.'

Grace turned on her Disney smile and walked towards the beanbag-filled kids' corner of the library, the bright colours of red and green and yellow welcoming her. Kids piled in, calling, 'Hi, Miss Grace' as they got ready for story time.

They settled, sat in the beanbags or strewn across the floor. There would be just enough time to get through *Room on the Broom* before Grace had to head down to the dock to meet Jeremiah. It was one of her favourite stories and was always a hit with the kids. They listened intently as she read them the sweet rhyming words.

As she finished the last page she realised she was holding her stomach. Was that it? The restlessness? All this living life to the fullest and there was still one thing – no matter how many bucket lists she wrote, how many planes she jumped out of, how many stable reports she received – that was forever out of her reach. She'd made peace with that when she was diagnosed. It was her ovaries or her life. The decision to have a hysterectomy had been straightforward.

She dropped her hand to her side.

Perhaps she hadn't made peace with it after all.

'Right, then.' She shook off the pervading sadness. 'Let's go on a bear hunt to the front of the library. I think I can see some grown-up bears waiting there for you.'

After she said goodbye to the reading group, Grace put the book club tub on a trolley and threw on her jacket.

'I'm heading down to the dock,' she said to Linh, smiling.

'You're getting such a kick out of this island book club thing, aren't you?' Linh said.

'It's different and that makes it exciting.' For the first time that day, Grace was genuinely looking forward to the task at hand.

Grace stood on the dock with the plastic tub of books at her feet, waiting to load it on to the *Seafarer III*. Captain Jeremiah Allen was on deck, making sure the deckhand was securing their cargo correctly. The books would go on last being the smallest and lightest of their load.

Jeremiah and the *Seafarer III* were as iconic symbols of Port Maddison as the echidna sanctuary in the west of town, though not quite as tourist friendly. The historical society had honoured him last year with a town service award for the *Seafarer*'s one-hundredth anniversary of running supplies to Wattle Island – through wars and the Depression, and storms that had retired two previous incarnations of the vessel and three generations of Allen men as captain.

Jeremiah hobbled off the boat and limped towards her. Grace had no idea how old he was, but if he was under eighty she would have been shocked. How he still operated the weekly supply run to Wattle Island was beyond her, though she suspected his deckhand probably did most of the actual work these days. Grace didn't know what would happen to the boat once Jeremiah retired, as he had no children of his own to take over.

'Ms Elliott.' Jeremiah tipped his head. Grace had known him since she'd started at the library twelve years ago and, despite the fact she could never get him to call her by her first name, he always had time for a chat with her.

'How are you, Jeremiah? Good seas today?'

'Looks like it. Have you got that tub ready for me?'

Grace handed him the book club set, worried its weight might be too much for him, but he took it with ease.

'Thank you for doing this,' she said. 'I had no idea how else I would facilitate the book club. Flights from Sydney would have been outside the library's budget.'

'Anything to help.' He looked at the label on the lid addressed to Anne and smiled. 'Just like old times.'

'Oh?'

'I haven't seen Anne at the dock in a very long time, though.'

'You're friends?'

He nodded. 'We go back a long way.'

It shouldn't be a surprise, Grace supposed. Jeremiah had been on the boat most of his life, as far as local legend said, and probably knew everyone on the island. He'd taken over from his dad as captain back in his thirties, so the story went.

'Brave of her to do this.' He shook his head.

'What's so brave about setting up a book club?'

A heavy sigh from Jeremiah sent a tingle dancing over Grace's skin.

'Did you know there's a rare type of bird on the island?' he asked. 'The Wattle Island gull. Only place in Australia they nest. Fascinating.'

Grace frowned. Of all the seniors who frequented the library, Jeremiah had his wits about him the most. This wasn't a 'senior moment' as Mr Bartlett liked to call them. This was Jeremiah emphatically changing the subject. But why?

'I'll make sure Anne gets it safely.' He tipped his head again and disappeared back onto the boat.

Grace hugged herself against a strong breeze blowing in off the ocean and watched the boat pull away from the dock, waving to the captain as he drew the vessel out past the break wall and into open water.

Later that night, curled up on the sofa, Grace turned off *The Greatest Showman*. Ever since her diagnosis three years earlier, Hugh Jackman had been her constant companion in one form or another – a movie to distract herself from the pain as she lay on the couch; an album playing through her earphones during treatment; his latest musical on repeat for six months now.

But tonight not even Hugh could lift the restlessness. It wasn't just the feeling that had come over her during story time. She knew that. Her life had shifted with her last couple of doctor's appointments and her thoughts had shifted too.

From the coffee table she picked up the bucket list journal that she'd kept since she was ten. The leather cover was worn in places, years of being opened and closed and read and written in showing in its mottled brown hide. Every bucket list she'd ever written was in there. Even her very first yellow crayon one was folded up and slipped between the first few pages.

She took it outside to her front veranda, and under a silky black sky peppered with stars, she opened it.

Grace Elliott's Bucket List, age ten:
- *Live on a desert island – no parents, no rules*
- *Build an awesome treehouse on the island*
- *Eat bananas every night for dinner*
- *Have a pet monkey in the treehouse*
- *Read every day in a hammock*
- *Solve a mystery like Sherlock Holmes – off the island, obviously*

Looking back on her earlier bucket lists always made Grace smile, seeing how much had changed, and how much hadn't. She never did manage to go to that desert island. But the first tub of books had started their journey to Wattle Island, and Grace wondered what it must be like to sail away and leave everything behind.

Five

Anne stood beside Sam on the dock as the morning sun peeked above the horizon, her arm linked with his. She could tell he wasn't altogether thrilled to be there that early – or at all really, given what it signified, but he was a good lad and wouldn't say anything. They watched the *Seafarer III* approach on the rising tide and Anne waved once the boat was close enough Jeremiah would be able to see who it was standing there.

'So, you really are going to do this?'

Anne knew her grandson was upset with her, but she'd hoped enough time had passed that he would be able to live with it, if not happily accept it.

'I know this is hard for you.'

'It's not that.' He gritted his teeth. 'I worry about you. If you're up to this.'

There was more to it than that, but she went along with it.

'Me? Up to it? Tsk, tsk, tsk.' She shot him a look he was well accustomed to, full of love and reproach. 'My dear boy, I'm insulted by your insinuation. Of course I'm up to it and you should know better.'

A wry smile crossed his face and he threw his hands in the air. 'Forgive me, Obaachan. You are a force, and I shall never doubt you again.' He bowed.

'You will doubt me again. You never learn. Who doubted me when I said I wanted to get a degree in fine art in my seventies?'

He hung his head.

'And who doubted me when I wanted to get the town hall refurbished, even though I managed to bring it in under budget?'

He looked at her, the spark in his eye something she didn't see nearly enough these days.

'And who doubted me—'

'Yes. Okay, you've made your point.'

'One can never drive home one's point too hard, my dear.' She patted him on the cheek – well, his straggly beard. She really wasn't sure about that thing on his face.

'Oh, yes one can.' He laughed and kissed the palm of her hand.

As the green steel beast lumbered into the dock, Anne held her breath. The young deckhand, Toby, waved to her, and Sam took the tub of books from him before the lad went on to unload the rest of the cargo.

'Anne.' Jeremiah nodded, his floppy white curls falling into his eyes as he hobbled off the boat. 'So glad to be dropping these off to you. Getting your old book club up and running again, then?'

'Thank you, Jeremiah. Yes, a brand new start.' She kissed him on the cheek and he squeezed her hand.

'I'm glad. It doesn't sit right, you without your books.' He clicked his tongue. 'A couple of old codgers like us need to make the most of the time we have left.'

'So'—Anne nodded to the boat—'you'll be coming off that soon?'

He shook his head. 'Tried that once, remember? I reckon my last breath will be taken on her.' He laughed. 'Good luck,' he whispered in her ear, then turned and started barking orders at Toby.

Luck. She'd need a hefty amount of that to pull this off.

Sam carried the tub of books to Anne's cottage in silence, and placed it on the kitchen table. He turned to leave.

'Before you head off'—Anne closed her hand around his—'why don't we have a cup of tea and then ring Miss Elliott to let her know the books have arrived safely.'

Sam moved about Anne's small pink kitchen with the ease of someone who'd made her tea many times.

'Oh, and grab some biscuits too.'

'It's barely nine am, Obaachan.'

'Well at my age, it's never too early for biscuits. Pop a few on the good china. Top of the cupboard. I only get to use the good china when you're here.'

'Not if you put it away in the cupboard under the bench. Then you could reach it whenever you want.'

'My dear Sam. One cannot put one's good china—'

'With one's everyday crockery.' He imitated her inflection infuriatingly well. 'You can if you can't reach the top cupboard.' He rolled his eyes.

She whacked him on his arm as he walked past carrying said biscuits on said good blue-and-white china.

'Here.' She handed him her phone. 'You make the call. My arthritis is acting up.'

Sam furrowed his brow, but did as he was told. He was a good boy. It wasn't totally wicked of her to take advantage of that.

Sam dialled the number and turned on the phone's speaker function. The first time Sam had shown Anne how to do this she'd been horrified. Why would she want everyone within cooee to be able to hear her private conversations? But she had to admit it did come in handy, especially when drinking a cup of tea with one hand, and holding a biscuit with the other. She just didn't have to admit it to anyone but herself.

'Port Maddison Regional Library, Grace Elliott speaking.'

'Hello, Grace. It's Anne Sato.'

'Hello, Anne.' Grace's pleasant voice rang through the cottage.

'Hello, pet. I'm sitting here with my grandson and a tub of beautiful books. Say hello, Sam. Don't be rude.'

'Hello, Miss Elliott.' He shot Anne a look, which she ignored and he moved to the sink.

'Hi, Sam. I'm so glad the books have arrived, Anne, and didn't end up at the bottom of the Pacific.'

Anne laughed. 'Sam, tell her how thrilled I am to start book club.'

'You're on speaker,' he mumbled from across the room. 'She can hear you.'

'Silly me. Of course. Technology, Grace. It will be our downfall. Mark my words.'

Grace's voice was light. Happy. It made Anne smile. 'Sometimes technology isn't my friend either,' she said. 'Today my email stopped working.'

Anne looked over to Sam. Normally he'd happily engage in a debate with Anne about the pitfalls of modern technology. Today he was silent.

'Grace Elliott, it is a pleasure to come across a kindred spirit.' Anne leaned back in her chair.

'Good luck with book club,' Grace said. 'If you need anything, don't hesitate to call me.'

'Will do, pet. Take care. Say goodbye, Sam.'

Sam didn't respond.

'Sam-kun, that was a little rude of you,' Anne said, after she ended the call. 'Grace has been very helpful.'

'To you. I said I'd help and I will. But I can't get involved.'

'Fair enough,' she relented. Clearly she'd underestimated how strongly Sam felt. Despite what others might say, Anne knew when to back off.

'Be a dear and distribute these'—she tapped the book tub—'to the people who've already said yes. And leave the rest at the pub.' Anne had made up flyers about the book club, saying that they'd be meeting in four weeks for a discussion, and how much they'd love people to join. She'd even created a sign-up sheet for Sam to place on the table.

'Why didn't you just get me to take them to the pub from the dock? It's a lot closer.'

'But then I wouldn't have had an excuse to have tea with you.'

All the tension left Sam's shoulders and his smile was soft and full of warmth. 'Obaachan.' He kissed her on her forehead before taking the tub.

Anne watched him head down the hill, wondering if anyone at the pub would even take a book. There was a very real possibility Anne would be sitting there in a month's time all on her own, dissecting character and plot inside her own head while she sipped quietly on a chardonnay. Yes, Maree had said she'd come. And so had a few others. But saying yes and actually turning up were two very different things. Her time on the town council had taught her that.

Pouring another cup of tea, she stepped out on to her veranda and cast her gaze down the hill, the coloured doors of Soldiers' Way bright accents in the morning sun. Well, there was nothing for it now. She'd made the choice and she had to live with however this turned out. At least, she supposed, even if she couldn't bring her book club back to life, she had something new to read herself. It had been far too long since she'd got lost in the pages of something new, her second greatest love interrupted by life. Well, third love. Family, art, then reading. But family was a given and therefore didn't need to be counted. A new book was always a thing of beauty in Anne's eyes. Always had been.

Wattle Island, 1948

Anne shuffled along the dirt path of Soldiers' Way, clutching her book to her chest. The kids from the end house were out the front playing marbles, but stopped and waved when she went past.

Most of the street was empty these days. The military families had moved on after the war, and only a few of those retired or discharged remained. Aunt Bess had chosen to stay on after her husband was killed in Egypt, and Anne wondered how she could remain trapped by so many sad memories.

As she approached the road that led into town – if you could even call it a town – Anne saw Hadley Follett heading her way, a cow following close behind.

'Anne.' He stopped and tipped his straw hat. 'Out for a walk?'

'Obviously.'

He didn't deserve her terseness. He'd been one of the few islanders her age to actually make an effort to be nice to her. She checked her manners and wiped her hands on her dungarees.

'Who's this then?'

She reached out and patted the cow he had with him. The trick to having anything other than a two-word conversation with Hadley was to steer remarks in the general direction of cows or hay.

'This is Daisy.' Hadley went on to give Anne a full run-down of Daisy's life to date. Not a milker, but his dad had, unusually, let him keep her as a pet. 'If you come by the farm tonight, the others from school are going to drop in for a hay ride. Just a bit of fun.'

Fun? Anne mostly found life on the island dull and uneventful. There were only so many rocks you could climb and stretches of sand you could walk before it all became one boring blur.

If she were back home, she'd be going to dances on Friday nights and passing time in the local milk bar on her way home from school every afternoon. But not here. There was no milk bar. And certainly no dances.

Anne didn't know why everyone didn't simply pack up and leave. She suggested as much once to Aunt Bess, but was met with a scowl and reprimand about not understanding the true value of home.

Anne understood perfectly well she'd been ripped from hers.

She would find a way out of here, somehow. Of course, that would require money and Aunt Bess was in charge of the small sum her parents had left behind until Anne turned twenty-one. Maybe she should think about getting a job. Except for one tiny problem. Where on this decaying island were there any jobs?

'Thank you, Hadley. I'll think about it.'

She knew she wouldn't go. There was no point forming attachments with people on the island when she was planning to leave at the first chance she got.

He bowed and moved on.

As she rounded the bend, right before the turn off to the beach, she saw them: Ruth and her little shadow, Maree. Anne braced herself and put on her warmest smile. And they turned their backs on her. Maree giving her a quick wave, possibly a sympathetic glance, before Ruth yanked her away.

Anne had made two fatal errors when she'd arrived on the island, as far as Ruth was concerned. The first was travelling to the island in the company of Jeremiah, which was apparently a sin in Ruth's eyes. If only Ruth had known how wretched that journey had been. None of the island boys were good enough for Ruth and she had her eyes set on the handsome deckhand. The second error was that, back on Anne's first day of school a year ago, she'd laughed when Ruth got a word wrong in the spelling bee. She knew it wasn't right to laugh, but honestly, what thirteen-year-old didn't know how to spell 'marvellous'? She'd tried to apologise, many times. But no matter how often she said sorry, Ruth still snubbed her.

Anne's shoulders dropped. Was there any point even trying anymore?

Dragging her feet, she made her way down to the beach to wait for the supply boat to come in. On the last Friday of every month, Anne sat on the damp yellow sand, her back against one of the rough wooden pilings of the dock, a book in her hand as she waited.

And this was strike three in Ruth's eyes.

Every month Jeremiah brought with him three or four books from the library on the mainland to lend her. All he wanted in exchange was an hour or so of her time to help him read better. Anne couldn't believe how low his level of literacy was, but she supposed if one was raised on the water as a third-generation seaman, there probably wasn't much call for Shakespeare or Hemingway or Austen. Anne had been introduced to such classics by literature-loving parents. Not everyone was so lucky.

She wasn't sure if he was genuinely interested in improving his reading or if it was merely an excuse not to hang out at the pub with his dad, who was partial to more than a drink or two as they waited for the tide to turn. But Anne didn't care what his motivation was, as long as he kept bringing her books.

There under the dock she opened a book of poetry by Emily Dickinson. It was her favourite of all the books Jeremiah had delivered last month, and she'd pored over the delicious pages many times throughout the past four weeks. There was something about the way Dickinson played with language that sent a tingle down her spine. She had her dad to thank for that. While her mum favoured novels, her dad had loved poetry.

A deep, haunting horn echoed across the water, announcing the *Seafarer*'s approach.

Anne stood and brushed the soft sand off her dungarees, running up the dune to get to the top of the dock.

Captain Allen pulled the boat up and Jeremiah leapt over the railing to tie the rope securely to the piling, throwing a quick wave in her direction. Once the boat was secured, Jeremiah ducked back aboard then emerged with her pile of books in a hessian bag.

'Here you go, Anne.' He handed her the bag and picked up the one at her feet with the previous month's books inside. She hugged the new bag to her chest with one hand. In her other, the Dickinson. She didn't want to give it back.

'Do you want to hang on to that one a little longer?' he asked.

She met his gaze, daring to hope. 'Can I?'

'I'll smooth it over with the librarian.' He winked.

'Thank you.'

'No problem.' He turned back to the boat and called over his shoulder, 'Same time, same place?'

'Yes,' Anne replied, and she skipped back up the dock as Jeremiah and his dad unloaded their cargo.

An hour later, Anne sat by the lighthouse, going through the bag of books to decide which one to read with Jeremiah. He'd come a long way in the past twelve months. She always chose one book from the pile, one that she was familiar with, to give back to him so he could read it and they could discuss it the next time the boat came to the island. She considered the selection. Perhaps *The Hobbit*.

From the rest of the pile, she selected one that would end up on her bedside table. *Northanger Abbey*. Had Jeremiah noticed her reaction last month when he'd given her *Sense and Sensibility*?

With *The Hobbit* in her lap she waited for Jeremiah to arrive. The lighthouse was her favourite spot on the island, an uninterrupted vista of grey or green-blue, depending on the weather; the white-washed lighthouse tall and strong behind her, cool against her back.

Anne couldn't get the thought of Jeremiah choosing a Jane Austen for her out of her head. She adjusted her long brown hair, pushing it behind her ears then combing it back out again, remembering how they stuck out from her head a little too far.

'Hello, Anne.' Jeremiah strode towards her, his broad shoulders relaxed beneath his navy-blue cable-knit sweater.

Her voice caught in her throat. This was new. Was she nervous?

'So, what work of literary genius are we attacking this month?' He plonked himself down beside her, his dark curls bouncing as he pushed them out of his eyes.

'This one.' She handed him Tolkien's work. 'It's got a bit of everything. I think you'll really like it.'

Jeremiah took it from her. His hands were large, strong.

Since when did she notice boys' hands? Men's hands. Jeremiah was practically a man now at eighteen. He leaned back against the wall of the lighthouse and began to read. Gone were the days when Anne had to sit beside him to help him through every passage.

Now, she left him to it, only needing to intervene if there was an odd word or phrase that tripped him up. He would spend an hour reading while Anne collected wildflowers or lay in the grass nearby and read her own book, soothed by the silent company.

But today she didn't get up and move away. And she didn't feel soothed at all.

Instead she watched Jeremiah read, the way he bit his bottom lip in concentration, the way his dark brown eyes crinkled at the edges every now and then, already fully engrossed in the world of Middle Earth.

Thankfully, he didn't notice her staring at him. She must have looked a right idiot fawning over him like that.

She shook her head and decided to move away from him to try to snap herself out of her trance. She stood up and stepped towards the edge of the cliff, peering over to the dark blue waves crashing onto the grey rocks below in an explosion of white spray. Breathing in great gulps of salty sea air, she tried to clear her mind.

'This is pretty amazing,' Jeremiah called, and Anne spun around as he stood up. 'Thanks, Anne. Great choice. I'm really going to enjoy this one.'

'I thought so.' She walked towards him and stopped mere inches away. 'I knew you'd like it.'

'You always pick just the right book for me. Thank you.'

She smiled and raised her chin, ever so slightly. She'd never kissed a boy before, but she was pretty sure that was what you did.

She closed her eyes.

And he punched her lightly in the arm.

'Where would I be without your help?' He put his hands in the pockets of his weathered and worn trousers. 'You're a good kid.'

Kid? She was fourteen.

'I have some news to share with you.'

Kid!?

'But you can't tell the captain.' He lowered his voice, as if his dad were somehow nearby, not off at the pub, drinking the morning away.

'I promise,' she whispered.

'I'm going to college. And it's all because of you.'

Anne smiled. *All because of her.* Then she frowned. College? There were no colleges on Wattle Island, that was for sure, or even in Port Maddison, from where the *Seafarer* sailed.

She stepped back. 'What do you mean?'

'Well, my aunt's a teacher and after you started helping me with my reading, she started tutoring me. She suggested I could sit an entrance test for teachers' college. So I did.' He looked Anne in the eye. 'And I got in.'

'You got in?'

'Yep. Thanks to you. And her. But especially you.' He hit her in the arm again. 'Shall we go get a scone or a cake from the bakery to celebrate?' He turned and headed down the headland; Anne had to jog to keep up with his long strides.

'That's . . . amazing. What does this mean, though? When do you start?'

Jeremiah stopped suddenly and Anne bumped into him.

'Steady there, sport.' He grinned.

Sport? Anne fought to quell the heat rising in her cheeks.

'Next month. In Sydney. I need to find a way to tell the captain that I've only got one trip left with him.'

Anne tried to gather her tumbling thoughts. *One trip left.*

'I thought you loved the boat?'

'I do. But I don't want to become an old seadog like my pa.'

Anne's bottom lip began to quiver.

'Hey.' Jeremiah touched her cheek. 'Are you going to miss me? I'll miss you too. You're like the little sister I never had.'

Little sister. Anne's head began to hurt. Was this what growing up was like? Realising one minute, quite out of the blue, that you liked someone, only to find out the next minute they think of you as a sister? Well, that didn't seem fair at all. And quite out of her control. Which was even less fair.

Afraid to look him in the eye in case she betrayed her feelings, she stared at the copy of *The Hobbit* in his hand. The last book they'd ever get to discuss now.

'Ah.' Jeremiah laughed. 'So you'll only miss my book deliveries.'

'Yes.' *No.* A thousand times no. She'd miss them, yes. But she'd miss him more, the kindness he always brought with him, the one friend who understood her love of books.

'I'll see what I can do about keeping you stocked in great stories, all right?' He patted the top of her head and she had to fight not to run away, fight to control the storm of fear, anger, loss and confusion that was raging through her. An awful lot of confusion. And happiness. For him. He was altering the course of his life. Just like she wanted to do with hers.

Was it possible to be completely happy for someone else and totally devastated for yourself at exactly the same time?

In town they stopped at the bakery and Jeremiah bought Anne a cream bun, which she forced herself to eat as they sat on the bench by the fountain. He spoke with such excitement about going to college; she couldn't let him see how upset she was.

He hugged her after they finished their morning tea. 'Thanks again, Anne. For everything. I'd better go check on the old man.'

He strode across the park in the direction of the pub and as soon as he was out of sight, Anne took off, ran up Soldiers' Way and locked herself in her room, reading page after page – skipping lunch, much to Aunt Bess's ire – well into the afternoon.

———

Twice now in her life Anne had missed the joy of something new to read. All those decades ago when she'd said goodbye to Jeremiah, and more recently when book club fell apart. Now, with the diary of a certain young Ms Jones in her hand, Anne crawled under the covers of her bed, hopeful that this was the beginning of a new era of literary discovery, however long the gods determined she'd be around. Book club had to succeed.

Six

The month passed all too quickly and before she knew it, Anne was standing outside the pub, breathing in deep gulps of air. She adjusted the sky-blue silk scarf wrapped around her head and made sure her left ear was covered just so. She'd worn her happiest lemon-coloured maxi-dress dotted with tiny blue forget-me-nots to help her portray a sense of joy and calm. This was it.

She pushed opened the heavy pub door and stepped inside. It hadn't changed much in all the years since Anne had arrived on the island as a child. The dark-red brick absorbed the soft orange glow of the fire that danced in the original black-and-white tiled fireplace on the western wall. The booths that lined the eastern wall had been refurbished once or twice, but the biggest change was the bar itself, clad in modern black panelling.

Thankfully over the years no one had touched the leadlight windows that reflected the fire in mottled greens and pinks in winter and that sent shards of rainbow colour scattering across the polished parquetry floor on bright summer days.

Anne could feel in her bones the distinct chill the night air promised and was glad the fire was already going. All the books Anne had left to encourage new members had been taken over the last couple of weeks. She didn't know by whom, but hopefully they'd come tonight and she would find out.

At the bar she accepted a rich red wine from Len and took a calming sip. Right. Time to get set up. She put her hands on her hips. The brass bell above the pub door tinkled and Anne turned around. It was Sam. She relaxed her shoulders.

'Obaachan.' He kissed her on her forehead. 'What do you need me to do?'

She directed him to arrange some chairs in a circle around the fireplace. She wanted to set out enough so that anyone and everyone felt welcome but not so many that it would look sad if only a handful of people came.

'How about ten?' Sam suggested.

'Sounds good.' She hoped they'd fill up.

The bell over the door rang again and she turned around to see Hamish grinning at her. Relief washed over her. 'When did you get back?'

He'd been off island for three weeks attending to his family's holdings on the mainland. She took his wrinkled hands and squeezed them. From beneath his white beard he smiled. 'This morning. Chartered a flight. I couldn't let you face this alone.'

Hamish. Her one constant in this life.

'Let me help with these.' He moved a few chairs into position with Sam. 'And we can keep some extras nearby, just in case.'

Next to arrive was young Shellie, Sam's best friend since childhood, her blonde bob tucked neatly behind her ears. Anne still marvelled that the little girl who used to run around her wading pool in nothing but her undies was now the island's only doctor.

Shellie bounced over and hugged Anne. 'I'm so excited you're doing this.' She took her hands. 'I know it can't be easy, but maybe it's what we all need.'

Anne smiled. 'Thank you for coming.'

Behind Shellie was her husband, Phil.

'I'm surprised to see you here, my lad.' Anne smiled.

'Doctor's orders.' Phil winked at Anne as he gave his wife an affectionate nudge.

Anne had suspected as much. Phil was far more at home taking tourists diving on the island than with his nose in a book. He leaned in towards Anne. 'I had to be here, you know,' he whispered, looking at Sam.

The strength and pain contained in that one look made Anne's breath catch in her throat. Nothing would ever come between those two.

Sam greeted Phil with a slap on the back.

'Where's my favourite girl?' Phil asked.

'Addie is all settled with Mrs Follett. They're playing Monopoly. Or a version of it, with some extra Addie rules.' Sam shrugged.

Poor Mrs Follett. Anne had learned long ago Addie's rules could be quite complicated.

Maree entered the pub next, her sapphire nose ring catching the amber glow from the fire. She was alone, though. In days gone by, Maree would come to book club with Ruth, and, despite how long it had been since their last book club meeting, despite what had happened, Anne had hoped it would be one thing that would stay the same.

Anne looked at her watch. There was still some time before they were due to start.

'Relax, Anne,' Maree whispered to her. 'They'll come.'

Minutes ticked by and the members of the new-look book club busied themselves with ordering drinks and taking their seats. Anne was about to give up hope that anyone else was joining them when the brass bell at the door chimed again. They all looked up to see Hadley Follett holding it open for an actual *stream* of people, including some real surprises such as Robbie from the airstrip. Ruth entered too, albeit with a scowl on her pinched face. She nodded hello to Anne, not a hair of her grey bob out of place, her thick pink cardigan buttoned tightly.

Anne was grateful Ruth had come. For all their ups and downs over the decades, there was something comforting about Ruth's presence.

Everyone bustled about saying hello, before the newcomers settled into their chairs. Anne's hands began to shake. There were four new members under the age of sixty there. And Hadley Follett was new too. Never in a million years would she have thought Hadley the type to join a book club. Anne shook her head, glancing at the copy of *Bridget Jones's Diary* in his hand. She had assumed he never read anything other than farming almanacs. It was true what they said: no matter how long you knew someone, there was still more to learn.

Anne cleared her throat, making gentle fists to try to stop the shaking in her hands. 'Thank you everyone for coming tonight. It's great to see some old and new faces for what I hope will be a regular fixture in your calendars.'

'Not much else to do,' Hadley said, shrugging.

'Count me in.' Robbie smiled.

'Me too,' Hamish added, pulling his copy of the book out of his jacket pocket. The warmth Anne felt for him in that moment was nearly overwhelming. And not for the first time in all the decades they'd known each other.

'Did everyone finish the book?' Anne looked around the circle. The only person with their hand down was Sam. He'd positioned himself away from the group, slumped over the bar, a glass of water in front of him.

Anne had hoped that with Shellie and Phil there he may have joined in, but the fact he hadn't left would have to do for now. Was he looking out for her? Or was he caught in his own memories, unable – unwilling – to leave?

Anne brought her attention back to the group. If she was going to help Sam, she had to make tonight a success. Create happy memories.

She pulled out the questions Grace had sent her.

'What similarities with one of the author's favourite reads, *Pride and Prejudice*, did you find in *Bridget Jones's Diary*?' she read.

Silence. Phil shifted in his seat and looked down.

Robbie stared with open eyes at Anne. 'Were we supposed to read another book as well?'

Ruth rolled her eyes. 'There was an attempt, clearly, to mirror certain aspects, but this'—she waved the book in the air—'was not a patch on Austen.'

The group was silent.

Hamish, who was sitting next to Anne, leaned in close to her ear. 'Maybe not everyone here has read Austen. Start with something easier.'

Of course. Silly her. She adjusted her glasses and skimmed the rest of the questions, most of which were convoluted discussion points. Book club never used to be this hard.

The silence turned into a low hum as people started talking among themselves.

Come on, Anne. Something easier. Right. As easy as it gets.

'Ah . . . did everyone like Bridget as a character?'

Phil shrugged. 'Wasn't my type. Not smart enough.' He winked at Shellie.

Robbie nodded. 'She was all right.'

'She was insufferable,' Ruth grumbled.

Shellie coughed. 'Look, she was a bit flighty, I'll agree. But aren't we often like that in our twenties?'

'She's thirty-two, I think you'll find.' Ruth shook her head. 'Similar to you lot.' She waved her hand in the general direction of Shellie, Phil and Robbie. 'None of you behaves that ridiculously.'

Silence.

Anne's heart sank. She shouldn't have been surprised. Ruth had always liked to find fault, if she could, with the books they read. And she usually could. In the past it had actually worked in the book club's favour, fostering interesting debate. But tonight it was the last thing Anne needed.

While Phil and Robbie chuckled about having behaved pretty badly last weekend, Anne reached over and touched Ruth's leg.

Her old friend met Anne's gaze with faded brown eyes. Anne shook her head slightly and Ruth's expression softened.

Hamish's voice called everyone back to attention. 'Okay. What about Mark Darcy? Why do you think he's attracted to Bridget? They're not exactly an obvious match.'

'Perhaps,' Shellie offered, 'because she's the antithesis of everything else in his world. The fun light to his stuffy dark.'

'Opposites do attract,' Maree added.

Ruth nodded. 'I concede there could be some appeal in that.'

'She is pretty funny.' Phil folded his thick arms across his muscled chest.

'Do you think it's a relationship that would last, though?' Ruth asked.

'There's never any guarantee a relationship will last,' Sam mumbled from the bar.

'They seem really cute together,' Robbie said. 'I reckon short of one of them dying, Bridget and Mark Darcy will stand the test of time.'

Everyone went silent. Robbie looked around, confused. He'd only been on the island for three years. He had no idea of the effect his words had.

Anne froze. She'd been careful to ask Grace about any content in the book that might cause upset, but she hadn't factored in rogue comments from book club members. She stared at Hamish, who quickly got the message and tried to smooth things over.

'Well, I believe there's a sequel so I guess we can find out if we want to. How did you all feel about the diary format of the book?'

Thank the universe for Hamish. Decades as a lawyer meant his brain rarely froze, unlike Anne's.

The discussion continued, although somewhat stilted after that. Sam slipped away from the bar disappearing into the night. Anne wanted to chase after him but she knew when to leave him alone.

Was he thinking about the sirens, the screams, like she was? He had so much of his grandfather in him – the way he furrowed his brow, the way he felt things so very deeply, the way he was at peace at his pottery wheel. He was probably headed there now.

Shellie broke Anne's reverie. 'So, what's our next book?'

All eyes turned to Anne.

'Well, I wasn't sure how keen people were, so I was going to see how tonight went before organising another book.'

Hamish was the first to respond. 'I'd say it was a success.'

'I'll talk to the librarian on Monday and get her to send over a set of books on Thursday's supply run.'

The semicircle rippled with murmured agreement, which turned to hugs and pats on the back as everyone took their leave.

Anne packed the books in the plastic tub, laying the book club questions on top.

'That seemed like it went okay.' Hamish put his arm around her shoulder. 'I think everyone really enjoyed themselves.'

'Really?'

'They're all coming back next month.'

True. But deep down, Anne was petrified everyone was simply putting on a front and right now, outside the pub, they were all rolling their eyes and trying to come up with excuses as to why they couldn't come next time.

'This will take time.' He picked up the tub of books. 'Sam will come round.'

Anne wasn't so sure about that.

Together they walked back to the cottages in silence.

Perhaps Hamish was right. Maybe the night wasn't as bad as she thought. Just not what she'd expected.

But then, life rarely did go as expected. She knew that all too well.

They slowed their stroll as they reached Hamish's cottage, the black door nigh on invisible in the dark. 'Would you like me to walk you up the hill, Anne?'

'Oh, I think I can manage the rest of the way on my own.' She kissed his cheek and said goodnight.

When she got home she slipped off her flowing yellow dress, put on her old house coat, and then padded out the back door and into her moonlit studio.

Memories of long ago had been haunting her lately, and not only in her dreams. Sometimes they were comforting, sometimes not. Tonight she had no desire for either. Tonight was not the night

for them. Tonight she needed to nurse her slightly bruised expec-
tations that the new Wattle Island Book Club would be an instant
success.

The old art shed with its wooden walls and tin roof was where
she needed to be tonight, the metallic smell of the ink dancing in
the night air around her. Surrounded by decades of paintings and
drawings and sketches of indigo landscapes and bright abstracts,
she pushed all thought from her mind.

She stood in front of the old drafting table and ran her fingers
over the notched, stained wood. It would probably be considered
vintage these days. Or perhaps antique. Like her.

She set up a large piece of parchment and her black and blue
inks and closed her eyes, twirling the old calligraphy brush in her
hand, the bamboo handle cold against her fingers.

Opening her eyes, she exhaled and pushed ink across the page,
her mind quieting, her heartbeat slowing.

Seven

Grace set out the last of the glasses on the circular table in the library's conference room and checked the laptop was properly connected to the big screen. The jugs of iced water were spaced evenly around the table, platters of fruit and chocolate biscuits between them. The Port Maddison Scribblers' Ink writing group would straggle in over the next fifteen minutes in a loud celebration of words, before they settled down to write. They'd been coming to the library for two years now, an eclectic mix of people who'd have never found each other if it weren't for their love of the written word.

A light tap on the room's glass door got Grace's attention. On the other side, Linh gestured that Grace had a phone call.

She took the call from her office.

It was Anne.

'Hello, pet. I'm calling to arrange our next title.'

'That's great. I take it the night went well?'

She'd been wondering all weekend how it had gone.

'Oh . . . well . . .' There was a slight quiver to Anne's voice.
'What happened?'

'It was fine. Fine. I suppose I thought people would be more . . .
open to discussion, I guess. It was a little like wringing blood from
a stone. Especially when Sam—Oh, don't worry, pet. I'm sure I'm
making far too much of nothing. Maybe starting this up again
wasn't a good idea.'

'A book club is always a good idea,' Grace said firmly.
'Sometimes it just takes a while for one to gel. You said something
about new members last time we spoke. Maybe once you get to
know each other—'

'We know each other well. Too well, perhaps.' Anne's voice
drifted off.

Grace paused. 'Anne? If you can tell me exactly what the
problem was, maybe I can help with the next meeting. Suggest a
different style of book, perhaps.'

'Thank you, pet. I don't think it was the book.'

'Is there any reason the book club would have trouble gelling?'

'Oh dear, is that the time? I'd better rush, love.'

'But we haven't discussed—'

Anne hung up.

What a strange conversation. Grace had heard the disappointment in Anne's voice. It may not have been a disaster, but
clearly it wasn't what Anne wanted. Grace was fairly sure it wasn't
the choice of book. More than likely they simply needed to
find their rhythm. Every book club had a sweet spot where the various personalities were in sync and discussion and debate could
take place in balance. But if the rhythm was off, a book club
could fail.

Linh came into the room. 'Everything okay?'

'Yeah.' Grace told her about the call.

'Sounds like they need some Grace Elliott Book Club Magic. You haven't met many book clubs you couldn't wrangle.'

No, she hadn't. In all her years doing this, there'd only been two book clubs whose rhythms she hadn't been able to help find.

Grace opened her computer and googled Wattle Island. If you wanted to help a book club find its rhythm, you had to know the book club. When the local clubs ran into difficulties, which happened from time to time – a reading slump, a reluctant husband, a difficult member, an out-of-bounds topic – she usually knew at least one person in the group personally, whether it was someone she'd grown up with, a regular at the library or a neighbour, and she could use that to figure out a solution.

This was different. She didn't know any of the members, and she'd never even been to the island. In the same way that many Australians travelled overseas before seeing any of their own country, not a lot of Port Maddison locals had visited Wattle Island. Its relative proximity made a trip there easy to put off, and far away meant exotic and that made overseas destinations more interesting. Grace was guilty of that. So many of her bucket list items involved travelling to far-off places.

She didn't know a lot about Wattle Island, but she'd have to change that if she was to help Anne.

Grace trawled through the visitor information website, which included a brief history of the island, its population – 503 – and its current attraction to tourists in summer. The photos of empty beaches and rolling hills were stunning.

There was a page for visitor comments, and Grace read through it.

very friendly locals – Jane & Jim, Sydney, March 2016

the diving is brilliant, Phil a great guide – Karen and Greg, Brisbane, September 2015

*loved the bakery and the pub serves the best counter lunches,
great for a couple of grey nomads like us – Terry & Turner, June
2005*

And then a comment that stood out.

*returned to the island for our 10th wedding anniversary, sad to
see the bookshop closed down three years ago – Nat and Henry,
February 2014*

Grace did the maths. The bookshop closed seven years ago, the
same year the original book club ended. That made sense, she supposed, as it would have been harder to source titles. Though there
was always the internet and the Port Maddison library. Why had it
taken Anne seven years to ask the library for help?

Setting up a new book club always had teething issues. But
this wasn't a new book club. And according to Anne, the members all knew each other well. If Grace wanted to help Anne, she
had to know why the book club stopped in the first place. Was it
simply a matter of logistics with the bookshop closing, or something else?

She rang Anne back.

'Hello, pet. I wasn't expecting to hear from you so soon.'

Grace didn't think jumping straight in was the correct tactic
so she stalled by saying, 'Well, I've been thinking about what to
suggest for your next book. Did you have a look on the library's
website?'

'Far too many choices, pet,' Anne said, and she was right. The
library had a lot of book club sets. 'And being such a mixed group,
to be honest, I'm a bit hesitant to pick.'

'Hmm. Well, what are the interests of the people in your
group?'

'Hadley, anything farming related. Ruth prefers the classics.
She's a bit of a literary snob. Shellie likes history. I wouldn't know

about Robbie. He's new,' Anne continued. 'And Phil, probably anything with a lot of action.'

Grace made notes.

'Maree is a hopeless romantic.'

Grace had an idea where she could go with this information.

'What about you, Anne?' Grace had learned over the years that if the person spearheading a book club was enthusiastic about a book, that enthusiasm was usually infectious.

'Oh, I'll read anything – it's one of my great loves. Reading and art.'

Art? A small bell rang in the back of Grace's mind, but she put it aside for now.

'And is there anything you all have in common?'

Anne paused. 'Book club.'

And with that, Grace knew the right title.

'Some of us are the original members going back sixty years,' Anne said.

This was Grace's chance. 'That's quite a long time. Do you mind me asking why book club stopped? Seven years ago, I believe you said.'

Anne cleared her throat. 'Oh. Ah. That's the oven timer.'

Grace hadn't heard any ding or chime.

'Whatever you choose will be perfect, Grace. Must run.'

Silence.

'What aren't you telling me, Anne Sato?' Grace murmured.

Anne Sato, who loved reading and art. There was that bell again.

Grace moved her computer mouse and her screen flickered awake. She searched the library's catalogue for 'Sato' and 'Anne'. Nothing. Then a memory of an old book flashed through her mind. What was it called? *Ink Master*? No. That was a TV show about tattoos. *Ink* something . . . *Liquid Ink*. That was it. How could she forget that? When she'd first checked the borrowed book back in, five years ago now if she recalled correctly, she'd thought it was a silly title. Ink was always a liquid. But then she'd never really understood art, despite it appearing more than once on her bucket list over the years – *age eighteen: visit the Mona Lisa; age nineteen: learn to paint like Monet.*

She had flicked through the large coffee-table book before putting it back on the shelf and thought nothing more of it. Until now.

Out in the library she navigated her way around the shelves and found the book exactly where it was supposed to be, wedged in tight between two other art tomes. She yanked it free.

Making use of one of the brightly coloured jellybean-shaped couches scattered throughout the library, Grace sat down and opened the book. The photographs were deep and luxurious, and the compositions so silky it was as if they moved. She'd not registered it last time, but it was as if the pictures were liquid. As if the scenes were flowing right before her. She turned the page and saw a river and mountain captured in black that dripped with detail, the leaves of the trees pouring into the water below. Grace was mesmerised.

Halfway into the book, she found a rendering of a cliff face jutting into the sea with a lighthouse perched above in broody tones of blue and indigo. It was as if she could dive into the page and be swallowed by the waves below, rising and falling with each swell, the lighthouse watching over her.

Grace closed her eyes. She was most definitely losing the plot now. Was this one of the side effects of her medication?

Opening her eyes again she looked at the caption of the painting. *Wattle Island Lighthouse*, A. Sato, 1972.

There you are, Anne Sato.

The book contained about a dozen of Anne's paintings. All were full of emotion, the dark sea calling to Grace, inviting her in. She imagined swimming in the waves, walking past the light-house, wandering the hills. Unlike the bright tourist shots Grace had looked at on the internet, Anne's renderings reached deep inside her.

She closed the book, unsettled by the yearning she felt.

For three nights Grace's sleep was restless, her dreams fitful with images of book titles and swimming in inky waves, being pulled towards something she couldn't see.

On the way to work she picked up a coffee for Gladys as she always did on Thursdays, but Gladys passed. 'You look like you need it more than I do.'

She probably did, but she hadn't been able to stomach coffee since her first round of chemo. She continued inside and the moment she sat down at her desk, she rang Anne.

'The boat is heading out this afternoon and I wanted to share with you what I've chosen.'

Anne clapped. 'Excellent, pet.'

Grace crossed her fingers. 'So, I think I've got just the book for your motley crew.'

'Intriguing.'

'There's a pig farmer, a lot of history, some action and romance, and it's an epistolary novel, completely told in letters, so that should give the literary snob something to mull over too.'

Anne let out a whistle. 'Well, I'd say you've outdone yourself.'

Grace swelled with pride. 'And they made it into a movie this year, though there were some quite significant differences.'

'Well, don't keep an old lady in suspense. What is it?'

'*The Guernsey Literary and Potato Peel Pie Society*.'

'My, isn't that a mouthful.' Anne laughed.

'It is. But it is one of my all-time favourites, so hopefully you'll all enjoy it too.'

There was a pause.

'Anne?'

'Sorry. I was just saying a quiet prayer asking for everyone to like it. I know that sounds silly, but it's very important book club is a success.'

'The importance of a book club doesn't sound silly to me at all.'

'It's not for me, mind you. A woman my age is on borrowed time. No, the book club is for everyone else.'

Borrowed time. Grace drew in a deep breath and let it out slowly. Was that it? Was Anne dying? Wanting to leave a legacy behind? Grace knew that a brush with your own mortality could make you reassess what was important in life. Maybe that was what Anne was doing. But that didn't explain why the book club had stopped seven years ago.

'Anne, is there anything I can do to help?'

'If you can somehow manage to wave a magic wand to ensure our next book club is a raging success, I'd be eternally grateful.'

If Grace had a magic wand, she'd have used it long before now on herself. But she did have a certain knack. And half a thought forming.

'I promise you it will be.'

Anne thanked her and hung up and Grace began to think about how to keep her promise.

Later that day, Grace stood on the dock watching the *Seafarer III* pulling into port. The afternoon sun was setting behind the hills of Port Maddison, casting an orange glow over the dark water in the harbour. Captain Allen waved to her as he stepped off the boat, followed by Toby, who picked up the plastic tub of books that was sitting at Grace's feet.

'Going well, I take it?' Jeremiah greeted Grace with a nod of his white curls.

'Well, they're up for another round, so that's a good sign.'

'It's good to see it back. They need it. Though I'm a bit surprised.'

Grace frowned. 'Really? Why are you surprised?'

'I never thought I'd see the book club together again. Especially after what happened.' He shook his head.

Grace nearly grabbed the man, and fought to keep her voice calm. 'Why did they stop? Was it because the bookshop closed?'

'Other way around, love.'

That didn't make sense. 'The bookshop closed because the book club stopped?'

He shrugged. 'Because of *why* it stopped. Terrible business, that.' He shook his head. 'I didn't know her well—'

'Her?'

He blinked and Grace could see him summoning his thoughts back from where they had wandered. 'I've been going to the island most of my life, but for a time I worked as a teacher in Sydney, did you know?'

'I didn't.'

He nodded. 'When my wife died, so young she was, I came back home and took over from my dad.'

'I'm sorry.' And she genuinely was, but her need to find a way to steer his thoughts back to book club meant she wasn't as empathetic as she should have been.

He shrugged. 'It's been a good life. Different to what I expected, I suppose, but life often is.'

Grace knew that better than most. 'I couldn't agree more, Jeremiah.' She lowered her voice. 'What was the terrible business?'

He stared straight ahead.

'And who is the *her* you mentioned?'

He shook his head. 'Not my business to share, Miss Elliott.'

Jeremiah tipped his head and stepped back on the boat. 'Better get on with it. The old girl won't sail herself.'

Grace stood on the dock until the *Seafarer III* moved past the break wall. Every bucket list she'd ever written since the very first had one common item.

Solve a mystery.

If she was going to help the Wattle Island Book Club find its rhythm, she needed to find out what had happened.

This may not have been what she'd had in mind over the years, but the half thought that had come to her this morning while talking to Anne was now morphing into the beginnings of an idea.

Two weeks after sending the books, a parcel arrived at the library for Grace.

'This is exciting,' Linh said, sitting next to her in the staffroom, the signature aroma of strong bitter coffee wafting around them. 'You don't normally get personal mail at work.'

Grace didn't normally get mail full stop. She opened the package. Inside, sitting on top of blue tissue paper, was a postcard. On the front of it was a series of photos of pottery pieces and a logo. On the back was a message. She read it aloud.

'*Thank you for the books, Grace. I've started reading and I'm hooked. I'm nervous about our next meeting, but fingers crossed. Please accept this piece of my grandson Sam's art as a thank you for helping me with book club.*'

Grace pulled back the tissue paper revealing a white pottery bowl decorated with tiny pink cherry blossoms dancing around the base in intricate patterns.

'Oh my.' She turned it around and over. On the underside the initials S. S. were stamped, next to some Japanese calligraphy.

'Oh my is right.' Linh nodded. 'That's stunning. Just for sending over some books?'

It was a lovely gift. And an unnecessary one for a regular old book club. But one thing Grace was beginning to suspect was that this was no ordinary book club.

Linh was leaning over her, looking at the bowl.

'Don't you have work to do?' Grace asked.

'Sorry, boss.' She grinned and slipped out of the room.

Grace pulled out her phone and searched the internet for 'Sam Sato' and 'pottery' and found a gallery in Sydney that sold his work. For quite a considerable price tag, in fact. She stared at his pieces on the screen. They were delicate yet bold, and had a similar sense of movement as Anne's paintings. There was a small portrait of Sam on the page. Warm brown eyes looked back at her; an easy, confident smile dressed a tanned face. The date in the caption read 2011. Seven years ago. There it was again.

The next morning Grace rang Anne to thank her.

'Oh, pet, I should be thanking you. I love this book. Love it. Hopefully the others do too.'

Grace doodled a lighthouse on the piece of paper in front of her. 'We never know if people will enjoy a book, but this one has a fair bit in it to unpack and discuss, so it should prompt the discussion you're looking for.'

'Do you have any tips for me? I never had trouble getting book club to talk before the— before.'

'Actually, Anne, I think maybe I can help.'

The thought that had turned into an idea had grown into a plan that took shape as Grace spoke with Anne. By the time they hung up, that plan was in motion.

Eight

Anne put the book down on the small wicker table beside the veranda chair and breathed in the heavily salted air. She had to hand it to Grace, *The Guernsey Literary and Potato Peel Pie Society* was an excellent choice. The entire thing being written in letters took some getting used to. But once she did, she found herself falling into the pages, swept along by a tale rich in emotion.

She'd been too afraid to ask anyone else what they thought of it when she'd run into them. She was trusting Grace was right. The plan they'd hatched over the phone was genius. Well, it was good, and Anne would take any help she could get. The meeting last month had been the first time the old book club members had all been together in one place in seven years. Even though Sam had remained separate, he was still there. And that counted. The people Anne loved most in the world being together again was what she was fighting for. People were better together. Isolation, loneliness – they were never good. And before her time to drop off the mortal perch came, she needed to fix things. To mend the wishy-washy version of themselves they'd been the last seven years.

Standing up Anne looked at the grey ocean.

From inside the cottage, the clock on the mantel chimed. Sam would be here any minute and she wasn't ready. She bustled inside, tossed the book on the sofa and hurried out to the studio to gather her things.

She made it back into the kitchen as Sam was arriving, and she draped herself casually on a dining chair, tapping her foot as if she'd been waiting for him.

'Hello, Obaachan.' He kissed her on top of her head. 'Are you sure you want to do this? Shouldn't you be resting?'

'Fiddlesticks.' Anne slapped Sam's hand away from her side. 'I'm perfectly fine.' She was tired. More than usual. But her nerves about book club, which was only a few days away, couldn't be eased by lying down or having a cup of tea. She needed to paint.

'Really? So I didn't need to bring in your washing last week? You haven't had trouble with your eyesight lately?'

'My dear boy. Getting you to bring in my washing is merely a ploy to get you around here more often so I can see your handsome, grumpy visage. And at my age, what do you expect of my eyesight?'

'I expect you to get it tested.'

'There is no force on this green earth that will get me to travel to the mainland. You were lucky when I had my stroke I was too weak to fight the air ambulance people.'

Sam shook his head and Anne knew she'd won. Or at least, she knew he'd given up, which wasn't quite the same thing, but she'd take it. Her aversion to the mainland was common knowledge, though only Hamish knew the real reason why she hated it so much.

'Now, are you going to help me carry these things down to the beach, or are you going to make me lug them all by myself? Have you seen the grey and broody sky today? The light is perfect this afternoon.'

'Of course.' He placed a gentle hand on her shoulder and a small smile broke through this thick beard.

She handed him her case full of ink and brushes. He picked up the easel along with the other equipment she'd need.

Anne tied her pink scarf covered in tiny hand-painted orange koi around her head, knotted to the left as always. It was the one Sam and Addie had given her for her last birthday. Eighty-something. She didn't bother counting anymore.

Together they ambled down Soldiers' Way and Sam helped her set up the camping chair and easel at the end of the dock, looking out to the churning ocean.

'Actually, I think I might like to look that way.' She pointed to the headland, the row of white cottages picking up the eerie light of the grey afternoon.

Sam moved her things around. 'What time should I come back?'

'As you know,' she said with a flourish of her right hand, the long sleeve of her kimono making a figure of eight in the air, 'creativity is no slave to time.'

Sam laughed, the sound warming Anne's heart.

'So before it gets dark, then.' He kissed her and walked up the dock.

Anne would have preferred to paint by the lighthouse; the rumbling weather would be bringing out all the colours of the grass and waves on that side of the island. But she couldn't ask Sam to take her there. If she'd been thinking, she might have rung Phil, but then he was probably working. Technically, so was Sam. But as a freelance graphic designer, he had a little more flexibility to be at her beck and call. Though she tried not to abuse that advantage. Not often, anyway.

She did paint from the lighthouse regularly, but only small, simple ink-on-parchment pieces. The feeling that had come over her this morning when the weather first started to turn was that of a much larger piece. Requiring an easel.

It had been a while since she'd painted anything so big. She hoped she was up to the task.

Sitting in front of the stark white paper she prepared her inks and then closed her eyes. And waited, taking in deep breaths.

Ah, there it was. The calm. She hadn't realised how much she'd missed it. So much a part of her life for so long now.

She picked up her brush and allowed it to dance over the blank sheet in sweeps of blue and indigo that brought back memories of a turbulent sea.

Wattle Island, 1949

Anne stood on the dock waiting for the supply ship to come in, the sun bouncing off the pale grey wood, the familiar tang of salt in the air. Jeremiah had written to her a couple of weeks ago, letting her know that teachers' college was going well, and that he was sending her some books on this week's boat run.

She was glad to still be in contact with her friend, and had put her embarrassing misunderstanding from a year ago behind her. Mostly. It still stung. A little.

The thought of new books had put her in the lightest mood over the past few days and even Aunt Bess had noticed. She thought it had something to do with the frequency with which Hadley

Follett had been coming round, but both Hadley and Anne knew that was all about Anne helping him stay on top of his schoolwork, especially maths.

She'd been attending the little island school religiously, determined to obtain a good intermediate certificate and somehow use it to make her way off the island. To do what, she wasn't sure. She had no desire to become a teacher, and nursing was the last thing she could see herself doing. She would have to get a good job in an office, perhaps. Her attendance and exceptional performance at school had attracted the attention of a few students needing a little help to get by. She didn't charge them much, but it was all adding up. One day she'd have enough to get off the island.

In the distance she could see the rise and fall of the familiar vessel coming into sight and her heart raced.

She hadn't had anything new to read since Jeremiah left – nothing decent anyway. The school's collection was rarely updated and when it was, it was with donations from the church. And Jeremiah was so busy adjusting to his new life; she hadn't wanted to bother him with something so trivial. Trivial as far as he was concerned.

Anne knew it was hard to tell distance when looking over the vast expanse of blue, but the boat seemed to be taking an inordinate amount of time to reach her. She walked the length of the dock and wandered onto the sand. There, she rearranged the shells into little tableaux. No one passing would have been able to recognise them, but in her imagination she created the Harbour Bridge, the Empire State Building, and a miniature farm with cows and sheep in a somewhat askew paddock, using slimy seaweed to represent bales of hay the shell-animals could eat. The lapping of the waves on the dock's pilings increased in rhythm until the droning sound of the *Seafarer*'s horn announced the boat's approach. Anne raced to the top of the dock.

Wringing her hands in anticipation, Anne watched as Captain Allen manoeuvred the boat in close. Behind her, two men from the pub walked up and took their positions to aid the captain with off-loading his cargo.

The *Seafarer* bumped to a halt and a young man jumped off the deck onto the dock. This one was skinnier than the last, the latest in a string of deckhands since Jeremiah had left. With speed and ease he tied the boat off and the captain started unloading. First, by throwing Anne's books, tied in a hessian bag, onto the pier with unceremoniously casual abandon. The loose knot that held the bag closed burst open and two books skidded across the wooden planks landing at her feet.

She let out a little squeal and bent down to pick them up. The new deckhand picked up the bag and took it to Anne, passing it to her with woollen-gloved hands, his beanie-covered head bowed down. 'Sorry, miss.' His voice was quiet and deep, but before Anne had a chance to thank him he jumped back on the boat and continued his job. Anne scurried away with her books held tightly to her chest, sad that Jeremiah wasn't there to deliver them, but excited to see what he'd sent.

Anne rushed through her usual roster of chores that morning – weeding the back path and cleaning the cloudy salt crust from the cottage's windows (the curse of being exposed to ocean winds) – and set off for the lighthouse, arriving as the sun passed its highest point in the sky. She settled in the grass beside the lighthouse, resting her back against the white-washed wall of the tall slim monolith. From this side, looking south, she was protected from the biting wind that had whipped up.

Jeremiah had done an exceptional job putting together the selection of books, six in total, including *Emma* and *The Grapes of Wrath*. She picked up *The Harp in the South*, and a note slipped out from the pages.

Everyone in Sydney is talking about this. Happy reading. J.

Anne had a hard time deciding which one to start with, so she got up and lay the books in a circle in the long grass that surrounded the lighthouse. Standing in the middle of the circle, she closed her eyes and spun around. When the risk of toppling over from dizziness became too much, she ceased twirling. But she stopped too quickly and her insides kept spinning even though her outsides had finished.

She opened her eyes, wobbled, stumbled and fell forward. A pair of strong hands caught her just before she thudded to the ground.

'Are you okay?' the voice asked.

'Yes.' She righted herself and turned around.

In front of her was a young man she'd never seen on the island. A man she'd never actually seen the likes of before. His dark brown eyes were kind, his smile slightly crooked but warm, his shoulders held tight, on alert.

'Hello.' She spoke very slowly, unsure if he'd understand her. 'Thank you for helping me.'

'I speak English, miss. I was born here.' His eyes hardened with resignation, and Anne wondered how many times he'd had to explain himself in this way.

Anne's cheeks burned with embarrassment. 'I'm sorry. I assumed . . . I shouldn't have . . .' She threw her arms in the air. 'I'm a numbskull. Sorry.'

The man's mouth turned up, his crooked smile disarming. Anne's cheeks flushed again.

'It's all right. I'm used to it. My name's Tadashi. But Tad will do. It's easier to say.'

Anne held out her hand. 'Nice to meet you, Tadashi. I'm Anne.'

'Nice to meet you again, Anne.'

Tadashi shook Anne's hand and warmth shot through her arm. 'Again?'

'At the dock. I picked up your—'

'Bag of books. Of course.' That was why she'd never seen him before. He was the *Seafarer*'s new deckhand. The woollen beanie that had been pulled down over his face this morning was now stuffed into the pocket of his overalls.

'And what were you doing here, Anne-san, before I came along? A new dance?'

Anne laughed. 'Hardly. Trying to decide which book to read next.'

'An interesting approach.' He crouched down to inspect the books. 'I've read this one.' He picked up *Emma*.

'You've read Austen? I don't know too many people who have. Not here on the island, anyway.'

'It's not bad.' He shrugged.

'Not bad? It's a classic. Everyone who's ever read it considers it a masterpiece. Or they have no brain to speak of.' She put her hands on her hips and Tadashi laughed.

'Yes. I know that's the widely held belief.'

'So what would you consider a classic, then?' If he was going to criticise, then he could at least back up his claim.

'Hmm.' He pressed his chin with his slender forefinger and thumb. 'English or Japanese?'

'You're Japanese?'

'I was born here, so that makes me a British subject, but yes, I'm Japanese.'

Anne had never seen a Japanese person before. Not even in Sydney. Not that that was surprising. All she knew about the

Japanese, and that wasn't much, were the things she heard about the war. She took half a step back.

His smile dropped. 'Sorry, miss. I'll leave you be.' He bowed and turned to go.

'No, wait!' Anne called out. She might not have understood much about the world or the war, but she knew about books and she knew how hard it was, especially here, to find others who loved them as much as she did. 'Both,' she said. 'English and Japanese classics.'

He stepped forward then back. Anne didn't know what to do so she plonked herself down and sat cross-legged in the cold grass. 'I'd love to hear your thoughts.'

Tadashi sat with her.

'*David Copperfield* would be on my list. Who doesn't love a scrappy orphan making his way in the world?'

Anne's mouth dropped open.

'You don't agree?'

'I . . . I haven't read it.' She hated to admit it and tried to think of something else to save her embarrassment. 'What about Swift?' she asked.

He nodded. 'I know he's often dismissed as simply a children's author, but he should be appreciated, for his critical and satirical view of—'

'—society.' Anne finished Tadashi's sentence, her mind reeling.

He bowed his head and smiled.

'What about Japanese classics?' Anne was desperate to hear more from this stranger. The idea that each culture had its own literary canon was a revelation to her.

He rubbed his chin with elegant fingers. 'My parents would say *Genji monogatari*, *The Tale of Genji*, is the pinnacle of Japanese literature. And they'd probably be right.'

Anne hung on his every word. A whole new world was opening up to her.

'It was written in the eleventh century about the son of an Emperor and a concubine.'

'I've never read anything that old before. Unless you count the Bible.'

He smiled. 'I've only read the modern Japanese version of *Genji*.'

'Modern Japanese?'

'A bit like English today compared with Shakespeare's English.'

'Right. Of course.' She felt foolish for asking.

Tadashi's eyes crinkled as he continued, passion in his voice. 'And there is *Kokoro*, my favourite. It means, roughly, heart.'

'I wish I could read them.' Anne looked up to the sky.

'Well, I can't help you there, but perhaps next supply run, I can bring you a copy of *David Copperfield*.'

'Would you?' She dared look him directly in his eyes but he turned his face to the horizon.

'Of course.'

Silence fell between them and Anne looked out to the deep blue ocean, heaving and falling below them. She wanted to keep the discussion going but was afraid she'd seem stupid if she opened her mouth. She glanced in his direction, his far-off gaze a mystery to her. One she wanted to solve. Casting her eyes down, she noticed indigo stains on his fingers.

'Do you write?' she ventured.

He smiled, a simple action that made her cheeks warm again. 'No, I don't have the talent for that.' He followed her gaze and rubbed his hands together. 'I'm an artist. Well, I'm a deckhand, obviously. But I'd like to be an artist.'

'What do you paint?'

'What I see. I sculpt sometimes too. I think maybe that is where my skill lies. And my passion.' He hid his hands in the sleeves of his jumper. 'I have taken too much of your time, Anne-san. I apologise.' He stood and waited for her to get up before bowing deeply.

Anne didn't know how to respond. Did she bow too? Curtsy? In the end she did an awkward mix of the two, and Tadashi was polite enough to hold back his laughter.

As he turned and walked down the worn dirt track that led toward the headland and back into town, Anne watched him until he disappeared, wishing she had said something to make him stay.

She looked down at the selection of books in the grass and picked up *Emma*. It wasn't overrated, like Tadashi had implied. She would re-read it, though, to make sure.

The next morning Anne waited by the dock before the turning tide. She smoothed her hands over the waistline of her yellow A-line skirt – the one she normally wore to church with Aunt Bess on Sundays. It was short on her now, and nowhere near as comfortable as her dungarees. When she saw Tadashi approach, walking a yard and a half behind Captain Allen, she wondered if she were making a fool of herself again, like she had with Jeremiah. No. She was simply giving him a gift. A friendly gesture towards someone who might appreciate it. Nothing more, nothing less. Despite the skirt.

'Anne-san.' Tadashi bowed towards her.

Desperate to avoid another bow–curtsy, Anne nodded at him. 'I thought you might like this.'

She handed him a book on nineteenth century art. She had found it ages ago on her way home from school in a pile of junk that one of the old biddies from the other side of town was throwing out, and thought the pictures were far too pretty to end up in the trash. She'd admired the Monets, but thought Klimt was a bit too strange. She'd even tried to copy some of the pictures, imagining that perhaps art could be her ticket off the island. She could travel the world and live off her paintings, having a bohemian adventure. But she'd failed miserably and hid the book so she wasn't constantly reminded of the brief fiasco.

With far more reverence than was required, Tadashi took the book in both hands. 'Arigato gozaimasu. Thank you, Anne-san.'

'You're welcome. It's all right if you don't like it.' Suddenly she felt foolish. 'I just thought after our conversation—'

'I will cherish it, and next month when I return I will have a book to gift to you.'

He turned and she watched him board the supply boat, waving them away as they set sail. Tadashi didn't look back to the dock, busy of course, doing what deckhands do, but Anne hoped he was a man of his word and would seek her out on his next return with his favourite classic for her to read.

The month dragged by in a monotonous stretch of school and chores. Anne read *Emma* three times in anticipation of Tadashi's return, ready for any debate that might arise about the novel's worth. He was most definitely wrong about it being overrated. She also re-read *Persuasion*, just in case, borrowing it from the school library. One of the few decent texts they had. She'd have to return it next week with the school year ending soon and her time there coming to an end. Her stomach tightened at the thought. Finishing school meant thinking about what was next to come. And that frightened her.

She pushed those thoughts from her mind. All she really wanted to think about was Tadashi's imminent return.

Finally, the time came. In the early morning light, she headed to the dock.

Waves crashed against the pilings in angry bursts. The night's storm had long passed but the ocean continued to heave and swell. Anne could see the boat's silhouette rise and fall and she hoped Captain Allen and Tadashi were okay being thrown around out there.

The violent waters made the approach slow, but the boat eventually pulled up alongside the dock and the men began to off-load their cargo. There were no books from Jeremiah this trip, just a letter Captain Allen thrust into her hands as he barked orders at Tadashi. She'd never heard him speak like that to Jeremiah all those times she'd waited for him at the dock. Tadashi avoided eye contact with the captain and didn't acknowledge her presence.

Sulking, Anne took her letter and trudged to the other side of the island. There, she sat on her rucksack to stop the moisture from the still-damp grass soaking through her clothes and read the words from her old friend.

Dear Sport,

Teachers' college is great and I'm actually doing well. Well, I'm not failing, at least. I'm sorry there's no book delivery this month, I've been mighty busy. I've met a girl, Corinne. I think you'd like her. She enjoys reading, like you. I might be serious about her. What do you think of that? Me, keen on a girl. Hope next month to send you books. J

Anne sighed. Jeremiah had changed the course of his life, just as he'd set out to. And she was still stuck on the island. She climbed down the hill and headed not towards town, but to the side of the island no one went to, to Rocky Beach. Surrounded by jagged rocks with no easy path to access it, it was nearly always empty despite its soft sand and gentle waves. She never ran into anyone here, and she didn't really feel like bumping into Hadley and being forced to discuss cows, or worse, running into Ruth and her side-kick Maree.

No, over here she'd be all alone.

School was all but over for her now and she'd saved a fair bit of money from her tutoring endeavours. But it wasn't enough. She could pay her way to the mainland, but then what? She'd been so focused on getting out of here, she'd forgotten to think about what would happen if she managed it.

That was a lie. Of course she'd thought about it. A lot. But since she'd been on Wattle Island, she'd lost contact with her friends in Sydney, and Aunt Bess was her only relative. Where would she go, all alone?

She knew Mrs Forster used to work in an office in Sydney before she got married and that she'd taught some of the girls on the island typing and shorthand and other skills that might help Anne secure such a job. She would speak to her tomorrow.

Perched on a rock she pulled out what was left of her sketch-book. Most of the pages had been torn out and incinerated. She didn't even know why she still kept it in her rucksack. Maybe she could make paper aeroplanes out of the last few leaves and send them into the sea.

'Anne-san. I apologise for the disturbance.'

She turned around to see Tadashi bowing to her.

'Oh. Um. That's all right. I was just contemplating the release of these offensive pages out into the wild.' She tore one of the sheets out and started folding it.

'Forgive me for asking, but what did the paper do to you?'

Anne laughed. 'It refused to accept my attempts to paint it with beauty.'

Tadashi held out his hand and she gave him the sketchbook.

'I cannot see any issues with the paper that would refuse ink or paint.'

Anne put a hand over her mouth to hold back a chuckle. 'No. You're right. It isn't the fault of the paper. I once tried to copy those pictures in that book I gave you and it didn't work. So I've been copying one of the art books at school, and that hasn't worked either. It isn't the paper's fault. That lies entirely with me.'

Tadashi nodded. 'Ah. Now I see the problem.'

'What?'

'You tried to copy other artists.'

'What's wrong with that?'

He lowered his eyes then looked back at her, his gaze warm. 'A true artist cannot copy another. They must find their own way.'

'Well, I'm fairly sure I'm no true artist.' She gave a bitter laugh. 'No roaming the streets of Paris or Florence making francs or lire to live off for me.'

'May I?' Tadashi indicated the rock next to Anne. She nodded and he sat beside her, close enough that she could feel the warmth of his body radiating towards her and smell the scent of salt and soap on his skin. From inside the bag he was carrying, more of a satchel than a rucksack, he pulled out a brush and a bottle filled with indigo liquid.

He handed them to her. 'Close your eyes.'

She looked at him, her head tilted to the side, then did as she was told.

'Now, what do you see?'

'Nothing. My eyes are closed.'

She heard him stifle a laugh. 'With your mind's eye. Describe the beach in front of us.'

She opened her eyes.

'No. Keep them closed.'

Shaking her head, she closed her eyes again. What kind of nonsense was this? She felt like a complete imbecile. But it was passing the time with Tadashi beside her so she continued.

'Now. Describe the beach to me, in detail.'

'The sand is soft. Yellow-white. There are grey rocks and blue water—'

'Is the sea really blue? When you really look into it?'

'Well . . . no. It's kind of grey-green. Kind of . . . nothing, actually.'

'Better.'

'And how does it make you feel?'

Feel? The ocean didn't make her feel anything. 'It's cold when I swim in it.'

'Good. But what does it make you feel inside?'

Inside? Anne focused. 'It makes me feel happy. Kind of . . .' How could she describe it? 'Like I'm free.'

'Ah. And what draws you to it?'

How did he know she was drawn to it? Her heart beat faster.

'With your mind, reach out to the water and feel the ocean.'

She took in a deep breath and tried to push her mind out. She felt the ocean, its depth, its colour. 'It's like it's pulling me in, pulling me home.'

A single tear fell down her cheek and she opened her eyes.

'I don't have the right words,' she whispered.

'Then don't use them. Use this.' He opened the bottle of ink and pointed to the sketchbook.

With a shaking hand Anne poised the brush above the white void. She closed her eyes, pushed her mind out again to see if it would happen once more. That altogether strange sensation of seeing without viewing. Her pulse slowed; her hand steadied.

When she opened her eyes she began to move the thick brush across the page in strokes that made no sense according to what she'd read about making art, but as she squinted her eyes slightly, she could see the picture take shape. Flowing lines, thick and thin, dark and light, she painted her response to what she felt rather than trying to replicate the image of what she saw. And it was working.

She got excited and moved her hand faster, but the brush slipped and she ended up with an unsightly blob in the top left corner of the page.

'Darn it.' She dropped her hand and the moment was gone. 'It's terrible.'

'No. It isn't.'

She frowned.

'What do you see?' he asked.

She tilted her head and looked at her painting. It was no masterpiece, that was for sure, but it had captured something. Hope? Uncertainty? The waves moved across the page, a new beginning. She could never say that out loud though.

'I see you on the page,' Tadashi said. 'A young woman full of hope. And doubt.'

She jumped up and the sketchbook fell off her lap. She looked at Tadashi, his smile full of warmth. And then she ran away as fast as she could.

Back at Aunt Bess's cottage, Anne paced the living room floor. What had just happened? When she closed her eyes she was transported back to the beach and that feeling of floating in the ocean that had overtaken her when she had pushed her mind out; to Tadashi speaking her truth. She should have been afraid. But she wasn't. Unnerved? Yes. But not afraid.

Anne spent the afternoon preparing a casserole for dinner and was ever so grateful for the distraction. She headed out to the front garden to pick some parsley and there on the steps was her rescued sketchbook, the brush and ink bottle and a copy of *David Copperfield*. There was also a note.

I apologise if I upset you, Anne-san. I think you have a real talent, so I hope you try again. Here is the book I promised you. T.

Anne hurried everything inside before Bess saw. Her aunt had no time for frivolous pursuits like art or reading. *They serve no purpose for a young single woman,* she was fond of saying.

From then on, every weekday after her chores, Anne would slip up to the lighthouse and pull the ink and sketchbook out of her rucksack. She used the technique Tadashi had taught her and it never failed her.

The lighthouse was her favourite place to paint. From up there, the colours of the ocean were more varied than anywhere else on the island – grey that bled into green, blue and black that danced with teal. Not that she painted in colour; she only had the indigo ink. But she found that by adjusting her stroke, applying or releasing pressure, she could conjure a different depth to the ink that created different hues.

Sometimes, on weekends when Bess was busy shoving her nose into other people's business in town, Anne would slip down to the beach, hide among the wattle trees and look up at the patterns the branches and leaves made against the sky. Then, at night, when Bess was snoring loudly, she'd pull out her supplies, close her eyes and summon the image, committing to ink and paper a rendering that rang true.

She kept her pictures and her supplies with her books in the trunk under her bed, hidden so Bess wouldn't find them.

And all night she'd dream in shades of blue and indigo.

———

Anne let the old memories slip away and Sam returned to the dock to collect her as promised, before darkness fell. It had been a productive afternoon and Anne was happy with the painting in front of her.

'I think that's one of your best,' Sam said, as he helped her pack away. He always said that, but it was their little ritual and she would have been upset with him if he didn't say it. 'We'd better get moving before this storm rolls in.'

The clouds had grown darker and angrier as the day slipped towards evening. Anne didn't know why everyone hated storms so much. They were so often followed by clear blue skies.

Anne's left hand began to tingle. It did that every now and then. She flexed her fingers a few times and the sensation went away.

Back at the cottage she said goodbye to Sam and went inside to wash up. The ink covering her hands swirled and mixed in intricate patterns under the water before slipping down the drain. An old duck like her found beauty and joy in the smallest pieces of life – a butterfly dancing on a soft breeze, the bright yellow wattle blooming every winter, any morning you woke with all your faculties intact.

With a cup of tea she set herself up in bed with her novel, pulling the brightly coloured quilt made from scraps of old scarves tight under her chin.

She would finish this Guernsey potato book tonight; determined to find out if Juliet and Dawsey would realise their feelings for one another. She'd never been one for needing a story to be tied up in a neat pink bow, often preferring they weren't. But sometimes she longed for a happy ending.

Nine

Grace stepped carefully down the metal stairs of the tiny ten-seater plane onto what she assumed was the airstrip, though it looked suspiciously like an ordinary open field. A man waving a light baton indicated she should follow the slightly worn path in the flattened grass towards a small shed. She looked for Anne but saw only a tall man holding a sign with her name on it.

'Grace?' His voice was deep and gentle. 'I'm Sam. Anne asked me to pick you up.'

He looked nothing at all like the photo on the pottery website. He had a wild black beard that was sprinkled with grey, and his dark eyes were lined at the sides. But there was warmth in his gaze, which reassured her.

'Hi, Sam. Nice to meet you.' Grace held out her hand and smiled. He took it in his and a bolt of heat shot through her.

'Yes. Um . . . yes.' He shook his head and cleared his throat.

'Is everything okay?'

'Sorry.' A dark cloud passed over his expression briefly. 'Yes. Welcome to Wattle Island.'

The man with the light baton brought over Grace's bag and Sam picked it up, slapping the man on the back. 'Thanks, Robbie.' He turned towards a field that seemed to double as the airfield car park.

'This way.' Sam nodded.

He led her across the flat expanse of green-yellow grass and opened the door of a white ute for her.

Soon they were rolling along the main road. 'I can't believe I'm actually here,' Grace said, watching the scenery around her change from paddocks to thick groves of dark green trees with heavy grey trunks.

Sam nodded. 'Anne has been talking about your arrival all week.'

'I was expecting to see her at the airport,' Grace said.

'She rang me this morning saying she wasn't feeling too good.'

'Oh. That's no good. Maybe I shouldn't have come, if this is going to be too much for her.'

'Hmm.'

Grace wasn't sure what that meant, but she got the feeling Sam agreed that maybe she shouldn't have come.

She was here now though and wouldn't be deterred. 'I'm looking forward to meeting the book club. Are you a member?'

'No.' He kept his gaze on the road.

'I can't wait to meet them all.' She hoped her enthusiasm might rub off on him.

He shrugged. 'They're a good bunch of people.'

Sam said no more in the seat next to her and she looked out the window at the passing view. The island was bigger than she'd imagined, with rolling green hills spilling on top of each other until they fell into the blue ocean. They drove along the top of the hills

with the water far below them, the deep blue crashing into long
stretches of soft yellow-white sand.

As they crested another rise they turned inland and the hills
melted into flat farms dotted with cows.

'Are they dairy or beef?' she asked.

'Dairy.' Sam said, without taking his eyes off the road.

Wattle trees in full golden bloom lined the road into town and
Sam slowed as buildings of brick and stone came into view. They
passed a fountain in the middle of a park and Grace noted the town
appeared to consist of one main street lined with buildings from
another era, each with a bronze plaque on its facade. She made
a mental note to explore the town and read every word of every
plaque once she was settled. She hadn't expected the island to have
a history. Well, of course it had a history. Everywhere did. But a
history worthy of brass plaques was something that surprised her.

She turned her attention back to Sam. 'Anne sent me one
of your pottery bowls,' she said, hoping to coax him out of his
silence. 'I looked you up, your work is stunning. It's a privilege to
own a piece.'

His skin flushed. 'Thank you.'

'Is that what you do full time?'

'No. I'm in graphic design. Mostly work outsourced by big
companies. Designing logos, marketing material, that sort of thing.
Websites. It isn't all that exciting but it pays the bills. Pottery is my
passion, though.' His expression softened, and Grace saw an echo
of the younger man from the website photo. Yet there was also
deep melancholy in his gaze.

'Art obviously runs in your family,' Grace continued. 'I looked
Anne up too.'

'You're not stalking us are you, Miss Elliott?' There was a
lightness to Sam's tone at this, which Grace liked very much.

'Only in a passive, checking-out-who-I'm-going-to-meet kind of way. Perfectly harmless.'

Sam shot her a side look, his dark eyes warm. 'Perfectly harmless? I suspect that's what all stalkers say.' He grinned.

'True. But my parole officer says as long as I don't act out any violent impulses, I won't go back to prison.'

Sam swallowed a laugh.

'You're a talented family,' Grace said. 'I don't have an artistic bone in my body.'

'That's not true, you know. Everyone has some form of creativity in them. You just need to find the right medium.'

'Are stick figures a medium? I can draw a mean stick figure.'

He laughed, a deep rich sound that sent warmth rippling over her skin. 'You and Anne are going to get along just fine.'

'Well, we do have a love of books in common. And now the Wattle Island Book Club.'

Sam's broad shoulders dropped ever so slightly. He tilted his head to the side and his expression hardened.

'She never should have started that back up.'

'Why not? It's just a book club.'

'She isn't well. She had a stroke a couple of months back. Hasn't been the same since. She tries to hide it – and thinks she's doing a great job too. But she isn't as stealthy as she believes.'

Grace could relate to that. The hiding part. She was pretty sure she was good at it, though. Unlike Sam, whose irritation was written all over his face, and Grace doubted it was because of Anne's stroke.

As they came to the end of the town, Sam pulled the car over to the kerb and got out, fetching her suitcase from the boot.

'Is this the hotel?' She pointed behind her to a tall, round concrete structure with no windows.

'No.' The stern look on Sam's face softened ever so slightly.

'Well I have to admit that's a relief. I had pictured something a little less prison-like.'

Sam's lips twitched. 'Well, by the sounds of it, prison would feel like home, Miss Stalker.'

'Yes, but that is exactly why I wouldn't want to stay in one when on holiday.'

'That's the old water tower.'

'And as I'm not a mermaid, I'm sure you have something far more suitable in store for me.' She laughed.

He looked into her eyes and paused. He nearly smiled, but that same cloud from before came over his expression and he turned away.

'We walk from here.' He indicated the hill that lay to the east with a salute of his arm into the air.

Grace stood still, not sure what had passed between them. She wasn't even sure if she wanted to know.

'Coming?' Sam was a few strides ahead of her.

'Sure thing.'

The path up the hill was narrow, no chance for cars to pass the string of white cottages that looked out to sea, each door a different colour. Halfway up the slope, Sam stopped.

'This is you.' He lifted her suitcase onto the veranda and the red door opened. 'And this is Anne.' He spread his arm in an arc as an old woman bounced out of the cottage dressed in a flowing silk gown covered in a pattern of peacock feathers, her head wrapped in a purple scarf.

Grace's image of a short Anne with grey curls and half-moon glasses couldn't have been further from reality. The woman standing before her looked like a seventies film star. Only the wrinkles mapping across her skin gave away her age.

'Welcome, Grace. I'm so thrilled you came. I hope my grandson was the perfect welcoming party.'

Beside her, Sam shifted his weight.

Grace avoided answering. 'I'm so glad to finally meet you, Anne.'

Anne hugged her in a tight embrace then stepped back, clutching Grace's shoulders. 'Come in and get settled. I've set up the cottage especially for you.'

She pulled Grace towards the door, leaving Sam to bring in Grace's suitcase.

'Oh, I can take that.' Grace turned to him, wriggling free of Anne's grasp. Reaching out to grab the handle, she brushed the tops of Sam's fingers. There it was again, heat shooting up her arm.

He flinched. 'It's fine,' he said, pulling the suitcase away.

'He knows I'll have his guts for garters if he doesn't show you the appropriate hospitality,' Anne said over her shoulder. 'I hope you like the cottage. It's the prettiest one on Soldiers' Way.'

'Soldiers' Way?'

Anne expounded on the history of the row of cottages from its humble beginnings as soldiers' homes to residences for the art classes she used to run on the island. 'Been a long time since then, though.'

Art classes? It was a shame they weren't still going. Maybe Grace could convince Anne to come out of retirement for a few private lessons while she was there. If Sam was right and everyone had a creative talent, maybe she could tick *learn to paint like Monet* off her bucket list.

'A few cottages are occupied by locals. Mine's the one up the top of the hill. But most get rented out during summer to tourists.' Anne patted Grace on the cheek. 'Would you like an exclusive tour of the island by yours truly'—she waved her hand grandly— 'now or later?'

Grace was tired, but didn't want to disappoint Anne. 'Now?' She hoped that was the right answer.

'Good idea.' Anne linked her arm in Grace's and guided her back to the door.

'Obaachan? Are you sure you're up to this?' Sam stood in their way. 'What about your turn this morning?'

'All better now. But maybe you should come with us, though, just in case.'

Sam shot his grandmother a look.

'And if Grace here has questions about the island I can't answer, you can jump in.'

Anne's face was a picture of serenity, which Grace suspected was a well-practised ploy.

Sam shook his head. 'There's not a thing you don't know about this place.'

Anne smirked at Grace. 'True. I've lived here all my life.'

'Not quite.'

'Shush, Sam. We don't count that. Either of the thats.' She glared at him with a look that put his earlier attempt to shame, then turned her back on Sam and led Grace down the path back towards town.

On the main street Anne pointed out the buildings – the post office where she used to work ('too many moons ago to count now'), the town hall, the pub. Grace grimaced, ever so briefly, as a dull twinge rippled across her lower back, but thankfully Anne was in full tour-guide mode and didn't notice.

'That's where we have book club. You'll see that tonight. Oh, I wish I had more time to prepare for our special guest.'

Grace smiled, pushing her pain aside. 'No need for any of that. I'll be just another book club member for the night.'

Sam had remained by Anne's side but at the mention of the book club he dropped back.

They wound their way through to the other side of town and Anne talked about the farms and the beaches. 'There's great diving on the other side of the island off Rocky Beach, isn't there, Sam?'

He nodded in agreement.

'But the best beach is on the other side of Wattle Avenue,' Anne continued.

They turned a corner and Grace realised they had reached the edge of town, where a row of wattle trees stood tall, branches laden with cluster upon cluster of soft yellow pompom flowers.

'Oh, that's stunning,' Grace gasped.

'Isn't it? I think of it as my own version of the White Way . . .'

'. . . of Delight.' Grace spun around, taking in the sight. 'The Wattle Way of Delight.'

'Ah.' Anne stopped. 'I see we have a kindred spirit among us.'

'One of my favourites,' Grace said. 'I was raised on the stories of the dramatic red-headed orphan growing up on Prince Edward Island. Gilbert Blythe was my first book boyfriend.'

Sam stifled a laugh.

'Never mind him.' Anne pointed her finger at her grandson. 'He's never been a fan of my eponym.'

'Do you read much, Sam?' Grace asked.

'I used to.' He pushed his hands into the pockets of his jeans.

Anne took Grace's arm and moved her along until they emerged from the Wattle Way of Delight onto the soft sand of a pristine beach, populated only by an old wooden dock that jutted out to sea.

'That's where your books arrive.' Anne pointed to the old structure. 'Back in the day the supply boat only came once a month. Now it's once a week. And we used to have a passenger ship, before the airstrip was built, that came in every two months.' There was a far-off look in her faded grey eyes and Grace wondered what memory had stolen her for that moment.

'We do still get charters that come in, fishing, diving groups and the like,' Sam said. 'Obaachan? Shall we head off?'

'Of course.'

They left the beach and headed back up Soldiers' Way.

'When were the doors painted? I can't imagine that was army standard.' Grace smiled at the rainbow.

'Back in the fifties. Sam's Ojiichan, his grandfather, started it. My Tadashi.'

The smile on Anne's face was full of love and sorrow at the mention of her husband's name and Grace assumed he was no longer with them. Anne must have been in her eighties after all, so that wasn't altogether surprising. Grace reached out and squeezed her hand.

'So, that's the tour.' Anne stopped in front of Grace's cottage. 'Well, most of it.'

'Thank you.' Grace smiled, then frowned.

'Unless there's anything else?'

'I was, kind of hoping . . .'

'Out with it, pet. I'm not getting any younger.'

Grace laughed. 'I was hoping to see the lighthouse. I noticed it when I flew in.'

Another look passed between Anne and Sam.

'That's on tomorrow's agenda,' Anne said.

'Great. It features so prominently in your artwork.'

'You know my work?'

'I looked you up. In the library. Your paintings are . . .' Grace searched for the right word, 'breathtaking. You said you don't run classes anymore, but do you have a studio?' It couldn't hurt to ask. Plant a little seed, perhaps.

Anne stood a little taller. 'I do.'

'If it's not too much bother, I'd love to see some of your work up close.' Grace clasped her hands in front of her chest.

Anne's eyes twinkled. 'Follow me.'

At the top of the hill stood the last white cottage in the row, its door a shade of deep ocean blue. Out the back was the studio, little more than a wooden shed really, but inside on every wall were Anne's paintings.

'Oh my,' were the only words Grace could manage.

The studio was covered in all sorts of artworks: drawings in coloured pencil, charcoal sketches, small paintings, but it was the blue and indigo ink flowing and rippling across pages and boards and canvasses that Grace was drawn to.

'These are even more wonderful in person.' She felt like she could dive into the water, run her hands through the lush grass. Climb the headland to the lighthouse.

'It's like they're alive. So full of emotion. Can we go now?'

Sam, who'd followed them into the studio and had been busying himself with nailing something on the table in the corner of the studio, became very still. The air seemed instantly heavier.

'I'm a little tired, pet. Besides, the anticipation will make it even sweeter,' Anne suggested. 'And the light is stunning in the morning.'

Grace sensed she shouldn't push. 'Okay. It's a date. Will you join us, Sam?' She turned to him.

He shook his head without making eye contact.

'Now, toddle back to your cottage and freshen up,' Anne said quickly. 'I'll swing by in an hour and pick you up for book club. The others will be excited to meet you.'

Anne gave Grace a hug, warm and genuine, like she really meant it. Grace didn't want to let go. Anne's hug reminded her of the way June used to embrace her, before she got sick. Before she was fragile in her mother's eyes.

'Thank you.' Grace stepped away, blushing, aware of the fact she'd probably held on a little too long.

'And thank you, Sam.' She held out her hand. 'For picking me up.' He took it, his hand soft and strong. Heat flowed over her skin again and she locked eyes with his. And, just for a moment, the world fell away.

He looked down, breaking the spell. 'You're welcome,' he said, and resumed hammering the nail.

With legs a little wobbly, Grace left the studio. She was most definitely not expecting that. Inside her cottage, she sank into the sofa, fatigue washing over her. From her handbag she took out her medication and swallowed two pills.

Ten

Anne may well have been getting older and becoming more frail as time passed, but her mind was still intact – mostly. And her heart – definitely. At least, enough to notice that something had happened just then, when Sam and Grace shook hands. Something that had unsettled Sam immensely. To the uninitiated – everyone but her – it was often hard to tell brooding Sam from happy Sam from shaken Sam. He kept his emotions so tightly corked. Not that she could blame him. But tiny changes in the look in this eye, the shape of his mouth, were all Anne needed to read her grandson.

'Are you okay, Sam?' she asked.

'Of course. I think you overdid it today though. What did Dr Hamer say?'

'Not to exert myself. But that was hardly exertion. I found it rather pleasant. Didn't you?'

He shrugged.

'Isn't Grace delightful?'

He pulled out the nail he'd just hammered in. 'Get some rest before book club, Obaachan.' He kissed her on the top of her purple scarf and strode outside with purpose, leaving her there alone.

She walked around her studio, her fingers brushing each of her pieces. She thought about opening her ink bottles, but Sam was right, she was tired. Not that she'd admit it to him.

Dr Hamer, the heart specialist, had actually said a lot more than she shouldn't exert herself. An awful lot. But there was no need for Sam to worry about her, so she'd glossed over most of it. Shellie was aware of the full story; knew about the new medication. And as far as Anne was concerned, that was more than enough people worrying about her. What was the point of all that worrying now anyway?

Life was what it was. Always had been. No one was in control, despite the human race being rather adept at fooling itself into believing it was. Anne had learned that lesson long ago.

She made her way inside the cottage and brewed a cup of tea, slipping onto her sofa with the delicate china cup in her hand. She'd rest her eyes, only for a minute. Just so she was alert and ready for book club.

Wattle Island, 1950

Anne sat against the lighthouse, palms sweating, heart pounding. Six months had passed since Tadashi had taught Anne to paint, and during that time their friendship had flourished. The *Seafarer* had docked hours ago and, as always, Anne was waiting for him to join her.

The sun was well on its afternoon descent by the time she heard footfalls in the soft grass coming in her direction, and when she turned around her heart did some sort of weird flip at the sight of Tadashi.

'Konnichiwa, Anne-san.' He bowed deeply.

She simply smiled in return. 'Hello.'

'Sorry I'm late. We had a lot of cargo to unload today.'

'No need to apologise,' she said. 'I know you can't always get away easily.'

'Have you explored your art any more?' he asked.

Anne exhaled. All week she'd been buzzing with excitement at the thought of sharing her latest pictures with him, wondering what he'd think, if she'd improved. But now nerves overtook her. What if she hadn't got any better? Or had got worse? She had so enjoyed the creating of them; she didn't really want his low opinion of them to cloud that joy.

'I have.' She pointed to her rucksack.

'You don't need to show me if you don't wish to.'

'No . . . I don't mind.' With trembling hands, she pulled out her sketchbook.

Tadashi flicked through the pages, and with each turn, Anne's pulse throbbed harder. She rocked on her heels. She turned her back on him, then spun around again to face him. She looked at the sky, then the ground.

'As I suspected, you have an artist's soul. These are very good.'

Anne exhaled.

Choosing a picture at random, one of her wattle renderings, he complimented Anne on her brushstrokes and delicate application of ink. There was, of course, much room for improvement, but she was, apparently, a natural.

Anne's cheeks flushed.

Tadashi offered to show her some more techniques and she agreed before he'd even finished his sentence.

Together they sat by the lighthouse and he showed her how to achieve incredibly fine lines. She marvelled at his skill with a brush.

'Where did you learn to paint so delicately?' Anne asked after he showed her one of his own pieces. It was a cherry blossom in front of some sort of temple, in miniature, yet so extraordinarily detailed. Anne had never seen anything quite like it.

'My mother was a very talented artist.' He cast his eyes down.

'Was?'

'She passed away when I was twelve. Six years ago now.'

'I'm sorry.' She reached out and touched his hand, pulling it back quickly. His body stiffened momentarily. 'I lost both my parents when I was thirteen.'

'Anne-san.' He lowered eyes. 'I'm very sad to hear that.'

'That's how I ended up here,' she said.

'Ah.' He nodded. 'How did they pass?'

'Car accident. I don't like to talk about it much. Your mum?'

His shoulders slumped slightly. 'The camps.'

'The camps?' Anne didn't know what he meant.

'During the war. They locked us all up.'

'Who?' Anne was confused.

'Any Japanese person. They rounded us up and locked us in camps. Enemy aliens, they called us.'

Anne squeezed her hands into fists. She'd only been eleven when the war ended, and they didn't teach much about it in school. She'd never heard of such a thing.

Tadashi continued with a soft voice. 'My mother got sick with flu. Conditions in camp were cramped, dirty. She didn't survive.'

'That must have been awful.'

He nodded. 'It was.'

'I didn't know about the camps.' Anne kept her voice soft.

'That is not surprising. They wouldn't want you to know what it was like, what they did . . .' Tadashi went very still, very quiet.

Anne had so many questions, but she wasn't sure how to ask them. A seagull flew past. Tadashi remained silent.

'What happened to your father?' She broke the silence.

'When the war ended, we were allowed to stay. Because I was born here, we had the choice.'

'A choice?'

'Those born in Japan were removed. Sent back. But those born here could choose to go or stay.'

Anne's mind was reeling. 'And you chose to stay?'

'My father said his homeland had been devastated by the war and we shouldn't return.'

Anne remembered the news stories about the bombings.

'But staying here . . . they'd taken everything from us. Everything we'd owned. We had to start again.' His gaze was distant. Sad. 'That was also when my father decided my education was most important.'

The cloud that had settled over Tadashi when he talked about the camps lifted.

'He made you read the English classics?'

A small smile touched his lips. 'He made me read everything. He wanted me to become a scholar. To have opportunities he never did. He didn't want me working as a pearler like him. But he didn't know. He didn't know what things would be like after the war. He died last year. I'm glad he'll never know.'

'You're young, Tadashi,' Anne said. 'There's still time for you to study.'

Tadashi shook his head. 'Time, yes. But there aren't a lot of options for someone like me.'

'Surely there are opportunities in the city?'

He shook his head. 'People like me don't get opportunities like that. The scars of the war still weep. I am still the enemy.'

'But the war was five years ago.'

He nodded. 'Yes, but people's memories are long. So, I work my way from job to job around the country. It isn't such a bad life.'

'Are you happy?' There went her runaway mouth again. It was far too personal a question to ask. But she had to know. How could he be already resigned to a life he wasn't meant for?

He shrugged. 'Happiness can be found anywhere. It's what you make it.'

Anne smiled. 'You sound like one of my favourite authors, L. M. Montgomery. Although I don't know if she got that one right. I've tried to be happy here, but I'd do anything to get off this island. Get back to Sydney.'

'Don't be so eager to venture into a world you don't know.'

'I know Sydney. I spent the first thirteen years of my life there.'

He shook his head. 'I think you will find it different as an adult.'

Anne opened her mouth to protest, but closed it again when she saw Ruth walking up the path towards them.

Ruth drew herself up to her full height, which was only four foot ten, and pushed her pointy nose a little further in the air. Her long black hair was tied back in a ponytail that was so tight she almost couldn't scowl. Almost.

Ruth had mostly left Anne alone since they'd finished school. Every now and then she'd throw a snide remark Anne's way and when she did, Anne would respond, 'Do you even know how to spell that?'

Her conjuring of the spelling bee fiasco always landed true and pierced Ruth's cold barrier.

Ruth passed them today without a word. But, just as Anne thought they might be able to escape unscathed, Ruth spat at Tadashi's feet.

Spat!

'What do you think you're doing?' Anne yelled at her.

'Trust you to be friends with a filthy Jap.' She tossed her head into the air.

Anne watched Ruth swan away then turned to Tadashi. 'I'm sorry about that. I've no idea what Ruth's problem is.'

He shrugged. 'Happens all the time.'

'Really?'

'The war, remember?'

Anne didn't understand this at all. 'I know, but you were born here. You're Australian.'

'It doesn't matter. I look different and that's enough for some people.'

'I'm sorry,' were the only words she could find.

'It isn't your fault, Anne-san. And for all the Ruths in this world spreading dark, there are enough Annes to maintain the light.'

Anne stared into Tadashi's deep eyes and the world around her fell silent.

When he broke their gaze, looking down at the ground, she let out the breath she'd been holding.

'We sail very early on the morning tide.' He cleared his throat. 'Will you accept a small gift?' He reached into his satchel and pulled out a tiny blue ceramic vase, a series of white cranes dancing across its curves.

'Did you make this?'

He nodded.

'It's beautiful.'

As he placed it in her cupped hands, their fingers touched, sending bolts of heat through Anne's skin.

'Thank you.' Her words barely a whisper.

He bowed and headed down the hill towards town.

That night, Anne tossed and turned, her thoughts a jumble of excitement, fear, hope and confusion. Finally, as dawn broke, she gave up on sleep and walked outside, her ink and sketchbook shoved into her rucksack. She wouldn't go down to the dock, even though she was early enough to see the *Seafarer* off. There was no way she could face Tadashi this morning.

She made her way to the lighthouse and set up the ink and brush. As the sun peeked over the horizon in the east, casting a soft gold sheen over the ocean, the black silhouette of the *Seafarer* picked its way west towards the mainland.

Anne opened her sketchbook and closed her eyes, allowing the kaleidoscope of emotions swirling inside her to dance. She picked out the colour and shape of them, and let her brush move across the paper.

A cold breeze blowing through the window drew Anne out of her dozing; dreams of her past dissolving. She reached for *Guernsey* and flicked through its pages once more, taking in phrases and sentences at random, a last-minute cram to ensure she looked like she knew what she was talking about.

She knew it was silly but she felt more nervous tonight, knowing Grace was going to be there, than she had been last month when she'd kicked off this crazy idea. Anne had been reading and discussing books all her life, yet the appearance of a friendly librarian from the mainland was causing her to unravel.

Enough of that. Grace was here to help and Anne needed tonight to be a success. She tied a blue scarf around her head; the tiny white waves dancing in the silk folds. Then she set off down Soldiers' Way. At the red door to Grace's cottage, she knocked.

Grace answered with a smile, though there were beads of sweat on her brow and her eyes darted around.

Anne knew nerves when she saw them, and was surprised. *Grace* was nervous? Anne thought she had the monopoly on that particular affliction tonight.

'Is our special guest ready to meet the Wattle Island Book Club?' She hoped her exuberance would put the girl at ease.

'Ready and rearing.' Grace smiled, though Anne wasn't comforted by her expression. There was something off about it.

So much for putting her at ease. What a pair the two of them were.

Anne hoped one of them would pull themselves together before book club got started. She knew the future hinged on tonight.

Eleven

Grace had heard Anne coming down the path and hoped she'd composed herself in time. She'd been putting off talking to her mum until tomorrow, after book club, but she should have known better. June's sixth sense rarely let her down and she'd rung Grace half an hour ago, wondering why she hadn't heard from her.

The call went even worse than Grace had anticipated.

'You're where?' June had shouted.

'Wattle Island, Mum.'

'You decided to up and take a holiday? On your own? Without telling me?'

Grace closed her eyes.

'I'm going to fly over on the next plane I can get. You can't be there on your own.'

This was what Grace had been afraid of.

'I'm not on my own. There's a whole town here.'

'Don't you sass me. That's not what I meant and you know it.'

'Mum, I'm fine. Really.' Grace could hear June shuffling about and pictured her mother pacing around her living room. She knew it was wrong not to tell her mum her plans, but June would have tried to stop her. Grace needed to do this, and she needed to do it on her own. It wasn't just about the book club. For the first time in three years, Grace was in control of her own life. Not a slave to appointments or chemo regimes or recovery spells.

These next few weeks were going to be completely on her terms. If June had come, she'd be worrying and fussing. For the first time in three years, Grace was going to live as if cancer had never hijacked her life.

'Mum, I know you're upset—'

'Upset? *Upset?* How can you do this to me?'

'To you? I didn't do this to you. I did it *for* me.'

'Well, this isn't only about you, is it?'

For three years Grace had put on a brave face for everyone else around her, especially for June. For three years Grace's cancer had been about everyone else. Just this once she wanted to be free to think of only herself.

'Why can't this be just about me? I'm tired, Mum. Of all of it. All I wanted was to have a break, to live, for a little while, like a normal person.'

'But you're not normal. You have . . .'

'Say it, Mum. For once say it. I have cancer.'

'But you're better, aren't you?'

Grace didn't answer that. 'Then why can't I do this?'

'I just— I can't— Grace Elliott, I want you home now, or else.'

'Or else what?'

Silence had met her question, and June had hung up.

When Grace had opened the door to Anne a few minutes later, she was still reeling.

Anne had greeted her with a sizzling smile – forced, perhaps – and Grace pushed the argument with her mother out of her mind.

As they walked into town, Grace was worried she was under-dressed. Her favourite jeans were no match for Anne's attire. Grace had assumed a book club meeting in a pub meant a casual dress code. But beside her Anne swished, actually swished, in a flowing sapphire-coloured satin gown with voluminous pleats falling from her shoulder, gathered at the waist by a gold belt. Around her head was a scarf of blue and white waves tied above her left ear like the one she had on earlier that day.

'Should I go back and get changed?' Grace asked.

'Why on earth would you want to do that?' Anne shook her head.

Grace shrugged and let it slide. Surely not everyone on the island dressed as extravagantly as Anne, but if it turned out she was completely out of place when they arrived, she'd make some excuse to leave early.

Actually, no she wouldn't. The new Grace would do no such thing. Just because she was on a strange island with a bunch of people she didn't know didn't mean she had to be something she wasn't. In fact, it was the perfect opportunity to be exactly who she was at her core. And her core had decided after her last operation to only dress in comfortable clothes, no matter the occasion.

Worry be gone.

She focused on Anne, chatting away beside her.

'. . . and then she clean dropped the glass off the bar top.' Anne laughed.

Grace joined her, though she had no idea what was funny. She was looking forward to meeting some of Anne's friends and the rest of the book club. She really should be paying attention.

They wound their way through town, past the pretty shop facades. Grace kept an eye out for an old bookshop but couldn't see one. There was a bakery with a pink-and-white striped awning over a large window with drawn pink gingham curtains. A carved wooden sign declared it to be Cutto's Cakes. Had that once been the bookshop? Probably not. It didn't seem new enough.

Next to the bakery was a dress boutique called Wattle Island Wears with three mannequins smiling out the window, clad in bright patterns of waves and wattles. A small, neatly written sign in the corner of the window read 'open Oct–Mar'. There was a camping store, a chemist, a general store, a medical clinic – all of them looking as if they had been there forever, their signs a little weathered. Only one shopfront was missing a sign, the one next to the general store where Grace spied a dusty window with a closed yellow polka-dot curtain.

'Ah, there we are,' Anne said, pointing at a figure emerging from a side alley. 'This is Hamish. He'll be joining us at book club.'

Much to Grace's relief, Hamish was dressed in chinos and a polo shirt. He greeted Grace with a polite nod. 'So lovely to have you with us. Everyone is talking about your visit.'

'Really?'

'Small island, pet.' Anne smiled. 'Word gets around fast.'

'Especially when Anne here has been telling everyone she can about our special guest.' Hamish's voice was deep and dripping with affection. 'Are you looking forward to joining us tonight?' he asked.

Grace nodded. 'I certainly am. Can't wait to see the book club in action.'

Hamish fell into step and when they reached the pub he leaned forward and opened the door for them.

The pub was warm; the low orange glow of an open wood fire filling the room. Around the walls of the pub were booths with leather bench seats, soft and comfortable, and wooden tables, aged with old nicks and scratches and ring marks from untold numbers of beer glasses, that held a hundred stories Grace would never learn of.

'If you're ever looking for a good dinner while you're on the island, the schnitty is top notch,' Anne said proudly.

The bell on the door to the pub dinged and a woman a little younger than Anne loped in, and introduced herself to Grace.

'I'm Maree. Nice to meet you.' She shook Grace's hand. Maree's relaxed demeanour was wrapped in a patchwork skirt of greens and blues topped with a white embroidered peasant blouse. As she pulled back, Grace tried not to stare at her nose ring. She'd seen many nose rings in her time. She'd even considered getting one at one point – *Travel to India and get a henna tattoo and nose piercing: bucket list, age twenty-three* – but she couldn't recall ever seeing one on a woman of Maree's age before. Not in Port Maddison anyway. And she'd never made it to India. She'd been due to go with Linh the year she was diagnosed, as part of a whirlwind world tour. First stop, Vietnam, then India, then on to Europe.

'Nice to meet you too.' Grace remembered her manners. 'Are you part of the book club?' There was a glint in Maree's bright green eyes that Grace wanted to know about.

'Indeed. I'm so glad Anne had the strength—'

Anne coughed.

'. . . so glad she brought it back to life.'

Bravery and strength had both now been used to describe Anne's resurrection of the book club. Strange choices. Choices, Grace suspected, that told another story.

The rest of the book club members arrived, smiling and chatting amiably among themselves as everyone got settled. There was nothing to indicate this wasn't a cohesive, happy group, as far as Grace could tell, and she wondered what Anne was so worried about.

Sitting very rigidly on a chair closest to the fire was a woman around Anne's age, dressed in a neat lilac twin-set. Her hands were folded in her lap and although she gave Grace the slightest of nods in greeting, the scowl across her thin face was less than welcoming.

'Don't mind my sister,' Maree whispered in Grace's ear. 'Her bark is worse than her bite.'

Never in a million years would Grace have picked the bohemian woman beside her and the pinched statue sitting by the fire as sisters.

The pub had filled up by the time Sam entered. But he didn't join them. He sat at the bar, the collar of his cable-knit jumper rising on his neck. He gave Grace a curt nod before turning his back.

Anne made the remaining introductions and Grace tried to commit as many names to memory as possible. Twin-set Ruth was easy to lock in. So was Nose-ring Maree.

'I'm sure you're all as excited as I am to have our special guest here tonight,' Anne said, which garnered applause from everyone.

Everyone except Ruth, whose neatly folded hands didn't budge from her lap.

Anne sat down and turned towards Grace. 'Perhaps, Grace, you'd like to kick things off. Show us how the professionals do it.'

So much for sitting back and observing.

Fifteen sets of eyes immediately focused on her. Then sixteen, when Sam turned around and fixed her with a wary glare. Grace didn't know what Sam's problem was, but she wouldn't let him shake her.

She took a deep breath. 'Well, firstly, there is no right way to do this. Every book club is unique, with its own way of doing things and its own dynamics. Its own quirks and its own secrets.' She winked, hoping a little joke might ease her nerves.

Ruth looked down, Sam moved slightly, as if he was about to get up and walk out. Anne stared straight ahead.

Right. Not the best start. Grace swallowed the lump in her throat.

Grace Elliott, you can do this with your eyes closed and your hands tied behind your back. All you need to do is go back to the basics.

'Well, I always find it best to start with something easy. Who's read the book?'

All hands went up.

'And who enjoyed it?'

There were quite a few murmurs of 'yes', a couple of 'meh's. Ruth simply rolled her eyes, as if Grace's questions were entirely beneath her.

Grace squared her shoulders. Challenge accepted. One thing she'd learned from six years with book clubs was that if you really wanted to get them talking about the book you needed to get them talking about themselves.

You're a detective, Mr Gerd? Did Harper portray Falk accurately in The Dry?

Mrs Arnold, you worked in catering before retiring. Is the catering business really the way Binchy described in Scarlet Feather?

Max, Oscar, you've been best friends since kindergarten. Would you put your lives on the line for each other the way Samwise did for Frodo in The Lord of the Rings?

No matter what the book was, there was always a way in. Without knowing the personal stories of the group in front of her, it would be harder, but not impossible.

And one thing in life was universal. Food.

'I don't know about you, but potato peel pie sounds positively vile. What's the worst thing any of you have ever eaten?'

It wasn't a very bookish question, she knew, but it was an ice-breaker, something to put everyone on the same level to start, regardless of their reading or personal background.

Ruth stared at her, her thin lips drawn tight. Anne looked confused; this was clearly not what she was expecting Grace to say. Sam folded his arms across his chest. Eyes darted around the room.

The man next to Hamish, the one who'd directed her plane in this morning, put his hand up.

Grace smiled. 'This isn't school, ah . . .'

'Robbie.'

'Just say what you think, Robbie.'

He patted Hamish's leg. 'Sorry, mate, but haggis is the worst thing I've ever had in my mouth.'

A ripple of laughter flowed through the group.

'I have to say . . .' Maree sat forward. 'I really didn't care for escargot when I was in France in the sixties. I know it's a delicacy, but it's not for me.'

'There's a maggot cheese in Italy,' the woman sitting opposite Ruth said. What was her name? Sharon? Shellie? Yes, Shellie. 'I've never tried it, but it sounds gross.'

The man with his hand on Shellie's back pulled a face. 'I would definitely prefer the potato peel pie over that.'

'I guess, though, if you were starving, like these poor buggers were,' the old man sitting next to Ruth said, holding up his copy of the book to illustrate, 'you'd eat whatever was available.'

Grace smiled. *Here we go.*

'I remember the rations,' he continued. 'Not as bad here as in England, but there were times we were pretty hungry. Even with the farm.'

'True, Hadley.' Ruth nodded.

'But there were some light moments during that time,' Grace said, seeing her opportunity. 'The society came together because of the shortage of food.'

'I'm sure they'd have preferred to stay strangers if it meant not having to endure the war,' Ruth said, frowning.

'Probably,' Anne spoke for the first time. 'But the war happened. And I loved the way they came together despite their hardship.'

'Because of their hardship,' Shellie chimed in.

Hadley nodded.

'Funny thing for me was,' Robbie said, taking another sip of his beer. 'I was reading about what Guernsey was like after the war. We read stories – well, for me it's mostly been film up until now – a lot of stories set during the war, but not so many about the aftermath.'

There was murmured agreement.

Grace leaned back in her chair. *Nearly there.*

'And this story was so personal, being all letters.' Maree nodded.

'I admit I found that tough going,' the man with his hand on Shellie's back said. 'The letter thing. That was hard work.'

'But, Phil, I don't know if it would have had the same impact if it was written in the conventional way,' Hamish chimed in. 'Would it have been simply another wartime story?'

'And we wouldn't have had the same number of voices – is that the right terminology, Grace?' Robbie asked.

Grace nodded.

'We wouldn't have had the same number of voices if it was a normal novel. I kind of felt I got to know them.'

'Oh I loved that.' Maree bounced in her seat. 'And I loved the way they found hope after tragedy . . .'

And there it was.

Grace sat back and watched on as the animated discussion got going. Maree was the story's biggest fan, it seemed. Shellie loved reading about a part of history she knew little about. Phil couldn't see what Juliet ever saw in Mark, arrogant git. And Robbie wanted to go to Guernsey now and see how much it had changed since the war. Ruth said very little. Sam said nothing at all.

Every now and then Grace chipped in with an opinion or a guiding question, but she enjoyed watching and listening far more. Besides, she was now somewhat superfluous.

Eventually the discussion died down and thoughts turned to the next book they'd do.

'Grace, what would you suggest?' Anne asked.

'Why don't I put together a short list of titles I think you might enjoy, now that I know you all a little better, and you can have a vote.'

'What about a classic?' Ruth suggested.

'Well, it is my firm personal belief that every book club needs to do an Austen once a year.'

Ruth appeared to approve.

'Ah, Mills and Boon of the nineteenth century,' Phil said.

'Wash your mouth out.' Anne waved a gnarled finger at him. '*Pride and Prejudice*?' She looked back to Grace.

'Can we watch the TV series, for Colin Firth and the lake scene?' Shellie asked. Poor Phil's face dropped.

Sam shook his head, the hint of a smile touching his lips.

'What about *Northanger Abbey*?' Grace suggested. 'Something a little different.'

Ruth stood up. 'That's one we never got to do . . . last time around. I vote yes.'

Hadley frowned.

'Or maybe we can see Grace's list first,' Hamish suggested. 'Weigh up our options.'

'Agreed.' Anne clapped.

After that, people took their leave, and as Shellie and Phil packed away the chairs, Grace's gaze was fixed on Sam over at the bar, now chatting quietly with Hamish, warmth nudging her back as she stood in front of the fire.

'So, how did you like our little book club?' Anne stepped up beside her and Grace realised she'd been staring.

'What a great bunch.' Grace smiled. 'But more to the point, how do you think it went?'

'Better than I'd hoped. Thank you.'

'Ruth alluded to the fact you might have done a few classics in the book club's other life.'

'Ah yes. We did. And she hankers after them. Once a literary snob, always a literary snob.' Anne began to pack the books into the tub with Grace's help.

Grace nodded. 'She did seem rather reticent about *Guernsey* at first.'

A faraway look came over Anne. 'Oh, it's not just the type of novels. She's still hanging on to . . .' Anne snapped out of her reverie. 'Ruth is old-fashioned is all.' The smile she donned was clearly forced.

'When did the Wattle Island Book Club start?' Grace asked. 'The original one.'

Anne let out a long breath and patted the fancy knot in her head scarf. 'It's been around in various forms since the fifties, pet.'

'Wow. That's impressive. I don't think I've ever known a book club that old. You must have covered some literary ground in that time.'

'Oh, we did. All sorts of books and all sorts of members over the years.' She laughed. 'This lot tonight – not the most eclectic bunch we've had.'

'Sam has never joined?' Grace asked. With Anne his grandmother, it seemed logical he'd have been raised with a love of reading.

Anne stiffened beside her. 'He used to be part of the group, before . . .'

This was Grace's opening. 'Before it stopped?'

Anne nodded.

'Why did you stop, Anne, before this reboot?'

With her hand resting heavily on the mantel over the fire, Anne looked down. There was sadness in her eyes when she looked back up. No. It was deeper than that. Sadness was finishing the final episode of your favourite TV show or leaving a job you loved for an uncertain future. In Anne's eyes, Grace could see real, deep, life-changing sorrow.

'Ah, see that?' She pointed to one of the framed pictures crowd-ing the mantel. 'There we are in our younger days.'

Taking a closer look, Grace recognised Ruth from the pinched look on her face, prim and proper in a neat swing skirt and bolero cardigan; and Anne with a yellow scarf around her head, wearing a loose-fitting dress Grace would call bohemian – a precursor, per-haps, to the seventies movie star look she now wore. They were sitting by the fountain in the park she'd been shown earlier that day on her tour, books in hand.

Grace spun around to ask Anne more questions, but she was nowhere to be seen. For a woman pushing ninety, she sure did move quickly.

The other pictures on the mantel moved through time. A sepia photo of the dock being built; men smoking pipes on the sand; children playing marbles in the churchyard; a black-and-white panorama of the main street; easels set up with canvasses in a field; the bakery sign being hung; a line of men drinking in the pub; soldiers in the early forties walking past the cottages, their uniforms neat and trim; a group of twenty-somethings donning scuba tanks, getting ready to dive into the ocean.

With a jolt, Grace recognised Sam's dark eyes, despite his youthful, clean-shaven face. Next to him was Shellie with her long blonde hair tied in pigtails, then Phil next to her pushing on his biceps. There was another blonde woman there too with piercing blue eyes, gorgeous in a polka-dot bikini lying on a towel.

'That was our first ever diving stint.' Sam's voice was low behind Grace and she turned around. 'Phil has made a good go of it ever since.'

'Back home, I joined an adventure group called MAW,' Grace replied. She could feel the warmth of Sam's body close to her.

'I know MAW. Phil's been in contact with them. He's hoping to bring in more groups like that to the island.' He smiled. 'They're a pretty wild bunch, aren't they?'

'They can be.' Grace nodded. 'Isn't it funny how we spend so much of our adult life craving certainty, yet sometimes what we need is the opposite?'

'Not me. I'd take certainty any day.' Sam's deep voice cracked with emotion.

'I used to feel like that. But sometimes certainty isn't all it's cracked up to be.'

Sam pressed his lips together and silence filled the space between them.

'I think Anne is pleased with how book club went.'

He shrugged. 'You certainly got them talking.'

'It's a great book. You should read it sometime.'

'I did read it.'

Grace wasn't expecting that. 'Oh? So why didn't you join us? Too much philosophical talk about hope and tragedy?'

'Some things should be left alone.' He turned and strode out of the pub.

Grace stood still, her mouth open. What just happened? What had she said? She looked around the pub. Other than Hamish, who was still at the bar, everyone had left.

She stepped out into the cold night air and heard urgent voices coming from the side of the pub. She inched along the veranda and stopped at the corner.

'Can't you see what this is doing to him, Anne? Bringing book club back, making him attend.' Grace recognised Ruth's clipped tone.

'Sam needs this as much as we do. More so. It's time, Ruth. For all of us.' Anne's voice, distraught.

Grace leaned forward, ensuring she stayed hidden.

'You shouldn't have done this without my okay first, Anne. You railroaded me. You always do that. Whatever you want, you get, without any regard for anyone else.'

'Don't you see? This *is* for everyone else.'

'We all loved her, Anne. You aren't the only one carrying this burden.'

Her?

Heavy footsteps echoed away from the pub and Grace scrambled back to the front door, pretending to come out. Anne would have to come this way if she was heading home.

'Oh, hello, pet.' Anne smiled when she saw Grace, but Grace could see the tears glistening on Anne's cheeks. 'Shall we stroll home together?'

'I'd like that.'

In silence they ambled along Soldiers' Way, Anne squeezing Grace's hand in farewell when they got to her cottage. Grace watched her new friend continue up the path, Anne's shoulders slumped, her step plodding.

What on earth happened here?

Twelve

Anne dragged herself up the hill towards her cottage. If Grace had overheard her fight with Ruth, she hadn't let on. Even if she hadn't, Grace was young and intelligent and had surely noticed the slightly fraught energy within the book club. She was bound to ask questions. Anne should have predicted that.

Although, would it be such a bad thing if Grace did prod? The whole island had been holding on to the past too tightly and it was clear that the unspoken pain that connected them was holding their futures captive. Maybe what they needed was an external force to unlock the silence – something they had been unable to do themselves. Or the force would destroy them.

Anne wasn't so worried about her and Ruth. They'd both lived long lives. And good ones, for the most part, if not always easy. But Sam and Addie – what was best for them? Was she hurting them, or saving them?

She'd always assumed that by this point in her life she would have all the answers. But one thing was for sure: age didn't necessarily bring wisdom. In fact, sometimes it seemed the longer she lived, the less she was certain of.

Opening the dark blue door to her home, she slipped off her ballet flats, unwrapped the scarf from her head and removed her belt, setting the folds of her dress free before flopping onto her soft sofa.

Book club could not have gone better. The chatter as the young ones left, talking about how much they were looking forward to next month, should have left Anne feeling joyful, relieved. But the meddling voice that lurked in the very back of her mind was whispering doubt. Doubt borne of so many moments in her life when great hope had been thwarted by great heartbreak.

Perhaps tonight's success was all down to Grace, and when she returned home, book club would fall apart. Maybe she could kidnap her. Keep her on the island. No one would suspect an old fool like her of such a crime.

Even with Grace's help, though, book club hadn't been a success for Sam. He still refused to join them and she'd seen his expression when Maree talked about tragedy and hope. She'd only spoken briefly, but sometimes small things had a habit of causing great big messy undoings.

Wattle Island, 1951

Every few days Anne picked wildflowers from the hills that surrounded the island and placed them in her tiny vase. It was perhaps foolish to harbour any kind of feeling about the delicate piece of pottery, or the man who'd given it to her, and she tried to push such feelings away and simply admire the vase for its beauty.

But it wasn't easy.

She painted often and thought she was improving, but it was hard to tell. All she knew for sure was that a profound peace came over her when she put ink to paper.

The sun was low in the sky as she walked home from helping one of the McCormack children with their maths. Although she had secured work in the post office with Mrs Forster, the old woman took the secretarial training out of Anne's pay. So she continued tutoring as much as she could.

When she arrived at the cottage, Bess was cleaning the floors and Anne tiptoed into her bedroom and pulled out her tiny metal tin where she kept her stash.

Her shoulders fell as she added the penny to her total. It wasn't nearly enough if she wanted to head to the city in a few months' time. She needed more. Maybe she could sell her paintings?

She laughed at this idea. As if anyone would purchase her silly little pictures. She would have to get a second job but she had no idea how she would do it. Landing the job at the post office had been difficult enough. She'd asked around – Follett's farm, the bakery, the milk bar – but no one had any work for her. Or at least they weren't willing to give her any. Captain Allen had sprayed spit in her face, so strong was his laughter when she approached him about helping him off-load the boat every month. 'No place for a girl,' he'd said.

Aunt Bess called her to supper and Anne washed up.

'So.' Bess banged a bowl of simple vegetable broth in front of her. 'You've been working for Mrs Forster a while now. Do you want to do that forever?'

'No,' Anne said. 'I'd like to go back to the mainland. Get a job. Maybe in an office.' The words came out of her mouth softly, as she feared Bess would tell her she was foolish.

'Hmm.' Bess thought a moment. 'Well, I'm not one to support the idea of a woman making her own way in the world. That's for the menfolk. But you're unlikely to find an appropriate suitor staying here.'

Anne didn't say anything about Tadashi. Even if there was something . . . more to his gift and his kindness, he was unlikely to be seen as suitable.

'But the city will suck whatever savings you have dry before you know it. Even when you do come of age and receive what little your parents left you, it won't be enough. Let me talk to the old army wives. I'm still in touch with many of them. They might be able to help us secure you a good position.'

'Really?

'Yes.' Bess almost smiled.

Anne almost cried.

Perhaps she should have asked Bess for help sooner. But, the whole time she'd been living here under her roof, this was the first hint of kindness her aunt had shown her.

When the month ended and the supply boat rolled back into the harbour, Anne was there to meet it to pick up the mailbag for Mrs Forster. It was the perfect excuse. Not that she'd ever had one before, but the safety of having a genuine reason to be on the dock as Tadashi tied the ropes off quelled her nerves a little.

Tadashi nodded his acknowledgement of her as he worked to unload the boat. When he picked up the mailbag, she approached him.

'I'm here for that.' She smiled as he handed it to her. Their fingers touched, sending heat rippling over Anne's skin. She studied him for some indication he was equally affected, but there was none. Dragging her feet, she took the bag and headed to the post office.

Anne worked a few hours in the morning, took a short lunch-break, and would work a few more hours in the afternoon.

She always took a book with her to read during the half hour in the middle of the day, eating her packed sandwich by the fountain in the park as she escaped into the pages of her novel.

Today, with the hot sun beating down, the cold spray from the fountain's splash was a welcome reprieve. As she sat there reading George Orwell's *1984*, a noise from behind made her turn around. Tadashi was walking towards her, hands in his pockets, eyes cast down.

She straightened her back and pushed her hair down over her ears.

'Good afternoon, Anne-san.' He bowed.

'Hello. How are you?'

'May I?' He indicated the space beside her.

She waved her hand inviting him to sit.

'Ew, look at this.' Ruth's shrill voice cut through the air. 'Book-girl and Jap-boy sitting together all cosy. Makes me want to vomit.' She twisted her hips, making her pink poodle skirt – new, Anne supposed, from the preening Ruth was doing – swish from side to side.

Maree was standing beside Ruth frowning. Not at Anne, but at her older sister. She opened her mouth to say something, but thought better of it and looked at the dirt instead. One day, thought Anne, Maree will step out of her sister's shadow.

'Good day, Anne-san.' Tadashi stood and backed away.

'He doesn't even speak properly.' Ruth rolled her steely blue eyes.

'Can I help you with something, Ruth?' Anne asked, holding back the harsh words she wanted to sling at her.

'You? Help me? Oh, I doubt that you could help me with any-thing.' She laughed. Last week, Ruth's dad, a widower now for five years, had been elected mayor of the island, making her even more insufferable than usual. 'Except maybe tell me what's going on between you and the Jap.'

'His name is Tadashi, and nothing's going on. We're friends is all.'

'Looks like more than friends. Does Bess know you've got a Jap boyfriend?' The sing-song in Ruth's voice belied her malice. 'I wonder what she'd do if she found out?'

Anne stood up, forcing Ruth to step backwards. She had no idea what Bess would do if she thought something inappropriate was going on with Anne and . . . well, Anne and anyone.

'There's nothing to find out, is there, Ruth?' Anne kept her voice steady, but she hoped her eyes conveyed all the threat she needed them to. Except Ruth had much more experience in threats than she did.

'Maybe not.' Ruth stepped further away and twirled her high ponytail. 'You know . . . I could get Daddy to get Captain Allen to fire your friend.'

'Why would you even care, Ruth? He's not a speck in your life.'

Ruth ran her thumbs over her fingernails. 'True. He's nothing to me. But he's something to you. Even if you deny it. And you took something of mine away once . . .'

Surely she wasn't still hung up on that.

Anne shook her head. 'How many times do I have to tell you, there was nothing between Jeremiah and me? Nothing.'

There was no reasoning with this frustrating girl. Up until now there had been the usual name-calling and snide remarks; banal threats Anne knew she had no intention of following through with. But there was something in her demeanour today – the set of her thin painted lips, the tilt of her head – that made Anne wonder if perhaps she might well tell Aunt Bess about Tadashi, or worse, plead for her father to do something totally uncalled for. There was a hardness in Ruth's eyes and stance. For the first time she actually had something she could use against Anne.

'I don't believe you. And I don't believe you about your filthy Jap, either.'

'Stop it, Ruth. That's horrible. You don't even know him.'

'I know he's Japanese.'

'So? He's a good, kind friend, which is more than I can say for you.'

Ruth's nostrils flared. 'I suppose one shouldn't expect an *orphan*'—she spat the word—'to understand the ways of the world. They did awful things in the war. Awful. How can you even associate with one of them?'

'Tadashi didn't fight in the war, Ruth. He was a child, like we were.'

'But they're all the same. Filthy Japs.'

Grace's anger rose. 'You narrow-minded little cow. If you took the time to get to know people before you judged them—'

'Why would I waste my time doing that?' Ruth leaned forward and knocked the book from Anne's hand. Maree bent down to pick it up, but Ruth grabbed her arm and spun her around, marching the sister she was practically raising these days down the main street.

Anne stood her ground until they were out of sight then gathered her book and ran back to the post office. The afternoon ticked by with only two customers visiting, for which Anne was grateful. She couldn't believe Ruth would behave like this. They were seventeen, not children.

When her shift finished, she headed to the lighthouse. As she'd hoped, Tadashi was there, waiting for her.

He bowed in greeting. 'I hope you weren't troubled too much earlier.'

Anne waved her hand. 'She's just a silly girl.' She stepped towards him, stopping inches away. He didn't retreat and Anne could feel the warmth of his breath dance over her forehead.

'If our friendship causes you grief from others, Anne-san, then perhaps we should see less of each other.'

'Is that what you want?' She held her breath.

He shook his head. 'I want you to be safe and happy.'

'I'm perfectly safe. And'—she wanted to tell him how she truly felt, how her heart sang when he was near and sunk when he wasn't—'our friendship makes me happy.'

'Really?' His eyes lit up.

'Of course.'

'It pleases me more than you'll ever know to hear this.'

Hope filled Anne's soul.

'It will not be easy, Anne.' He brushed her cheek.

She tilted her head into his soft touch. 'Nothing worthwhile ever is.'

He nodded and let her go. 'I've got to get back, the captain is waiting for me, but when I return next month, will you meet me here?'

'Of course.' Anne breathed the words and he turned and ran down the headland. As she watched him disappear, excitement pulsed through her veins.

The next four weeks passed in a monotonous haze of work and avoiding Ruth whenever she could. Anne sat by the fountain reading each lunchtime, and for the most part Ruth left her alone. That probably had more to do with Hadley Follett's handsome cousin, Ray, visiting the island than anything else. And Anne made sure she didn't even meet the man in person, just in case Ruth got a bee in her bonnet about some falsely perceived connection.

Aunt Bess had been surprisingly keen to secure a position on the mainland for Anne, but then, Anne supposed it would mean Aunt Bess would be free of her completely. A blessing in Bess's eyes, no doubt. And that suited Anne just fine. She made sure she went above and beyond for Mrs Forster, in case any of Bess's old army wife friends heard of a position going in Sydney and needed a reference.

The end to her time on the island was in sight, and nothing would stop her.

When the *Seafarer* came in four weeks later, she wasn't due for a shift in the post office, but offered to bring Mrs Forster the mailbag anyway. Standing on the dock, her skin tingled as the familiar silhouette of the boat pushed through the sunrise. A month was too long without his face, without his thoughts on this book or that, without his encouragement of her painting. But hopefully it wouldn't be long now till she was on the mainland and would be able to see him more often.

Captain Allen threw the mailbag at her when the boat docked, and barked angry orders at Tadashi, who didn't look in her direction. Anne was confused. Had she misread his intentions? Were they not at the very least close friends?

She told herself that he was simply busy unloading the boat, and slipped off to deliver the mailbag to the post office. Then she trudged up to the lighthouse to watch the remainder of the sunrise through salt-veiled eyes.

He would come. She knew it. She wiped her tears away, remembering the soft touch of his hand on her cheek, his breath tickling her forehead. He would come.

Hours passed, and the sun reached higher into the sky. There was no sign of Tadashi, but still she waited, until long shadows spread across the grassy headland.

Right before dusk settled over the island, Anne stood on stiff legs. She'd been a fool.

From her rucksack she pulled out her sketchbook. As she

flipped through it, tears fell down her cheeks. Her artwork, her connection to Tadashi, was nothing more than childish fancy.

She tore out the first page. Her breath caught. She screwed the piece of paper up into a ball and flung it over the cliff. The next page came more easily. And the next. With increasing ferocity, each crumpled page sailed into oblivion. She hurled the final page into the ocean and fell to her knees, letting out her pain and sadness in a short, guttural scream.

Then she turned her back on the lighthouse, straightened her shoulders, swallowed the last pitiful sob, and headed home.

'Ah, there you are,' Bess greeted her at the front door of the cottage. 'Come in and have some dinner. I have news.'

Anne plonked herself down at the small dining table opposite her aunt.

Bess handed Anne a piece of paper.

'This telegram came for you today.'

It was from a Mrs Harris, who had an opening for a secretary at one of the wool companies in Sydney. Anne looked up at her aunt, hardly daring to believe it.

'You'd be a very foolish girl if you didn't take it. Mrs Harris can give you lodging too.'

Tears pricked Anne's eyes. She would never be foolish again. She'd take the job, leave the island and all memories of Tadashi behind.

'Thank you, Aunt Bess,' she managed to say.

'I know it seems I've been hard on you, girl.' Bess's voice faltered slightly. 'But I couldn't let you get too attached here.'

Anne frowned.

'I've never been one for emotions. But I did my best for you. You have the chance to leave the island, find a good husband, make a better life for yourself.'

Anne's eyes rimmed with tears. But she wouldn't let them fall.

*

After a light supper of roast beef and day-old bread, Anne excused herself from the table and sat on the end of her bed, staring out of the small salt-encrusted window into the night.

From down the corridor she heard a light tap on the front door of the cottage. She knew Aunt Bess would answer it and shoo away whoever it was. One of the many things Bess couldn't abide was people calling unannounced. Especially after suppertime.

Anne padded out of her room and into the kitchen to fetch a glass of water. 'Who was at the door?' she asked.

Bess didn't look up from her knitting. From the kitchen window Anne could see a shadowed figure moving down Soldiers' Way, but it was too dark to see who it was.

Bess waved her hand dismissively. 'Just one of the farmhands asking if we needed eggs. I sent him away.' She shifted slightly in her chair, adjusting the knitted rug that hung over her lap.

But the figure Anne had seen from the window didn't have quite the right silhouette to be any of the farmhands. It was too tall, too slim.

'Off to bed then.' Bess waved Anne out of the room.

Sitting on her bed, Anne re-read the telegram. Since she'd arrived on the island four years ago all she had wanted was to get back to Sydney and this was her chance. In two weeks' time the passenger ship would take her to a new life.

No tears came, but no smile either. A hollow in the pit of her soul where excitement should have been.

In the morning, she watched from the lighthouse as the *Seafarer* departed, the sun beginning to light up the world. Leaning against the rough rendered whitewash of the tall beacon she watched the boat grow smaller as it sailed away. There was a lone figure standing on the stern of the boat, tall and slim, and if she were her childish self of yesterday, still prone to silly fancies, she would have imagined it was Tadashi, looking for her there.

———

Anne's body ached all over as she hauled herself up off the sofa and away from her memories.

Tonight had been good. Book club had been a success. She needed to hold on to that, not her disagreement with Ruth or the fact that Grace may know things she shouldn't. Anne's task at hand was to ensure that book club would continue long after she was gone. Long after her memories of a lifetime ago faded with her.

She yawned. Her left arm tingled, but she ignored it. It would go away.

The chime of the old clock on the shelf behind her spoke of the late hour. She'd need a good night's sleep before the walk to the lighthouse tomorrow. Especially if she was going to have her wits about her to hide her emotions; to conceal the past from Grace.

Thirteen

Grace had tossed and turned all night. It wasn't because of the bed, which was comfortable and soft. Or the fact that it was her first night in the cottage, which was quiet, with only the faint sound of waves crashing below beating a rhythm through the night. And it wasn't the book club. Apart from a few awkward moments, it had been rather successful.

It wasn't even the fight with her mum, though she'd have to deal with that at some point.

It was those dark, piercing eyes, where only fleeting hints of joy danced. *His* eyes. And Anne and Ruth's fraught whisperings caught on the night air. *Can't you see what this is doing to him?*

She shook her head as she poured peppermint tea into a delicate cup painted with red swirls.

Perhaps today she could find out some more. Do a little digging. When she finished her cup of tea she dressed in a white long-sleeved T-shirt and jeans and grabbed her red cardigan. She hadn't worn that old favourite in a long time. As she pulled on her walking shoes there was a knock at the door.

'Good morning, pet.' Anne greeted her in a floating kaftan in shades of green, and a white-and-yellow scarf around her head. Grace wondered if Anne had thermals on underneath, as the day carried with it a definite winter chill. 'Did you sleep well?'

'It was a very comfortable night.' Not strictly a lie.

'Shall we?'

Grace walked beside Anne on their way up to the lighthouse, the morning sun warming her face. The only noise other than their footfalls was the breeze and the waves crashing below them. The sweeping vista of green hills and blue ocean cast a swell of peace over her.

'It's exactly like your pictures,' Grace remarked when they reached the lighthouse. She walked around the base of the structure, running her hands along the rough, white-washed surface. It was a silly thing to say, perhaps, given that the blues and purples Anne used to paint with were nothing like the stark white lighthouse sitting on its green blanket dotted with tiny white flowers. But standing here, Grace could feel Anne's paintings, sense the movement.

'Thank you, pet. It is my favourite place on the island.' A light hitch in Anne's voice caught on the last few words and Grace looked at her, hoping for more. But no more came.

'In your earlier works there was such a sense of joy,' she said carefully. 'But in the pictures in your studio, there was . . . sadness.'

'You are perceptive.' Anne nodded, her gaze distant. 'If a place is part of your life for long enough, part of your soul, then it holds the good memories and the sad. A lot has happened here.' She placed her hand on the wall of the lighthouse and closed her eyes, as if she was feeling its heartbeat. 'So very, very much.'

Grace put her hand on Anne's back and felt her shaking. 'Are you okay?'

'Oh, yes, pet. At my age the weight of those memories, even the good ones, can be heavy. And there were lots of good ones.'

'It's a shame Sam couldn't join us this morning.' Grace hadn't meant for those words to be spoken out loud. She'd just been thinking that if he were here, his presence might have soothed his grandmother.

'He never comes to the lighthouse.' A brief moment of anguish flashed in her eyes.

Before Grace had a chance to ask why, Anne straightened her shoulders.

'Now, have you got something to occupy yourself with for the afternoon? I have a meeting with the town council I can't get out of. They'd be lost without me, you know.'

The moment had passed. Grace made a mental note to find out why Sam never came to such a beautiful part of the island.

Grace assured Anne she'd be fine on her own. She had a town to explore; all those plaques to read. Air to breathe in deeply. She escorted Anne back to the cottages and then headed down Soldiers' Way towards the beach. As she emerged from the yellow veil of wattle trees she stopped dead in her tracks at the sight before her.

Was she hallucinating? She closed her eyes for a moment and opened them again.

There on the beach was a young girl, walking a caramel-coloured cow on a pink lead.

Grace hadn't known what to expect when she arrived on Wattle Island – but she certainly hadn't expected this. Over the years, she'd added many interesting things to see to her bucket lists – *age sixteen: see the Northern Lights; age eighteen: visit Pamukkale in Turkey; age fifteen: see the Nazca Lines of Peru; age twenty: witness Kati Thanda–Lake Eyre when full* (tick, age twenty-two, partially filled) – but she hadn't ever imagined anything like what was in front of her.

Stepping onto the soft sand, Grace walked towards the girl, who she guessed was maybe around eight or nine.

'Hello.' She waved.

The young girl smiled at her. 'Hi.'

'I'm Grace.'

'My name's Addie.'

'Nice to meet you, Addie. And who's this?' She reached out and patted the cow's nose.

'This is Emmeline Harris.' At the mention of her name the cow nuzzled Addie's shoulder.

'Well, never a better name for cow I've heard.' Grace put her hands on her hips. 'Do you have any other pets?'

'She's not a pet. She's my friend. I had a chicken once.'

Grace smiled. 'Was his name Gilbert Blythe?'

Addie's eyes grew wide. 'You know *Anne of Green Gables*?'

'I do,' Grace replied. 'I'm a librarian.'

'A librarian?' Addie's eyes grew even wider. 'We don't have a librarian on the island. We don't even have a library.'

'Do you like to read?' Grace asked, as Emmeline Harris pushed her nose into Grace's chest, shoving her off balance.

'She doesn't like to stand still,' Addie explained.

Grace laughed. 'Does she like water?'

'Yes.' Addie smiled.

Together they walked up to where tiny waves lapped at their ankles at the edge of the shore; a sensation Emmeline Harris appeared to enjoy.

'I wish we had a library.' Addie trailed her toes in the sand. 'My Obaachan's collection is good, but she has mostly grown-up books.'

Grace had heard Sam use that term before.

'Is your great-grandmother Anne?'

Addie nodded.

'And Sam is your dad?'

'He is.' The girl exuded love in her expression.

Grace pursed her lips. Sam was a dad. His wife hadn't been at book club, though. She wondered what she might be like, the woman who had Sam's brooding heart.

'Do you read a lot?' Addie asked. 'You must if you're a librarian. I can't imagine how excellent it would be to be surrounded by books all the time.' She looked up to the sky, her arms spread wide.

'Tell you what, Addie, why don't I send you some books when I get back home?'

Addie held the pink lead to her chin. 'You can do that?'

'I can.'

The little girl let out a long breath. 'I'd like that. Very much.'

Grace held out her hand and they shook. 'Deal.'

Addie giggled.

'I'm going to head into town, now. It was nice to meet you, Addie. Make sure you get Mum and Dad to clear you a shelf for your new books.'

'It's just Dad.' Addie swept her foot in the sand.

'Oh?'

Emmeline Harris started walking off and Addie followed. 'Bye, Grace.'

'Bye.' Grace's voice drifted to nothing.

She walked back up the beach. *Just Dad.* Where was Addie's mother? Then she remembered more of Ruth's words to Anne when Grace had heard them talking after book club. '*We all loved her.*' Had Sam's wife left? Died?

Grace thought of the looks on everyone's faces at book club when she had mentioned secrets; the recurrence of seven years everywhere she turned. Something had happened here on the island seven years ago – something shared, something painful. The Wattle Island Book Club was shaping up to be quite the mystery.

The golden pompoms of the wattle trees rippled in the light breeze, their dance pulling Grace from her thoughts.

She wound her way past the buildings on the main street, reading the brass plaques that adorned each one. All were inscribed with an intricate font, and most of the dedications were simple, displaying the year the buildings were built and by whom. A few, though, had little additions: *This stone was laid by the dishonourable headmaster Mr Dober, may he never return;* 'Ouch,' Grace said. *In honour of G. M. Hart, a true lover. Of all.* Grace raised an eyebrow. All of the plaques were older than Grace would have assumed, some of them dating back nearly one hundred and fifty years.

She passed the fountain – unchanged from the photo of a much younger Anne and Ruth sitting by it that Grace had seen at the pub – and took in the park. From there, she could look back on the whole town with its maze of Federation-style shops, filigree terraces with intricately worked balustrades, red-brick structures with painted wooden fretwork, intermittently interrupted by Californian bungalows. Physical snapshots of history.

To her left was the back of a row of shops, their plain rear facades nowhere near as interesting as their preserved heritage fronts. Not beautiful, but sound of structure. Except for the building in the middle. It seemed duller in colour than the others, as though it was covered in an extra layer of grime and dust. A layer of neglect. Grace walked over to it.

Through a partially boarded-up window she could see shelves along the walls inside, lots and lots of shelves. She hadn't noticed a boarded-up shop from the other side of the building where all the facades were postcard-perfect. She stepped closer and peered more intently through the dirt-covered glass.

A few books were scattered along the dusty floor. Tables and chairs were set up as if they were waiting for guests to come and sit. On one table sat a single teacup on a saucer, a serviette folded neatly by its side.

Her view was obstructed, but she could just make out a stack of books sitting forlornly on a counter at the far end of the room, next to a sign she couldn't read.

To her left was an old door and Grace pushed against it. It gave way easily against her weight.

Stumbling back, she looked around. There was no one about.

The door's hinges squeaked.

Grace went to pull the door to and noticed the lock that should have held it shut was broken. She leaned inside to take a peek. The musty smell of old books and dust assaulted Grace's senses. This had to be the closed-down bookshop.

She knew she had to go in. Which wasn't the same as breaking in. Not really. The door opening like that was practically an invitation. She crept into the old shop.

To her right was the cluster of chairs and tables she'd seen from outside. She could see now they were part of a little cafe set-up. There was an old menu on one of the tables, one chair pushed out, another tucked neatly away. An empty saucer sat on a yellowed doily, a fork flung off to the side as if whoever had been sitting there had taken off in a hurry.

On the opposite wall to where she was standing was a cabinet with ceramic candle holders and coffee mugs for sale with the same swirling pattern as the one from which she'd drunk her tea this morning. Grace turned one of the mugs over. The initials S. S. were etched into the bottom.

To her left, shelves she hadn't been able to see from outside were heavy with books. Grace ran her fingers through the dust, revealing handwritten labels. *Fantasy, Romance, Second-hand.* There was one labelled *Island recommendations,* with postcard-sized signs stuck to the shelf. Taking out the hanky Grace always carried in case of hot flush emergencies, she wiped the printed signs. Each revealed a title – *Wattle Island Book Club recent reads* – followed by a paragraph about a book. There was one written by Ruth W. for *The Count of Monte Cristo: three and-a-half stars – a little overrated,* one by Anne Sato about *The Red Tent: five stars – my favourite book of all time* and one by Felicity, no last name or initial, for *Frankenstein: four stars – my first classic and it resonated . . .*

It appeared that, in its day, the Wattle Island Book Club had been bigger than a few mates sitting in a circle having a friendly chat about books. It had been more important than Grace had realised.

In front of the shelves, chairs were set up in a semicircle around a coffee table stacked with twenty books in two neat piles. *Moby Dick.* Grace's heart beat harder as she realised she'd stepped back in time to where the book club used to meet.

She moved towards the counter she'd spied earlier from the door, dust dancing through the air, making her cough. On top of the counter sat an issue of the *Wattle Island Times*, dated Friday 28 January, 2011. Seven years ago.

The newspaper's front page displayed a picture of the book-shop, a slightly younger Anne and a blonde woman who looked vaguely familiar.

Grace took in every word of the article.

Today will mark the third annual Book Club Under the Stars on Wattle Island. Locals and visitors alike are expected and a screen has been set up in Commonwealth Park for the post–book club viewing of the film adaptation of Moby Dick.

A favourite on the island event calendar, and the brainchild of Felicity Sato . . .

Grace drew in a deep breath. Felicity Sato.

. . . Book Club Under the Stars has grown from strength to strength and we are all looking forward to island doyennes Anne Sato and Ruth White leading tonight's discussion. The evening will finish in true Wattle Island style with Hamish McKenzie playing us all out with his beloved bagpipes echoing across the hills.

Grace spun around, taking in the full sight of the abandoned bookshop, imagining the book club sitting here discussing white whales and revenge and fate and madness. She ran her hands over the backs of the chairs and along the bookshelves. She pictured Anne sitting over there on the left, talking about the characters; Ruth in the opposite corner, shaking her head; faces unfamiliar to her chatting and laughing and nodding; the tourists milling around, waiting for the movie to start.

The ghosts shimmered and faded and the hairs on the back of Grace's neck tingled.

Grace may not have believed in the universe sending signs, or in destiny; in any of that nonsense. But she did believe in her bucket lists. She'd been waiting her entire life to solve a mystery. Sure, this wasn't exactly *Murder on the Orient Express* but there was most definitely unfinished business here. Detective Elliott was now on the case.

She took some photos of the space with her phone, then stepped back outside into the blinding sun of the clear winter's day, straight into Sam.

She bounced off his solid frame and laughed as she took his outstretched hand to steady herself.

'Sorry,' she said. 'My fault.'

'Are you okay?' The deep tone of Sam's voice warmed her skin.

'Yes, thank you.' Their hands were still clasped.

He frowned. 'What were you doing in my shop?'

'Your shop? Oh . . . I . . . just . . . I was walking past and looked in the window, and the door kind of gave way.'

'So you went inside?' The dark cloud she'd seen before came over his face again, but this time it stayed. He dropped her hand.

'Well . . .' She looked down at the ground.

'You shouldn't snoop.' His voice was low, halting.

'I . . . I wasn't snooping.'

'What were you doing, then?'

Grace paused, not knowing what to say. Technically she had been snooping, but that sounded so underhanded and wrong.

'That's what I thought.' Sam shook his head.

'Sam, is this where the old book club used to meet?' she asked, even though she already knew the answer.

He nodded.

Grace lowered her voice to a whisper. 'What happened in there?'

'Nothing.' His words were gruff. 'You've got no business sticking your nose in where it doesn't belong.'

He turned and strode away. Grace stared after him, her mouth open.

This was most definitely not nothing.

She shuffled through town, all sorts of scenarios running through her head.

A: Sam's wife, Felicity Sato – speculation, at this point – left Sam, ending their marriage, in the middle of book club. Possible. But surely the pain Grace knew plagued her new friends was deeper than an explanation as simple as this.

B: Addie's mum – speculation, Felicity – had died in child birth. Tragic. Yes. Though the dates didn't add up. If Addie was born in 2011 she'd only be seven, and Grace was sure she was older than that. A second child perhaps?

C: Some sort of terrible accident had happened the night of Book Club Under the Stars . . .

'Lovely day.'

Grace looked up as Anne stepped out of the town hall.

'Isn't it?' It was, though Grace was still a little shaken by Sam's reaction to her being in the bookstore. *His* bookstore.

'Is everything all right?' Anne frowned.

Grace shrugged. 'Oh, I think . . . I think maybe I upset Sam somehow.'

'Oh?'

'I found my way inside the old bookshop. At least, I assume it was the bookshop . . .'

Grace didn't need to say anything else. The look on Anne's face was enough.

'I'm sorry.' She touched Anne's arm. 'I've upset you too. I didn't mean to.'

Grace could see the pain in Anne's faded grey eyes.

Anne took in a deep breath. 'It's okay, pet.'

'Anne?' Grace's voice was gentle. 'What happened in there?'

Anne closed her eyes. 'Some stories aren't mine to tell.'

She turned and walked away, her green kaftan billowing behind her.

Grace wandered up to the lighthouse and sat with her back against the flaking curve of the wall. She wasn't sure it was such a good idea to delve so deeply into other people's lives, but she felt drawn in. Almost as if – she couldn't believe she was about to admit this – as if she were meant to be here.

From below her the sound of crashing waves floated up on the cool breeze and she drew in deep salty breaths. There was a peace here by the lighthouse, a vastness she found comforting. She knew she had no right to pry into these people's lives. And yet, she knew without a doubt, she couldn't leave until she'd learned the truth.

Fourteen

Anne entered the cool, dark solace of her studio and leaned heavily on the workbench. She'd avoided Grace's questions, rather pathetically, for now. But how long would that last? She didn't get the sense Grace would let go easily.

It isn't my story to tell. Why had Anne said that? She could have said anything else – *Oh nothing, pet; economic downturn, you know how that goes; hard to keep a small business open in a town like this; sometimes Sam wakes up on the wrong side of the bed.* Anything else.

Her words may have got her out of there, but they were also an admission there *was* a story hiding in the shadows. It was Sam's story, yes. But they all felt the repercussions. Perhaps not in equal measure, but Anne certainly felt its weight every day.

Did a person's story exist on its own, in isolation? Or were their stories all connected? The joy, the guilt, the pain, the love. Story upon story. Moment upon moment.

She looked around at her art, her story all around her;

her present, her past. She picked up a paintbrush and tried to filter the images, the memories, shifting in her mind.

Sydney, 1951

Anne stepped off the train at Central Station, tired and filthy from twenty hours on a boat followed by five hours on a train. Mrs Harris had told her she would be waiting on the platform, and sure enough, Anne spotted a burly woman dressed in a plain yellow dress and sensible brown shoes searching the faces of the train passengers.

'Mrs Harris?' Anne waved.

Mrs Harris nodded at her but didn't smile. 'Welcome, child. Come along now.'

On the way to her new living quarters in Pyrmont, Anne listened to Mrs Harris's instructions on what time she'd be expected at her desk at the wool company, when supper was served at the boarding house, what time curfew was, and that there were no allowances for lateness. Her golden rule, that would see Anne immediately evicted if she broke it, was that there were absolutely no male visitors allowed. Not even relatives.

Anne didn't bother telling her that was a rule she had little hope of breaking.

The cab drove through streets crammed with buildings and people; sandstone and wood and brick and steel all around them. Eventually, they pulled up outside a row of two-storey terrace houses, all a similar shade of dusty grey-brown.

'It's nothing fancy,' Mrs Harris said, as they entered the terrace. She gestured that Anne follow her up the stairs. 'But it's clean and fine enough for a single working woman.' The last three words dripped with judgement. 'This is your room. Keep it tidy. Supper in an hour.'

Anne closed the door behind her and inspected her new lodgings. The room was half the size of her room back on Wattle Island. Against one wall stood a rickety iron bed and thin mattress; against another, a small wardrobe. There was one tiny grime-covered window, and a small washing urn sat atop an old wooden hallstand. She unpacked her suitcase and slid it under the bed. *This is temporary*, she told herself. *At least you're back in Sydney.* A stepping stone to her new life. She would work hard, save all her money and eventually she'd be able to create a nice life for herself. Sitting on the end of the bed, she opened her copy of *Anne of Green Gables* and let the familiar passages wash over her.

On Monday morning Anne stepped into the foyer of Walsh and Walsh, her palms sweating. The polished floor gleamed, and the grand wooden staircase in the centre of the foyer was rimmed by an intricately carved balustrade.

Anne was greeted with a smile by a girl a couple of years older than her, with bright titian hair set in a perfect bob with Rita Hayworth waves framing her fine features. With her red pencil skirt and crisp white blouse, she could have stepped right out of *Vogue*.

Anne ran her hands over the blue shirtdress Bess had given her as a leaving present, hoping she didn't look as out of place as she felt.

'You must be the new secretary.' The woman smiled, although she was unable to shake Anne's hand as she was holding a large stack of files.

Anne pushed the wayward strand that had fallen out of her ponytail behind her ear. 'Would you like me to take some of those?'

The redhead handed her half the stack. 'Thank you. Follow me and we can put these away, then I can show you to your desk.'

'Of course.'

'I'm Simone, by the way. I'll be your supervisor. Welcome to Walsh and Walsh.' Her footsteps were light and fast; her open-toed Oxfords tapping sharply on the polished wooden floor in their shiny black patent leather. Anne tried to mimic her movements, although she was unable to create any kind of click-clack sound with her slightly worn loafers.

'I'm Anne. It's nice to meet you.'

After they finished filing, Simone showed Anne to a small desk that sat at the top of the stairs – the first port of call for anyone visiting the wool store's office – and ran Anne through her tasks: answering the phone, making coffee, filing, greeting visitors. Simone's desk was right outside the office of Walsh Senior, who was hidden behind a thick oak door that Anne wasn't allowed to enter.

Anne had no idea what to expect from a big corporation like Walsh and Walsh, but it wasn't long into the day before she discovered how much coffee businessmen liked to drink, how quickly they expected it to be made, and that there was no correct way to prioritise answering the phone versus making a coffee, as the expectation was that they both be done without delay.

The morning slipped by in a blur of coffee-making and phone-answering, but once Anne had mastered these fairly straightforward tasks, she quickly became bored, and the afternoon dragged. Focusing on the thought of her first payday helped get her through, though. Finally, five o'clock rolled around, and Simone appeared at her desk.

'Shall we walk out together? You did well today, Anne,' she said, as they passed through the foyer, the doorman bowing slightly as he held the large door open for them. 'Thank you.'

Simone nodded in his direction. 'Keeping Walsh's coffee hot is more important than most people realise.'

Anne frowned. 'Really?'

'Happy boss, happy workers. And he is decidedly unhappy without his coffee.' She laughed. 'Where are you lodging?'

'With Mrs Harris, up on—'

'Ah, Mrs Harris. She runs a tight ship.'

'You've heard of her?'

Simone nodded. 'We've had a lot of girls come through from Mrs Harris.'

'And where are they all now?'

'Married, of course. They catch the eye of one of the merchants and *poof!* They up and marry and we never see them again.'

Anne turned to face her. 'They stop working?'

She shrugged. 'Well, yes, that's usually how it goes.'

Anne supposed she'd never really thought about it. On the island everyone – married or single, male or female – had a job. There was no other way to keep things running. And, while she may not have had her pulse set racing from today's coffee and phone tasks, she understood the value of her newfound independence and couldn't imagine giving it up for a husband. Not that there was much likelihood of that. Hers was a heart that couldn't be trusted when it came to the male species.

'What about you?' she asked Simone.

'I'm engaged.' She held up her hand, showing off a simple yet elegant diamond ring. 'To Colin Walsh Junior. He's happy for me to keep working after we're married, until we're blessed with children.'

Anne nodded, though she didn't quite understand why Colin got to make that decision, not Simone.

'Do you have a beau, Anne? Someone special waiting to sweep you off your feet?'

'Ah, no.'

'Well, maybe we can fix that. Colin has a number of single friends.'

Anne wasn't sure how she felt about that prospect. 'Oh. Well, maybe once I'm settled. This is all a rather big adjustment for me.'

At Simone's tram stop, not far from the wool store, they bade each other goodnight and as Anne walked back to Mrs Harris's, a broad smile swept across her face. This was going to take some getting used to, but with Simone taking her under her wing, she might actually make a go of it.

It didn't take Anne long to notice that she was smarter than many of the suits, but she held back, imagining they wouldn't respond well to their arithmetic being corrected by a secretary. But, after three months, she was presented with an opportunity she couldn't resist when she overheard an argument over a report in which the numbers didn't quite add up. Intrigued, Anne sneaked a look at the report, which was sitting on Simone's desk while she was at lunch. It was a straightforward mistake, one any one of the suits should have picked up, but apparently between them they couldn't interpret a simple graph. She scribbled the correction onto a piece of paper, left it on top of the file and went back to her desk.

When Simone returned to her desk, Colin in tow, she picked up the piece of paper and read it. It was clear from her expression that she didn't understand what was written there, but she passed it to Colin, who most definitely did. He looked around the room and Anne made sure not to make eye contact with him. He burst into his father's office and within minutes all the suits bustled in, one by one.

Anne could hear the raised voices, though they were muffled. And she could feel Simone's eyes on her.

In the end, the fact that the problem had been solved overrode the fact that a mistake had been made in the first place, and the suits left Walsh Senior's office in single file, seemingly appeased. All except the last suit.

'Rodney.' Walsh's stern voice boomed out from the open door. 'I don't need to tell you what's at stake if you make this kind of error again.'

Rodney's pockmarked face was red, his lips pursed. With his hands shoved into the pockets of trousers that appeared to be one or two sizes too large, he stormed past Anne's desk, knocking off the files that were perched close to the edge. He didn't stop to pick them up.

Anne quickly bent down and gathered the loose papers.

'Thank you, Colin, for picking up what happened.' Mr Walsh patted his son on the back. 'We would have been in big trouble if you hadn't found that.'

Colin nodded, but said nothing. His father disappeared back into his office.

As Anne returned the files to her desk, Colin leaned in to Simone.

'It wasn't you?' Anne heard him ask her.

'Of course not. You know I don't have a mind for figures and facts like that.'

'Then who?'

She shrugged, but looked over at Anne, who quickly turned her head.

'If you find out, let me know. We should be rewarding minds like that.' He kissed Simone's hand and headed off to wherever his office was. Anne wasn't quite sure; the building was so vast and she'd seen very little of it so far.

Simone slid over to Anne's desk. 'Is there anything you'd like to share with me?'

Anne shrugged.

'It was you, wasn't it? If it was one of the men, they would have taken credit for it. And unless one of the sorters came up from downstairs there aren't too many other people who'd be wandering past my desk.'

Anne shrugged again. 'I've always been good with that sort of thing.'

'Why didn't you say anything?'

'Would they have believed it was me?'

Simone tilted her head. 'Good point. But, Anne, you're wasted in this role making coffee and filing. If I had your smarts, I'd be marching into Walsh's office and demanding a better position.'

'Really?'

'Okay. So I wouldn't march in there. But surely there's something we can do to get you noticed around here. I'll talk to Colin tonight. He's a little more open-minded than most of them.'

Anne dared to hope. She was appreciative of what she had, but the chance to do something more with her job excited her. A lot.

'I don't want you to stick your neck out for me,' she said, but she was lying. She really would love a more challenging role and if Simone helping meant it was possible, then she was okay with that.

Simone took Anne's hands. 'No necks being stuck out. Colin isn't like that. You'll see.'

Three days later, Anne stood in front of Mr Walsh Senior in a blue skirt and blouse Simone had lent her for this very meeting. She folded her hands in front of her to stop them from shaking and wriggled her toes inside her low pumps, also borrowed from Simone, fearing her legs would go numb and she'd collapse onto the floor right there in front of him.

'So, Miss Webb, am I to understand correctly that you are the employee who discovered the error in this month's report?'

All she had to do was say yes. The word formed in her mouth but refused to come out. She swallowed hard, hoping to dislodge the blockage.

'Well, out with it, lassie.'

'Yes, sir.' Ah, there was her voice, cracked and small as it was.

'Where were you educated?' he asked, looking over his glasses at her. 'Queenwood? Miss Rennie is a fine educator.'

Anne pressed her lips together before answering. 'No, sir. I was not educated in Sydney. Not my final years of school, anyway. I was sent to live with my aunt on Wattle Island when I was thirteen.'

'Wattle Island? Where's that? Do they have a school?'

'A small one, sir.'

Walsh frowned. 'Never mind. If anyone asks, we'll tell them you were tutored by a wonderful governess. I'm fairly liberal, you understand, Miss Webb. I've been employing women since before the war. But this is an old industry and with it comes old ideas. I can't have some random woman educated at a backwater school working under Colin. They simply won't take you seriously.'

Anne nodded. She didn't care what Walsh told his colleagues about her education, if it meant getting out from behind that desk, away from making coffees. Working as Colin's operations assistant meant learning everything about the business, an idea that excited her more than she was willing to admit.

Walsh outlined what her duties would be: reading and checking reports, running through numbers and charts. 'But anything you find has to go through Colin, you understand? While I have no problem listening to a woman, some of the others certainly do. And I can't pay you any extra. That wouldn't be fair on the men.'

While it would have been nice to have a pay rise so that she could earn enough to move out of the boarding house, Anne certainly wasn't expecting it. She was simply grateful not to have to make coffee anymore.

When Walsh finished with her she packed up her things and moved them to the desk outside Colin's office on the floor below.

She wasn't quite sure what to do once she got there, as Colin was in a meeting with buyers, so she organised her desk and familiarised herself with the layout of the floor.

'So it's true.' Rodney came around the corner and stopped in front of her desk, pulling his skinny chest up tall. 'The old man has given Colin his very own plaything.'

'Excuse me?'

'You don't really expect us to believe you're a whiz with numbers and have landed this job because of your smarts?'

'Why not?' Anne snapped.

It was one thing to allow herself to feel small in front of Walsh. He had power, money, a clear intelligence and business acumen and held her fate in his hands. This Rodney fellow, who apparently didn't even understand simple mathematics, was a different matter altogether.

'Don't you get too big for your britches, missy. The men around here don't take too kindly to skirts with smart mouths.'

'Perhaps I should wear trousers then.'

Rodney's nostrils flared and with a sweep of his arm he knocked Anne's pens and a pile of paper off her desk.

'You'd better watch this one, Walsh,' he said, as Colin exited the meeting. 'Cute, but clumsier than a bull in a china shop.' He shook Colin's hand and headed off down the hallway.

Bending down to help Anne, Colin smiled at her. 'Sorry. Right buffoon, that one. The old man owes his dad a favour, so keeps him around. The minute I take over running this joint, he's out on his ear.' He helped Anne up – not that she needed it, but she appreciated the chivalry.

'Thank you.' She smiled.

'I'm happy to have a quick mind like yours on board,' Colin said, looking at Rodney's retreating figure. 'But this isn't going to be easy.'

Anne smiled. Little in her life so far had been easy. She was ready for whatever came her way.

———

Anne closed the studio door behind her, her inks and canvasses untouched. Usually her art was her escape. A way to process old memories and stories; a way to face new challenges. But Grace's questions had rattled her so thoroughly, she couldn't even paint.

She leaned her back against the cool shed door and drew the night air deep into her lungs. So many memories. Some she shared for all the world to see. Some she carried deep inside her where no light could reach.

Fifteen

Grace spent the next three days wandering the island by herself. Anne was constantly busy, it seemed, running this errand or that. She was always polite when Grace ran into her, but Grace got the distinct impression the old lady was avoiding her.

And, as much as she wanted to, she didn't dare go back to the bookshop either, for fear of upsetting Sam any further. Not that she'd seen him. He was probably working. Though Grace couldn't help but wonder if he was avoiding her too.

Thinking of working, she hadn't been missing the library as much as she'd thought she would. She missed seeing Gladys every morning and hoped Linh was bringing her coffee like she'd promised. And she missed her reading groups and the kids' smiling faces. But she didn't miss the longing deep in her soul that had started to surface every Monday morning when they raced into the library, jostling for the best beanbag.

And she certainly didn't miss the admin. There was something a little daring about not knowing what each day would bring, not having a plan. She'd never taken a spontaneous holiday like this. Even before she'd got sick, she'd planned the few holidays she'd taken down to the last second, not wanting to miss anything. Coming to Wattle Island on a whim, having no plan at all – it was liberating.

Okay. Technically she did have *a* plan: to find out what had happened to the Wattle Island Book Club. But perhaps *plan* was overstating it a little. Plan meant you had a direction, steps to follow, a clear path to reach your goal. Goal. Yes, at this stage what she had was a goal.

Every day Grace had explored a different part of the island, partly to fill in time, partly in the hope a clue might suddenly appear out of nowhere. She'd read every plaque in town. Twice. Nothing useful there.

The day before yesterday she'd explored the beaches and had seen Shellie and Phil fishing from the dock at midday.

'Wrong time of the day to catch anything,' Phil had shouted to her. 'But a perfect excuse to make the good doctor here take a proper lunchbreak.'

Shellie had smiled and waved, a half-eaten sandwich in her hand. Grace wondered what they knew about the Wattle Island Book Club. Surely something. But would they be willing to tell Grace anything? Probably not.

Under the dock Grace had taken out her phone and snapped a picture of the criss-cross pattern formed by the pilings and cross-beams – dark where the water caressed the wood, lighter as they reached higher, an orange stain around the bolts that held them together – beautiful in its repetition.

Today she walked past the farms on the far side of the island, spotting Hadley in the field, broad-brimmed hat pulled low over his eyes. He didn't see her.

As the sun reached its peak in the sky, trying in vain to warm the winter day, Grace headed back into town for lunch, thinking she might sample the pub's famous schnitzel.

After ordering at the bar, she took a seat in one of the booths. In the light of day the old hotel looked very different than it had on book club night; no soft orange glow, very few people. There was washing hanging in front of the fireplace to dry, and Grace hid her smirk behind a fake cough.

The bell above the door rang and in walked Sam. Grace smiled at him, half rising out of her seat ready to apologise once more. But he saw her and turned around, walking right back out again. She was surprised he was still so mad at her. Surprised even more at how much that hurt.

The bookshop and whatever had happened there was definitely a corner piece of this puzzle. She'd done many puzzles when she'd been receiving treatment – when she wasn't busy throwing up – and the corners were always the key. She'd find them first, do the edges and then work her way into the middle until the picture was complete. All the pieces were here somewhere. She just didn't know how to find them.

Lunch arrived and Grace could see before even tasting it that the schnitzel was, indeed, top notch. And massive. She had no idea how she was going to get through it.

The door dinged again and Grace looked up. She'd have been lying if she'd said she hadn't hoped it was Sam returning. But instead, in walked Maree – a bohemian splendour of yellow and purple and aqua – and Ruth, in a grey twin-set over plaid trousers.

Maree hit Ruth on the leg when she saw Grace, and Ruth swatted her away. After some intense whispering between the two, they walked towards Grace, a broad smile on Maree's round face, a less enthusiastic one on Ruth's thin visage.

They asked if they could join her – well, Maree did – and Grace happily agreed, grateful for the company, as she'd spent so much of the past few days alone.

Ruth ordered for her sister and herself at the bar and when she returned, she eyed Grace up and down, while Maree prattled on about how much she'd enjoyed book club and had Grace explored the island properly yet?

Grace couldn't get a word in edgeways. Maree only seemed to take a breath when her lunch arrived.

'So, tell us, Grace.' Maree attacked her beef burger in a manner Grace had never seen before, pulling it apart, piece by piece, eating the patty first, then reconstructing the tomato, the cheese and the bun. 'What's it like working as a librarian?'

Maree listened attentively as Grace told them about her job, genuinely interested in what she had to say – unlike Ruth, who clearly wanted to be anywhere else.

'Never had a library on the island, have we, sister mine?' Maree looked at Ruth.

'No. Never really had the means or support for one.' Ruth's words were clipped.

'But you did have a bookstore once,' Grace said.

Maree coughed, and Ruth elbowed her.

'It closed. A while back now.' Ruth looked straight ahead, a deep sorrow momentarily appearing in her gold-flecked irises before the hard gaze Grace had associated with her since book club night returned.

'What is it you do for fun in Port Maddison, Grace?' Maree changed the subject. 'It must seem like a regular metropolis compared to our quiet corner of the world.'

Grace told them about MAW and Maree leaned forward. 'That

sounds amazing. Probably too much for an old duck like me, though.' She shrugged.

'My sister the daredevil.' Ruth rolled her eyes. She was very good at that.

'Don't bet on that. There is an eighty-year-old in the group,' Grace said, ignoring Ruth's comment.

'Oh, how ridiculous,' Ruth said. 'At that age.'

'Age is merely a number,' Grace responded, looking directly at her. And if she wasn't mistaken, Ruth appeared to appreciate the challenge.

'That's easy for someone as young as you to say.' She pushed her chest out and almost smiled. 'You have all the time left in the world.'

Grace choked slightly on her mineral water.

Maree rubbed her shoulder. 'You wouldn't know it now, but I used to be quite the adventurer.'

'I can see that about you.' Grace nodded.

Maree's face lit up. 'Really?'

'It's in your eyes.'

'And what do you see in my eyes?' Ruth fixed her with a glare.

The old Grace would have backed down at this point. But not the new Grace. And not the Grace who suspected Ruth respected someone who could hold their own.

'Intelligence. Hard work. Loyalty.' She was pulling that last one out of nowhere, but she figured if Anne had been friends with this woman for decades, there had to be a reason. 'And'—she softened her voice—'loss.'

Ruth's glare faltered, as Maree jumped in. 'Oh, you've got her pegged.'

As they talked about Maree's travels in her younger days, Hamish entered the pub wearing a kilt and Maree waved him over.

He stopped by the bar and grabbed a takeaway coffee, then joined them.

'Good day, ladies. Enjoying lunch?'

Maree and Grace nodded.

'Anne was right about the chicken schnitzel. Best I've ever had,' Grace said.

'It is indeed. And how are you liking your stay on the island?'

'Very much.'

Maree leaned forward. 'And isn't the view from your cottage beautiful? It used to be Sam's, you kn—'

Another elbow from Ruth cut her sister off. Grace wondered how Maree had any ribs left if this was an indication of their life as sisters.

'Will you join us?' Grace asked Hamish.

'I'd love to, but I've got a date with a classic mature lady.'

'Anne?'

Hamish laughed and Ruth almost cracked a smile. 'A droning old bag, you mean,' she said to Hamish.

'That's my cue to leave.' Hamish bowed and headed off.

Grace turned to Maree. 'Is Hamish going on a date with Anne?'

Maree shook her head and laughed, a sound full of mirth and mischief. 'Not at all. Though I can honestly say that there is an old bag Hamish has been in love with for as long as I can remember.'

Grace frowned. 'Who?'

Maree smiled. 'It will all become very clear soon.'

'Painfully clear,' Ruth added.

The sisters took their leave, Ruth with a curt nod, Maree leaning in to Grace. 'Don't mind her. Really. She's always cranky.'

Ruth came back and dragged Maree away.

Grace watched them go, feeling disappointed. She'd been hoping to steer the conversation back to the bookshop or to the new revelation that Sam owned the cottage in which she was staying, but she'd have to wait.

With the sun against her back doing little to warm her, Grace wound her way up the gently sloping rise on the east side of the island that led to the lighthouse. She stopped along the way, taking photos of the tiny pink, yellow and white wildflowers that dotted the long wispy grass on either side of the dirt path.

She moved to the far side of the bluff, the lighthouse behind her, and stood there looking out to sea, the whole world melting away. The wind blew off the ocean, lifting white spray into the air that danced and floated, suspended momentarily, before falling back to the churning waves below.

She breathed deeply, watching the inky waves crash in and out, their depths calling to her, dark and frightening; their white foam teasing her, light and playful.

There was something about this place that was both peaceful and menacing. What had Anne said? That a place can hold memories. That a lot had happened here. Grace could almost feel it. She couldn't understand why Sam refused to come up here. Was the lighthouse the fourth corner piece of the puzzle? The book club; the bookshop; the seven-year timeframe; the lighthouse?

A noise from behind made her turn around. Hamish was striding towards her, a large set of bagpipes under his arms.

His droning old bag. Grace held back a laugh, remembering Ruth's words from the pub.

'Hello there, young Grace.' He smiled.

'Hi, Hamish. Do you play up here often?'

'Not too often. I play up the top of Soldiers' Way on the last Friday of every month. This beauty's song floats all over the island from here.' He spread his free arm out in a sweeping arc and Grace remembered the note in the newspaper article about Hamish play-ing bagpipes at the Book Club Under the Stars. 'But every now and then I like to come up here to practise and stare at the view.'

Grace could understand that. The view part, not the bagpipes part.

'I've always played, though, any chance I get – weddings, birth-days, anything. I haven't yet convinced Anne to let me intro the book club each month but I'm still working on her. How long can she keep saying no to me, really?'

This time Grace did laugh. 'I suspect she's stubborn enough to say no for a very long time.'

'You don't know how right you are.' He winked. 'I don't nor-mally have an audience, but you're welcome to stay.'

'Actually, do you mind if I do?' Grace had never been a particular fan of the bagpipes herself but Uncle Craig had been and together they'd dreamed of going to the Edinburgh Military Tattoo one day. It had been on every bucket list she'd made since she was twelve.

A private bagpipe concert in front of a lighthouse wasn't quite the Tattoo, but she'd take it. And it was another tick against the varied entries in her journal of concerts and live performances: *age sixteen: go to a rock concert* (tick, Jet, mind blown); *age seventeen: attend a poetry reading in a small Parisian cafe; age twenty-one: see an opera at Sydney Opera House* (tick, didn't really enjoy); *age nineteen: see a musical in a Sydney theatre* (tick, age twenty-seven, *Les Misérables*, loved it).

She sat down on the grass a few metres away from Hamish and he turned his back on her to face the ocean. After a couple of warm-up notes – were they even called notes? – he settled into a song full of melancholy and longing.

Grace never thought the bagpipes would be able to inspire any kind of emotion in her, but that afternoon she was proved wrong. She closed her eyes. Her chest rose with the music as she remembered the mouth ulcers, the nausea and the intractable fatigue following her first round of chemo; June by her side, nursing her day and night. Her chest fell with the soft melody as she let the memory dissolve. The crescendo of the tune was a reminder of the fight she'd had with her mother just days ago; the fade of the last notes an echo of the fragile peace she'd made with her cancer.

When Hamish finished, he turned around and took a bow.

Standing, Grace clapped. 'That was beautiful, really. But so sad.'

Hamish nodded. 'I've found over the years that burying one's sadness does one no good. But by letting it sing, giving it wings, in my case though music, you set it free.'

Grace had never heard anyone express the idea of letting go quite so eloquently before. 'I like that. A lot.'

Hamish touched Grace on the shoulder. 'Thank you. Not everyone sees it that way. Some people hold on to their pain, their darkness, for too long.'

Grace knew what it was like to live without light, and everywhere she turned on this island, pain was lingering in the shadows. Surely there was a way for her to help.

As she walked back to her cottage – *Sam's* cottage – her thoughts turned to June. She really should call her.

She was hanging up her jacket in the bedroom wardrobe when she felt a dragging pain in her lower back, wrapping around to her pelvis.

No. Not that. Grace wasn't ready for *that.*

She couldn't call June now. Her mother would know something was up. Grace took the pain medication out of her bag, swallowed it and counted her breaths until the pain passed and then fell against the closet. A thud echoed behind the old piece of wooden furniture.

Once the pain subsided, she reached behind the closet to see what she'd knocked down. She pulled out an old book.

Frankenstein.

Grace opened the cover and there in the opening chapter, a sentence was highlighted in pink.

There is something at work in my soul, which I do not understand . . .

In the margin of the book a heart was drawn in pink highlighter, the initials F. S. small inside.

Grace's eyes went wide. Her pulse raced.

Sixteen

As Anne stood up from her crouched position in the bushes behind the row of cottages, her knees protested, reminding her that a woman her age had no business ducking behind bushes to hide. It was foolish, she knew, to avoid Grace. She was abandoning her, really. She'd seen her in the pub at the mercy of Maree and Ruth – well, at the mercy of Ruth – and she'd left the poor girl there to fend for herself. Then she'd seen her heading back to her place and Anne had ducked out of sight. She was a coward.

She'd brought this upon herself, openly welcoming Grace when she'd suggested coming to the island to help with book club. Anne wondered if, on some level, she had hoped Grace's presence would stir things up. That Grace would ask the questions Anne was too afraid to ask. So many things from that night seven years ago, and so many things since, didn't add up. Anne knew, deep down, it was time to uncover the truth so they could all make peace.

But could they? Could she? Could Sam?

Could you ever truly make peace with the painful parts of

your life? She thought she had with her own past. Long ago. But her wretched memories had been resurfacing so often over the past few weeks that she was having trouble some days distinguishing the now from the then.

Anne dragged her tired and sore legs up the bluff until she reached the lighthouse. She eased her back against its sturdy wall and watched the ebb and flow of the ocean.

The then, the now, the next. How was she supposed to sort it all out?

Sydney, 1952

For three months after she was promoted, Anne was either ignored in meetings, spoken over or asked to fetch coffee, despite Walsh Senior introducing her as Colin's operations assistant. She quickly learned to pass notes to Colin, and when he presented her idea as his own, it was listened to with respect. Frustration was not a strong enough word, but at the end of each day, Colin made sure to thank her for her contribution, so she took comfort in the knowledge that one day he would be running the company and then she would be given rightful credit.

Patience is a virtue. Bess's words ran through her mind. Anne hated patience, but knew its value here.

It was a Friday afternoon in autumn, and dark clouds were rolling in over the harbour when Colin came by her desk.

'Webb, Simone and I are going for a drink at the Monty with a couple of others. Care to join us?'

While she may have socialised a little with Simone over the last few months, being invited out directly by Colin was new. And not a small deal.

'Thank you, yes,' Anne said immediately. 'Sounds like fun.'

In the dark pub Colin shouted the first round, and Simone and Anne sat on the high bar stools while he and his three mates stood, shoulders back, sleeves of their crisp white shirts rolled up, talking around them. Hamish, the man to Colin's left, smiled at Anne, though wasn't so bold as to speak to her directly.

'How are you liking working with Colin?' Simone leaned forward and touched Anne's knee.

'I'm loving it. I'm learning so much.'

'Colin said you were a quick study. The men aren't giving you too hard a time, are they?'

Anne shrugged.

'It's a man's world all right.' Simone nodded, her red hair waving ever so slightly. 'But look at you, forging your way through. You're doing it for every one of us, you know.'

'Oh, don't put that responsibility on me,' Anne laughed. 'I simply want to work and pay my own way.'

Colin leaned in and asked Simone if she wanted another drink, kissing her on the cheek. The way he looked at her reminded Anne of that one perfect moment on the island when . . . oh my, she hadn't thought of that – of *him* – in quite a while.

'Are you all right?' Simone asked.

'Yes.' She'd cordoned off that part of her heart the moment she'd left the island. And now, a world away, there was no point opening old wounds. 'A distant memory, is all. One I'd like to forget.'

Colin handed her a wine. 'This might help.'

Anne took it and smiled. She didn't drink much – she found the taste of wine terribly unappealing – but she didn't want to be rude. Perhaps if she took only tiny sips, they wouldn't buy her another.

Hamish adjusted his stance, inching closer to Anne, when a rowdy group of men burst into the pub. One of them knocked into Hamish, sending him into Anne's lap, spilling his drink all over her.

Head down, she tried to mop up the beer that had soaked her skirt.

'I'm so sorry.' Hamish's face was stricken with concern.

'Not your fault.'

'Bloody wharfies,' Colin grumbled. 'Why aren't they up at the Anchor?'

The group of wharf workers shouted their drunken apologies as they moved to the back of the pub to the men's only section.

A tingle ran up Anne's neck and she turned to look at the group. They were jostling past the other pub patrons, tightly packed together, indistinguishable from one another in their identical blue overalls and blue woollen jumpers.

Colin turned to his mates. 'How about we move on from here?'

Simone and Anne followed the men outside. Anne turned back once, the tingle at the back of her neck refusing to go away.

'Come on.' Simone slipped her arm around her waist. 'We don't want to lose them.'

There was no chance of that. Colin would never leave Simone behind. Anne may not have known much about how romance worked – Lord, look at her history – but she knew men found beauty like Simone's enchanting, and rarely let it go once they had it.

'So, where to next?' Colin asked.

A few suggestions were thrown about, but Anne looked at her watch. 'Actually, I'd better get back. Mrs Harris's curfew.'

'Are you sure?' Simone stepped over to Colin and he put his arm around her shoulder.

'Yes. Thank you, though, for inviting me tonight.'

Colin hit Hamish on the back. 'Why don't you walk Anne home? There are a lot of larrikins about tonight.'

Anne put up her hand. 'Oh, it isn't far.'

'Nonsense. I can't have my star employee walking home alone at night. Hamish, we'll head to the Commercial. See you there.'

Hamish nodded.

'It really isn't necessary.' Anne smiled.

'It's no trouble. I wouldn't feel right about you walking around this late by yourself.' Thunder clapped loudly. 'Especially with this storm rolling in.'

Silence filled the space between them and a light rain began to fall as they navigated the few streets back to the boarding house. At the front door, Anne turned to Hamish. 'Thank you. Enjoy the rest of the night.'

Hamish's smile was warm and sweet. 'Sleep well, Anne.' He tipped his fedora.

She watched him head back down the street, now a glossy black in the wet, and once he was out of sight she opened the front door to the boarding house. The hairs on the back of her neck stood up again and she spun around. Another crack of thunder. From the corner of her eye she noticed a movement in the shadows and she wished she'd gone straight inside without waiting for Hamish to leave.

With her heart racing she fumbled with her keys and fell into the foyer of the boarding house. She slammed the door behind her and locked it. Through the glass panel on the door she looked out into the dark night, illuminated by a flash of lightning. A lone figure scuttled down the street and Anne let out a long breath before scampering into her room. On her bed was a telegram from Wattle Island. Mrs Forster was writing to let her know that Aunt Bess had passed away unexpectedly in her sleep.

Anne couldn't believe the words she read. She'd written to Bess every month since arriving in Sydney. Only last week she'd mailed her latest update. Bess's replies were always short, to the point, but Anne had enjoyed the tiny glimpses of island life.

Sadness washed over her. The last tie to her family was now gone.

She wouldn't be able to afford to attend the funeral. The cottage was now hers, according to Mrs Forster, but Anne couldn't see any point in moving back. There was nothing there for her anymore.

From beside her bed she grabbed the notebook and pencil she kept there to make lists of things to ask Colin about, or questions for Simone, or random thoughts about her life in Sydney.

She turned to the next blank page and closed her eyes. At first, the images that came to her were grey and loud – the buildings of Pyrmont that lined her way to work, the bustle of the docks, the flurry of the sorting room. Then her mind reached further, to the rolling green hills and the ebb and flow of blue waves caressing the soft yellow-white sand of the island.

Lead pencil was not her preferred medium, but it was all she had. With tentative strokes, she moved it across the page, no idea what would come out of her. With each rise and dip of the marks she made on the page, her heart slowed and her nerves settled.

When she finished, she studied the drawing in front of her. The Wattle Island dock was so familiar to her, though askew and obscured by swelling waves. The lighthouse peered at her from the edge of the page. The *Seafarer* sailing towards her, on its bow a figure hidden in shadows.

Since the day she'd purged her life of her foolish art she hadn't felt any urge to paint or draw. Until tonight.

She closed her notebook and climbed under her thin bed covers. As she waited for sleep to take her, images danced through her mind. The path to the lighthouse, reading by the fountain, the wattle heavy in late winter, weighing the branches down. The tiny, beautiful vase sprinkled with cranes. Dark eyes, a crooked smile. His face.

Anne spent the weekend doing chores around the boarding house, as all the girls were expected to do: washing linen, preparing meals, cleaning windows.

When they had free time, most of the girls went to Hyde Park, strolling the paths in small groups hoping to catch a young man's eye. Anne had no interest in catching anyone's eye, so she mostly stayed in her room reading. Until this weekend, when she couldn't stop sketching.

It felt good to let her hand flow across the page again, although she was surprised by how many vignettes of Wattle Island she seemed to be drawing. The only problem was, when she sketched, she thought of Tadashi.

When Monday rolled around, she dressed in her new grey wool pencil skirt that stopped mid-calf, and a lemon-coloured blouse. Walking to work, she pushed any thoughts of Wattle Island from her mind. Colin had a day of important meetings and she needed to be at her best, not distracted by silly memories.

At work she spent the morning reading reports and trying to anticipate Colin's need for this file or that, while he barked requests at her between meetings and phone calls.

By lunchtime Anne was exhausted and ever so grateful when Colin headed out with his dad. She rested her head on her desk when she was alone and breathed deeply.

Click-clack, click-clack. She looked up to see Simone coming her way.

'So,' Simone said, stopping beside Anne, her long legs pouring out from under her tight pink pencil skirt. 'It was good of Hamish to walk you home on Friday night.' Her voice was dripping with mischief.

'Yes, it was.'

'He's a very good catch, you know.'

Anne was sure he was. He seemed decent enough, not that she'd spent long enough with him to really know.

Simone picked up the notebook that Anne had sitting in the middle of her desk. 'What's this?' She flicked through the book and stopped a few pages in.

Anne reached out to take the notebook back. 'Oh, nothing.'

Simone snatched it away. 'These aren't nothing. They're beautiful. Did you draw them?'

Anne nodded.

'Well, I wonder if Hamish would like them?'

For the next ten minutes Simone stood there, talking up Colin's friend. By the end of the conversation, which Anne, for the most part, wasn't entirely sure she needed to be there for, Simone had decided that when the time was right, they'd go on a double date. Anne agreed. If nothing else, it was a night away from the boarding house.

A little after two Colin returned. 'Ready, Webb?' It was time for the weekly meeting with Walsh Senior.

The men crowded around the large round table inside Walsh's office and, as usual, Anne sat behind Colin's right shoulder, gently fanning away the plumes of cigarette smoke. She passed notes to Colin when needed, but remained silent.

Halfway through the meeting, Rodney, his black hair caked with too much Brylcreem, snapped his fingers at her, demanding she fetch him a coffee.

Colin put his hand up. 'Ida can get that.' He called out to the girl who'd replaced Anne on the front desk. Rodney shot Anne a look, but said nothing.

At the end of the day, after everyone but Walsh and Colin had left the building, Anne packed away her desk.

She bade good afternoon to the doorman and turned the corner towards home. And there, waiting for her in the fading twilight, was Rodney. He looked behind him, then over her shoulder.

'I know what you're playing at, missy, and I won't let you get away with it. Smooching up to Colin to get ahead. You'd better learn your rightful place. You're not taking my job.'

Anne stood tall. So that was his problem. 'I don't want your job.'

Men in grey suits bustled past on their way home, manoeuvring around the two stalled figures in their way without disrupting their step.

He frowned. 'What *do* you want?'

'I want to be given a go. One day, maybe make it to management.' She'd never really thought about that before, only saying it to annoy Rodney. But as the words came out of her mouth, she found she liked the idea. Perhaps one day she could be a manager.

Rodney spat on the ground in front of her and laughed. 'A woman manager? I'd never work for a woman manager.'

'Then one day you might find yourself looking for a new job. Now, excuse me, please.'

She pushed past him with her head held high and stepped back into the path of a group of burly men in grey overalls carrying tin lunchboxes.

'Watch it, lady,' one of them grumbled.

She didn't dare look back, lest Rodney see the uncertainty in her eyes. She knew there wasn't really anything to worry about at work, as Colin saw right through him, and valued her. But making enemies was never a good idea, and Colin wasn't around to protect her right now.

She quickened her step to get away, hoping to get lost in the throng. She turned a corner and looked behind her, letting out a long breath when she saw that no one was there. It was another block and another corner until she reached the boarding house, and with each step her pulse slowed. As she neared the boarding house – she couldn't bring herself to think of it as home – the heaving mass of workmen dissolved and the streets became much quieter.

Anne nodded at familiar faces as she joined the regular handful of women coming back from their office jobs. They never stayed long – a few weeks, sometimes a few months – before they moved to other jobs or found husbands.

At least that's how it went with the ladies in the boarding house. Exactly as Simone had said.

Anne looked up at the darkening sky. Soon the street lamps would come on, casting soft yellow pools of light onto the footpath, and today would be over.

Heavy footfalls sounded behind her and her heart quickened. Had Rodney followed her?

She spun around. 'If you don't leave me alone I'll have to tell—'

She stopped. And blinked. And blinked again.

Looking back at her were those dark soulful eyes and the crooked smile of her dreams.

'Anne-san?' Tadashi bowed, stepping out of the shadows of the large Moreton Bay fig across the street from the boarding house.

Anne stared at him, her thoughts incoherent.

'I didn't mean to startle you,' he said.

'Tadashi?' Anne rubbed the back of her neck.

'I asked about you. On Wattle Island. They said you'd left. Come to Sydney.'

'Yes.' She nodded.

'I saw you. At the Monty last week. At least, I thought it was you. I've been . . .' He cast his eyes down. 'I'm not proud to say, I followed you here that night.'

Anne cast her mind back to that evening – the tingle at the back of her neck; the figure in the shadows. 'Why?'

'To see if it was you. And it was. It is.' He removed the blue knitted beanie from his head and shoved it into the back pocket of his overalls. 'I didn't know whether you'd want to see me. You left Wattle Island without telling me.'

Anne stepped back, then stopped. 'But you didn't come.' The words burst forth without any chance of her stopping them. 'That day, to the lighthouse. I waited.'

Tadashi cast his eyes down. 'I couldn't. The captain was in a foul mood. The worst I've ever seen him. He took it out on me. I couldn't see you like that. I explained it in my letter.'

Anne frowned. 'What letter?'

'I stopped by the cottage that night, after . . . well, once I was cleaned up. And I left a letter with your aunt.'

Silence echoed between them. She hadn't received a letter. Why was he lying to her?

And then it dawned on her. The knock at the door late that night. Aunt Bess's story about a farmhand selling eggs.

Anne's stomach tightened and she doubled over. *Oh no.*

'Are you all right?' Tadashi closed the gap between them. He reached out to help her, his touch heating her skin.

'I never received your letter.'

'Oh, Anne.' Tadashi's eyes bore into her.

Breathing deeply, Anne righted her posture. 'You're working here?' Simple questions. Easy questions.

He nodded. 'On the docks.' Simple answers. Easy Answers. 'And you?'

'For Walsh and Walsh. In the office.'

'And you're well?'

'Yes. You?'

He smiled at her, and the thudding in Anne's chest sounded in her ears. If she stood here much longer the questions would become more dangerous; the answers harder to bear.

'I need . . . I should . . .' She pointed to the door of the boarding house.

'Of course.' He bowed and she turned to go, but then he spoke again. 'Wait!' His voice was urgent and she faced him. 'Anne, please.' Gentleness returned. 'I have something for you. I've kept it . . . in case . . .'

From his pocket he pulled out a tightly folded piece of paper, and handed it to her.

As she unfolded it, her hands began to tremble. It was one of her paintings. The ink was smudged, the image distorted with bleeding lines, but it was unmistakably hers. One she'd torn from her sketchbook and flung into oblivion. She stared at it, the brush strokes conjuring memories so full of meaning.

'How . . . where . . .?'

'After I left your cottage that night I went for a walk. This had washed up down on Rocky Beach. I salvaged it. Kept it.'

The ground beneath Anne's feet began to sway and the early evening sky above her spun.

'Anne-san?' Tadashi caught her, his arms around her waist, before she folded onto the ground. 'Are you all right?'

She nodded, unable to trust her words.

'I'm sorry. I shouldn't have turned up unannounced like this.'

'No.' She spoke slowly as he helped her back to standing. 'It's . . . I'm . . .' She breathed out. 'It's good to see you.' She steadied herself and as Tadashi let go of her, she missed the warmth of his embrace.

'I can see I've upset you. I'll go.'

'Wait.' Anne forced her voice out. 'How can I find you, speak to you again?'

He looked down. 'Where I'm staying is no place for a woman. Maybe . . .' He looked up. 'Maybe I can meet you near your work?'

'I'd like that. Walsh and Walsh.'

He nodded. 'As soon as I can get time away from the docks, I will find you. Good evening, Anne-san.'

'Good evening,' she whispered.

Inside her dark room, she sat on the end of her bed, cradling her ruined artwork, her thoughts tumbling over each other. The letter she never received. The painting she'd thrown away. And Tadashi. Here.

———

A rush of cool air swirled around the lighthouse and Anne shuddered. From the cold or the memory, she wasn't sure.

She dragged herself back to her cottage, leaning against the door momentarily as she locked it behind her. Without turning on the lights she moved to the small writing desk in the living room and from the drawer pulled out the old sketchbook she'd kept from those early Sydney days. In the middle was a loose piece of parchment and she took it out, running her wrinkled fingers over the now yellowed painting Tadashi had rescued from the sea so many years ago.

She didn't look at it often. The memories it held were both too happy and too sad. Too much.

She hadn't made peace with her own past and she had no right to force Sam to, either. But she knew how draining it was to hang on to pain and sorrow and guilt. Sam was young. He deserved a second life, even if he didn't think he did.

Seventeen

*G*race wrapped her red cardigan tightly around herself to ward off the cool morning chill. She'd woken early and had been turning over in her mind what she knew about the Wattle Island Book Club so far: the book club had stopped seven years ago after decades of meetings; the island's bookshop had also been abandoned seven years ago, but was still there, frozen in time; it was Sam's shop and he was upset that Grace had been in there; Ruth was unhappy that the book club was back; Felicity was not on the scene and Addie only had Sam; Anne was keeping something from her; and everyone seemed to have a shadow over them.

The Case of the Wattle Island Book Club was taking up so much space in her head, Grace had to do something about it. None of her literary sleuth heroes ever solved a mystery by sitting back and simply hoping the clues fell into their lap. They went out and found them. It was times like this Grace loved the internet.

Unfortunately, the internet connection in her little holiday cottage was slow and unreliable, and after a morning of trying, she was getting nowhere. The pub had a strong signal, but she didn't think such a public space was the best place for this sort of thing. Time for a new approach.

Step One – enlist Linh's help.

So, what is it exactly I'm looking for? Linh's text came with a shrug emoji.

Well, that's part of the problem. Grace tapped her phone screen. *I'm not exactly sure. Any reference you can find about the Wattle Island bookshop online. Maybe any major news stories from around seven years ago. Anything on a Felicity Sato. That sort of thing.*

Oh. And the lighthouse. Anything you can find out about the lighthouse.

Who knew if that would help, but it was worth a try.

On it, super sleuth. Thumbs-up emoji.

With Step One in place, Grace decided to clear her head before putting Step Two in motion.

She headed down Soldiers' Way to the beach lined with wattle trees, kicked off her shoes and let her toes sink into the sand. She figured while she stayed on the island, she could start every day like this. She still wasn't sure how long that would be, though. When she'd decided to come, she'd booked an open ticket, not wanting to be bound by a plan. And Anne had told her she could have the cottage as long as she liked, unless she was staying into summer. They'd need it back by then.

The lack of a return date hadn't helped smooth things over with June when she'd called last night.

'When will you be home?' June had asked.

'I don't know.'

'For goodness sake, Grace. How can you not know? You have appointments you need to keep.'

Grace had lowered her head. 'Mum. I won't miss my next appointment. This is just something I need to do.'

'And I'm supposed to be okay with that? Not knowing when you'll come back? Not knowing if you're all right?'

'I am all right. And I really wish you could be okay with it.'

June had hung up.

Grace knew it wasn't fair keeping her mum at a distance, in the dark. But she knew she had to do this her way.

She let her toes sink into the sand. Memories of her childhood spent on the beaches of Port Maddison with the gritty grains between her toes flooded her mind and she took a moment to reconcile this new feeling beneath her feet, which was more like cotton wool. The painful electric shocks she'd felt during the time she was having chemo had left her with a permanent loss of sensation in her feet. Still, it wasn't altogether unpleasant, this cotton-wool touch. She hadn't walked barefoot on a beach in a very long time. And despite this strange new sensation, she resolved to bring back this piece of her old life and walk barefoot on the beach each day, for as long as she could.

A deep lowing from behind made her turn around. There was Addie with Emmeline Harris. She waved to the young girl and smiled. Maybe Grace should get a pet cow. That would be one for the bucket list. She laughed. She hadn't been able to keep even a goldfish alive when she was a child. Perhaps a cow was too big a step. A budgie, maybe. They'd be easy to look after.

Balancing on the rocks that sat under the dock where it met the sand, Addie waved back, her little hand a blur. Then she swayed. Then teetered. Then fell.

Grace ran towards her. 'Are you okay? What happened?'

With stifled sobs Addie pointed at her knee, which was badly scratched.

'Oh dear, that's a nasty cut.'

Addie nodded, trying hard to stop her tears.

Grace adopted her best Florence Nightingale expression. 'It's okay, sweetie. It's okay to cry. I do it sometimes.'

'Daddy does too.'

Grace tore her eyes from Addie's wounded leg and looked in her eyes. 'Does he?'

Addie nodded. 'Mostly about Mum. She left.'

'Oh?'

'He cries after book club sometimes, too.'

Grace was dying to know more but was also acutely aware that she needed to manage a wounded child and a cow. She took off her cardigan and wrapped it around the gaping wound that the sharp rocks had torn into Addie's knee.

She helped Addie up. 'Can you stand on it?'

'Sort of.' Addie winced with the effort.

Grace could see the pain the little girl was in, despite the brave face she was putting on. She looked around to see if anyone else was on the beach. No. Just a cow on a pink lead. Well, needs must.

Grace coaxed Emmeline Harris over and lifted Addie onto the cow's back. Taking the pink lead with one hand, she steadied Addie with the other. She had no idea if it was okay to use a cow as a horse, but Addie was only small, so she hoped Emmeline would forgive her.

'They don't think I know what happened to Mum,' Addie said, as her tears began to subside. 'But I do. Adults sometimes forget that kids have ears. They say things. I listen. I know.'

Grace looked at Addie. There was such grown-up sorrow staring back at her from such young eyes. And in that moment, The Case of the Wattle Island Book Club became personal.

Somehow Grace managed to get Addie and Emmeline Harris into town and to the medical clinic. She knocked on the door and Shellie came out, stopping dead when she saw Addie on Emmeline's back.

She took Addie into her arms. 'What happened?'

'I fell.'

'I think she might need stitches,' Grace said.

Addie held out her hand to Grace as Shellie took her inside. 'Come with me, please?' she asked, her bottom lip quivering.

Grace looked at the cow and back to Addie.

'Tie Emmeline to that post,' Shellie said. 'She won't wander off.'

Grace did so, hoping that the knot would hold. Of all the things she'd wanted to learn over the years – *age sixteen: learn French* (tick, intermediate level); *age fourteen: learn to play chess* (tick, thank you Uncle Craig); *age thirteen: learn to fly a plane* (apparently very expensive) – how to tie knots was never on her list.

Inside the clinic she held Addie's hand while Shellie called Sam.

'She's fine, yes . . . yes, but she will need stitches . . . of course I'll wait till you get here.' Shellie hung up the phone and prepared her equipment. 'Daddy will be here in a minute.'

As Shellie got everything ready, the all too familiar smell of antiseptic triggered a wave of nausea that Grace fought to hold back. She had to be strong for Addie until Sam arrived. Which thankfully wasn't very long. Within minutes, he came bursting into the room.

'Adrienne? What happened?'

With a lollipop in hand, Addie painted him a rather detailed picture of her and Emmeline looking for mermaid treasure among the rocks and a sea troll attacking them when they got too close.

'The troll cast a spell with his trident and then I fell.'

'Right.' Sam nodded, trying not to laugh, his initial anguish abating. 'And Grace helped you?'

Addie ginned and nodded. 'She scared the troll away and rescued me. Like a knight. Can a girl be a knight?'

'If she wants to be.' Sam and Grace answered in unison. They locked eyes.

Addie laughed and Sam mouthed his thanks. Grace smiled and removed herself for a much-needed gulp of fresh air. Emmeline Harris had worked Grace's knot loose, but seemed perfectly content to stay right where she was.

A few minutes later Sam carried Addie out of the surgery, her knee stitched and bandaged, a big grin on her face as she sucked on the rainbow lollipop.

Sam adjusted Addie's weight in his arms and looked at Grace. 'Thank you for your help.'

'Oh, don't mention it. I'm just glad she's okay. And it was kind of my fault.'

'You were looking for mermaid treasure too?'

'I wish, but no. If I hadn't waved she wouldn't have lost her balance.'

'It was the sea trolls, Daddy.' Addie puffed up her chest.

'This isn't out first visit to Dr Shellie after an encounter with the trolls. They're tricky characters.' He winked at Grace. His whole expression was warm.

Addie nodded.

'Really?' Grace laughed. 'I shall be wary of any trolls then, if I see them.'

Sam tried to wrangle Emmeline Harris's lead with his free hand, but Addie wobbled in his arms.

'I can take her,' Grace offered.

'Thank you,' Sam replied. 'That would actually be great.'

They walked through town, towards the side of the island where the farms were. Grace was surprised; she hadn't picked Sam as the farming type. Though that would explain the cow.

They approached a quaint little farmhouse and a large shed nestled in a grove of wattle trees. Sam took Addie inside and got her settled, while Grace looked after Emmeline Harris, following very specific instructions from Addie about hay and water. After she walked the cow in wide circles, as directed, she closed the gate and headed back to the house, stopping outside the shed. Its door was ajar, inviting her to take a peek.

Before she had much of a chance to peer inside, Grace heard soft footfalls and she turned to see Sam walking towards her. Oh god. He'd caught her snooping again. But he didn't seem annoyed.

'Thank you for looking after Addie today,' he said. 'She's on the couch with a cup of hot chocolate and asked me to see how you were getting on with Emmeline.'

'Happy in her pen. I'm sorry again,' Grace said. 'For distracting Addie, and for being in the shop the other day.'

'No, I'm the one who should be saying sorry. Sometimes I let my demons get the better of me.'

Grace looked him in the eye. 'We all have demons.'

Silence fell between them as Sam held her gaze, the edges of his eyes soft.

Grace coughed. 'Well, I should go.' She glanced at the shed again.

'It's my studio.' Sam reached across her and shut the door. 'Can I offer you a hot chocolate too? And not just for helping Addie today. Consider it an official apology for my rudeness.'

'Thank you. But technically I was trespassing, so a hot chocolate is more than generous.'

'Hmm. Trespassing. I wonder what your parole officer would say about that.' Sam smiled.

Grace was surprised he remembered their little joke. And even more surprised by how it made her feel. Special. And a little light-headed.

'I won't tell him if you don't.' Grace hoped her response was as witty out loud as it had been in her head.

Thankfully, Sam laughed. 'Shall we?'

'Absolutely.'

Sam's house was large, with a wraparound veranda and two large barn doors that led inside. The open-plan living room was warm and inviting, with a big, soft sofa in the middle of the space, currently occupied by Addie. Her wounded leg was propped up on pillows and a chocolate milk moustache covered her upper lip.

'That looks delicious,' Grace said.

Addie nodded. 'Daddy makes the best hot chocolate this side of Lilliput.'

Grace smiled. 'Does he now?'

'Uh huh.'

'I'll make you one and you can judge for yourself.' Sam motioned for Grace to join Addie on the sofa and he went in to the kitchen. Grace leaned forward as Addie went into extraordinary detail about Gulliver and his adventures. As Addie got to the part where he put the fire out, a little giggle escaping her lips, Sam returned with Grace's hot chocolate.

'And then . . .' Addie yawned, her eyes drooping. 'And then . . .' She leaned back against the sofa.

'And then . . .' Grace continued the story while Addie closed her eyes, her breathing slowing. By the time Grace got to the part where Gulliver was rescued and sailed back home, Addie was fast asleep.

Sam slipped his arms under his daughter and carried her to her room.

Alone in the living room, Grace stood up and looked at the wall of photos opposite the sofa. Picture after picture crowded the space. There were photos of Addie with Emmeline; Addie and Sam on the beach; Addie at a pottery wheel, Sam standing beside her, clay caked in his dark curls; Addie on Anne's lap reading a book together. The photo in the middle of the wall was a picture of a baby in the arms of a pretty woman. Grace recognised her from the photo on the pub mantelpiece of Sam, Shellie, Phil and the group of divers. She also recognised the blonde curls and blue eyes of Addie in her. This must be Addie's mother, who had left.

'Nurofen always makes her tired.'

Grace spun around to see Sam coming back into the room.

'That and a good story,' he added.

'I imagine the shock of her fall has taken a bit out of her too,' Grace smiled.

Sam looked at her and then at the photo in front of which she was standing.

'That's Felicity, Addie's mum. My late wife.' His voice caught on the last word.

'I'm so sorry.' Late. Not left. Grace's heart broke for Sam and Addie. That explained a lot. 'She and Addie look a lot alike.' Grace's voice was soft.

'The bookshop. It was Flick's. After she . . . well, I . . . it still hurts. Seeing you come out of the back door like that . . . I'm sorry I was so rude to you. It was uncalled for.'

Sam had closed the distance between them and he was now standing close to Grace.

'I never meant to upset you.'

He shook his head. 'I know. I'm just a cranky idiot. Guilt can be a bastard to live with. It makes you do stupid things.'

Sam's eyes bore into her, and her skin tingled. Yes, this was definitely personal now.

'I'm no stranger to doing silly things,' Grace said. Like coming to this island, she thought.

'With MAW?'

'Bungee jumping, throwing myself out of a plane.'

Sam took a sip of his hot chocolate. 'You are a surprise, Grace Elliott.'

'A surprise?'

'Yeah. A bungee-jumping librarian who can wrangle a book club and fight off sea trolls while searching for mermaid treasure, all while on parole.' Sam's eyes crinkled at the edges when his smile was genuine.

Grace really needed to stop looking in his eyes.

'Daddy? I can't get comfy.' Addie hobbled into the room.

Sam strode over to her and picked her up, wrapping her tightly in his arms.

'I'll let you two settle,' Grace said. 'Thank you for the hot chocolate. Definitely the best this side of Lilliput.'

Addie giggled.

With Addie on his hip in one arm, Sam took Grace's mug, their hands touching, lingering a moment too long.

'I'll see myself out.' Grace turned and left.

Grace couldn't get back to the cottage fast enough and once inside, she paced the wooden floor, shaking her head. She had no room in her life for . . . for whatever it was Sam was stirring in her. She was here to help the book club. Nothing more. She was in no position to open her heart to anyone.

Her phone chimed with a message from Linh.

Nothing to report, super sleuth. Sad-face emoji. *How's it going your end?*

I found out Felicity is Sam's wife and she died.

He's a widower? Poor guy.

Yeah . . .

What's he like?

Grace wasn't sure how to answer that.

A flame emoji followed by heart eyes pinged on her phone.

That's inappropriate, she responded.

So he is hot??????

Grace thought about turning off her phone to avoid having to tell Linh anything more, but there'd only be a string of texts waiting for her when she turned it back on. And probably a lot of angry-face emojis.

I'm not going to answer that.

You don't need to.

You know I don't have time for anything like that.

Shrug emoji. *Not even a fling?*

No.

What would Romanov do?

Grace exhaled and tossed her phone onto the couch. She couldn't have this conversation.

Grace visited Addie the next day and together they read books from Addie's collection. She begged Grace to come back again, and three days later Grace found herself on the front veranda enacting a scene from *Anne of Green Gables*. Addie had also enlisted her father in the role of Gilbert.

'You be Anne, Grace, and I'll be everyone else,' Addie insisted. 'This can be the slate.' Addie handed Grace a cushion. 'Make sure you hit him hard, just like when she cracks it over his head when he calls her carrots.'

They threw themselves into the scene and Grace looked at Sam and mouthed 'sorry' when it was time to hit him over the head. Sam rubbed his head and looked suitably hurt.

'And we all take a bow,' Addie declared, and Sam and Grace did as they were told.

The sound of clapping made them spin around. Anne was walking towards the house.

Sam's face turned red. 'How much did you see?'

'Enough.' She laughed. 'I'd better get planning my red carpet outfit.'

'Hi, Obaachan.' Addie waved.

'Hello, Gumnut. How's that knee feeling?' Anne embraced her tightly. 'Grace.' She nodded in greeting. 'Are you staying for dinner?'

'Oh, I . . .' Grace didn't know where to look.

Addie clasped her hands in front of her chest. 'Yes! Please, Daddy?'

Sam smiled. 'Please stay. After that performance, you deserve a good meal.' He touched Grace's shoulder ever so briefly and she really wished he hadn't.

'And you make a good meal, do you?' she replied. Running away at this point probably wasn't an option. Better to use humour.

'I can hold my own in the kitchen.'

'Then I'd love to stay.'

Addie clapped.

The four of them headed inside. Addie and Anne began to assemble a salad at the kitchen table, and at the benchtop Sam pulled out the ingredients for a bolognaise sauce.

'It's Addie's favourite and one we always have with Obaachan.' Sam handed Grace a bowl of tomatoes. 'How are you at chopping?'

'It's one of my specialties.'

He smiled.

Grace got to work. She wasn't the world's greatest cook, but she could chop vegetables with the best of them. After each cycle of chemo was done the first sign she was getting over the treatment was being able to watch cooking shows without succumbing to nausea, and when she got her appetite back, she'd try out the recipes and techniques she'd seen. Her knife skills were excellent, only three tiny scars proving her persistence.

'Wow,' Sam whistled. 'That was fast. Are you sure your stint in the slammer was only for stalking?'

'I plead the fifth.' Grace put her hands in the air, still holding the knife.

Sam laughed. 'Remind me not to get on your bad side.'

She put the knife down. 'Don't ever underestimate a librarian.'

'Especially one with a record.' He grinned.

Without thinking, Grace playfully hit Sam's arm. He stopped laughing and looked at her with gentle eyes.

'Salad's done,' Addie called out.

'Why don't we go check on Emmeline before dinner?' Anne took Addie's hand in hers and the little girl limped beside her as they headed outside.

'They're really close,' Grace said, desperate to take the attention off herself and the fact she'd just hit Sam.

'Yeah. I don't know what I'd do without Obaachan. After Flick . . . well, Anne has helped out so much.'

'Addie's a sweet girl. You've done a wonderful job with her.'

Sam shrugged, the hint of the cloud that was never far away touching the edge of his expression. 'Sometimes I wonder if we should move to the mainland. Broaden her horizons.' He stared out the kitchen window. 'Get away from my memories.'

'Memories can be tricky.' Grace narrowed the distance between them.

'I'm just glad she doesn't remember what happened.'

Grace thought about Addie's words on the beach. *Adults forget kids have ears sometimes. They say things. I listen. I know.* She may not have memories, but she knew more than Sam thought.

'I tell her about Felicity all the time,' Sam continued. 'The good bits.'

'I can't imagine how hard it is.' Grace kept her voice low.

'Do you have children, Grace? A brood back home missing you?' He angled his body towards her.

'No. Unless you count the kids at the library who come in every week for story time.' *Keep it light, Grace.*

He nodded. 'Maybe one day, then? There's nothing like parenting.' A brief smile touched his lips, as Grace's face fell.

'Oh no.' He frowned. 'What have I said? I've upset you.' He brushed the single tear that fell down her cheek and the gentle touch released painful words she never usually spoke.

'I . . . I can't have . . . children.' She couldn't believe she blurted that out. Only Linh and June knew. Grace had never told anyone.

'I'm so sorry.' His hand cradled her cheek. She leaned into his touch. He breathed deeply.

'Daddy?' Addie burst into the room. 'Is the sketti ready?'

Sam cleared his throat. 'It won't be ready for a bit yet, Gumnut. Why don't you and Obaachan set the table?'

Grace turned around slowly. Anne stood in the middle of the room, one hand on her hip.

So much for keeping it light.

'Emmeline's happy and my stomach is rumbling,' the old woman said, not taking her eyes from Grace.

'Hold your horses.' Sam turned back to the pot of mince. 'Perfection takes time.'

'A woman my age doesn't have a lot of that.' Anne sat herself at the table.

While they waited for dinner, Addie fetched a book and pulled Grace to the couch to read. While Grace was reading the story, Addie inched closer and closer until she'd worked her way under the crook of Grace's arm. Grace's heart melted at the simple intimacy of the act and she gulped down the lump in her throat.

'Grace?' Addie looked up at her with big blue eyes. 'Is something wrong? You stopped reading.'

'I'm fine, Addie.' Grace brushed the loose blonde curls away from Addie's round face, her chest tightening. 'I'm fine.'

How was it possible when everything was wrong for there to be nothing wrong at all?

'Where's my chief taste-tester?' Sam's voice boomed across the room.

Addie jumped out of Grace's arms and Grace felt the sudden absence keenly.

Halfway to the kitchen Addie stopped and turned around. 'Would you like to be chief taste-tester tonight?' she asked Grace.

Grace blinked, flexed her fingers and stood up. 'I'd love to be.'

'But only for tonight.' Addie frowned. 'Not for keeps.'

Grace smiled. 'The job is definitely yours for keeps.'

Addie clapped.

Grace approached Sam, who was holding a spoon above the large bubbling pot. She breathed in the rich, comforting aroma.

'Mmm.' Grace closed her eyes.

'Wait till you taste it,' Addie said, sitting higher on her chair.

Sam gave Grace the spoon, their fingers touching. Tangy tomato and sweet basil danced in her mouth.

'Oh my.' She moaned, not breaking eye contact with Sam. 'That is delicious.'

'Secret's in the basil,' he whispered, holding her gaze.

'Sketti time,' Addie called.

Grace didn't say much at dinner, content to watch on as Sam, Addie and Anne talked and laughed with joy and tenderness.

At the end of the meal, as Sam cleared away the dishes, Addie reached across the table and shook Grace's hand. 'Best chopped tomatoes ever.'

'Why thank you.' She doffed an imaginary cap. 'I've had a wonderful night.'

Sam smiled at her from the kitchen sink and she knew if she stayed any longer, she might fall apart, happiness and despair tearing her in opposite directions.

'I should probably head off. Don't want to outstay my welcome.'

'Sam?' Anne stood up. 'Why don't you walk Grace home?'

'Oh, no.' Grace raised a hand. 'That's not necessary.'

'Fiddlesticks.'

Sam put his dish cloth down. 'A walk after all that food might be a good idea.'

Anne moved behind Sam and Grace and started pushing them towards the door. 'I'll stay with Addie. Maybe we can play a game.'

'Yay.' Addie clapped.

And before she knew it, Grace had kissed Anne and Addie goodnight and was outside in the cool night air, walking right beside Sam.

'Are you cold?' He offered her his coat.

'Thank you.'

He wrapped the warmth around her, his hands moving over her shoulders, and they walked on in silence.

When they reached her cottage, Sam stepped up on the veranda as Grace fumbled for her keys.

'Should this be out here?' He leaned over the small wicker table and picked up Grace's journal. 'I hope that's not your secret diary.' He handed it to her.

'No. It's my bucket list journal.'

'A what now?'

Her bucket list journal was very much a private thing; she wasn't sure how to explain it to him. But she couldn't very well pretend she hadn't just said that.

'My bucket list journal. It's where I keep a record of all my bucket lists and tick them off if I manage to achieve them.' Apparently tonight was the night she told Sam all her deepest secrets.

Well, not all her secrets.

Sam frowned. 'That's a bit morbid, isn't it? Aren't you worried you're tempting fate?'

She managed not to tell him that fate had long been snubbing her. 'My Uncle Craig introduced me to the concept when I was seven. I've kept this journal since then.'

'May I?' He held out his hand.

She should have said no, put her journal away, shooed him off her veranda. Instead she gave it to him.

He opened it at a random page and read out some of the contents.

Grace Elliott's Bucket List, age sixteen:
- *Marry Justin Timberlake*
- *Get a belly button piercing*
- *Re-read all five Harry Potter books before the next one comes out* (tick)
- *Solve a mystery à la Veronica Mars*

Sam raised an eyebrow.

'They've evolved over time.' Grace knew her cheeks were red.

He laughed. 'You mean you no longer want to marry Justin Timberlake?'

'Well, I wouldn't say no if he asked.' She shrugged. 'But I did move on to things like learning languages and going bungee jumping.' She turned to a random page later in the journal. 'See?'

He read out loud. 'Have a romantic seafood picnic on a tropical beach. Written when you were twenty-one. Not ticked, I see.'

Yep, cheeks definitely red.

'So it's kind of like a diary.' Sam tilted his head to one side. 'A snapshot of Grace Elliott – her interests and dreams over time.'

She'd never really thought of it like that, but she supposed he was right. And she liked that thought. Snapshots of her life.

Sam gave her back the journal. 'Maybe one day you'll let me read more, let me get to know you more.'

'Maybe.' She hugged her journal to her chest. 'Goodnight, Sam.'

'Goodnight, Mrs Timberlake.' He kissed her on the cheek and headed back down the track.

Grace leaned against the doorway, watching Sam walk down the path, the echo of his tender lips lingering on her skin.

Eighteen

Anne sat at her grandson's kitchen table, playing Scrabble with Addie. Addie's rules, of course. She laid down a tile and tallied her points.

Addie shook her head. 'Pay attention, Obaachan. When there's an "s" on the end of the word, the extra point *doesn't* count. I told you that.'

She probably did. At the best of times Anne had trouble keeping up with Addie's extra rules. And tonight she was distracted by what she'd seen in this very room not fifteen minutes earlier.

A spark.

Could she allow her ageing heart to hope?

No, she didn't have time to hope. She had to act. A little nudge, perhaps.

'When will Daddy be back?' Addie asked.

'He shouldn't be too long.' Although, the longer the better, Anne thought.

'I like when Grace is here,' Addie said.

'Me too.'

'Daddy's light is on when she's around.'

Anne paused, her hand holding the tile she was about to play stopped mid-air. Where had that come from? What did a nine-year-old know about a person's light?

She was right, though. Anne had noticed too.

'Maybe we can invite her to dinner again,' Anne said.

Addie looked up from the Scrabble board. 'I'd like that.'

Yes. A nudge.

Thinking about people's sparks and lights and having to concentrate on Addie's rules left Anne feeling a little light-headed. While Addie made her next move, Anne got up to brew a cup of tea, but that made things worse. She stopped, her head spinning.

'Obaachan?' Addie's voice seemed far away and the light around her faded to black.

Sydney, 1952

The day after her encounter with Tadashi, Anne had trouble focusing at work. She had no idea if she'd see him again or if his promise to visit her was simply a placation. She should have set up a day, a time. But he'd caught her off-guard and she hadn't been thinking straight.

She hated waiting.

A not-so-subtle cough from Colin brought her wandering thoughts back into the room, where an important meeting with buyers was taking place. What had she missed?

Colin held out his hand. The graph. She handed it to him, whispering an apology.

Later at her desk, Colin approached, frowning. 'Is everything okay, Webb?'

'Yes, of course.'

'You seemed a little distracted.' He leaned on the back of her chair.

'Sorry. I didn't sleep well last night.'

He tapped the chair with his index finger. 'Whatever is going on, don't let it interfere with your work.'

She nodded. 'Of course not.'

Colin was right. She couldn't let Tadashi's reappearance jeopardise her job.

Put him out of your head, Anne told herself.

Except she couldn't. Every lunchbreak for the next three days, Anne went for a walk around the block, looking for Tadashi. He wasn't there.

Every evening she waited outside the boarding house. He didn't come.

It seemed that it was an empty promise after all.

On Friday morning, Anne walked to Walsh and Walsh with renewed purpose, determined to close the chapter on Tadashi once and for all. She turned the corner that lead to the office. And there, standing in the shadow the large building cast, stood a familiar figure.

'Anne-san.' Tadashi approached her.

She pushed her nose into the air. 'Good morning.' She walked past him.

He grabbed her arm and spun her around. 'Anne-san. Wait. Please.'

She looked him in the eye, resolute.

'I'm sorry I haven't been by. Work. It's been—'

'Miss Webb?' A booming voice reverberated down the street. Colin was striding towards them, Simone click-clacking behind. 'Are you all right?'

Tadashi dropped her arm as Colin moved in front of Anne, grabbing Tadashi by the collar.

'Miss Webb, did this Jap hurt you?' Colin craned his neck to look at her.

She shook her head, rubbing her arm where she could still feel Tadashi's grip. 'No. He's an old . . . friend. From Wattle Island.'

'So, you're okay?' Colin let Tadashi go and turned to her.

'Yes.'

He brushed Tadashi's crumpled overalls. 'Sorry, mate. No hard feelings?' He extended his hand and Tadashi shook it.

'None.' Tadashi frowned, resignation fleeting across his face. 'I'm glad Anne has good people looking out for her.'

Simone linked her arm in Anne's. 'Are you going to introduce us properly?'

'Of course.' Anne made the appropriate introductions.

'Sorry about the misunderstanding.' Colin nodded. 'Webb, let's get to work.'

Anne nodded. 'Yes, of course.'

'Mr Sato, are you on your way also?'

The pointed question wasn't missed by Anne. Colin may well have been liberal enough to accept a woman in the workforce, but his open-mindedness didn't quite extend to his employee associating with a man of Japanese origin.

'Yes, sir.' Tadashi bowed.

'You're a wharfie?' Colin asked, the blue overalls and jumper common on the docks.

'Yes, sir.'

'On your way then.'

Tadashi bowed. 'Anne, it was lovely to run into you.'

'You too. Stay well.'

There was so much more she wanted to say. So much to ask. But she couldn't; not here, not now. She watched him walk away, her heart aching the same way it had the morning she watched the *Seafarer* sail from her for the last time.

Simone shot Anne a quizzical look. If Colin hadn't been there, Anne was certain Simone would have peppered her with questions. There wasn't too much that escaped that woman's attention.

Colin placed an arm on both Anne's and Simone's backs and herded them in to the office.

Anne worked the morning in silence, head down, focusing on the reports she'd been given to work on, not daring to think about anything else.

At lunchtime, Simone made her way to Anne's desk.

'So, who was that Tadashi fellow, really?'

'Just someone I met a few times on Wattle Island. We barely know each other.'

Instead of pressing further, Simone leaned over and lifted Anne's chin with a perfectly manicured finger. 'You can't fool me. I saw it in your eyes. His too,' she whispered. 'Best you put him out of your mind, though. It's hard enough to make our way in a man's world, without other . . . hindrances.'

Anne saw kindness in Simone's gaze.

'They'd never accept him,' Simone said. 'Many of the men here fought in the war, including Walsh Senior.'

Simone was right. Tadashi would never be accepted here.

Not that it mattered. He was unlikely to return after what happened this morning, and Anne had no way of contacting him other than hanging out down by the docks. And here in the city, a young lady hanging out at the docks was not the same as back on Wattle Island.

Try as she might, though, she couldn't push thoughts of Tadashi from her mind. In the afternoon meeting she was slow to react and pass notes to Colin, and, while he didn't say anything, she was sure he'd noticed.

As she packed away at the end of the day, he walked past and stopped, a few steps beyond her desk, his back to her. 'We're not going to have a . . . problem after this morning, are we, Webb?'

'No, sir.'

'Good.'

The following Wednesday, Hamish stopped by her desk after a meeting with Colin and asked her to lunch, which she accepted, if for no reason other than to break up her day. Colin coughed from his office doorway, and she realised he'd been watching the brief interaction. He winked at her before ducking back into his office.

Hamish took her to a small coffee shop a block away from the Walsh and Walsh building. It was full of suits and women in elegant pencil skirts, white gloves and single strands of pearls.

He ordered them a hamburger and milkshake each. Anne was excited; she'd never had a hamburger before. From her seat opposite him, she was able to study his features in more detail: pale blue eyes that seemed kind, if unsure; strong jaw; thick brown hair touched with red. He played with the serviette in front of him, his gaze not quite meeting hers.

'Do you like working for Walsh?' he asked, daring to glance up briefly.

'I do. Every day is different.' She opted not to share the truth that some days the monotony got to her, or that some of the suits were less than accepting of her. Talk like that always had a way of making its way back to the office. Besides, whatever the challenges, she was ever so grateful for her job.

'That's nice.'

Silence.

'And what about you, Hamish?' Anne asked. 'Do you enjoy being the company's lawyer?'

He did, but didn't expound any further. Anne supposed he might be equally concerned about any complaint he made getting back.

Their food arrived and Anne looked at the hamburger, unsure how she was supposed to eat it without spilling half of it down the front of her blouse. She took a knife and fork out of the basket in the middle of the table and began to cut into it. Hamish, meanwhile, had picked his up with both hands and took a whopping big bite.

The speed with which Hamish ate his lunch was astounding. He wiped his mouth with the serviette before taking a sip of his chocolate milkshake. Not once since the food arrived had he stopped to chat with her.

Was this how people dated in the city? Without actually speaking to each other? Or maybe this wasn't a date. Maybe Colin had sent Hamish to be her minder.

Anne had put Hamish's lack of interaction that first night at the pub down to shyness. But he'd asked her here today, so why wasn't he saying anything?

Clearly it was up to her. 'So, Hamish, what do you like to do when you're not working?'

He looked at her, seemingly contemplating the question, which Anne thought should have been relatively easy to answer.

'I like to read,' he finally said.

Anne sat up taller and a grin spread across her face. 'Really? Me too. What do you like to read?'

'The newspaper,' he replied. 'To stay abreast of the market.'

That made sense, but it was not where she hoped the conversation was going. She nodded and waited. But nothing more came. And he didn't ask her anything about herself. Still, she wouldn't give up. She had to fill in the time somehow.

'Do you read novels?' she asked.

'Nope.' He shook his head. 'Can't say I see the point.'

Any chance of a spark that Anne was certain Simone and Colin were hoping would ignite was extinguished right there and then. She looked up to the large clock on the wall. There were ten minutes until she had to be back at work. Even factoring in the walk, that left them about eight minutes to fill.

As it turned out, eight minutes filled with nothing but silence was a very long time indeed.

'Thank you, Anne,' he said, when he eventually dropped her back at her desk. 'I had a lovely time.'

Was that sadness in his eyes? He pushed his thumbs into the suspenders beneath his grey suit jacket and bade farewell.

Anne had never been so happy to see her desk. If that was dating, she'd resign herself to being a cranky old spinster for the rest of her life.

The day dragged on and went from awkward to bad in Colin's weekly meeting when she managed to upset Rodney again by pointing out yet another of his mistakes. Technically Colin brought it up, but Rodney knew Anne had alerted him.

At the end of the day, Rodney glared at her as he passed her desk but Simone's timely presence prevented any other action he might have been considering.

Apparently, Simone was ready for a debriefing of the lunch date. Things were going from awkward to bad to worse.

'So, you don't like him?' Simone frowned.

'Rodney?'

'No, not Rodney. Nobody likes Rodney. *Hamish*.'

How was she supposed to navigate this? 'He's a lovely man. I'm not sure we have much in common, though.'

'Oh, that will come. Don't give up just yet. He's shy. Always has been.'

Anne nodded. It was more than him being shy, but she couldn't say that to Simone. The whole date hadn't made any sense but she had no idea how to explain that to her friend, especially seeing as Simone was clearly invested in the matchmaking being a success. All she could do was hope that it would die down in a few weeks and Hamish would lose interest. And Simone too.

On her way home that evening, Anne stopped to buy a new sketchbook with thick paper. As she left the shop, she found Tadashi outside waiting for her.

'Anne-san.'

'Hello,' was all she could manage, her heart racing.

Tadashi bowed. 'I saw you go in. Will you walk with me?'

'Of course.'

He wore a heavy woollen coat and a beanie, and in the fading light, no one looked at him twice.

The silence between them was soft. Neither one, it seemed, wanted to break it.

Tadashi was the first to speak. 'Thank you for allowing me this time.'

'I'm sorry about my boss today.'

'No need. I'm used to it. Down on the docks it isn't too bad. As long as you work hard, they leave you alone. But elsewhere . . .' His voice trailed off. 'It will take time for the wounds of the war to heal.'

'It isn't fair.' She touched his arm, letting it linger longer than propriety allowed.

'It is what it is.' He took hold of her hand. 'What isn't fair is how we left things back on the island. I'm sorry it caused you pain.'

'You don't owe me an apology.' She shook her head. 'I never got your letter. Perhaps Bess is the one who owes me an explanation.' Except there was no way of getting one. While Anne nursed disappointment and heartache when it came to Tadashi, her anger was levelled at Bess.

'Was there anything else in the letter other than an apology for missing our appointment?' she asked, afraid to look him in the eye. 'Appointment' was such a formal word, but Anne was afraid to use one with more meaning.

'Yes.' He nodded.

She held her breath.

'There is much to speak of,' Tadashi said. He stopped and tilted his head.

They were outside the boarding house and Mrs Harris was sweeping the steps of the entrance.

'If you'll allow, perhaps . . .' he cast his eyes down. 'I may call on you.'

Anne swallowed. 'We aren't allowed male callers at the boarding house.'

'I understand.'

She lowered her voice. 'But if you want to meet me on Saturday, in Hyde Park, maybe we could take a proper walk.'

The smile she'd dreamed about so often returned to Tadashi's face. 'I'd like that. Very much.' He kissed her hand and walked off into the night.

After supper, which Anne hardly touched, she sat on her bed drawing the sweeping arcs of the beaches of Wattle Island, rendering the lighthouse with fluid strokes. Later, she fell asleep to fitful dreams of hope.

*

Back at work on Friday, it appeared Hamish hadn't been as dis-
heartened by their lunch as Anne had been and a bunch of flowers
was delivered to her desk, with a card saying he hoped she'd join
him for drinks after work.

'We'll finally get that double date,' Simone had cooed.

'Double date?'

'You can't go out with Hamish by yourself at night. Propriety
dictates Colin and I must join you.'

Anne was fairly sure Simone's interest in chaperoning the
evening had far more to do with ensuring Anne didn't pull out
and that she didn't make a right meal of the evening, rather than
anything to do with propriety, but she didn't mind. At least with
Simone there, there might actually be some conversation.

So, together with Colin they headed to the Monty after work
and met Hamish there. He greeted Anne with a light peck on the
cheek, then immediately engaged Colin in a detailed discussion
about the new wool contracts, leaving the girls to talk together,
which Anne didn't mind one bit.

A group of wharfies sauntered into the pub and Anne turned
around, searching for a familiar face. He wasn't there. And what
would she do if he was?

She let out a breath.

The evening passed pleasantly enough. In a group, Hamish was
charming, polite, even amusing. But the moment it was just the
two of them, he retreated into himself.

'He gets nervous around women,' Simone said, while the men
were at the bar. 'He's always been like that. Ever since I've known
him. I think it's rather charming. Better than those brash, confident men.'

Anne smiled. Though she wouldn't exactly describe Colin
as brash, he was most definitely confident. But she didn't point

that out. And while it was an idea she was sure Simone, out of friendly loyalty, wouldn't entertain, perhaps Hamish simply didn't find Anne attractive. Next to Simone, how could any other woman be considered beautiful?

A new group of dock workers arrived into the pub, and Anne took another look over her shoulder.

'Are you expecting someone?' Simone leaned into her.

'Of course not,' Anne said quickly, hoping the dim lighting in the pub would hide the red in her cheeks.

When it was time to call it a night, fifteen minutes before Anne's boarding house curfew, Colin and Simone skipped ahead down the street, leaving Hamish alone with Anne. Hamish said little other than commenting on what a mild night it was. Which was true. And under different circumstances, the warm breeze over the water and the dark, fluid sky peppered with stars might have been romantic.

Hamish walked her to her door, while Colin and Simone waited on the corner of her street, in each other's arms, blissfully unaware of the world around them.

'Thank you, Hamish, for walking me home.' Anne smiled.

He nodded. 'You're welcome.'

She turned to head inside when a thought struck her. She spun around. 'Are you being forced into this?'

'Forced into what?' He frowned, but the slight twitch at the corner of his mouth gave him away.

'I'll be no charity case, Hamish. Despite whatever those two'— she pointed down the street—'have cooked up.'

He at least had the decency to avert his eyes. 'It isn't that, Anne. I swear. I'm sorry you're caught up in this. I've been friends with Colin since we were children and he just wants me to be as happy as he is with Simone. But I'm not—'

'Attracted to me. That's fine. I understand.' She didn't mind. Not on any real level. Though it still stung a little on the surface. Rejection always did.

'No, Anne. That isn't true. You're beautiful, truly you are. And you're smart. Smarter than any woman I've ever met.' This was the most he'd ever spoken to her on his own.

She shifted her weight. 'You don't have to say that to make me feel better. I'm made of tougher stuff than that.'

He reached out and grabbed Anne's hands; the urgency with which he gripped her giving way to a tender touch.

'I'm not just saying it. You are amazing. Truly. You're simply . . . not . . . for me.'

'So why agree to this?' she asked. 'I mean, why put yourself through this, if you know I'm not for you?'

Casting his eyes down, he sighed. When he looked back up at her, they were full of sorrow.

'Simone.' It dawned on Anne. Of course, it was obvious. 'You're doing this to be closer to her?' That made sense. 'I won't tell them, I promise.' A broken man stood before her; she didn't need to be insightful about relationships to see that. 'But maybe you should give yourself a little distance from her.'

He shook his head. 'Simone is stunning. But no.'

'Then . . .?' she asked. He was clearly trying to tell her something, but she couldn't figure out what.

'Goodnight, Anne. I'm sorry you got messed up in this.' He kissed her on the cheek and headed down the street, back to Simone and Colin. Simone jumped up and down and Colin patted him on the back. They must have seen him kiss Anne goodnight and misconstrued what was simply a polite gesture.

What they didn't see though, but Anne most certainly did as she watched on, was the slight way Hamish pulled away at Colin's touch.

Anne raised her hand to her chest. Everything suddenly became very clear.

———

Images faded and blurred. Muffled sounds swirled around her.

'Anne?' Tadashi's sweet voice, so distant.

'Obaachan?' Sam's familiar lilt.

A heavy weight across her chest. Soft. Warm. A faint scent of lavender.

Anne blinked.

The softness was Addie's doona, dotted with pink and yellow flowers.

She blinked again.

Beneath her was a hard . . . floor. She was on the floor.

A dull ache in her hip as she forced her eyes open became a blinding pain as she came to.

'Slowly, Anne.' Shellie's hand was on her shoulder. Shellie? What was she doing here? And why wouldn't she let Anne sit up?

'What . . .' Why was her voice so croaky? 'What's going on?' The rest of the room came into focus. She was lying on the floor of Sam's kitchen. Sam and Shellie kneeling beside her. Addie was standing in the corner, tears staining her cheeks. Hamish was there too, with his arm around Addie.

'Anne. You've had a nasty fall.' Shellie was feeling for her pulse. 'Do you remember anything?'

She remembered everything. Though Anne knew Shellie didn't mean *those* recollections. She pushed the images of Tadashi aside and forced her mind into the present.

'Addie and I were playing Scrabble. I got up . . . to make a . . . cup of tea. And now you're all here.'

Shellie nodded. 'You collapsed. Addie came and got me. You hit your head, it seems.'

But her head didn't hurt. Her hip did.

'Your vitals appear stable,' Shellie said, her fingers still on Anne's wrist. 'But now you're awake I'd like to give you a proper check. You may have had another stroke.'

'Fiddlesticks.' It didn't feel like a stroke to her. But the stern look from Shellie told her it was probably best not to protest. 'Well, not with this lot gawking at me.'

'If you can give us a minute?' Shellie addressed the room. Sam and Hamish and Addie shuffled out.

Shellie checked Anne's neck and spine first. Once she was comfortable it was safe to move her, she helped her up.

Anne groaned. The pain in her hip made it hard for her to get onto the chair.

'I'm fine, Shellie,' Anne insisted.

'Clearly not.' Shellie took Anne's blood pressure, and while she asked a series of questions any buffoon could answer, she made her raise one arm then the other, then asked her more questions. She shone an annoyingly bright light in her eyes. Then she checked Anne's hip, her poking and prodding doing nothing to ease Anne's pain.

'Your speech is fine. Clearly your mind is functioning. But—'

Anne raised her hand. 'No buts.'

'While I see no evidence it was a stroke, I'm not happy you lost consciousness. Even if it was only brief. You'll need an ECG, and lucky for you I'm the only doctor on the island so I keep the machine in the car.'

'Lucky me,' Anne groaned.

Shellie called out to Sam to get the portable machine out of her car boot. 'And I'll try to organise a Holter monitor for you to wear.'

'I'll do no such thing.'

'Yes. You will.'

Sam came back in with the machine.

'Back out you go,' Anne said to him as Shellie hooked her up to the ECG machine. This was embarrassing enough as it was without an audience. After a lot more – unnecessary, if you asked Anne – fuss, Shellie allowed Sam and Hamish and Addie back in the room.

'Not a stroke, and no sign of a heart attack or arrhythmia,' she said and Sam and Hamish visibly relaxed. 'I've given her some meds for the pain. That hip took the brunt of the fall. She's lucky she didn't break it. If she can stay here tonight, Sam . . .'

'Of course.'

'I'll be back tomorrow to check on her. And if everything's okay, then I'd like her to see the heart specialist when they're on the island next.'

Sam nodded. Addie stood next to Anne, holding her hand.

Shellie and Sam moved to the far side of the room, their heads bent in hushed conversation. It wasn't right to be talking about her like that. Surely Anne should know whatever it was they were discussing. She'd have told them so, but she was terribly tired.

Sam and Hamish helped move Anne to Sam's bed and Shellie did a series of further unnecessary checks before she agreed to leave.

Addie kissed Anne goodnight and went to bed.

'Sam, do you think you can give Hamish and me a moment, please?' Anne asked.

'Of course, Obaachan.' He kissed her on the forehead and left the old friends together.

Hamish sat on the side of the bed. 'So, old girl. I take it something's cooking up there in your brain?'

'You know me too well.' She patted his hand. He was such an old and dear friend. 'I'm not too proud to admit that was a little frightening.'

'For us all.'

'Hamish, I need you to take care of some things, if I . . . if I can't. Promise me you'll see to it?'

'I promise.' There was no hesitation. 'What things, exactly?'

Nineteen

Stretching in bed, Grace's face was warmed by the morning sunlight streaming in the cottage window. She turned over and looked at the little alarm clock on the bedside table. Make that midday sun.

She'd slept better – and longer, it seemed – than she had in ages. That was, once she'd managed to stop thinking about Sam and that kiss. She reached a heavy arm up and touched her cheek.

Stop it. Friends kissed each other on the cheek all the time. So did relatives. Work colleagues. It was nothing more than a friendly gesture.

At least that's what she had to tell herself last night in order to nod off. And once she did, she'd drifted into dreams that were saturated with images of Sam's smile, his eyes, his hand brushing hers.

She pushed thoughts of Sam aside. There was a task she needed to achieve today and distraction wouldn't help.

Today she needed to put Step Two, of her plan to solve The Case of The Wattle Island Book Club into motion. And for that she needed Anne.

She pulled on a mustard-coloured long-sleeved T-shirt and her jeans. The waistband was a little snug. She smoothed her hands over her bloated stomach. Such an innocuous thing, a part of many women's lives at certain times of the month. So innocuous that Grace had dismissed it at first when the bloating had hung around longer than usual three years ago. Now she knew better. She hung her head and counted to ten in French. Now she was even more determined to tackle Step Two.

After a quick brunch of toast and peppermint tea, she headed out the door.

As she stepped off the veranda she saw three familiar figures coming up Soldiers' Way: Sam, Hamish and Anne, who was in a wheelchair.

Grace raced towards the trio. 'Is everything okay?'

Anne swiped her hand in front of her face. 'Perfectly fine. A lot of bother about nothing.'

'She had a fall,' Sam said. 'Fainted.'

Sucking in a sharp breath, Grace looked at Anne. 'Are you all right?'

'Of course I am. Takes more than a little fall to keep me down.'

'Did this happen last night?' Grace asked, realising Anne was in the same flowing pink dress as yesterday.

Sam's face was steely. 'Yes. While we were . . . before I got back home.'

Grace's eyes went wide. 'Oh, Anne. What can I do?'

'Tell these two oafs to stop fussing over me.'

Hamish put his hand on Anne's shoulder. 'Never going to happen.'

'You're a dear.' She looked up and patted him on the cheek, running her fingers through his white beard.

'Come on, Obaachan. We need to get you inside to rest.' Sam urged her forward.

'And you're a worrywart. I love you. But I'm okay. If you don't believe me, believe Shellie.'

With that, Anne made Sam push her up the hill and Grace and Hamish followed.

Inside Anne's cottage, they set her up on the sofa – she refused to go to bed – with a cup of tea and a book. 'And get that awful contraption out of my sight.' She pointed to the wheelchair. 'I can walk,' she said to Grace. 'Sort of. That thing is unnecessary.'

'And how would you have got up the hill?' Sam asked, returning from moving the chair into the kitchen.

'Sam,' she said. 'Haven't you got work to do? Off you toddle.' She dismissed him with a wave of her hand.

Sam rocked back and forth on his heels. 'But . . . I . . .'

'I can stay with her,' Grace offered.

'Okay.' His shoulders slumped. 'But I'll be back in two hours.' He kissed his grandmother on the forehead, and took Grace's elbow, guiding her outside. 'Promise you'll ring if anything happens. If she gets a headache, starts mumbling, her face droops . . . anything.'

Grace rested her hand on Sam's shoulder. 'I promise.'

He took her hand and squeezed it tight, holding it for a long moment. 'Thank you.'

Sam turned back three times as Grace watched him walk down the path, keeping her eyes fixed on his retreating figure until he was out of sight. When she went back inside, Hamish and Anne were deep in whispered conversation.

'Ah, there you are.' Anne sat up straighter, rearranging the crocheted rainbow afghan over her knees. Hamish nodded at Grace and took his leave.

'Is there anything I can get you, Anne?' Grace asked.

She shook her head. 'No, I'm fine. It really is a lot of fuss about nothing. No breaks. My hip is sore, I'll grant you, but at my age you get used to pain.' She paused. 'Though . . .'

'Yes?'

'Tomorrow the new books are arriving, correct?' Anne winced as she tried to adjust her position.

'Correct.' Linh had confirmed yesterday that they'd be on the boat, as directed, along with a little surprise Grace had organised. In the end the book club had decided against Austen and chose something a touch more modern. Grace couldn't wait for the tub to arrive.

'Maybe you can help Sam when they come in.'

'Of course.'

Anne asked for a sandwich – ham and cheese, extra pickles – and by the time Grace returned with it, Anne was snoring softly, snuggled into the sofa.

Grace placed the plate on the coffee table and settled into the armchair opposite. She pulled out her phone. Step Two was now in tatters. She could hardly trick Anne into giving up her secrets now.

Grace pocketed her phone, stood up, and turned her attention to Anne's bookcase that stretched across the breadth of one wall.

Dotted among the volumes of books were pieces of pottery, old photos in frames – Grace recognised a very young Sam in many of them – and some interesting-looking craft projects. She ran her fingers over an egg-carton butterfly. Or was it a crocodile?

'Addie made those.' Anne's voice was weak. 'We haven't found her artistic talent quite yet.' She smiled and closed her eyes again.

Grace perused the titles, many classics among them, and pulled down a copy of *I Capture the Castle*. A tale of love not meant to be. Perfect. Inside the cover was an inscription. *With all my love, T. 1953*. Grace sat in the armchair and started to read.

Two hours later, Sam arrived with Addie.

'Shh.' Grace put her finger to her lips as they entered the cottage, and motioned that Anne was sleeping. Addie curled up next to her great-grandmother and pulled a book out of her schoolbag, the pages so well read they were falling out of their binding.

Grace gestured for Sam to follow her out to the veranda.

'Thank you for staying with her,' said Sam. 'I know she's tough, but I still worry about her.' He ran his hands through his hair.

'We always worry about the ones we love. Even the strong ones.'

The now familiar cloud passed over Sam's face, and Grace knew he was thinking about Felicity. '*Especially* the strong ones. They're good at hiding when they're in pain.'

Grace swallowed hard. She knew all too well that it was beneath the surface – beneath the glowing skin, the healthy-looking hair, her Disney smile – where the dark truths hid.

She cleared her throat, her dark truth too close to the surface. 'I'll let you spend some time with Anne.' She turned her back to him, but Sam took her hand and she stopped.

'Grace?'

The warmth in his voice as he said her name tore at her heart.

'Are you okay?'

'Yes.' She couldn't turn around. She couldn't look at him. 'I'll see you tomorrow.'

'Tomorrow?'

With her back still turned to him she looked at the ground. 'Anne asked me to help you with the book club set.'

'Tomorrow, then.'

She pulled her hand away, descended the steps and walked down the path not daring to look back.

*

The next morning, as the sun reached over the ocean, bathing the island in a soft yellow glow, Grace headed to the dock to meet the supply boat. Sam was already there, standing tall next to Addie, who was in her school uniform. Relief washed over Grace at the sight of the little girl. At least she didn't have to face him alone.

Addie spotted Grace first, dropped her father's hand and ran towards her, wrapping her arms around Grace's hips tightly.

'Are you here to watch the boat come in?' Addie asked as they walked along the dock back to Sam.

'I am. Anne asked me to help your daddy with the book club set.'

Sam smiled at her, his eyes crinkling at the edges, and Grace felt the tension leave her shoulders.

'Well, once we get Gumnut off to school we'll start the drop.'

'Do I have to go to school?' Addie swept her foot in an arc along the dock.

'Do you have to ask me that every morning?' Sam copied her movement and Addie shot her dad a cheeky grin.

The boat pulled up to the dock and Addie clapped at its arrival. Jeremiah nodded in greeting. 'Miss Elliott. Sam.' Toby handed Sam the tub of books, placing a second, smaller box on top.

'What's this?' Sam asked Grace.

She grinned. 'You'll see a little later.'

They walked over to Sam's ute, which was parked a little way up from the beach. Sam put the book club tub on the tray and the extra box next to it.

'Night-vision goggles for better stalking?'

'Something even better. But it's a surprise.' Grace didn't want to tell him what it was yet. Now wasn't the right time.

'I love surprises.' Addie jumped up and down before climbing into the cabin of the ute.

They drove the short distance into town and stopped outside Addie's school – a converted church hall on the south side of town, the seat of learning for thirty island children.

Addie held Grace's hand as she skipped beside her until they reached the school gate.

'Have a good day.' Sam kissed her on the cheek.

'You too, Daddy.' She kissed him back. 'Bye Grace.'

Back at the ute Sam opened the tub from the library and pulled out three copies of *Big Little Lies*. 'Easier to walk from here,' he said to Grace. 'Plus it's a lovely morning.'

'Lead the way.'

First up was Maree, whom they found standing in her kaleidoscope front garden, in which every plant you could think of was growing wildly all around. Maree was doing tai chi in a flowing white kaftan.

'Oh, thank you, dears,' she said when Sam handed her the copy of the book. 'How's Anne? I'll pop by later to check on her.'

'Shellie says she'll be okay. A little bruised.' Sam smiled.

'Would you like to join me?' Maree looked at Grace. 'Good for the soul.'

Grace had tried tai chi during the first year of her illness and hadn't really taken to it. 'Thanks, Maree, but I'm helping Sam,' she said.

Maree smirked. 'Of course. Anne's idea?' She went back into white crane stance and started to spread her wings.

Sam stiffened beside her and Grace coughed. They'd been set up, it seemed.

After Maree, they visited Ruth, who was sitting on her veranda in a grey knitted top over black culottes. Grace gazed at the neatly trimmed rose bushes and the lawn cut perfectly to hug each stepping stone that lead to Ruth's small house.

'Thank you, Samuel. Grace.' She turned the book over in her hands and rolled her eyes at it. 'I do hope Anne is resting. She does too much. I tell her. Not that she listens.' She shook her head. 'It's her pride, you know. Thinking none of us can survive without all that she does.'

Grace watched closely as Ruth spoke. Her words were harsh but her expression was full of concern.

There were a couple more deliveries to make in town and Sam and Grace filled the silence between them with small talk – the weather, the beauty of the wattle in bloom – before they headed up Soldiers' Way.

They knocked on Hamish's black door, but there was no answer.

'We'll head to Obaachan's and leave the rest of the books there for anyone else to pick up, instead of at the pub,' Sam suggested. 'That way there'll be no shortage of visitors to fuss over her.' He winked.

When they got to Anne's cottage, they found her sitting on her front veranda sipping tea with Hamish.

She hit Hamish on the leg before calling out. 'Hello you two.' She waved. 'Is that our next read?'

'Good morning, Anne. How are you feeling?' Grace asked as she handed her a book. Sam placed the tub inside the door.

'Oh, much better now. Much better. Look at this.' She held up a white walking cane. 'Hamish brought it over in case I need it. I think it will make me look quite distinguished indeed.'

Sam returned and kissed her on her forehead. 'And no doubt garner just the right amount of sympathy.'

Anne put her hand on her chest. 'Well, I never.' She huffed, though her eyes danced with mischief.

Hamish tried to stifle a guffaw but couldn't hold it back.

Sam joined in. As did Anne. Grace shook her head and smiled, the warmth between the three of them so natural, so joyous.

'Now, you two young'uns head off and Hamish can start reading our new book to me.'

Hamish narrowed his eyes but opened the book.

Halfway down Soldiers' Way Sam angled his body towards Grace.

'Thank you for your help this morning.'

'Well, I'm sure you didn't actually need it, but Anne asked me to and she seems to have a way of ensuring her will is carried out.'

'You've learned quickly.' His eyes crinkled merrily. 'She's a force, to be sure, but her heart is always in the right place.'

Grace nodded. She'd figured that out about Anne nearly straight away. 'Besides, it was fun,' Grace said.

'Fun? Bungee jumping, skydiving . . . surely delivering books pales in comparison to that.'

Grace laughed. 'Well, that's a matter of perspective.' She had genuinely enjoyed herself this morning.

'Anyway.' Sam slowed as they neared the steps outside Grace's cottage. 'Thank you. That box of yours is still in the ute, though.'

'Would it be okay to leave it there? Maybe I can pop over tonight. It's actually for Addie.'

Sam frowned. Then smiled. 'Okay then. We'll be at Anne's for dinner. I can bring it with us, if you want to join us there?'

'Great. I'd, um, better get inside.'

He leaned in closer. 'Thanks again.' He kissed her on the cheek, lingering a moment before stepping back. The scent of clay and basil filled Grace's head. 'See you tonight.'

'Bye.' Her voice cracked.

Inside, she sat on the sofa and called Linh.

'I think I'm in trouble.'

'The broody one?'

'Yep.'

'I knew it.' The triumph in Linh's voice was almost enough to make Grace smile. 'You really like him, don't you?'

'Yes.' Grace paused. 'But—'

'Nope. No buts. I won't hear any buts.'

'How do I . . . when . . .' She buried her head in her hands. 'It wouldn't be fair.'

Linh lowered her voice, her words soothing. 'Grace, I know. But maybe he's come into your life for a reason. Don't shut it out, whatever it is, because of *fair*. Nothing in life is fair. You know that.'

Grace nodded. 'I know.'

'Take happiness when and where and how it comes.'

'But what if it comes with pain?'

'It always does.' Linh never sugar-coated things. 'But that's why you have to embrace it tightly, unapologetically, when you can.'

Grace stood and paced the living room floor. 'How did you get so wise?'

'I was born that way.'

Grace laughed. 'Ah. That explains everything.'

In the afternoon, Grace headed into town. She didn't want to see Shellie, not in a professional capacity, but she had no choice. Her body was telling her she needed medication. More than what she had with her.

Sitting in the surgery, which was decked out in warm wood tones and soft cushions on soft armchairs, Grace rubbed her hands together.

'So, Grace.' Shellie sat at her desk. 'What brings you in today?'

'I . . .' Grace knew Shellie was bound to confidentiality, but she never liked telling anyone her situation. 'I need some medication.'

'Right. What's giving you trouble?'

Grace told Shellie everything. Nearly everything. And she listened without interruption.

'Do you mind if I give your oncologist a call?'

'Of course.' Grace nodded.

The pharmacy on the island didn't carry the medication Grace needed, so Shellie arranged to have it flown over on the next morning's flight.

'It should help keep you more comfortable,' she said to Grace as she walked her to the surgery door. 'Does Anne know?'

'No.'

'Does Sam?' Shellie's voice was tight.

Grace shook her head. 'Only you.'

Shellie pursed her lips. 'Right. Well, you ring me if there are any changes.'

'I will. Thank you.'

Grace headed back to the cottage to rest up before dinner, her burden weighing heavily on her mind.

Anticipation was a funny thing. Sometimes it made Grace ravenous to the point where she ate everything in the fridge. Sometimes it tied her tummy in knots and the thought of eating made her sick.

That afternoon, for the first time in her life, it did both to her at the same time. Her excitement at giving Addie the surprise made Grace want to eat but her nerves about seeing Sam made her want to throw up.

She watched the old brass clock on the mantel tick over. The hands seemed to be moving both painfully slowly and excruciatingly quickly at the same time until, all of a sudden, it was time to head up Soldiers' Way.

She stepped off the veranda and was greeted by a puffing Addie, barrelling up the path.

'Daddy says you're coming to Obaachan's for dinner.' She entwined her tiny soft hand in Grace's.

'I am.'

'We're both very happy about that.' Addie beamed.

Grace looked at Sam, whose long strides had allowed him to catch up quickly.

He smiled at her and she willed her cheeks not to give her away.

'Anne will be pleased too,' Sam said, reaching for Addie's other hand.

'One, two, three!' Addie counted and Sam lifted her in the air, tipping her sideways as she held fast to Grace, who hadn't moved her arm. 'Grace, silly, on three you're supposed to swing me too.'

'Oh, sorry. I wasn't ready.' She mouthed 'oops' to Sam over Addie's head.

'That's okay. We can try again,' Addie said. 'One, two, three!'

This time Grace swung her arm in sync with Sam, and Addie sailed high into the air and back down again.

'One, two, three!'

Again and again, Grace and Sam swung Addie, and, despite it not being far to Anne's place, by the time they got there Grace was exhausted. She hadn't exerted herself so much since before she was diagnosed. Dr Puddy was always telling her to get some gentle exercise. Shellie had repeated the sentiment a few hours earlier too. But swinging a child in the air was certainly not on the list of recommended activities. Perhaps it should be. Although it had taken the wind out of her, it was a lot of fun.

Addie ran up the veranda steps and inside ahead of them. Grace stopped, resting her hands on her knees to catch her breath.

'Are you all right? She loves doing that.' He put his large hand on her back, the warmth of his touch penetrating her top through to her skin.

'Just out of condition.' She smiled.

'Shall we?' He spread his arm in an arc towards Anne's door.

'Wait.' Grace stood up. 'You didn't bring the box?'

Sam walked up the two steps to the veranda. 'It's already inside. I dropped it off earlier. Come in.' He held his hand out and she hesitated, only for a moment, before taking it.

Inside, Addie was already setting the table while Anne gave instructions to her great-granddaughter from her seat near the kitchen window. The wheelchair was nowhere to be seen, but the white cane was leaning against the dining table. At the kitchen bench, Hamish was serving up a roast lamb with all the trimmings, the smell of mint and gravy pushing aside any nervous stomach knots Grace may have had.

'First we eat.' Sam helped Hamish carry the plates to the table. 'Then Grace has a surprise for you, Addie.'

The little girl's face lit up. 'For me?'

'For you.' Grace tapped Addie on her tiny button nose.

Addie ate her dinner so fast she had to wait for the grown-ups to finish and as soon as Grace put the last forkful of roast potato dusted in rosemary into her mouth, Addie sat forward.

'Now?'

'Manners.' Sam's reproach was gentle.

'Please.' Addie sat back.

Sam got up and disappeared, returning with the box Grace had sent over on the supply ship.

Opening the box, she turned to Addie. 'I noticed most of your books have been very well loved, I thought maybe . . .' She reached in, pulled the first book out – *The 117-Storey Treehouse* – and handed it to Addie. '. . . you'd like something new to read.'

Addie clasped the book to her chest. Book after book, Grace pulled out of the box and Addie hugged each one. Ten new books in total.

Then the room went very quiet. Addie closed her eyes and lowered her head. Panicked, Grace looked at Sam with pleading eyes. He touched his daughter on the arm. 'Addie?'

She dropped the books she was holding and threw herself into Grace's arms, sobbing 'thank you'. Grace held back her own tears.

Addie dragged them all into the living room and made each one of them read to her. When it was Hamish's turn, Grace stood by Anne's bookcase, watching on, an idea forming very quickly in her mind.

Sam came and stood so close to her that she could feel his body heat.

'Thank you. That was such a thoughtful thing to do.' His breath danced down her neck.

'You're very welcome.' She dared not twist around to face him.

'Did you see the joy in her face? I'll never forget you did that for her.'

Grace had indeed seen the joy, and the idea that had sparked was now in full bloom.

Twenty

With quiet settling over her home, Anne hobbled on her walking stick around the living room. The pain in her hip was bearable. Just. But she wouldn't use that god-awful wheelchair. No sir-ee. Even if it meant she could get around more easily. She was going to hang on to her physical independence as long as she could. Once she came to rely on that thing, she may never get out of it.

She brewed a cup of tea, the joyous glow of the evening – the look on Addie's face, the softening of Sam's outer shell – still warm inside her. Hamish wouldn't have noticed the shift in Sam. Neither would Grace. But Anne certainly had. Echoes of the grandson who'd once exuded love and happiness and life had resurfaced. Grace had done more than she realised with her gift for Addie.

Perhaps a nudge wasn't necessary after all. Although, one never could trust fate in circumstances that mattered.

She carried her tea – only half filled so she didn't spill any, given her wobbly gait – to the small table beside the sofa and then fetched her photo album.

With her throw rug pulled up tight, she sank into the sofa, summoning memory lane. She'd been doing that a lot lately. Sometimes consciously, sometimes not. It was the old-age equivalent of pregnant women nesting. When you knew your time was coming to an end, you wanted to surround yourself with memories. They were all you had left.

As she often did, she opened the album to a random page. The bright blue eyes of a younger self stared back at her, her hair pulled back off her face in a fashionable pony tail. Hamish stood next to her in a crisp grey suit as they posed outside Walsh and Walsh. She tried to remember the date.

Ah, yes. That was right before everything changed.

Sydney, 1952

Hyde Park was throbbing with couples walking and families playing, the warmth of the spring sun perfect for a Saturday out. Anne walked past an ice-cream vendor but declined the flavours he was spruiking, even though her mouth was dry. As she approached the Archibald Fountain she saw a familiar figure standing off to the side under the shade of a tall weeping fig tree.

He bowed as she approached. 'Good morning, Anne.'

'Hello, Tadashi.'

His straw hat was pulled down low over his eyes, obscuring his face somewhat.

'Shall we?' He started to walk and she fell into step beside him. 'Tell me about your job.'

Anne tried to make it sound more exciting than it was, and he listened to every word.

'And do you like it here, Anne? Working in Sydney?'

She thought for a moment before she answered. 'I do. For the most part. It is harder than I thought it would be, living in the city, and I do miss the open air of the island. But there is a definite satisfaction to working and earning an income.'

'But you are not happy.'

She didn't respond.

'Do you still paint?'

'Yes. I gave it up for a while, but I've started again.'

'Good. A talent like yours shouldn't be wasted.'

They wandered through the paths of the park, stopping every now and then to admire a flower or step out of the way of running children.

'What about you, Tadashi? Are you still making beautiful things?' She thought about her vase stashed away under her bed back on the island and wished she had it here.

He shook his head. 'There's not a lot of opportunity. I don't have the space for it where I live and work keeps me busy.'

'Tell me more. What's it like working on the docks?'

'I load and unload the big container ships that come in. It's hard work, but honest work. Mostly.'

His words were measured and Anne suspected it was a lot harder than he was letting on.

'Mostly?'

'There are some men, some gangs, who don't like to follow the rules. If you stay out of their way, though, they leave you alone.'

'Oh. And where do you live?' She had to keep the topics simple. Safe.

'There are residences for wharfies. Those of us with no family or no other place to stay.' He cast his eyes down.

'Tadashi?'

'It isn't very clean. The men are often drunk. Giuseppe and I, we share a room. We don't tend to associate with the rest of them.'

Anne's heart ached. If this was the polite version for her sake, what must his reality be?

'It sounds . . . tough.'

He shook his head. 'It could be worse. I'm saving my money. I will make a better life. For myself. For . . .' He looked her in the eye. 'For a family.'

His words hung between them, and they paused for a moment before continuing their stroll.

As the sun moved across the sky, they walked through the Botanic Gardens, past Government House towards the harbour, letting the hours slip by in gentle conversation.

The Fort Macquarie tram terminus at the end of Bennelong Point was bustling. Anne desperately wanted to ride one all the way to Bondi Beach, but when you were saving every penny, walks closer to home had to do.

A cool breeze lifted through the air and she shivered.

'It's probably time I got you home.' Tadashi offered her his jacket, exposing his blue overalls beneath.

'Thank you.'

As he lifted it over her shoulders, he winced.

'What is it?'

'Nothing.'

She touched his arm and he flinched. 'Tadashi?'

'Just some trouble at work.'

'Regular trouble, or trouble because of the colour of your skin?'

'It's nothing for you to worry about.' He pulled his hat further over his eyes.

The walk back to the boarding house was slow but Anne didn't mind one bit. They talked about books and art and imagined how lovely it would be to maybe visit the Art Gallery of New South Wales one day together.

Every now and then, their hands brushed together, sending a jolt right through Anne.

The sun dropped low as they passed the Monty, a crew of rowdy wharfies spilling out of the heavy wooden doors.

Tadashi stepped to the other side of Anne, putting himself between her and them.

'Is everything all right?' she whispered.

'It's one of the gangs.' He rolled his shoulder. 'And they're drunk. Keep walking. We'll be fine if they don't—'

One of the men stumbled into Tadashi. 'Sorry, mate,' he slurred, putting his hand on Tadashi's chest. He reached up and tipped Tadashi's hat back. 'Oh, it's you. The filthy Jap. Killed our men in the war, they did. Now this one is taking all our work.'

Tadashi started to steer Anne away.

'Where are you going, filthy Jap?' The man shoved Tadashi but he stood his ground.

'Mike, I don't want any trouble,' Tadashi said softly. 'Go home. Sleep it off.'

'You want no trouble? Why'd you dob Rex in to the boss, then?'

Tadashi guided Anne backwards, never taking his eyes off the agitated men. 'I already told you, that wasn't me.' He rubbed his arm.

'Of course it was you.' Mike came towards Tadashi. 'None of the Aussies would have dobbed. We don't dob on mates in this country.'

'I didn't do it.' Tadashi backed up further.

'Yeah, right.'

A few of the men flanked Mike. 'You lot'—he pushed Tadashi— 'have got no honour.'

Anne put her hand on Tadashi's shoulder. 'Let's go,' she whispered.

'You tortured and killed our men.' A shove from the left.

'You take our jobs.' A push from the right.

'Dob on mates.' A heft from straight on.

'And now you're having a crack at our women.' Mike eyed Anne up and down, his fist balled up tight. 'You filthy Jap.'

He punched Tadashi in the jaw. The force sent him flying into Anne and she crashed to the pavement, her head hitting the kerb with a crack.

'Oh shit,' one of the men called out. 'You've killed the sheila.'

Another group of men came running out of the pub and the drunk wharfies scattered.

Tadashi scrambled to her side. 'Anne? Are you okay?'

Another voice rang through the evening. 'Anne?' A blurry Hamish crouched beside her.

Anne didn't know who to answer first. She was all right. Though her left ear throbbed. And she was having trouble focusing her vision.

'You're bleeding.'

She didn't know which one of them said that.

'We need to get her to a hospital.'

One of them picked her up and took her inside the Monty. Anne barely registered the shouting voices around her; the talk of telephoning an ambulance. The words were swirling around her throbbing head.

'You shouldn't be here.'

'I have to stay.'

'If they think you're involved . . .'

The voices faded and so did the light.

*

When Anne woke up she was in a hospital bed, tucked tightly into cool sheets while a stark white ceiling loomed brightly overhead. Simone was sitting in a chair beside her.

'Oh, Anne. You're okay.' Simone jumped up and hugged her, making her wince. 'Sorry. Does it hurt?'

Anne didn't know which 'it' Simone was referring to, but answered yes because everything hurt. Especially her head. She reached up and found a bandage wrapped around it.

'Oh, it's awful what they did to you last night. But you're going to be all right. And Hamish is a hero for saving you from them.'

'Hamish?'

'He'll be back a little later. He's hardly left your side.'

Anne tried to focus on Simone's words, but they made little sense. She had been with Tadashi when she fell. Not Hamish.

'Rest now.' Simone patted Anne's hand. They were the only words that made any sense to Anne.

She woke again as the sun was sending long shadows across the hospital floor.

'Hey there,' said a gentle voice. 'You took quite a knock. How are you feeling?'

'Hamish?' Anne's voice cracked. 'What happened? Where's Tadashi?' She tried to sit up, but her swirling head had other ideas.

'It's okay. He's okay,' Hamish whispered. 'What do you remember?'

Not much, apparently. She remembered falling and everything before that, but hardly anything after. There were snippets, at the edge of her mind, but they were grainy and disjointed.

'He wanted to stay but I sent him away,' Hamish continued.

Anne forced herself higher on her pillow and frowned.

'It was for his own good. Imagine what they'd think, what

questions would be asked, how he'd be implicated. I'll make sure he knows you're all right.'

'But you know what happened. Surely people will believe you.'

Hamish shook his head. 'I *know* what happened because I believe Tadashi. But I didn't *see* it. My testimony, if it ever came to that, would never hold up.'

'But he did nothing wrong.' Anne shook her head, and it ached.

'It won't matter. It's the word of one Japanese man against a group of white men.'

'The war was so long ago, Hamish.' She sighed.

Hamish took her hands in his and rubbed them gently. 'For a lot of the men, a lot of the families, the war isn't over. It never will be. It doesn't matter where someone like Tadashi was born. They need to hate someone for what happened.'

'I'll go to Walsh. He must have some—'

Hamish put up his hand. 'Mr Walsh's eldest son was killed in Changi, Anne. He won't help.'

'So, the men who did this?' She touched the bandage on her head.

'If we report them, they'll blame Tadashi. There are . . . other ways to deal with this. Best to keep Tadashi, and the law, right out of it.'

She wasn't sure she wanted to know what that meant.

'As far as anyone else is concerned, you were taking a stroll and were set upon. You didn't see who did it.'

Anne nodded. Reality settling over her.

'Thank you.' Her voice was soft.

He squeezed her hand, and Anne knew, without doubt, what a true friend Hamish was.

After Anne was discharged from the hospital, Simone wouldn't let her go back to the boarding house. In fact, she arranged to have her things picked up and moved her in to Simone's parents' guest room.

While Anne didn't like the idea of giving up her independence, she did find the thought of no longer living under Mrs Harris's iron boot rather appealing. But how would she see Tadashi now?

A week after the accident, the doctor made a house call and removed Anne's bandage. The stitches would need to stay in a little longer, but the laceration that ran the length of her hairline behind her left ear was healing nicely. The crippling headaches had gone. Finally.

'You will have a nasty scar,' the doctor said, and Simone gasped, clapping her hand to her mouth. She ran down the hall and came back a moment later, her hands behind her back.

Once the doctor left she sat beside Anne. 'Here.' She handed her a silk scarf. 'We can use this to hide the scar.'

Anne had no idea how to wrap it properly, so Simone taught her.

'This was my grandmother's. It came all the way from France. If we . . .' she put it behind Anne's head, '. . . and then we . . .' she wrapped it over the bandage and tied it. 'Voila.'

Anne returned to work a few days later, her scarf a fashionable and permanent addition to her wardrobe.

'Good to have you back, Webb,' Colin said, knocking on her desk. 'We have a meeting with a buyer in ten minutes.'

It felt good to be back.

'Trying to keep your brains in?' Rodney teased her as he passed her desk in the afternoon. She simply ignored him.

Just before closing, Hamish came past her desk. 'I have to speak with Colin for a moment. Then would you like to go for a walk?'

She hadn't had the chance to thank him properly since the hospital, so she happily agreed.

Half an hour later he held out his arm to escort her out of the building. 'Shall we?'

'Thank you, Hamish, for everything,' she said, as they left Walsh and Walsh, and walked up the street.

'It's nothing.' He guided her around a corner, then another. Anne hadn't been in this part of town before and she wondered where he was taking her. 'Tell me about this fella of yours.'

Anne's cheeks burned, but she told Hamish everything. If he was going to lie for her, she owed him that much.

'He means a lot to you, then?'

She cast her eyes down and nodded.

'I figured so.'

They rounded another bend and came to the rusted iron gate of a little park. Tightly packed trees skirted the perimeter, tall and dense, with foliage hiding people in their shadows. Over there, two men holding hands; over there a white man and a black woman, their heads pressed together in hushed conversation. The middle of the park was open, a bird bath in its centre, surrounded by four wooden bench seats facing the perimeter of the park. On one bench a man sat alone, his eyes closed, face tilted to the sky.

'This is lovely.' Anne smiled. 'But I'm not sure why you've brought me here.'

'I'll give you twenty minutes, then I'd better get you back to Simone's.' He sat on one of the benches.

'What?' She frowned.

'Anne-san?'

She spun around. Tadashi walked towards her and stopped, an inch away from her. He touched her scarf. 'I'm so sorry.'

She shook her head. 'It wasn't your fault.'

'Yes it was.'

She reached out and took his hand, her boldness coming from somewhere deep inside. 'Walk with me.'

In silence they took a turn around the park on the edges of the shadows, Anne not letting go of Tadashi's hand.

'I would not have been able to forgive myself if anything had happened to you, Anne,' Tadashi finally said.

'Nothing did happen.'

He looked at the scarf.

'Okay, nothing too terrible.' She smiled. 'I'm all right now, and we have an ally.' She glanced over at Hamish, and he tapped his watch. She turned back to Tadashi. 'I hope . . . I hope you'd like to see me again.'

'More than anything in this world.' He cast his eyes down, then looked up at her with passion in his gaze that took her breath away.

She hugged him tightly and ran back to Hamish. He returned her to Simone's house and she kissed him on the cheek. 'Thank you.'

He shrugged. 'I know what it's like to love someone you're not supposed to.'

'Oh, I don't . . . we don't . . .'

He raised an eyebrow and smiled. He was right, of course. She'd loved Tadashi since the moment she'd met him and it now seemed possible that they might be able to be together.

———

Anne closed the photo album and removed her scarf, running her fingers along the bumpy scar above her left ear. It had faded over the years, like memories sometimes did. But it was still there, part of her story, no matter how much she tried to hide it.

So much had happened; so many memories that had paved the way to here and now. She wondered what would come next, as she entered the final days of the winter of her life. What would happen with Sam, with book club?

If life had taught her anything, it was there was no knowing. No predicting. No certainty. And she didn't like that one bit.

Twenty-one

Grace stood in front of the old bookshop, her mind racing through all sorts of possibilities. The size and location were exactly what she was looking for. It was perfect. She moved away and sat on the bench beside the fountain. Some people on the island might not like her idea. But she felt it in her soul: Operation Words for Wattle was the right thing to do and she was determined to stay until she saw it through.

She texted Linh.

What? Shocked-face emoji. *You're staying? Like, indefinitely? Does this have anything to do with a brooding potter?*

No.

Maybe.

Of course not. Rolling-eyes emoji.

Really!

Okay. Tell yourself whatever you need to. Is there anything I can do to help Operation Words for Wattle?

Grace told Linh she'd send her an email when she had more of an idea of how to turn her thoughts into a plan.

There was no point telling her mum yet. If Grace couldn't get her idea off the ground then she might well be returning to Port Maddison sooner than expected. No point worrying June about nothing.

Operation Words for Wattle was going to need all her attention if she had any hope of pulling it off. And she'd better get started.

She jumped up off the bench and headed up Soldiers' Way, arriving at Anne's cottage slightly out of breath.

Before she could knock on Anne's door, it swung open.

'Oh, Grace. Well, isn't that fortuitous. I was just on my way to see you.' Anne's smile was genuine, if a little hesitant. She was leaning heavily on her cane.

Grace waved her hand in dismissal. 'You should have rung. You shouldn't be moving about so much.'

'Fiddlesticks. Besides, Shellie said gentle walking is good for me. Still, it seems fate brought you to me instead. What can I do for you?'

'Well, I was hoping maybe to engage your services for . . . I suppose you could call it a bit of a pipe dream.'

Anne's shoulders relaxed and she leaned in a little. 'Oh? Do tell.'

'Well, you mentioned you used to teach art, and I saw the photo at the pub . . .'

'You'd like an art lesson?' Anne's face lit up.

'Yes. And I was thinking about staying around for the next book club too. Especially if you're still recovering.'

'Well bless your cotton socks.' Anne smiled, a hint of mischief behind her eyes. If only she knew Grace had ulterior motives, she might not be blessing her socks. One key element in Grace's new plan involved the old bookshop. That meant Grace had to understand more about the place and the people involved. And she was starting with Anne.

'So, if it's okay, let me know when I can come to your studio and you can laugh at how much artistic talent I don't have.'

'Everyone has a creative talent.' She sounded just like Sam. 'But the studio won't do. We need inspiration.' She waved her arm in the air. 'This time of year the farms are glorious.'

'What about your hip?' Grace asked. 'How would we even get the art supplies there?'

'Let me worry about that.'

They arranged to meet the following day at 3 pm at Follett's farm. Apparently the afternoon light was much better for painting than midday glare.

Grace took her leave and headed for a stroll around the island. She'd come to enjoy her daily walks and the gentle exercise was helping with her pain.

She made her way to the far side of the island and took her shoes off as she settled into the sand at Rocky Beach. With bare feet and her jeans rolled up, she walked along the damp grains, stamping deep footprints into the shoreline. The waves that tickled her toes were warmer than the air that surrounded her and she stopped, looking out at the ocean.

With every wave that lapped her ankle, her feet sunk deeper into the sand and with the rising tide, the footprints she'd left behind disappeared, erasing all traces of her having been there at all. A flock of seagulls flew past her with expert precision, an inch from the water. She followed their path with her gaze and they banked at the cliff where the lighthouse stood tall and headed out to sea.

As she stared at the lighthouse a shiver ran down her spine, just like last time. She turned her gaze to the waves and took in deep breaths of salty air.

The *woosh-boom-roar* of the waves filled Grace's ears as they broke, melting from teal to white as their crests crashed in on themselves. How was it possible a place so loud and wild and restless could be such a haven of calm?

Grace breathed in for four counts and out for six – a technique she'd learned not long after her diagnosis. She closed her eyes and concentrated on the feel of the cool water against her skin.

It was the right decision to stay, whether she could pull off her plan or not. Here, her reality was so far away, it was almost possible to forget it entirely. With the waves soothing her, she thought perhaps she might never leave.

The next day, wearing an old navy-blue T-shirt and tracksuit pants – the perfect outfit for painting – Grace made her way to Follett's farm.

Her mother's shock at her decision to stay longer played on her mind as she wandered through town.

What is so important about this book club? Why can't they look after themselves? What about your job? Does Dr Puddy know? All very valid questions her mother had hurled at her last night.

Grace had assured June that her leave from work was fine and Dr Puddy was aware of her extended absence.

'Maybe I could pop over there for a visit, then. See for myself that you're okay,' June had suggested.

Part of Grace wanted to say yes. But if June were here, she'd see the pain Grace was disguising, and Grace couldn't have that.

'Actually, Mum. Maybe you can come over.' She heard June take in a sharp breath. 'In a couple of weeks. Let me get this project off the ground first.'

'Right.'

Grace imagined June giving her *The Look*.

'We'll talk about this more, Grace,' June continued. 'Mark my words.'

When Grace arrived at Follett's paddock, she found Anne set up in the middle of a field of long green grass. Two easels, two chairs and two canvasses had already been set up. By Sam.

He gave her an awkward wave as she walked across the field towards them, the long grass swaying in the light breeze, brushing against Grace's legs.

'Hi.' She smiled, not trusting herself to say more.

'Ah, here she is,' Anne said. 'My budding little Monet. Or maybe you're more of a Klimt. We shall see soon enough.'

Grace laughed. 'Is there a famous stick-figure-ist? I think that's more my style.'

'Nonsense.' Anne handed Grace a paintbrush and a palette that already had some paint on it. 'Everyone can paint. Some just do it better than others.'

Well, there was no arguing with that.

'You can apply that to most things in life, you know.' Anne smiled.

'Are you joining us, Sam?' Grace wasn't sure what she hoped his answer would be.

'No, I have to work.' He ran his fingers through his thick curls. 'But I'll be back to help pack up when you're done.'

'Off you toddle, grandson-mine.' Anne held out her hand and he took it, leaning in to kiss her on her forehead. 'Leave us *artistes* to it.'

'Right, see you later, then.' Sam laughed. 'Good luck.' He winked at Grace.

Grace grimaced. 'Thanks.'

'Ready?' Anne raised her paintbrush.

'We're jumping straight in?' Grace asked, taken slightly aback.

'I find it best not to think too much about it.'

She told Grace to close her eyes and recall what she could of the field they were sitting in. Other than grass, not much else came to Grace's mind. Except for Sam. And she didn't think that's what Anne meant.

With a soothing voice Anne encouraged her to use her mind's eye rather than her actual eyes. Which made no sense at all. Slowly and with the patience of a goddess, and a lot of 'that's it's and 'good work's, Anne stepped her through it, bit by bit, as Grace turned the greens and yellows of the farm into strokes on the canvas in front of her.

'You're very good at this,' Grace said softly, as Anne sat beside her painting her own masterpiece while still giving gentle instruction. 'The teaching. How long did you give art lessons for?'

'Oh, well, let's see. I started the winter of 2000. We were trying to think of ways to increase the number of tourists to the area in the off-season. There was a town meeting to come up with strategies. Some were more successful than others. Maree, god bless, tried to get a circus troupe to come to the island and run a circus school.' She winced and Grace laughed.

'It was actually young Felicity's idea that I start giving art lessons. I was teaching her at the time. She was only eleven or twelve, and she said I was so good at it, I should teach everyone.'

Anne's brush stopped mid-stroke. Only for a moment. Grace held her breath. Was this her way in?

'Anyway, they were very successful and I did them right up until . . . well for around eleven years.'

Grace did the maths in her head. Seven years ago. This was her chance.

'Sam told me about Felicity. I don't hear people talk much about her,' Grace said, careful not to look at Anne. Eye contact often made people nervous.

'No.' A small pause. 'I suppose not.'

'You stopped the lessons when she died?'

'Yes.'

'And that's when book club stopped too.' Grace made it a statement more than a question. She turned her head just enough to see Anne wipe a tear from her eyes.

'Oh, Anne. I'm sorry. I didn't mean to pry.' A tiny lie.

Anne shook her head and pushed her shoulders back. 'It's fine, pet. It was a while ago now. But you know how memories can be. They sneak up on you sometimes. Especially when there are unanswered questions.'

Grace reached across the short distance between them and took Anne's frail hand in hers. 'Questions?'

Grace had assumed she was the only one who didn't know the truth of why book club had ended, and that everyone was simply keeping it from her. It appeared there was much more to the story, more that needed to be revealed.

'Oh, listen to this old fool prattle on. A young thing like you doesn't need an old sour goat like me depressing you with sad philosophy. At your age it should be all rainbows and lollipops.'

Grace looked down at the space between them. She'd given up on rainbows and lollipops long ago. Looking back at Anne, she forced a smile.

'I'm here if you ever need to talk,' Grace said. Such an empty statement, really. It was one she'd heard many times herself. But she meant it.

'Thank you, pet.' Anne stood up, leaning on her walking stick, before Grace could ask anything further. 'Let's take a look at this masterpiece of yours, shall we? A few steps back and you can often see things more clearly.'

Grace rose and joined Anne, full of confidence from an afternoon of encouragement. She looked at her painting.

And laughed.

'Hmm,' was all Anne could say.

'It's okay, Anne. I can see what a disaster it is. Maybe we don't really want to see this particular . . . thing . . . more clearly. Step closer, Anne, before it's too late.'

Anne laughed. 'Maybe we need to find you a different medium.'

'Or maybe we shouldn't inflict me on any more of the arts.'

They doubled over in fits of giggles.

It was not pleasant to look at. At all. Yet Grace was proud of it nonetheless. She'd given it a go, and had fun too.

She would pull out her journal tonight and turn to the correct page – *age nineteen: learn to paint like Monet* – and she would amend the entry. *Attempted age thirty. Failed. Miserably. Happily.*

'How'd we go?' Sam's deep voice rang out behind them. 'Oh,' he said. 'A different medium, perhaps?'

The two women doubled over again.

'Did I miss something?' Sam frowned. Neither Grace nor Anne could answer, they were still laughing so hard.

Sam packed away the equipment and helped Anne back to the ute. 'Hop in,' he said to Grace.

Sitting between Anne and Sam on the vinyl bench seat of the Holden, Grace could feel Sam beside her, the rise and fall of his chest, the brush of his leg as he changed gear. He parked at the bottom of Soldiers' Way.

'Sam,' Anne said before getting out. 'Why don't you take Grace to the lookout? It's hard to access without a car. Lovely view.'

'Would you like to?' He looked at Grace. 'We might have time to catch a phenomenon that only happens in winter.'

'Sure.' She knew it was dangerous to say yes. But she couldn't bring herself to say no.

'Wait here while I get Obaachan home and—'

'No need.' Anne got out of the ute. 'Here's Hamish. Right on time.'

Right on time? Grace narrowed her eyes.

'Bring the easels back tomorrow.' She waved goodbye as Hamish escorted her up Soldiers' Way.

In silence, Sam and Grace drove to the southernmost part of the island. Unlike the other scenery Grace had observed since arriving – lush displays of nature or the bright colours of human settlement – this peninsula was bleak.

No grass. No trees. No colour. Just a narrow gravel road winding between grey rocks.

Grace had no idea why Anne would want her to see this part of the island.

Sam parked the ute and led the way to a small metal platform on the edge of the cliff.

'Down there'—he pointed to a tiny corrugated iron shed perched precariously on a rock shelf jutting out from the cliff face—'is where scientists, in about six weeks' time, will spend a month documenting the nesting habits of the Wattle Island gull.'

'I've heard of them,' Grace said. 'The gulls. Not the scientists.'

Sam laughed.

'Is that what I'm here to see?'

'Just wait,' he said, looking at his watch. 'Another five minutes. Trust me.'

She looked into his eyes. 'I do.'

Between them the air stilled, and then a cold wind whipped up. Grace shivered. Sam opened the front of his coat and Grace stepped in. He closed his arms around her.

'Better?'

She nodded, her hands pressed into his chest.

Moments passed, during which neither of them moved or spoke.

'Now,' Sam whispered in her ear. 'Turn around.'

Without leaving his embrace, Grace turned.

'Oh my.' She exhaled.

The setting sun had lit the sky on fire in bursts of orange that melted into red at the horizon.

'Look down.'

The grey rocks below had transformed into shining orbs of pink and purple and orange.

'Only in winter. Something about the angle of the sun and the minerals in the rocks . . .'

Grace turned back to face him.

He smiled down at her with soft eyes and he took her hand in his. 'I should probably get you back.' He released her from his coat and stepped back, the dark cloud flashing across his expression.

They drove back in silence, and neither spoke as Sam walked Grace to her door.

'Goodnight,' he said at the bottom of the steps.

She watched him walk away and when she got inside, she collapsed onto her bed, her concern about how complicated things had just become being pushed aside by the magic of the moment shared with Sam.

Twenty-two

Anne had forgotten how much she loved teaching art; how much she missed running retreats. She'd recaptured an old joy, if only briefly. If events of seven years past hadn't stalled her life, would she still be running classes? Perhaps.

She hadn't planned to say anything to Grace about Felicity, though. She'd relaxed too much into the moment and said something that she perhaps shouldn't have. But maybe it was exactly what she needed to happen.

Sending Grace off with Sam into the sunset had been a stroke of genius. She puffed out her chest, careful not to overbalance on her walking stick.

She'd never got to the truth of that night herself. Perhaps Grace could help her find it. She clearly had a connection with Sam and he hadn't been this open since he'd lost Felicity. If pushing them together helped the truth come out, then Anne wouldn't apologise for that. Maybe Grace was exactly what Sam needed. Anne had noticed the haunted look in Grace's eyes when she thought no one was looking. Maybe she could get through to him. Souls that knew real pain often recognised each other. Often came together.

Sydney, 1953

Since the attack outside the pub, Anne's world had changed dramatically.

At work she kept her head down, the scarf around her head a constant reminder not only of what had happened, but also how she needed to keep her relationship with Tadashi a secret. Outside work, for the last few weeks Hamish had acted as a go-between, organising meetings in the park with Tadashi, bringing Anne notes.

'Oh, a love letter from Hamish.' Simone snatched one such note out of Anne's hand one day at work. Thankfully Tadashi was wise enough to never sign the notes. Technically, Anne supposed, it was a love letter, and technically, she had received it from Hamish, so she wasn't really lying to her friend when she didn't correct the misassumption.

'Wow-wee.' Simone whistled. 'Who knew Hamish had this side to him?' She fanned herself with the letter. 'I knew all it would take was the right woman.' She grinned, handing the note back.

How very wrong you are, thought Anne.

Every night in bed, Anne re-read Tadashi's letters, his words as beautiful as his art.

I long for the day we can sit in a park under a blinding sun and read together . . .

You are my north, my truth . . .

Without you there is no air to breathe . . .

Every night she held them to her chest, praying they could find a way.

*

One Friday evening, early in the new year, Anne and Tadashi were walking around the secret park, hand in hand.

'Anne, I have something I'd like to give you.' Tadashi stopped and moved in front of her.

'If it's another one of your letters, I might swoon like a lady in one of those gothic romances you refuse to read.'

He laughed. 'I've read them. But that's not the point.'

'No? What is?'

'This.' With outstretched hands he presented her with a fan made of dark-blue silk, tiny white blossoms sprinkled across its top. 'It was my mother's.' He bowed.

'It's beautiful.'

'In Japanese culture, in days long past now, such a gift was given during . . . a yuino. An engagement celebration. It symbolises a happy future.'

Anne's hand began to shake. 'What . . . what do you mean?'

'I know I should have a ring, but this means more to me. I have nothing to offer you, Anne, except my heart. Will you accept it?'

She threw her arms around his neck. 'Of course I will.'

'I love you, Anne. With every part of my soul.' He reached behind her neck and pulled her close.

'I love you too,' she whispered and he kissed her, his lips soft, full of want.

Hamish was waiting for them at the edge of the park, and as they approached, he simply nodded at them. Tadashi turned left, Anne and Hamish right. Directly into the path of Rodney.

He eyed them up and down and craned his neck to see behind them. Anne dared not turn around to see if Tadashi was still in sight. She held her breath.

Hamish held his hand out in greeting. 'How are you, Rodney?'

Rodney shook his hand, swaying slightly as he did so. 'Evening.' He looked past Hamish's shoulder, then down at the fan in Anne's hand. She moved it behind her back.

He looked from her to Hamish and down the street again, then at the park, a moment of recognition crossing his glazed eyes.

'Can I help you with something?' Hamish asked.

Shaking his head, he turned down the next road.

Anne let out a long breath. 'We're going to have to be more careful.'

'Yes, we are.'

On Monday at work, Rodney approached Anne's desk.

'Morning.' His voice was dripping with spite. 'Did you enjoy your evening on Friday?'

'I did, thank you. You?' She kept her eyes down on her file.

'Strange part of town you were in.'

'You were also there.' Anne thought perhaps she could use her wits to get his measure, but he didn't even flinch.

'Very interesting.' His eyes narrowed. 'Like that fan you were carrying. Where did Hamish get it?'

'He didn't tell me. A gentleman never reveals from where his gifts come. Perhaps you need to ask him yourself.' Her heart began to race and she hoped Rodney wouldn't notice the slight darkening of her orange silk scarf as tiny beads of perspiration formed on her forehead beneath it.

'Maybe I will.' He bumped the desk, giving Anne a jolt and sending her pencils rolling onto the floor.

At the weekly meeting that afternoon, Colin chastised Rodney for turning his report in late and he immediately glared at Anne.

'I put it in on time. Maybe your sorry excuse for a secretary misplaced it.'

Anne held her tongue, the hairs on the back of her neck standing up.

'Miss Webb is incredibly efficient.' Colin's voice was firm. 'She doesn't misplace files.'

'Maybe she's distracted thinking about her beau all day.' He wasn't going to back down.

The heat in Anne's cheeks rose. As far as Colin knew, Rodney was talking about Hamish, and therefore there was nothing to worry about. But the look Rodney gave her unnerved her.

For the next few weeks Anne and Tadashi didn't see each other, just to be sure. Hamish called round to Simone's parents' house regularly, to keep up appearances and to check on her, bringing notes from Tadashi with him.

Being apart from you is sorrow too heavy to bear . . .

Soon we will be free. Have patience, my dearest . . .

Snatched moments with you will never be enough . . .

Anne retreated into her books for solace.

Week after week passed and slowly Rodney seemed to let go of the phantom he was chasing.

On a Friday evening in spring, Hamish deemed it safe enough to arrange another meeting. He escorted Anne to the park and told her he'd return in twenty minutes, like always.

Under a weeping willow Anne stood in front of Tadashi. His hand played with the knot of her blue-and-purple scarf.

'How much longer must we sneak around like this?' Anne asked.

'Once I've enough money saved, we can leave. Start our lives together. I promise.'

'I have some savings too. But where would we go?'

'Together we'll figure it out.' Tadashi lifted her chin and kissed her tenderly, deeply.

It felt like hardly any time at all had passed before they had to leave the park. They reached the rusty iron gate, but Hamish wasn't waiting in his usual spot. As Anne spotted him striding up the road with fierce determination, Rodney stepped out of the shadows.

'I knew you were up to something, Little Miss Smug.' Disgust oozed with his every word. 'But I did not expect you to be whoring yourself to a filthy Jap.' He spat out the words.

Tadashi stepped forward. 'Don't speak to her like that.'

'Why not? It's true. Do you know what his kind did? My family, all of them, slaughtered in the bombing of Darwin. Wait until Walsh hears about this.'

Anne grabbed his arm. 'Please, Rodney. Please don't.'

He tore himself from her grip and ran away.

Hamish was running as fast as he could, but by the time he got to Anne and Tadashi, Rodney had disappeared.

Anne stood there, unable to move.

'Go,' he said to Tadashi. 'I'll get her home safe.'

'Not headaches again?' Simone pouted, when she greeted Anne at the door.

'She just needs a rest.' Hamish supported Anne around the waist as he led her inside.

'Thank you, Hamish.' She turned and hugged him, tears in her eyes.

'It'll be all right,' he whispered in her ear.

But Anne didn't believe him. She fretted all weekend and sure enough, first thing Monday morning, Walsh Senior strode towards her desk. He rarely came to this part of the office and Simone was scampering behind him, worry etched across her face.

Anne's heart beat faster and her palms began to sweat.

'Miss Webb. In my son's office. Now!' Walsh bellowed.

Colin was waiting for them inside, and once Simone had firmly shut the door, Walsh threw a photo onto Colin's desk. A photo of Anne and Tadashi in the park.

'Care to explain?'

Simone looked at the picture. 'Oh, that's just an old friend of Anne's from home. She's seeing Hamish McKenzie now. They're very close.'

Anne had no words. Her pulse continued to throb.

'That's right,' Colin added.

'I have it on good authority that Miss Webb is in fact seeing this, this . . . Jap.'

Colin and Simone looked at her.

'B-but what about Hamish?' Simone stuttered.

All Anne had to do was lie. Colin and Simone would believe her and Walsh would believe his son. Hamish would back her up. She knew that beyond doubt. But how long could this go on before Rodney had more evidence, or someone else found out? How much longer could she skulk in the shadows?

And it wasn't fair on Hamish. There were already rumours circulating, probably started by Simone, that he was going to propose to Anne very soon. They were all expecting it now. She couldn't let it go that far. There was no clean way out of this.

Anne's squared her shoulders and looked Walsh in the eye. 'His name is Tadashi, and we're engaged.'

'Oh, how could you be so blind, Simone.' Colin's voice was low as he pieced together the truth.

'What? No.' Confusion and doubt played across Simone's face.

'It isn't Simone's fault.' Anne looked to Colin.

'And you pulled a decent fellow like Hamish into your web of deceit, too.' Colin threw a newspaper across the desk. 'That poor bastard.'

Simone let out a sob.

'You . . . you . . . hussy,' Walsh growled. 'I won't have any employee of mine ruin this company's reputation. I should have known some uneducated island orphan would bring trouble. Get out of my sight.'

The next moments happened in a blur. Anne's desk was packed up. Simone and Colin escorted her to Simone's parents' house to get her things, and then she was out on the footpath where she cried silent tears, her suitcase with all her belongings thrown at her feet.

Simone broke free from Colin's grip and hugged her tightly, slipping something into her pocket. 'If you'd come to me, I could have helped. But Colin feels betrayed now. There's nothing I can do. This will be enough for a hotel for a few nights. I can't do any more.' She ran back to Colin's side and with his arm around her, they went back inside the house.

'I'm very disappointed in you, Webb,' he said over his shoulder.

Anne stood there alone shivering in the warm sun as cars drove by. She hugged herself tightly, trying to stop the shaking, her mind racing. Where would she go? What would she do? How would she find her way back to Tadashi? As the sun moved lower in the sky, she forced herself to stop her tears, picked up her suitcase, and squared her shoulders.

Anne stayed in a hotel on the edge of Pyrmont for a few days. She made contact with no one, except to send a letter to let Simone know where she was. She didn't dare contact Tadashi in case Rodney or one of Walsh's associates was watching. When things died down, she'd find him. She had enough savings for a month or so, but without a job, that would soon dry up. And without a reference, she was unlikely to get another one. Not a decent one. She had no idea what she was going to do.

She could go back to Wattle Island; there was an empty cottage waiting for her. But, despite the obstacles in their path, she couldn't make any decisions without Tadashi.

For the next few days Anne slept and drew and read and slept. On Sunday afternoon a message was slipped under her door.

Meet me in the foyer. H.

She couldn't run downstairs fast enough.

Hamish greeted her with a smile. He looked exhausted, and he hadn't shaved.

'How much trouble are you in?' she asked, standing before him.

'It will blow over. My family have money and contacts, both of which Walsh needs. Besides, they're all blaming Tadashi for bewitching you and you for bewitching me with your feminine wiles.' He laughed, slightly forced.

She would have laughed too if it weren't all so needlessly tragic.

'Apparently I'm a victim in this.' He shrugged.

'I'm so sorry.' She held back tears. He *was* a victim in this.

He shook his head. 'I'm never going to have the love I desire, Anne. I was simply trying to help you get yours. Don't ever be sorry for that.'

'And now all is lost.' She bowed her head.

With a gentle touch he lifted her chin. 'Not necessarily. What is it you really want, Anne?'

She looked him in the eye. The answer was easy. 'To marry Tadashi. Live a simple life.'

He nodded. 'What if I can make that happen? The marrying part, at least. The simple life would be up to you.'

'But where?'

'I know a place.'

Hope rose in her then fell. 'And then what?'

'Well, the two of you would need to figure that out. Come to this address on Saturday.' He handed her a piece of paper. 'Your room here is paid for.'

Anne followed his instructions the following week and, with a cool breeze at her back, she found herself knocking on the door of a terrace house in The Rocks. She was let in by an old lady, who seemed to be expecting her.

Anne waited in the drawing room, taking in her surroundings. Heavy-looking brown leather sofas sat in the middle of the room, and the walls were lined with shelf after shelf of old books. There were law tomes, classic novels, works on psychology, modern paperbacks. Anne could have lost herself in their volumes for an eternity.

'I'm glad you came.' Hamish stood in the doorway.

Anne turned around. 'Is this your place?'

'One of them.'

'I thought you didn't read.'

'Well, I couldn't tell you the truth and have you fall madly in love with me, could I? I saw that look in your eye when you asked me if I read. If I'd said yes, you would have swooned.'

Anne allowed herself a small grin. She quite possibly would have.

There was a knock on the door and Hamish left the room returning moments later with Tadashi.

'What happened?' Anne gasped when she saw the bruises on the right side of his face.

'Just some people wanting to send me a message. I'm okay, though.'

Anne looked at Hamish, his brow furrowed, and he shook his head slightly. Walsh's people? Anne's stomach tightened as she touched Tadashi's cheek. This wasn't fair. None of this was.

'You two have some things to work out.' Hamish backed out of the room.

Tadashi held Anne's hands in silence for a long time. She wanted to tell him everything would be okay, but she didn't know if it would be. Hope was all she had, and perhaps that wouldn't be enough. With a low voice, Tadashi finally spoke.

'Anne, I'm sorry I've brought this trouble into your world. All I want is your happiness. Say the word and I'll disappear forever. You can have a chance at a beautiful life.'

'Is that what you want? To disappear from my life?' The thought crushed her.

He shook his head. 'No. I want you, Anne. Always. But I love you and want to make your life better, not worse.'

'I love you too. And you do make my life better.' The warmth of his touch on her cheek radiated through her and she knew this man with his crooked smile and kind eyes was all she'd ever need.

When Hamish returned an hour later, Anne's tears had stopped and she and Tadashi had agreed on what to do next.

'And you're sure?' Hamish asked, when they told him their plan.

'Yes,' they said in unison.

It was a perfect winter afternoon under clear, crisp skies; the sun shining through the Moreton Bays that lined the narrow street in Newtown. The church was a small stone building tucked away off a side street. Standing at the entrance in a simple white skirt suit, Anne took Hamish's arm. She held a small bouquet of wattle, mixed with some Queen Anne's lace that Tadashi had found her. His Queen Anne.

Together they stepped inside and walked towards Tadashi, who was dressed in a suit borrowed from Hamish. The minister performed the ceremony without fuss. With simple words he proclaimed Anne and Tadashi man and wife, and Anne's heart swelled with love as Tadashi smiled at her.

She had never been one to imagine a big white wedding, so to her, the day, with the sunlight pouring in through the stained-glass windows, sending pools of red and blue and green light dancing onto the stone floor, was perfect.

Outside the church, Hamish embraced them, his eyes full of love and sadness. 'Helping you has been an honour. I can't bear to say goodbye, so I'll have my driver drop you at the station.' He handed Tadashi a plain white envelope. 'My wedding present. Don't open it till you get where you're going.' He winked, a smile returning to his face, and he gave Anne a pink one. 'From Simone.'

Anne looked at him with wide eyes, but said nothing.

On the train heading north from Sydney, as the rattle of the wheels on the tracks filled Anne's ears, she opened her pink note from Simone.

I'm sorry for how things worked out. I tried to talk to Colin, but there was nothing he could do. In the eyes of his father, the wrong was too great. I do hope you'll be happy together. Truly.

Hours later, standing on the pier at Port Maddison, Anne watched their luggage being loaded onto the passenger ship bound for Wattle Island. Nerves and excitement coursed through her veins.

It was an obvious choice in the end. A simple one.

'Mr and Mrs Sato?' The deckhand checked their tickets. 'Welcome aboard.'

Slipping her hand into Tadashi's, Anne squeezed tightly.

———

Anne opened the drawer of the small writing desk in the living room and pulled out the blue fan Tadashi had given her so long ago. She ran her fingers over the folds and smiled.

Funny how entwined pain and joy were. If life had taught her anything it was that one didn't come without the other. She wondered who she had to speak to about that.

Sam had had more than his fair share of pain. She hoped it was now time for his joy. She hoped the sunset had done the trick.

Twenty-three

As the sun reached into the sky, Grace left the beach after her walk, and strolled through the Wattle Way of Delight. Soft golden pompoms dancing on the gentle breeze fell on her shoulders and in her hair.

All night she'd gone over what had happened with Sam on that clifftop, trying to make sense of his reaction and her own thoughts and feelings.

There had been a moment shared, of that she was certain. But he'd pulled back. What did that mean? And would she have withdrawn, if he hadn't? She certainly should have.

She wandered the still-sleeping streets of town, the sun drawing back the curtains of morning and illuminating each building as it climbed higher in the sky.

She paused as she passed the bookshop. This is what she needed to focus on. Operation Words for Wattle. Not a foolish heart and feelings that had no business being felt.

She decided to make one more loop of the island and then head back to her cottage to work on her plan. Avoiding Sam's place, she skirted the edges of the farms and made her way to Rocky Beach. Looking up at the lighthouse, she saw someone leaning against the southern wall, and she froze.

It was Sam. Without question. She knew his shape; his stance.

Sam never comes to the lighthouse. Anne's words echoed in Grace's mind.

She watched for a moment. He tilted his head towards the sky. Then, lowering his gaze, he turned, and Grace ran. As fast as she could. Hoping he hadn't seen her.

Back in her cottage, she drew in deep breaths.

Focus, Grace. She had a job to do.

She opened her laptop and, as she'd hoped, there was an email from Linh.

Excellent. Her fingers started to move across the keyboard and she stayed there for hours, gathering information, sourcing statistics, collecting inspiration, only breaking to stretch or make a cup of tea.

By the next morning, she was ready. She called Anne and arranged to meet for lunch.

Grace sat nervously in the pub waiting for Anne to arrive. They could have met at the cottages, she supposed, but she thought a good meal might make Anne more open to her idea. She knew technically it wasn't Anne she should be speaking to. But she also knew if Anne liked the idea, she'd have a shot. If Anne was against it, there was no hope.

She drank her sparkling water, her hand shaking ever so slightly. She hadn't slept well last night; too busy thinking of the best way to present her idea. Tired didn't begin to describe how she felt today, and the discomfort in her back was not helping.

Maybe she should have postponed this meeting, but she believed so strongly in her idea that she really wanted to see if it might work. And if Anne gave her the green light, then they'd have to get started straight away. It wouldn't be easy to pull this off in a short timeframe.

The bell above the pub door rang and Grace smiled as Anne walked in. Then she tilted her head as Hamish followed behind.

'Well, pet.' Anne slid into the booth. 'You've certainly piqued my interest. A plan to "breathe life into the literary pulse of the island"? Let's hear it, then.'

Grace looked at Hamish.

'Oh, he knows everything about my life. Runs half of it, truth be told. If you need my help with something, then you probably need his too.'

Grace took a deep breath. 'I've been thinking about book club and the lack of resources here on the island and when Addie reacted the way she did when I gave her those books . . . well, every kid should have the chance to experience that. Every adult too.'

Anne leaned in.

'So I was thinking we could set up a community library. I've done the research.' Grace pulled out her laptop. 'And it will take some doing, but I think we can make it happen.' She opened her files and continued.

'You can see from this graph here where most community libraries get their funding. It's different to public libraries.'

Anne nodded.

'Donations.' Hamish scratched his beard. 'I can help with that.'

Grace ploughed through, afraid to stop. 'We need to get your local council involved.'

Anne smiled. 'I think I can manage that.'

'I was hoping you'd say that. And I have plenty of experience writing grant applications . . .'

They talked about the finances at length.

'Staffing would be another big challenge, but if you look at this model'—she opened another file—'you can see there are ways to do it with a predominantly volunteer staff.'

Anne frowned.

'I know Wattle Island is small.' Grace had thought of everything. 'But I figure with the book club contacts, that would be enough to get started and once the community sees what an asset it is, that should encourage others.'

'We'll need premises to house the library.' Hamish stroked his white beard thoughtfully. 'Not a lot of options around here.'

Grace pressed her lips together. All the other logistics were paperwork and manpower. This was the part she was most worried about. This was the part wrapped up in emotion.

She looked at Anne and understanding flickered in the old woman's grey eyes.

'I was thinking the old bookshop might work,' Grace said gently.

Anne didn't respond.

'It's a good size. Perfect location.' Grace opened the pictures of libraries she'd bookmarked as examples of her vision. 'We'd need to renovate, of course, but I really think—'

Anne raised her hand. 'Those are all matters of fact. But there is another issue.'

Grace looked down at the scratches in the old wooden table. 'I know.' She looked up. 'I was hoping you might have some ideas on how to broach it with Sam.'

Anne glanced at Hamish and he cocked his head.

'Why?' Anne asked.

'Sorry?'

'Why do you want to do this?'

'Like I said, I think kids like Addie should have access to books. I saw her face light up when I gave her that box. Well, that's when the idea first struck me.' She emphasised each beat of her sentence with an exaggerated hand movement.

'And?' Anne put her elbows on the table and rested her chin on her clasped hands.

Grace took a deep breath. It was time to lay it all out. 'And while I don't know what happened here seven years ago, I can see you're all still hurting. I believe in the power of books. Not only for education. They bring people together, they allow you to escape, allow you to heal. And maybe a library on the island can help with some of that.'

Anne's expression remained neutral. Then slowly, the corners of her mouth turned up.

'It's time,' she said to Hamish and he nodded.

Turning back to Grace, she grinned.

'I think your idea is inspired. I can't predict how Sam will react, but why don't we talk to him together over dinner tonight?'

'Yes?' Grace's eyes went wide. 'Yes.'

'Now, about some of your models. Grants take ever so long and are boring and tedious. We will need them, of course, ongoing. But if we want to get moving on this, then the funds we can take care of, can't we, Hamish?'

He nodded.

'So why don't you two talk some more about that stuff. I have a grandson to start laying some groundwork with. I'll have to be subtle about it.'

Both Grace and Hamish snorted.

'Oh, really? The two of you? I expect it from you Hamish McKenzie, but I thought better of you, Grace Elliott.' She spun on her heel and shot them a wink before exiting the pub with a swish of her red silk kimono dress and gold scarf, her white cane clacking on the slate-tiled floor. 'See you both at my place, six sharp.'

Hamish leaned back and held his stomach as he guffawed, while Grace leaned forward and laughed.

Squeezed around Anne's dining table, Grace and Hamish presented the idea to Sam. At the mention of a library, Addie stopped her colouring in on the sofa and came to stand beside Anne.

Sam sat very still, his eyes blank, staring at the now empty bowl of korma curry in the middle of the table.

'Why the bookshop?' he asked, not looking up.

Hamish started with all the logical reasons but Grace put her hand on the old man's arm and he stopped.

'Books are a part of its soul,' she said, her voice soft. 'I could feel it the day I went in there. It seems like that's where a library should live. That only a library can bring that space back to life.'

Silence.

Addie walked around the table and climbed into Sam's lap. She reached up and patted him on the cheek, her tiny fingers lost in his thick beard.

'Mummy wouldn't want you to be sad anymore. That's not why she left.'

Anne shot Grace a look, full of fear. Sam lifted Addie off his lap and pushed his chair back, standing.

'I need to leave.' He turned and walked out.

Addie ran after him, but Hamish held her back. 'Daddy needs a little time to think. Come read with your old uncle Hamish.'

Grace sat in silence at Anne's dining table as the old lady made a pot of tea. Easing herself onto the chair next to Grace, Anne poured them each a cup and took a sip.

'What do you know, Grace, about what happened to Felicity?'

'Sam told me she died. But I've pieced together other fragments. The bookshop and the book club both have something to do with the story.'

Anne nodded. 'Felicity was killed seven years ago in a terrible accident after book club. We never met again after that. Until now. And Sam had no desire to keep the bookshop open.' She added another sugar to her tea and stirred. 'Sam took Felicity's accident so hard. I know losing her was tragic, but I've always sensed there was something more to it. Something he's never shared about that night. He's always carried the burden so heavily.'

'What do you mean, Anne?' Grace's mind was racing. Did they have a fight? Was Felicity's accident Sam's fault?

'I don't know. But I'm hoping you might be able to help.'

'Me?'

Anne pushed her teacup aside. 'Grace, I know it's a terrible ask, but maybe you can find out for me.'

Grace reeled. Yes, she'd wanted to solve the mystery of what happened to book club, but that was when it was an item to be ticked off her bucket list. Now there were real people involved, real feelings. Very real feelings. She couldn't cheat Sam out of secrets. 'Oh, Anne, I don't think . . .'

Anne raised her hand. 'I know, I know. I feel terrible asking. But as I creep towards the inevitable, I have to know Sam and Addie will be all right. And I don't think he can be if there's something awful hanging over him.'

Grace stood and paced the room. 'Anne. I understand where you're coming from. But sometimes people keep things to themselves for good reason.' That was one thing Grace understood in her bones.

'But—'

Grace stopped in front of Anne and took her hands. 'I won't force Sam to tell me anything. But if he does, I'll encourage him to talk to you too.' She could see the disappointment in Anne's eyes. 'That's the best I can offer you.'

Anne shook her head. 'If we can't get Sam to move past whatever it is that's holding him back, we won't convince him to use the shop for the library. Your idea will sink before you even start.'

It was a low attempt at manipulation and Grace should have been mad at Anne. But she understood why Anne was trying to coerce Grace in this way. Desperate people did desperate things.

'Anne. I'm sorry. I realise how worried you are, but I can't do that to Sam.'

Tears glistened in Anne's eyes. 'I understand. You are a true friend.'

'Then maybe that friendship will see him open up to me.'

'Maybe.' Poor Anne looked so defeated.

Grace only hoped there was enough time.

Just before sunrise, Grace padded into the small kitchen of the cottage and made some toast. She'd tossed and turned all night and finally gave up on the idea of sleep. It was 5 am. Not long till the winter sun would be rising. She flicked through her journal and stopped at one of the latest entries.

Could she? Should she? She would never be brave enough to do it back home.

Yes. She could. She grabbed a towel and headed out into the pre-dawn hour.

Standing on the sand of Rocky Beach on the far side of the island – safer than the beach near town, she figured – Grace looked at the dark ocean before her.

She was really going to do this.

She stripped off her clothes and ran into the water completely naked.

The cold took her breath away as she jumped through the waves, dolphin-diving a few times before she got used to the chill. Then she turned over on her back and floated on the ebb and flow, looking up at the waking sky, watching the stars disappear one by one.

She watched the sky turn from pale indigo to grey to orange as the water lapped her bare skin, a sense of calm surrounding her.

'Grace!' Shout. Splash. Shout.

Grace startled at the frantic sounds coming from the direction of the shore. Suddenly a pair of arms wrapped around her body. She folded over, trying to get away. Her head went underwater as she gulped for air, then she came back up. 'What the—'

'It's okay, Grace. I've got you,' a familiar voice said as she was dragged, spluttering, coughing and gasping, onto the sand.

'What the hell are you doing, Sam?' She spat seawater out of her mouth. 'Are you crazy?' Salt stung her eyes, her nose. 'You nearly drowned me.'

'I thought you were—'

'Thought I was what?' She suddenly remembered she was completely naked, and wrapped one arm across her breasts and used the other used to cover her lower region.

'I'm sorry.' He turned his back. 'I thought . . . I couldn't let you . . .'

Grace scrambled over the sand to where she'd left her clothes and wrapped the towel she'd brought with her around her body.

'What are you doing here?' She marched back to Sam. 'And why are you trying to kill me?'

He shook his head, his back still turned. 'I was walking. Couldn't sleep last night. I needed to clear my head. And I saw your clothes on the sand.'

'Look at me, Sam.'

He turned around. 'And you were so still in the water, I thought—'

'I was swimming.' Grace's anger gave way to confusion.

'What? Oh god. I'm so sorry. It's just, when I saw your body, it all came back. I . . .' His eyes narrowed. 'You're shivering.'

'Yes.'

He went to wrap his arms around her but she pushed him away. 'You're wet'

'Oh.' He looked down at his sodden clothes as if he hadn't realised. 'Yes. I'm sorry.' He stepped back, then forward again.

'Sam? What's going on?'

His shoulders slumped, his chest heaved with gulping breaths. 'The kiln is on.'

'What?' He had really lost his mind.

'You need to dry off. You're shaking like a leaf. My kiln is on. My studio will be warm.'

As strangely as Sam was acting, the promise of imminent warmth appealed deeply to Grace. She followed him up the beach and along the path to his studio. Sam opened the door to his garage and the rush of heat took Grace's breath away.

'I started the kiln before going for a walk,' he said. 'I thought working today might help sort through my thoughts.'

Grace nodded. She had been trying to do the exact same thing.

All thought stopped, though, when she looked around the open space. This wasn't a studio. It was a gallery. Every wall was lined with shelves, and every shelf was covered in bowls, vases, plates, cups and sculptures of every possible size and style imaginable. It was incredible.

Sam wrapped a heavy blanket around her; his gentle touch in complete contrast to his frantic thrashing down at the beach.

He moved away from her into the centre of the studio. As her eyes followed him, she took in his work.

She recognised Anne's influence on one shelf, the blue and indigo ink flowing over the white clay. On one wall she saw bowls like her own, with delicate flowers sprayed around the edges. On another wall, modern, abstract pieces sat beside traditional ones. Large bright pots full of joy. Smooth, delicate teacups made with love and gentleness. Rough, rugged bowls with jagged, angry ink marks. Every shelf told a story, and Grace felt every emotion emanating from each piece. Joy. Love. Pain. Heartache.

Then she turned around, and her breath left her body. One corner of the garage was occupied by shelf after shelf of the most exquisite art Grace had ever seen. Bowls and plates and cups of blues and pinks and greens, with veins of gold running through them. There seemed to be no two pieces alike. In some the gold was thin as hair, in others thick as ribbon.

She reached her hand to touch them, then pulled it back.

'That's kintsugi.' Sam's deep voice was soft.

She turned around and he was standing there, right behind her.

'It's beautiful. I've never seen anything like it.'

He reached past her and grabbed a bowl, his arm brushing her shoulder, her skin tingling at the touch.

'I found a kintsugi master in Sydney to teach me the traditional way, to learn a little about my heritage. My Ojiichan – my grandfather – was a potter.'

'Tadashi?'

He nodded. 'Kintsugi is the art of fixing broken pottery with gold. It translates to *golden joinery*.' He took a bowl and placed it in her hands, his eyes boring into her. With his other hand he guided her fingers over the smooth lines of gold.

She couldn't breathe, couldn't move.

'They believe by using gold . . .'

His sweet warm breath danced over her cheek.

'. . . the broken pieces become more beautiful. The scars are a part of its history and make it unique. I had quite a few scars there for a while. Still do.'

She turned her back to him. 'What do you do when the pieces are so broken there isn't enough gold to put them back together?'

'I haven't figured that bit out yet.'

'Even with all this practice?'

Warm air danced down her back and she turned around. Sam had stepped away, his eyes dark. The space between them was thick with emotion.

'Sam? What happened just now? In the water?' Even if he had thought she was in trouble, that didn't explain his frenetic tearing at her.

Grace could see the conflict in his eyes. He opened his mouth, then closed it.

Grace rested her hand on his damp chest. 'Sam?'

He looked into her eyes. 'When we're both dry and warm, will you come for a walk with me?'

'What?'

'I'll wait outside for you to get dressed.' He pointed to the pile of her clothes he'd put on a stool by the studio entrance. 'And I'll get changed.'

Once dressed, Grace stepped outside to where Sam, now dry, was waiting for her. 'Do we need to get Addie?' she asked, glancing at the house.

He shook his head. 'She stayed overnight with Anne.'

In silence they walked across the island. Grace didn't know why they couldn't talk in the studio, but she figured there must be a reason. Then they reached the lighthouse and it became clear.

'I hate this place,' he growled. 'I came up here the other day for the first time since Flick died. After our sunset together.'

Grace nodded, not wanting to mention that she'd seen him.

'I didn't think I'd ever return to it, but then you . . . you're here and everything is . . . different.'

She understood. Meeting Sam had changed everything for Grace too.

'When Addie was born,' Sam continued, 'Flick struggled, you know, adjusting to a newborn. But we'd got through it. At least, I thought we had.' Sam reached out and brushed the lighthouse wall, his hand falling with a thud to his side. 'But before Addie's second birthday . . .' His voice lowered and cracked. 'Felicity walked off this cliff.'

Grace gasped. Oh god. Her stomach clenched.

'After book club. As we were packing up the chairs in the book-shop, she slipped away. None of us noticed at first. When I realised, I went looking for her and as I rounded that hill'—he pointed behind Grace—'I saw her. She jumped.'

The weight of Sam's words landed on Grace, the last piece of the puzzle dropped into place.

There is something at work in my soul, which I do not understand . . .

The line from *Frankenstein* Felicity had highlighted.

Grace's heart tore open. 'Oh, Sam.'

'I knew. I knew something wasn't right, but I made excuses. Little things mostly. Like when I'd catch her crying in Addie's room in the middle of the night, she said it was hormones. And I believed her. The house was always spotless. Too spotless. But I just thought she was Superwoman. She'd pull out of plans at the last minute, even with Shellie and Phil, and say she was tired. Of course she was tired. She had a baby.' He paused. 'A million little things. All perfectly reasonable. And what mum doesn't get the baby blues? None of those things ring alarm bells, right? But all together?'

Big pleading eyes stared at Grace. She moved towards him but he turned away.

'There was one night.' His voice was soft, broken. 'I didn't think anything of it at the time, but now, every day I wonder, was that it? Was that the point she decided?'

Grace rested her hand on his back.

'I woke in the middle of the night to Addie crying. It was about a month before . . . before *that* night. I never heard Addie cry in the night. Flick always had it covered. I got up and Flick was standing in Addie's doorway, hugging a pillow to her chest, staring blindly into the room. I put Flick to bed, figured she was just exhausted. And I settled Addie. In the morning Flick was fine. Seemed better than she had in ages.'

Sam sank to the ground, his knees swallowed by the long grass, his tortured face staring out at the water.

'Everything was fine in those weeks before book club. I thought. But then . . . and when I got home after she jumped, I found a stuffed toy in Addie's cot. A superhero bear. And a note. *Because Mummy will always protect you.* How did I miss it?' He sobbed. A guttural sound escaped from deep within. 'How did I not see?'

His back heaved under Grace's touch. Kneeling beside him, she ran her arm across his shoulders and he turned, burying his face in her chest. She held him there till his body eventually stilled.

'When I saw you floating in the water this morning, I was back there, to that night. I couldn't save her. I had to save you.' He pulled back, his face drawing level with hers. 'Why? Why couldn't I save her?'

With a soft voice, Grace found her words. 'When someone wants to hide something, something important, something from deep within them, nothing can stop them. They can hide it so deep, no one will see it or sense it. If Felicity didn't want you to know how much pain she was in, even if you had suspected something wasn't quite right, she never would have let you know how badly she was hurting.'

Sam's cheeks were stained with tears, his eyes red. 'But why? Why didn't she come to me, ask me for help?'

'I don't know what was going on deep inside Felicity, but I do know that people often keep their pain to themselves so they don't burden others. They don't want to hurt the ones they love the most. I suspect Felicity was trying to protect you.'

Pushing himself up, Sam stood, shaking. 'Protect me? How is losing her protecting me?'

Standing, Grace took a step back, allowing the air between them. There was never enough air. Her chest tightened.

'Sometimes . . .' She chose her words carefully. 'Sometimes the darkness is stronger than the light. And when darkness is within, it can take away all hope. And without hope . . .' She paused. 'When you believe, when you *know* the darkness isn't going to fade, it can feel like there's no choice.'

Sam looked into her eyes. 'How do you . . . you sound like you know . . .'

Grace had to tell him. She had to try to help him understand.

'I have cancer.' She watched his face cloud over as her words sunk in. 'There was a time about two years ago I lost hope. The treatment was beating me up, it was too hard to take. I wanted out. I wanted the pain to stop. And not just the physical pain. The despair. And I wanted for everyone around me to be able to get on with their lives. My mum put everything on hold for me. I didn't want her to have to endure it anymore. I wanted to protect her from the pain I was causing her. I didn't want to be a burden anymore. And I wanted my pain to stop. I never told anyone how I felt. Never let on. No one knew the darkness inside me.'

Sam touched her cheek with a shaking hand. 'But you didn't . . .'

'No. Nearly though. I was moments away.'

'What stopped you?' His voice was barely a whisper.

'Honestly? I don't know. Chance? I hesitated. Only for a moment. I don't know why. And I caught a glimpse of my journal. I opened a page and read a list. Then another. Then another. Then it was morning. I picked up the phone and called my doctor.'

He wiped the tear that fell from her cheek.

'I was lucky.' She shrugged. 'I found one small moment in each day to get me through to the next. That's all there is. One small moment after the other.'

'Why, Grace? Why couldn't I help Felicity find the small moments to hold on to?'

'Because she didn't want you to.'

Grace let the words sink in.

'This is not your fault, Sam. And it isn't Felicity's either. She was sick.'

He lurched forward, gulping air. With shaking arms Grace caught him and together they sank into the grass. Time stood still. Minutes passed. An hour.

'Does anyone else know?' she whispered eventually. 'That it wasn't an accident?'

'No.' He shook his head. 'How can I tell anyone what happened? How can I possibly explain it to Addie?' His face contorted in despair.

Addie. Grace swallowed hard. Is this what she knew? The pieces of Grace's shattered heart dissolved. How could she help him unpack so much turmoil? There was so much hidden within the wounds of his soul.

'Sam.' She wiped the tears from his cheeks. 'You haven't even told yourself the full story yet. Telling me this today, sharing the agony you've been holding on to for seven years, is big and painful and difficult. And only the beginning. You need to be gentle with yourself. It's okay to take the time to work through this and heal and forgive yourself. And then, when the time is right for you, out of the love you remember, instead of the guilt, then you'll find the right words. You'll be able to tell Felicity's story. Tell Addie how much her mum loved her. ' She held him tight until his tears subsided.

He gulped. 'How do I ever move on?' His voice cracked as he pulled away slightly.

'Maybe you don't. Not completely, anyway. I know that doesn't help. I know you want answers. But sometimes there aren't any.' Grace searched for the right words. 'And maybe that's not what it's about. It's like your pottery, and my scars.'

She took his hand and pressed it against her belly. Looking down, she swallowed hard. 'We can't move on from our scars. They are part of who we are. It's only when we accept that, that we can be whole again.' She drew in a deep breath. 'Pieced together with beautiful, tragic gold.'

Twenty-four

Anne poured Addie a glass of milk while her great-granddaughter slathered a frightening amount of Vegemite onto her toast. Anne could barely stomach a thin scraping of the sticky, salty black spread, but Addie preferred hers as thick as concrete. Always had. Just like her mother.

Oh Felicity. Anne had lost count of the number of times she'd seen the young Felicity she'd watched grow up in Addie. The way she tilted her head when reading, the way she said sketti, her penchant for unpalatable foods – the only two people she'd ever known to put Milo on their muesli.

Without Grace's help, she didn't know if she'd be able to find the answers to the questions she had. She didn't know if she had the strength to. She couldn't be mad at Grace though. What she'd asked of her was sneaky and manipulative. If anything, the fact Grace had refused to be her spy proved she was a true friend to Sam. Perhaps something even more. Anne's phone chimed with a message from Sam. Relief washed over her. Could she keep Addie for a bit longer?

Of course.

Addie took the last bite of toast, her mouth ringed with Vegemite.

'What do you say to a Saturday morning painting session with your old Obaachan?'

'I say yes.' Addie punctuated her agreement with a short sharp nod of her head.

Inside the studio, Anne set Addie up with inks and brushes and canvas offcuts, and settled herself in front of her sketchbook.

With Addie humming beside her, she closed her eyes waiting for inspiration to strike. But all that came were memories.

Wattle Island, 1953

'Welcome home, Anne.' Hadley Follett stood on the dock with his hands in the pockets of his brown corduroy trousers. He nodded at Tadashi. 'Congratulations on your nuptials.'

Anne smiled. Before they'd left Sydney she'd wired Mrs Forster to see if there was a chance of getting her old job in the post office back. Obviously the island grapevine was working well.

Hadley shook Tadashi's hand. 'The eldest McCormack kid left the island last month. It's rendered Dad and me a bit shorthanded, to tell you the truth. If you're not afraid of some hard work, I've got a job for you.'

'Thank you.' Tadashi bowed.

While they were in no danger of starvation, thanks to Hamish's very generous wedding gift in the envelope Tadashi had opened as Wattle Island appeared on the horizon, and they would have a roof over their heads thanks to Bess's cottage, they were both keen to find work. They wanted to lead simple but productive lives.

'Good. Young ones these days don't like getting their hands dirty. I'll help you with those.' Hadley picked up Anne's suitcase and they headed towards Soldiers' Way.

Anne took a deep breath before stepping inside the cottage. It felt somehow empty without Bess's stern presence. Tadashi walked around acquainting himself with the place.

Anne couldn't bring herself to take Bess's larger room as her own, so she unpacked their things in her old room. She placed the empty suitcases on top of her wardrobe and reached under the bed for the box she'd left there, pulling out the blue-and-white vase she'd stashed away when she'd fled the island.

She was home. Funny. She'd always thought that Sydney was home. But in leaving the island, in finding her life with Tadashi and returning now, she realised Wattle Island was where she belonged.

She walked out of their bedroom and found Tadashi at the back door looking out at the garden shed.

'That would make a great studio,' Anne whispered in his ear, placing the vase on the window sill next to the door.

'It would.' He turned and wrapped his arm around her waist. 'We can set that up another day, though.' He kissed her, pulling her body into his, sliding his hand down her back. 'Mrs Sato.'

Through the kiss Anne smiled and Tadashi picked her up, carrying her into the bedroom.

Life on the island settled into a routine of work and art and reading, and a year after Anne and Tadashi had returned, Anne was heavily pregnant with their first child.

At the post office she had to manoeuvre carefully around the counter, her bulging belly always in the way now. Every day for the past year she'd taken her lunch by the fountain, a sandwich in one hand, a book in the other.

She lowered herself down on the bench with a groan.

'That looks heavy.' Maree strode by, no longer the little girl she had been when Anne left the island three years ago.

'It is.' Anne smiled.

'When are you due?'

'Another month.'

'Nifty.'

It was very nifty. She and Tadashi couldn't have been happier.

'And what are your plans, Maree?'

'I'll be off this island faster than you can say Jack Robinson. I'm not going to end up like Ruth. Three kids already? No thank you.'

'She seems happy, and Ray is a decent guy,' Anne said. He and Tadashi had formed a tentative friendship, despite Ruth's scowling and whispers that Anne's husband was 'not one of us'.

'Maybe. But I'm going to travel the world before I even think of settling down. Maybe I'll go herd goats in Mongolia.'

Anne had no idea if it was even possible to herd goats in Mongolia, but she could see Maree doing it if it was. Chalk and cheese, her and Ruth. It was hard to believe they were sisters.

'I think you should.' Anne nodded.

'What's that?' Maree pointed to Anne's book.

She handed it over. '*Little Women*. One of my all-time favourites. A tale about sisters, and about one in particular who has very strong ideas about not settling for what's expected of her, but rather following her own path. Have you read it?'

Maree shook her head.

'I think you'd like it. Why don't you take this one and see how you go.' Anne ignored the face Maree pulled. 'Give it a try. You never know.'

A week later Maree found her on the bench by the fountain again. She handed Anne the book back. 'Do you have anything else?'

'Come by the cottage this afternoon and you can have a look.'

When Anne returned home there was a parcel waiting from Hamish. Tadashi must have grabbed it directly off the boat this morning. A note inside read, *I hope these make lovely additions to your shelves.*

Over the past year, Anne's collection of books had grown considerably. She'd been writing to Hamish every month since arriving back home and he'd been sending her novels with each reply. His letters often seemed sad to her, but if she asked him how he was he simply brushed it aside. Every now and then he shared news of Simone and Colin, now married. Both had forgiven Hamish, though their friendship hadn't been quite the same since, and they didn't socialise much anymore.

He'd thrown himself into his work and would soon be leaving Walsh and Walsh to become a partner in his father's firm. The last few letters he'd mentioned a chap named Tristan, whom he'd met at the Scottish Society. He enjoyed the bagpipes and was teaching Hamish how to play them.

Come visit us here on the island, she wrote to him many times, and he always promised that one day he would.

When Maree stopped by, Anne had just finished putting her new titles on the shelf. Maree let out a whistle.

'And you'll lend me any of these I like?'

'Of course.'

After Maree left, *I Capture the Castle* in hand, Anne pottered around the cottage until Tadashi came home from his day on the farm. Their evenings usually started in the studio where Tadashi would teach Anne new techniques or they'd each work on their own projects, followed by dinner, often a picnic at the lighthouse by lantern-light. Their lives were simple. Happy.

As the last of winter melted into spring, the change in weather saw the wattle trees that skirted the town in full bloom. The soft yellow pompoms formed golden clouds that hugged the trees. Anne had stopped working, her belly too cumbersome, and she spent her days at the cottage completing projects, including, at Tadashi's suggestion, painting their front door a deep shade of ocean blue.

At the beginning of spring, Anne went into labour. Ruth attended, as well as Mrs McCormack. The combined experience of their own births helped Anne bring her baby boy safely into the world.

Hamish Samuel Sato was the most perfect baby ever to exist, according to Tadashi, and Anne was inclined to agree. And he grew and amazed them every day.

A warm northerly breeze heralded the orange days of summer and change. Maree had left the island and was travelling the world. The last postcard Anne received had been sent from Italy. Anne had no doubt she would make it to Mongolia after all. Ruth was pregnant again, and while they were still not what Anne would call friends, there was an easy truce between them since she'd helped deliver baby Hamish.

With the sun beating down at midday, Anne made her way to the lighthouse, baby Hamish on one hip, a picnic basket on the other. The lighthouse was undergoing major repair work and the whole town was chipping in. While no longer operational, it was an icon on the island and the residents wanted to maintain it.

Ruth's children sat on a blanket in the grass on the headland as she poured cold drinks for the men. Mrs McCormack and Mrs Forster handed out sandwiches. Anne placed baby Hamish down and Ruth's eldest daughter Betty came bounding over to play with him. Anne opened the picnic basket and offered everyone fruit and more sandwiches.

'Come on, men,' Ray said after lunch, clapping his hands. 'These repairs aren't going to take care of themselves.' He kissed Ruth's forehead and the men got back to work on the jobs scheduled for the day – removing flaking paint and fixing broken windows.

Hadley and Ray climbed up the scaffolding, followed by Tadashi. Two of the McCormack kids joined them.

On the ground, the women and young children chatted and played. Anne looked around, committing the scene to memory. Perhaps she'd paint it tonight. She still wasn't very good at rendering figures, but there was a feeling here today she wanted to capture. Change. Hope. Joy.

Ruth sat beside her and handed her a book: Jane Austen's *Emma*. 'Maree left this for me to give you before she took off overseas.'

'Have you read it?' Anne asked.

'No.'

'Why don't you hang on to it, then? I think you'll like it.'

A crack echoed over the headland and Anne turned around. Ruth screamed.

Part of the scaffolding had collapsed and Ray was hanging from the top of the lighthouse, in the gap that had opened between two sections.

'Ray!' Ruth ran forward, as her husband dangled precariously by one hand.

Just before Ray lost his grip, Tadashi swung from the other side of the scaffolding and grabbed his arm. Ruth gasped. Anne stepped up beside her and put her arm around her shoulder. Mrs McCormack sent one of the older children into town to get more help. Betty held onto baby Hamish's hand, both too young to know what was happening, of course, but sensing the fear in the air.

There was a creak and the part of the scaffolding to which

Tadashi was clinging with one hand swayed. Ray was still holding tightly to his other arm. With the strength a lifetime of physical labour afforded, Tadashi managed to fling Ray safely to the other side of the scaffolding. Hadley caught Ray in an awkward embrace that saw them both tumble onto the landing. They scrambled down to the ground and Ruth ran to her husband, embracing him fiercely.

The effort to swing Ray to safety, though, had caused the scaffolding Tadashi was still on to sway even more.

'Get down!' Hadley shouted. 'Now!'

But the wooden supports were still shifting, making increasingly loud groans and creaks, until there was a terrifying snapping sound and the supports gave way. The platforms collapsed on top of each other, tumbling to the ground below, swallowing Tadashi in the rubble.

'Tadashi!' Anne screamed, and her world went black and cold.

––––––––

'Obaachan?' Addie pulled on Anne's voluminous sleeve. 'What do you think?'

Anne blinked and looked at Addie's picture. 'It's lovely, pet.' She had no idea what the blue lines and black blobs were meant to be.

Addie frowned and pointed to the blank page in front of Anne. 'Why didn't you paint anything?'

'Oh, I got a little lost in my memories there for a bit.'

Addie patted her hand. 'But if they're your memories, how can you get lost in them? You already know the way.'

'Well, you know how sometimes you need to go to the bathroom at night and it's dark and you stumble around a bit?'

Addie nodded.

'It's a little like that.'

'So why don't you just turn the light on?'

Anne had no answer.

Voices from outside floated on the breeze and Addie ran out of the studio, recognising them. Following behind, Anne made her way to the side of the cottage and there on the path out front was Sam, with Grace very close beside him.

Sam picked Addie up into a tight embrace, and kissed Anne on her forehead. He appeared a little harrowed, though not upset exactly. Grace seemed exhausted. Anne looked between the two of them, unsure what had happened, but certain that whatever it was, it was big.

'Good morning.' Anne narrowed her gaze.

'Grace and I have been talking. A lot.' Sam squeezed Grace's hand. 'I think we should do this library thing.'

Anne threw her arms around Sam and Grace, squishing a clapping Addie somewhere in the middle.

Twenty-five

Grace left Sam at Anne's. He needed to be with his family right now. Even if he couldn't tell Anne the truth yet, he'd find comfort in her presence.

Opening the door to her cottage, Grace kicked off her shoes, took off her clothes and crawled into bed. Pulling the red striped doona up under her chin, she closed her eyes and fell into a deep sleep that lasted all day and through the night.

In the morning she woke to find a text message from Sam.

Lunch at the pub with Hamish? Addie is pressing me to have the library finished by tomorrow! Grace laughed at Addie's enthusiasm.

When Grace got to the pub, it wasn't just Hamish and Sam waiting for her. Anne was also there. And Ruth. The scowl that usually adorned her face was replaced with – could it be? – a smile. That made Grace very nervous.

'Wonderful idea, Grace,' Ruth greeted her as she slid into the booth next to Anne, and opposite Sam, who'd trimmed his beard close. Grace's heart quickened.

They spent the afternoon discussing detailed plans and then they went to the shop, where Sam had organised Robbie from the airfield to meet them all in his other role as the island's best contractor.

Before opening the shop door, Sam paused.

Grace touched his arm. 'It's okay,' she whispered.

He reached for her hand, and they entered the space together.

Inside, Grace took the lead, explaining her vision to Robbie, while Ruth, Hamish and Anne sorted through the pots and pans in the cafe kitchen. Robbie took notes and measurements and said he would get back to them tomorrow with an estimate.

'I haven't thanked you. For yesterday.' Sam stood beside Grace after Robbie left.

'You don't need to.'

'Yes. I do. For the first time I'm seeing what happened in a different light. I don't know if I'll ever forgive myself for not realising how much pain she must have been in. But this morning when Addie crawled into bed to wake me up, well, I think that's the first time in seven years that anger and guilt and pain weren't gnawing away in the pit of my stomach.'

Grace let out a slow breath as Sam ran the back of his hand over her cheek. 'Thank you.'

Before she could say 'you're welcome' or anything else equally banal, he turned and left the shop.

Outside, Ruth and Hamish bade them goodnight, but Anne hung back.

'You've worked a miracle here, Grace.'

'Not yet, I haven't.' Grace shook her head.

'I'm not talking about the library. Though it is going to be fabulous. I'm talking about Sam. Whatever you two discussed the other night, he's a changed man.'

On the surface, yes. And perhaps inside, the initial spark of healing had begun. But Grace knew it would take time before he was ready to share his story, Felicity's story. Grace wished she could tell Anne what she wanted to know, but it wasn't her truth to tell. It was Sam's, in his own time. 'I hope that if I tell you Sam is going to be okay, that maybe that will be enough solace for you.'

Anne ran her hand over the scarf wrapped around her head. 'I—'

'Can you trust me on this, Anne?'

'I don't know. But I can trust what I see in him.'

Grace nodded and hoped that would be enough for Anne. 'Shall we?' She held out her arm and Anne took it. Together they walked up Soldiers' Way.

For the next few days, Grace spent most of her time on the phone or her laptop, filling out paperwork, applying for council permits, ordering from suppliers. Trades were pretty thin on the ground on Wattle Island. If she had all the time in the world then it wouldn't matter how long the fit-out took. But she didn't. Thankfully, Hamish was around to help her.

Every afternoon Addie popped by Grace's cottage and together they planned the children's section of the library. Some of Addie's ideas were great (caterpillar-shaped lounges); some not so much (a vending machine dispensing fairy floss into the air to make edible indoor clouds).

Sam picked Addie up each evening, and each evening he lingered at the door, talking to Grace. He would never come inside, yet he didn't seem to want to leave.

It would take him time, she knew.

On Thursday night, for the third time that week, June rang.

'You need to slow down,' she said. 'What's the hurry with this library?'

Grace shifted in her seat. 'Well, the sooner it's done, the sooner I can come home.'

June let out a sigh. 'Do you want me to come and help? Surely there's something I can do.'

Grace did want to see her mum. She missed her. But there was still so much to do before it was time for that.

'There's not really much you can do. Unless you know how to rewire a building.'

'Ha, ha. I could look after you.'

'I'm being looked after, Mum.' And she was. Between Anne and Ruth bringing her food and Hamish helping with the mountain of paperwork, she had all the looking after she needed. And Shellie checked in on her when no one else was around.

'It's been so long since I've seen you, Grace. If you don't come home soon, I'm swimming over there.'

Grace laughed. 'Goodnight, Mum.'

Book club was on again tomorrow night, which meant it had already been a month since she'd arrived on Wattle Island. How had that happened? Luckily, she'd read *Big Little Lies* ages ago, as there'd been no time lately to enjoy such pleasure.

The following evening the book club was abuzz with talk of the new library. There were four new members who joined, even though they hadn't read the book. Sam took part too, sitting in the book club circle, a copy of the novel in his hands.

With encouragement from Grace, Anne led the discussion, taking a leaf out of Grace's playbook by asking a question first up that anyone could answer. 'If we had a theme for a school fundraiser, what would it be?'

Grace sat back and watched, relieved not to have to think or speak. Her exhaustion was overwhelming.

Ruth, of course, didn't like 'those random snippets of police interview. What a silly gimmick', but Hamish thought they added some needed colour. The character of Celeste was discussed at length, and Grace let her attention drift.

'Hey,' Sam whispered in her ear. 'Are you okay?'

'Yeah.' She forced a smile and focused on the group once more.

'Well, I loved Bonnie.' Maree leaned into the semicircle. 'The way she bottled everything up for so long and then *boom*, it exploded. I thought that was pretty realistic.'

Sam took Grace's hand.

'And the way her friends stood by her.' Shellie nodded. 'You can get through anything with the right people beside you.'

Sam tightened his hold.

'Oh, rubbish,' Ruth interjected. 'As if not one of them would turn.'

Grace laughed. So did Sam.

With the discussion in full flight, Grace got up to slip away. Sam followed her to the door.

'Early night?'

'Yes. This lot will be going for hours at this rate.'

'I'll walk you home.'

'No, stay. Anne will skin you alive if you bail on her book club your first time back.'

'She won't skin you?'

'I'm building her a library. I'm pretty sure it's my get out of jail free card.'

He laughed. 'Do you have plans tomorrow?'

'Nope. I was intending to take most of the day off from all this library stuff.'

'Would you like to have lunch?'

Grace narrowed her eyes. 'What do you have in mind?'

A broad grin spread across Sam's face. 'Meet me on Rocky Beach at midday.'

Despite her fatigue, Grace felt a little thrill at the idea of seeing Sam again so soon. Just the two of them.

Grace had no idea what to wear to a mysterious lunch on a beach in late winter with a guy she'd realised not too long ago that she genuinely liked. There wasn't a book or magazine in any library that could help her with that. She went for casual. Jeans and her mustard-coloured long-sleeved T-shirt. As she left the cottage she smoothed her hands over her short hair, checking in the mirror that none of it was sticking up in clumps as it sometimes liked to.

She checked her face, too, though she wasn't sure why. She hadn't worn make-up since her diagnosis – easily irritated skin being one of the fun side effects of her condition – so there wasn't much she could do about what nature had given her.

Right. Stop stalling, Grace. She breathed out and headed towards Rocky Beach as slowly as she could. She knew what Linh would say: 'Just go for it.' And she wanted to, but with everything she now knew about what Sam had been through, everything she was going through, it wasn't that simple.

As she rounded the hill past Follett's farm the black boulders that surrounded this stretch of the island came into view, glistening in the bright midday sun. Then she saw Sam, standing on a red checked picnic blanket in the middle of the cove. Next to him were two deck chairs on either side of a small white table laden with food.

She raised her hand to her mouth and stared at Sam.

'I know this isn't exactly what's in that journal of yours, seafood picnic on a tropical beach, but I figured . . .' He shrugged.

'You can't go chasing your bucket list items while you're stuck here building us a library, so I thought I could bring a bucket list to you.'

'Oh, Sam.'

Grace kicked off her shoes and walked down the sand, stopping an inch away from him. She reached up her hand and ran it along his beautifully trimmed beard. 'It's perfect.'

'Sorry it isn't . . .' He looked around.

Grace took his hand. 'It's perfect,' she repeated.

He pulled a chair out for her. 'Would you like to take a seat?'

She did, and he moved his chair to sit beside her.

Over a lunch of fresh prawns, salad and bread rolls, they talked about their childhoods and jobs, all the things they didn't know about each other yet. Well, nearly all the things.

'Shellie, Phil and I once set fire to Hadley Follett's hay bales.'

Grace widened her eyes. 'You did not.'

He nodded. 'Yep. It was an accident. We were sixteen, seventeen. Phil was showing off in front of Shellie – he'd had a crush on her since we were ten – and he'd found some old fireworks. We were in Hadley's main paddock and I had the great idea to make a castle out of the bales from which to launch them.'

Grace smiled. 'Oh no.'

'Oh yes. He lit the cracker and it fell over, exploded right into the bale castle and *whoosh*, the whole thing went up.'

'You're lucky none of you were hurt.'

'Phil was. Burned his hand and Shellie had to patch him up. I reckon that's the day she decided to become a doctor. And the day she realised she loved him.'

'And they're still together.' Grace shook her head. 'They seem such an unlikely couple.'

'Yeah, I guess. But they were destined for each other.'

'I don't know about destiny.' Grace took a sip of water. 'But clearly they're happy together.'

'They are.' Sam opened a container of strawberries and offered them to Grace. 'You don't believe in destiny?'

She took a strawberry and bit into it. 'I guess I think relying on some mystical force doesn't do you any good. If you want something, you make it happen. Don't wait around for fate, or for the time to be right. Because you never know how much—'

'Time you have.' He wiped away the sweet sticky strawberry juice that dripped down her chin and traced the line of her jaw. 'Hence the bucket list, huh? Not leaving those dreams to chance.'

'Something like that.' Her pulse throbbed at his touch.

'Well, whether it was fate or not that brought you here,' he said, leaning in, 'I'm very grateful.'

He moved his hand behind her head, pulling her closer. He stopped, looked in her eyes. She closed the distance and they kissed. His lips soft, the sweet tang of strawberry lingering. She pressed into him. And the world around them dissolved.

After their picnic they walked along the beach, hand in hand. Grace had no desire to put a stop to this, even though she knew she should. A few stolen moments of happiness after everything she'd been through. Was it selfish of her to want that so desperately?

They reached the end of the beach and turned back and, with the afternoon sun lengthening their shadows, they packed up their picnic.

'Thank you.' Grace hugged Sam. 'You have no idea how much this day has meant to me.'

Running his hands down her back, he pulled her in tighter. 'We don't have to let the day end here.'

'Actually, we do. I have another date.'

Sam drew himself up to his full six-foot-three height. 'Is that so?'

Grace smiled. 'With a very gorgeous book lover, who's going to help me with some online ordering of caterpillar lounges.'

Sam grinned. 'Of course. Addie has been talking about that for days.'

They headed into town to pick up Addie from her playdate and when they arrived home, Grace and Addie got to work on the computer, sitting up at Sam's dining table. Sam watched on from the sofa.

On Sunday morning Sam and Grace stood in the middle of the bookshop.

'Are you sure you're ready for this?' Grace wrapped her arm around his waist.

'To be honest, I don't know.' He looked down at her and lifted her chin with a gentle movement of his hand. He drew in a deep breath and exhaled. 'Yep. Let's do this.'

From the doorway Ruth called out, 'They're here. Shall I let them in?'

Without taking his eyes off Grace, he called back, 'Yep. Let them in.'

Thanks to Ruth, half the town had turned up to help clear out the old bookshop and start the refurbishment. She'd placed herself in the doorway and directed the volunteers in from there.

Grace's first job was to sort through all the books that had been left there these past seven years. Many of them were damaged, moisture having seeped into the pages, causing mould to grow in them. It broke her heart to have to throw them out. The few that were salvageable she dusted off and would put into the library once it was complete.

For the rest of the week, teams of volunteers came in, removing this and tidying that. Phil came every day, as did a small team of tradies led by Robbie. Maree appeared every lunchtime, providing a feast of sandwiches and fruit for the hungry workers.

What surprised Grace, though, was how very helpful Addie was. She had insisted on contributing, and had shown up every day after school, ready to do whatever she could. Grace had been worried she'd get in the way – unintentionally, of course. But Addie worked as hard as any of the tradies, lifting things, carrying things, fetching things for anyone who asked for her help.

On Friday evening, after the tradies had gone and Grace was alone, Shellie popped in.

'This is looking great,' she said, taking in the space. 'How are you coping with the workload?'

There was no point lying. 'It's taking its toll. But it's worth it.'

'Is it?'

'Yes. Have you seen how happy Addie is? Sam?'

Shellie leaned her back against the new counter that had been put in. 'I have. Sam is . . . Sam again. It's wonderful. But I'm worried how much this will take out of him. You two are getting very close.'

The familiar tentacles of guilt wrapped themselves around Grace's heart. 'I won't hurt him.'

'You can't promise that.' Shellie frowned.

'No. But I can promise you I care about him a great deal.'

'I hope that's enough.' Shellie left Grace to wallow in her thoughts. Messy, loving, fearful thoughts. Shellie had every right to look out for Sam. Grace should walk away. She knew that. But she couldn't.

She dragged herself up Soldiers' Way and fell into bed, exhausted. She ached everywhere and found it hard to breathe, her four–six breathing technique getting a serious workout.

June rang as she was about to nod off.

'I'm not liking this. You're working too hard. I can jump on a plane and be there in a heartbeat.'

Grace could hear the concern in her voice. 'I'd love you to come for the opening. Then you can see what all this has been for.'

'When will that be?'

'In a few weeks.' Grace hoped she could pull it off in that time.

June breathed heavily. 'A few weeks then.'

Grace's heavy eyes closed and she drifted off with images of June and the library and Sam dancing through her mind.

On Monday, Grace's hopes of finishing on time were dashed. She'd met with Robbie to go through the numbers and he didn't have good news.

'Six more weeks? That's too long.'

'Maybe a month with more manpower. Three weeks, even.'

Grace shook her head. There was no budget for more men who'd have to be brought over from the mainland. The volunteers had been brilliant so far, but the build was at a point where the only way to move forward quickly would be with a larger team of qualified sparkies, chippies and plumbers.

She thanked Robbie and dragged herself to the fountain, slipping onto the bench, her head bowed into her hands.

'Grace?'

She looked up to see Anne and Hamish strolling towards her.

'Is something wrong?'

Grace filled them in.

'Well, that's how long it will take, I guess,' Anne shrugged. 'Robbie is very good at what he does. You can't rush perfection.' She took Grace's hands. 'And this has to be perfect.'

Grace stood and paced back and forth. 'I just . . .' She looked at Anne and turned away. 'I guess I had it in my head we could have the next book club there.' Not a lie. Not the complete truth.

'We can shift book club to fit in.'

'No,' Grace said with more force than she'd meant to. 'No,' she whispered again.

'Grace, pet, is everything all right?'

'I'm sorry. Once I get an idea in my head . . .' She shrugged.

'Maybe we can work something out.' Anne turned to Hamish.

'I can chat to Robbie. Find out what he needs to get this done by book club.'

Grace pressed her lips together. 'We don't have the budget.'

Hamish took hold of her shoulders. 'What's the good of having money if you don't spend it, hey? Let me take care of it.'

She shook her head. 'I can't let you . . .'

'Hush, lassie. I can't take it with me.'

Anne whispered in Grace's ear, 'And he has *plenty* of it, trust me.'

Grace threw her arms around both of them. 'I'll make sure everything my end is ready too.'

Sitting on the cottage veranda in the late afternoon, Grace looked down to the sea below. It was green and calm today; no wind to whip up white foam. She'd spent the entire day on the phone chasing orders and making sure everything from here on would go smoothly. She had checked, double-checked and cross-checked everything.

And if all went well, in three weeks' time the Wattle Island Community Library would be open. It was amazing what could be achieved when you threw money at a problem.

She stretched her neck and rolled her shoulders, and took another painkiller.

Bouncing up the path came Addie, Sam loping beside her.

'Hey,' he called.

'Hi, Grace.' Addie waved.

When they got to the veranda, Sam embraced Grace and kissed her, his hands tight against her back.

Addie giggled.

'We thought we could cook you dinner, didn't we, Gumnut?'

Addie held up a shopping bag. 'Sketti for three.' Her grin was broad.

Grace forced a smile. She didn't have much of an appetite; hadn't had for the last few days. But she wouldn't disappoint them.

'Excellent. Let's get cooking, then.' She held the door open, the pain in her back still strong, and they headed to the kitchen. 'We can celebrate Hamish coming through with the goods again.'

Grace smiled. Hamish's money could solve a lot of problems, but even it had its limits.

Twenty-six

Anne had no idea why Grace was in such a hurry to get the library finished, though she had to admit she was rather impatient for it herself. Thank god for Hamish.

How many times in her life had she said those words?

Too many.

She hoped Grace wasn't looking to finish the library so she could go home; hoped she wasn't having second thoughts about her connection with Sam. Any idiot could see they were meant for each other. It wasn't in the outward displays of affection. It was the quieter moments – a gentle touch here, a smile there. So much of life's good stuff was in the quiet moments.

As the day's light began to fade, Anne opened the door to her studio, her hip still aching. Shellie had suggested a trip to the mainland to investigate a possible replacement but Anne had swiftly dismissed that idea.

'The only reason I let you get away with sending me to the mainland for treatment when I had my stroke was because I was unconscious,' she'd said.

She set out her ink bottles and closed her eyes, pushing her mind out. Ah. There it was. A memory. An open book. Water splashing off a fountain.

Anne picked up a brush and held it poised over the page.

Wattle Island, 1954

Anne sat alone in the dark, ignoring the knocks at the door; the pleas to be let in.

'Anne Sato.' Ruth's voice pierced the cold night air. 'Open up this minute. You've indulged in self-pity quite long enough.'

Quite long enough? It had only been three days since the accident at the lighthouse. Three years wouldn't be enough for Anne to get used to the idea her Tadashi was gone. Three lifetimes wouldn't be enough.

'Anne.' Ruth's voice softened. 'I have a little someone here who'd very much like to see his mum.'

Ruth had taken baby Hamish into her care the afternoon of the accident. Anne had been too distraught to look after him.

Through the door she could hear his sweet gurgling. The sound pulled at her heart. She placed her hand on the lock. Turned it. Opened the door.

Ruth pushed her way in, the baby on her hip. 'Good god, woman. You look a fright.'

Anne hadn't eaten. Hadn't bathed. Hadn't changed out of her nightdress. She went to take her child, but he recoiled from her. Ruth instead put him on the rug in the living room and he sat there, playing with his rattle.

'You need to clean yourself up.' Ruth angled Anne towards the bathroom. 'I'll make us some tea.'

When Anne came back into the kitchen, showered and in fresh clothes, Ruth handed her a tea in one of the cups Tadashi had made when they first returned to the island. Her breath caught in her throat.

'Drink up,' Ruth ordered, and Anne complied.

When they finished their tea, Ruth stood and smoothed down the front of her blue-and-white floral coat dress.

'I'll be back tomorrow to check on you. There's a casserole in the oven.'

Only then did Anne notice the rich, meaty aroma that was filling the cottage. She picked up baby Hamish and held him close to her chest.

True to her word, Ruth came back the next day. And the next. And the next. And Anne made sure she was presentable each time. Outside she began to look like her normal self. Inside she was numb.

Seven days after the accident, Anne stood on the dock, a strong wind whipping her dress about her legs, the taste of sea salt in her mouth.

The *Seafarer* approached with a long drone of its horn. It wasn't due for another two weeks, but Hamish had chartered the vessel to get to the island in time for Tadashi's funeral.

His funeral. So final. Until now, Anne was able to pretend Tadashi was simply away. That any moment he could walk through the door, embrace her, hug his son.

After the funeral, though, there'd be no more pretending. A headstone in the churchyard would make his death so horribly real.

As the *Seafarer* docked, Anne tried to suppress her tears.

Hamish stepped off the boat and wrapped Anne in a tight embrace.

'You look terrible.' He smiled.

'Thank you.' She touched his cheek. 'I'm glad you're here.'

'Me too.' He turned slightly to the man now stepping off the boat, dressed in brown corduroy trousers, carrying two small suitcases. 'This is Tristan.'

Anne hugged him. Though they'd never met, Anne felt she knew him through Hamish's letters.

'I'm sorry we couldn't meet under more pleasant circumstances,' Tristan said, his blonde hair flopping over his eyes as he spoke.

'Me too.' Anne led the men to Soldiers' Way, where they'd be staying.

The church service that afternoon was a simple farewell. Ruth and Ray, his arm broken but otherwise okay, brought flowers. Hadley read a passage from the Bible. Mrs McCormack and Mrs Forster provided food for the wake afterwards, and looked after baby Hamish.

Anne had no tears; no words. In silence, she watched Tadashi's coffin enter the ground in the yard behind the tiny church on the edge of town.

As the sun began to set, Anne, Hamish and Tristan climbed the hill to the lighthouse. When they got there, Anne knelt in the grass and placed a sprig of Queen Anne's lace at the base of the tall slender building.

Dressed in kilts, Hamish and Tristan stood on the edge of the headland and hauled their bagpipes out of their cases. They began to play, a haunting tune that danced over the island on the evening air.

Hamish and Tristan stayed for two weeks, their gentle company providing comfort to Anne. Tristan was a quiet man of intelligence, and she liked him very much. It was clear Hamish was content, in love. Happy was a word she couldn't use, though, as they had to keep their relationship secret from their families. It was a sorrow each man carried silently.

The two weeks passed quickly, and before Anne knew it, they were gathering on the dock, preparing to say their goodbyes.

Hamish hugged her tightly. 'We'll come visit again. I promise.'

'You'd better.' She frowned.

'Ach, who else will grace these shores with such musical culture, if we don't?' Tristan patted his bagpipe case.

'Oh, you can leave those at home next time,' Anne laughed.

Hamish touched her cheek and she grabbed his hand and squeezed it tightly, closing her eyes. The men boarded the boat.

Anne watched it sail away until it was a mere speck in the bright blue water.

That night, after she put baby Hamish to bed, she walked out into the dark with heavy limbs and entered Tadashi's studio. Staring at the shelves lined with pottery, she sunk to the ground and sat there in the middle of his work. And her tears finally fell.

A month after Hamish's departure, life had returned to normal – at least on the surface. Mrs Forster's youngest daughter looked after baby Hamish during the day while Anne worked and every Sunday Anne attended church, sitting next to Ruth and her family.

Under the surface, though, life without Tadashi was colder, paler, less vibrant and Anne knew it would always be so.

One mild day in spring, she sat by the fountain in her lunchbreak, eating her sandwich, reading her book.

Ruth walked across the grass towards her.

'May I?' she asked, holding up the copy of *Emma* Anne had loaned her the day of Tadashi's accident.

'Of course.'

'Anne, I haven't yet . . . Ray wouldn't be here if . . .'

Anne knew Ruth would have trouble finding the words, and she didn't need to hear them. 'It's okay, Ruth.'

'No. It's not. He saved my Ray's life. I was never a good neighbour towards your Tadashi and I will never forgive myself for that.' Her bottom lip quivered.

Anne patted Ruth's knee. 'It's just as well I will, then.'

Ruth straightened her posture and smoothed her dress over her legs.

'Is this the best of Austen's work?' Ruth asked, waving the book in the air.

'Opinions vary on that. I have the complete collection if you want to read more.'

Ruth nodded. 'That would be nice. Do you have other classics, too?'

'Absolutely.' Anne smiled. 'Why don't you come over tonight and pick one off my shelves?'

The following month Ruth joined Anne by the fountain again, a borrowed copy of *Pride and Prejudice* in her hands.

'I found that Darcy fellow altogether too arrogant.' Ruth pursed her lips.

Anne smiled. 'I think you might be in the minority there.'

'Handsome and wealthy, sure. But unpleasant.'

'He did save Elizabeth's family from ruin, though. And he genuinely loved her.'

Ruth frowned. 'Maybe. But do you think Miss Bennett will be happy with a brooding ill-mannered man like that?'

'I like to think their love lasted.'

'You would.' Ruth shook her head and Anne laughed.

Mrs McCormack and Mrs Forster happened to be strolling through the park at that moment, and Ruth called them over.

'Ladies, have either of you read *Pride and Prejudice*?'

They both nodded.

'Excellent. Then perhaps you can settle something between Anne and me. What do you think of Mr Darcy?'

'Insufferable,' said Mrs Forster.

'Darcy?' Mrs McCormack put her hand to her chest. 'If only my Ed were more like him.'

'Then you'd probably have even more children,' Anne joked and Mrs Forster spat with laughter.

'I do enjoy reading,' said Mrs McCormack, 'but rarely find the time these days.'

'I always try to make time,' Anne said. 'A little escape from the world.'

Ruth nodded.

An idea struck Anne. 'I have a wonderful collection of books. If you ladies like, maybe you could all borrow something and we could meet back here this time next month and chat about what we've read.'

'Splendid idea, Anne,' Ruth said. 'Absolutely splendid.'

The very first ever meeting of the Wattle Island Book Club was set. And for the first time since Tadashi's passing, Anne felt the smile that adorned her face actually touch her heart.

———

Anne ran her hands over the artworks that lined her studio walls. Not all memories were bad, but even the good ones, the beautiful ones, could make your heart ache.

The trick, not that she had mastered it, was to allow the good memories to shine so bright they cast their light into the shadows of the dark.

Twenty-seven

The men Hamish had helped secure from the mainland arrived a week later and Robbie put them to work immediately. Most of them were staying in the cottages on Soldiers' Way and on their first Friday on the island, Hamish treated every one of them to a round of beer at the pub, much to Len's delight. Winter was usually a slow time for the publican.

Grace sat in one of the booths, pushing her schnitzel round her plate while Addie leaned against her. With her free hand, Grace played with the girl's hair, twirling the blonde curls around and around before letting them go. Sam looked on and smiled.

After ensuring all the tradies had a drink, Hamish slid into the booth next to Sam.

'We're on schedule.' He raised his glass of beer in the air. 'When's the furniture coming?'

'Next week.' Once Grace had had the brainwave to get Hamish's tradies to custom-build the shelving and desks and any other cabinetry, instead of shipping over pre-packed units, the logistics had become a lot easier. And, thanks to Linh, the books would arrive the week after that.

Addie stretched out on the bench seat and lay her head in Grace's lap, yawning.

'Do you think we should get this one home?' Grace asked Sam.

'Probably.' He came around the table and lifted his daughter into his arms as if she were light as a feather. Addie snuggled into her father's neck.

Back at home, Sam put a stirring Addie to bed and Grace read her a story until she settled and drifted off into a deep slumber.

In the kitchen, Sam made two cups of hot chocolate and together they sat on the couch, Grace's legs over Sam's, his hand tracing lines up and down her thigh.

It had become a bit of a routine of theirs – hot chocolate on the couch after dinner. Grace never wanted to leave once the hot chocolate was finished, but always did.

She got up and stretched her arms into the air.

'Stay.' From behind Sam wrapped his arms around her waist.

'I shouldn't.' She pulled away.

'You should.' He kissed her neck, his breath warm, his hands moving down her hips. 'You really should.'

She turned around, their eyes locking. There was nothing else she wanted more than him. Nothing else but to stay in his arms forever; nothing else but to plan a future with him. Nothing else, except one thing.

He touched her nose and brushed her cheek. 'Grace, I lo—'

She put her finger to his lips.

'Don't say it. Please.' She so desperately wanted to hear the words come out of his mouth, but she couldn't let him. This had gone too far already. 'You can't.'

'Why? I know it's fast, Grace, but it's real. Tell me it's real for you too.'

She drew in a breath. 'It is.'

'I haven't felt this . . . haven't felt anything except pain and numbness for so long. But when I'm with you, the pain stops. And there's joy. I know how rare happiness is. And now I've found it again.' He held her head in his hands. 'I don't want to let it go. I don't want to let you go.'

Grace shook her head, her heart aching. She ran her fingertips through his beard. 'You've lost so much already. I can't be the one to bring you more pain.'

He frowned. 'Your cancer? Okay. Not a small hurdle. But together we'll fight it, Grace.'

She wriggled free of his embrace and stepped away.

'I've never liked that term,' she whispered. 'Fighting one's cancer. Fighting makes it sound like we're on a level playing field, that there's an even chance of success and failure. And if I fight hard enough I will win. And if I lose, it's because I didn't.'

Sam closed the gap between them. 'So we don't fight. We face it. Together. I know the future is uncertain. But as a very wise and beautiful woman once said to me, there's no point waiting around for the time to be right. Because you never know how much—'

'Time you have. The thing is . . .' She exhaled. 'The future *is* certain.'

He shook his head. 'I don't understand.'

'I haven't been completely honest with you.' Her bottom lip started to tremble and she bit down to make it stop, unable to say the words. Unwilling to say them. But she had to. She rested her hands on his chest. 'We've stopped treatment.'

She let the words sink in.

'So . . . you're in . . . do they still call it remission?' His words were hopeful but he sounded scared.

'No, Sam.'

'No they don't call it that? Or no you're not in it?'

She could feel his chest rising and falling, his breath faltering. She opened her mouth but the words didn't come. Instead, a single tear escaped from her eye. 'I'm palliative.'

'Grace? Are you saying . . .'

Her face contorted.

He shook his head. 'But if treatment buys you more time . . .'

She tore her gaze from him. 'Time I'd only spend so sick, I may as well have no time at all.' She looked up and met his tortured gaze. 'That's not living, Sam. It's simply not dying. Whatever time I have left'—she breathed in—'I want to spend it living.'

Sam backed away. 'I . . . I don't . . . I can't . . .' He raised his hand and turned, storming out into the night.

Grace hung her head.

When Sam didn't return, she went outside and stood on the veranda, wrapping a blanket around her against the cold night air. Against the pain. She looked up at the sky, at the happy stars twinkling in the liquid black. Stars that burned so bright, their light lived on long after they'd perished.

Minutes passed, and then an hour.

From the shadows of the shed Sam emerged, hands in the pockets of his jeans, shoulders slumped beneath his dark green jumper.

'I'm sorry,' he said, stopping at the bottom of the veranda steps. 'I needed to think. To take that in.'

'I understand.'

'Grace?'

'Yes?'

'I need you to be completely honest with me.'

'Of course.'

He took a step closer. 'Are my feelings for you one-sided?'

'No.' She walked down the steps and stopped in front of him. 'I love you, Sam. I didn't mean to. And it would be easier if I didn't. But I do. With all my heart.'

He cupped her chin in his hand. 'I know what it is, to exist without living. It's cold and it's dark and it's lonely. And I can't ask that of you. I understand why you've stopped treatment. I don't know where we go from here. But I do know that I love you.'

He tilted her head so her lips met his and he kissed her slowly and deeply. She melted into his embrace.

Morning sun filtered through the leaves of the gum tree outside the kitchen window, sending dappled light onto the dining table. Sam hugged Grace from behind as she poured three glasses of chilled water. He kissed the base of her neck.

In pink fluffy slippers, Addie padded into the room, carrying a stuffed cow. 'Good morning, Daddy.' She yawned. 'Good morning, Grace.'

'Good morning, Gumnut. Toast and Vegemite?' Sam picked her up and sat her on the kitchen bench.

'Yes please. Is Grace staying over today?'

Grace and Sam looked at each other and smiled.

'Yes,' Sam said. 'It that okay?'

She nodded. 'It's very okay.'

On Monday, Grace and Sam headed into town to check on what was fast beginning to look like a community library.

Hamish, Robbie and the tradies were already there.

'Looks like everything here is under control,' Sam said, shaking hands with the two men.

'Of course.' Robbie saluted.

'Then I might leave you to it.' He took Grace into his arms and kissed her deeply.

Robbie whistled as Sam left. Hamish smiled. Grace blushed.

'Well, about time,' Anne said as she walked in the door, hitting Sam on the back on his way out.

As the week drew to a close, the progress in the library was both thrilling and exhausting. Grace was there every day spending hours overseeing things. In the evening she had dinner with Sam and Addie – not that she ate much of it – and at night she lay in Sam's arms, soothed by his rhythmic snoring.

On Friday at lunchtime, as she was directing the chippies where to put the last of the tables, Sam came bursting through the library door.

He picked Grace up and put her over his shoulder.

'You've got this, right, Robbie?' he called.

'Yes, sir.'

Outside, Sam bundled Grace into his ute and without a word drove to the north side of the island.

'What on earth are you doing?' Grace asked.

He smiled but said nothing.

'Where are we going?'

Again, there was no reply.

They pulled up beside Rocky Beach. Sam opened the door for Grace and she got out.

'What is going on?' She put her hands on her hips.

'Well, I figured you wouldn't come if I asked. You'd make some excuse about installing a light or painting a shelf.'

'I wouldn't exactly call those excuses.'

'Maybe not.' He closed his hands over hers. 'But you've been working too hard lately and I thought you might like a special treat.'

'A special treat?' Grace narrowed her eyes.

Sam handed her a bag. Inside was a wetsuit. 'Put this on.'

'What? You're mad.'

He kissed her. 'Madly in love.'

'That's the cheesiest thing I've ever heard.'

Sam's laugh was warm, infectious. 'I know. But it's true. Get changed anyway. It'll be worth it. I promise.'

Grace did as he asked, hoping they weren't about to go surfing. Balance had never been one of her strengths. Once she'd wriggled into the wetsuit, with a little help from Sam – okay, a lot of help – she stood on the sand, her toes sinking deep.

'Right then. What's this all about? I don't see any surfboards about. Or waves.'

From inside the backpack he'd been carrying, Sam pulled out some flippers and two snorkels. 'It's not the Great Barrier Reef,' he said, 'but I'm hoping it still counts.'

Grace's eyes grew wide. 'You read more of my journal that day than I realised.'

He ran his hand through his hair and cast his eyes down. 'Actually, you left it open the other night and I might have had a peek.' He looked up. 'Forgive me?'

Grace threw her arms around him. 'There's nothing to forgive.'

Hand in hand they waded into the calm water, the cold seeping into Grace's bones despite the wetsuit.

'Ready?' Sam asked.

She nodded.

Immersed under the water, Grace travelled with slow smooth movements. Sam was never far from her, pointing to this fish or that stingray. And Grace was enveloped in stillness. Peace. The orange and purple coral was vibrant, tiny blue fish swimming in between its twisted tendrils. Grace almost choked seawater into her snorkel when a huge turtle swam so close she could have touched it.

Eventually they surfaced and dragged themselves back up the sand.

'That was . . . amazing,' Grace said with breathy excitement. 'I didn't expect there to be coral. And the turtle! Where did he come from? He was magnificent.'

Sam unzipped his wetsuit, pulling it down, and Grace ran her fingers through the hair on his strong chest.

'We're just far enough north. The reef is only on this side of the island, though.' He captured her hand and raised it to his lips, kissing each of her fingers in turn.

'Thank you, Sam. This was unbelievable.'

'It's not over yet.' He carried her up the sand and lifted her onto the open tray of the ute. 'Grace, I love you. When we first met we talked about nothing in this life being for certain. We're both too aware of that. But there is one thing I am certain of.' He reached behind her into a bag and pulled out a small box.

Grace gasped, her hands covering her mouth.

He opened the box and held out a turquoise and silver ring. 'Grace, will you marry me?'

She stared at him.

'Grace?'

'You've gone completely mad,' she blurted.

Sam tilted his head. 'Of all the possible responses I imagined, I've got to say, that wasn't one of them.'

Grace took his hands. 'I love you, Sam and if it wasn't for . . . I'd say yes in a heartbeat. But—'

'No buts. I don't care if we have a day, a month, a year, a decade. If your cancer and my past has taught us anything, it's that we need to grab happiness when it comes. To really live, not just exist.'

'You're using my own words against me.'

He nodded. 'Yes. Whatever it takes. I love you. I want to be your husband. I want you to be my wife. For however long the universe decides.'

For the last three years Grace had thought it impossible for someone to love her; never thought being a wife was in her future. Yet here was Sam, a man she loved deeply, a man fully aware of what their future held, asking her to marry him.

She breathed out slowly. 'Aren't there . . . processes? Paperwork? Applications? Don't they take time?'

'Yes. But I've already spoken to Hamish and Len – he's the island celebrant. There are exceptions. We can be married next Friday. All you have to do is say yes.'

She stared at him in disbelief.

'Grace?'

She blinked. Then smiled. 'Sam Sato. I'd be honoured to be your wife.'

He threw himself at her, knocking her back into the tray of the ute.

'Okay. Okay. No need to kill me before we get married,' Grace laughed.

He lowered himself down, his weight pressing onto her. 'I love you, Grace.' He kissed her. And she wrapped her arms around him, holding him as tightly as she could.

Planning a wedding in only a few days was not as hard as Grace first thought. In fact, without all the lead-up it was surprisingly simple, as all the extras, the nonsense, the drama that usually accompanied such events had to be put aside. And all that was left was what mattered.

A simple ceremony with the people they loved.

Addie had squealed with delight at the news. Anne had cried. The whole island was abuzz.

On the Wednesday before the wedding, Grace and Sam waited at the airstrip. At first, June had thought the whole idea ludicrous, but if Grace was going to go ahead with the idea, then she wouldn't miss out on her only daughter's wedding.

When the plane touched down, Grace squeezed Sam's hand.

Linh was the first off the plane and she ran into Grace's arms, hugging her tightly. She hugged Sam too, the force of her embrace making him stumble back a step.

'I wholeheartedly approve,' she said, looking him up and down.

June, her hair in a neat bob, walked off the plane next and stopped in front of Grace, holding her at arm's length. Then she pulled Grace towards her and held her for a long moment.

When they separated, Grace introduced her to Sam.

He kissed June on the cheek and she stepped back, sizing him up. He held her gaze with a soft expression.

She smiled. 'I guess you two have a lot to catch me up on.'

After dinner that night, Sam put an overly excited Addie to bed while Grace sat with June on the sofa, each holding a cup of tea.

'I can see that you love him.' June sipped her Earl Grey.

'I know it seems fast,' Grace tried to explain, 'but I—'

June put her hand on Grace's leg. 'But your time is running out.'

Grace's mouth fell open. 'How did you know?'

'I didn't, at first. But when you flew out here without a word, I figured something was up. I just wasn't sure what. Why do you think I was so desperate to get you home?'

'Then why didn't you come and try to drag me back?'

'Because it wouldn't have worked.'

True.

'And after I got over the initial hurt . . .'

'Sorry.'

'I thought maybe it was my fault. That you were trying to get away from me.'

'No, Mum—'

June waved her hand. 'It's okay, Grace. I know you needed space from me.'

'I needed space from my life.'

'I know.' June nodded. 'I started to put together the pieces. You sounded so tired. And then you told me about Sam . . .'

'I'm sorry I shut you out.' Grace gulped back her tears.

'We have no time for sorry now.'

'I love you, Mum. I'm glad you're here.'

'I love you too, my Gracie.' June hadn't called her that since she was a child. 'Now tell me about your plans. Is there anything I can do?'

Wildflowers of yellow, pink and lilac were sprinkled over the sand, forming an aisle.

Grace, dressed in a flowing white cotton dress, carried a small posy of wattle picked from the Wattle Way of Delight and Queen Anne's lace picked from beneath the lighthouse. She walked on her mother's arm towards Sam, who was standing under an arch made of driftwood draped in chiffon. The aqua sea behind him was calm and glistened in the afternoon sun. He looked at her with so much love in his eyes that her breath caught in her chest. His pale-blue shirt was open at the neck, the cotton soft against his tanned arms, his white trousers rolled above his ankles, his feet bare. Phil stood beside him.

In front of Grace, Addie, in a tiered white dress, led Emmeline Harris down the sand, a bouquet of wildflowers tied to the cow's pink collar. Each step of Addie's silver glitter shoes was slow, deliberate – the responsibility of being flower girl taken very seriously.

The beach was lined with faces that felt like home – Maree, Hadley, Shellie, Hamish, Ruth with a smile on her face. Linh, dressed in a traditional silk áo dài of aqua and white, was Grace's bridesmaid and Anne, eyes glistening, looking resplendent in her pale blue kimono sprinkled with white cherry blossoms, stood at the front of the gathered family and friends in her rightful place.

June passed Grace to Sam with a kiss on her daughter's cheek, and joined Anne, who embraced her. Len began the ceremony with little fuss, just the legal formalities before going straight into the vows.

Sam went first. 'Grace. You have brought light back into my life where I thought only darkness could dwell. I am proud today to become your husband and I promise that no matter what our future brings, I will strive to always be the light in your dark. Addie and I love you very much.'

'We sure do.' Addie beamed and the gathered loved ones laughed.

Sam patted her on her shoulder. 'And we couldn't be happier than we are right now, as the three of us become a family.'

Grace's hands began to shake. She could hear sniffles behind her, but was determined to hold it together.

'Sam. Addie. I never thought today was possible. That standing before a man I love and becoming his wife, that being able to love and cherish a child I adore, would ever be part of my life. But here we are, the two of you my future. Today, tomorrow, however long the universe decides and even after that, I will love you . . . both, with . . . with all my heart.'

Addie hugged Grace around the waist and Sam kissed her.

'Hang on, mate.' Len laughed. 'Still a few more steps. Let's make this official.' He smiled. 'Do you, Samuel Tadashi Sato, take Grace Elizabeth Elliott to be your wife?'

'I do.'

'I do too.' Addie grinned.

'Oh bless.' June wiped away a tear.

'And do you Grace Elizabeth Elliott, take Samuel Tadashi Sato to be your husband?'

'I do.'

Len clasped his hands. 'Right, now you can seal it with a kiss, you two.'

Sam leaned in to Grace, putting his hand behind her back and pulling her close. As they kissed, a loud cheer erupted from the guests.

Grace and Sam walked back up the sand to where Hamish had repositioned himself, bagpipes at the ready.

Sam lifted Grace into his arms and carried her under the wattle trees and through town to the pub, the guests following behind, Hamish's melody floating on the air.

Inside the pub people mingled and drank and ate, the atmosphere relaxed and joyous. Someone turned on the jukebox in the corner, and Addie, who'd left Emmeline Harris tied up outside, was the first to start dancing, dragging Sam onto the dance floor with her.

'Grace.' Anne put her arm around Grace's shoulder. 'Welcome to the family.'

'Thank you, Anne.' Grace had to hold back tears.

'Oh, none of that "Anne" business anymore. We're family now. Call me Obaachan.'

Well, that did it. The tears flowed.

As the night went on, Grace sat by the fire. Three dances had been more than enough for her. June pulled a chair up beside her.

'Are you okay, love? You look tired. A little pale.'

Grace took her hand. 'I'm all right, Mum.'

'Grace?'

'Okay, I'm more tired than I should be. But I won't let anything spoil tonight.'

'You need to look after yourself,' June said. 'Now more than ever.'

Grace nodded. 'I'll go see Shellie tomorrow. Maybe we can adjust my meds.'

'I know I'm only here for a few days, but if there's anything you need . . .'

Grace lifted her head and looked into June's eyes. 'Actually, do you think maybe you could extend your stay? Hang around for a week or two?'

June squared her shoulders and exhaled slowly. 'As long as you want.'

Twenty-eight

In the morning Grace sat on the veranda sipping a tea, her aching legs over Sam's lap as he rubbed them gently. Light footfalls tapped on the wooden surround. Wiping her eyes, Addie came into the morning light, carrying Grace's journal in her hands.

She plonked herself down beside them on the wicker bench seat and placed the journal in Grace's hands. 'This is a very strange story.'

'Ah, that's because it's not a story. It's a journal.' Grace smiled.

'Hmm. What's with all the lists?'

Sam stifled a laugh.

'Well'—Grace opened to a random page—'they're called bucket lists. They're things you want to do with your life. Some of them are realistic, like this one . . .'

She pointed out an item on the page.

Age seventeen: Go to university (tick, ages eighteen to twenty)

'. . . and some of them are just a bit of fun.'

Age twenty-one: Be part of a flash mob, hopefully with a musical theatre theme.

Addie whistled – or at least she tried to, not having quite perfected the art – as they turned the pages together. 'There are a lot of purple ticks.' Her eyes were wide.

'I've been very lucky,' Grace said. 'This one'—she turned to *seafood picnic on a tropical beach*—'and this one'—she turned to *snorkel with turtles*—'your dad helped me with.'

Addie stared at her father with obvious pride, then she returned to the book.

'What's this one?' she asked.

Age nineteen: Start a library for underprivileged children in Cambodia.

'I don't know what under . . . underpr . . .'

'Underprivileged,' Grace helped out.

'. . . underprivileged means. And this isn't Cam . . . Cambodia. But we are building a library, right?'

'Yes. We are.' Sam nodded. 'And it will be a beautiful one at that.'

'So,' Addie climbed into Grace's lap. 'I'm helping you tick off one of your bucket list items, too? Just like Daddy.'

Grace smiled, her heart warm. 'You sure are. And those caterpillar lounges you chose should be arriving this week.'

Addie smiled.

'All right, Gumnut.' Sam untangled himself from Grace and Addie. 'Today, you and I are going to play in my studio, while Grace has a rest.'

'No,' Grace protested. 'It's okay . . .'

Sam shook his head. 'Yesterday was a big day. And you've got a massive week ahead.' He kissed her.

'But—'

'Remember, no buts.'

Addie jumped up and Sam piggybacked her to the studio. Grace stretched out on the seat in the winter sun. Actually, a rest sounded perfect.

*

On Monday morning, refreshed after a languid weekend, Grace met the small group who had volunteered to staff the library for a training session. Addie, now on school holidays, sat beside her, taking notes in an old notebook with a unicorn pen, nodding every time Grace made a point, even though Grace was sure she had no idea what she was nodding about.

As they broke for lunch, and a much-needed rest for Grace, Hamish pushed the library door open. 'I have something for you, Grace,' he called out. 'Addie, come hold the door for me.'

Addie ran over to get the door and Grace saw a huge grin spread across the girl's face. 'Come quick, Grace.'

Tears filled Grace's eyes when she saw boxes and boxes outside the door. The books had arrived.

She turned to Hamish. 'How did you . . .? I thought . . . I didn't think they were arriving till next week.'

'I may have made a call or two,' Hamish said, with a wink.

The rest of the afternoon was spent beginning the mammoth task of starting to catalogue and shelve the books. It was going to take days, maybe weeks, even with a team of helpers.

Addie was put in charge of making sure the kids' section was being stocked properly, with a little help from June.

'What do I call you, Grace's mum?' Grace heard Addie ask as they shelved the Clementine Rose books. She watched on from behind a shelf shaped like a wave. 'Technically Grace isn't my mum, so can you still be my grandma?'

June put her hand on her chest. 'I don't mind what you call me. In my heart, I'm your grandma, but if you're not comfortable with that, we can come up with something else.'

Addie tilted her head to the side.

'It's what's in the heart that counts, Grandma.' She nodded and Grace had to turn away.

*

By the end of the week the library was nearly ready. The final paperwork outlining the agreement with the council and the now established Wattle Island Community Library Association, of which Sam had been nominated president, were signed off. In two weeks' time they would be ready to hold the grand opening.

Anne had moved book club to coincide with a series of events she and Ruth had taken charge of.

There was little left for Grace to do now and she and Sam and Addie settled into a comfortable routine. In the mornings they would have breakfast together around the kitchen table, and then Addie and Grace would walk Emmeline Harris or collect driftwood or visit the baby chicks at Follett's farm while Sam worked; then lunch in the pub with Anne and Hamish, sometimes Ruth, often Maree, always June; and afternoons by the fountain, Grace lying on the bench with her head in Sam's lap as he read to her, Addie playing in the grass, and, quite often, in the fountain.

Four days before the grand opening of the library, Grace couldn't get out of bed. Sam, tracks of worry etched into his face, called Shellie while Anne took Addie for a walk. June stayed by Grace's side.

When she arrived, Shellie took Grace's temperature and blood pressure; asked her question after question and eventually decided to tweak her medication.

'I have limited resources here,' Shellie said. 'All I can do is manage the pain.'

Grace smiled. 'That's all I need.'

For the next few days Sam barely left her side, reading to her when she was awake, as the laughter of Anne and June and Addie floated through the house. And Grace committed every trill to memory, holding on to the joy that filled her breaking heart.

Twenty-nine

Anne tried to make herself useful without getting in the way, helping with the finishing touches on the library, looking after Addie, preparing meals. Sam was looking tired, which was to be expected. She was worried this was all too much for him, watching Grace suffer, but he reassured her he was fine.

She didn't believe him. None of them were fine.

A few days after Grace had taken ill, Anne popped over to Sam's to clean the kitchen and living room. Sam and Addie were at the library; a rare moment away from Grace. She tiptoed in, careful not to make too much noise. Before she left, she knocked on the bedroom door to see if Grace needed anything. There was no answer, so she pushed the door open quietly.

Grace was not in bed.

Panic tore through her. Where was she? She raced around the house but there was no sign of Grace. Outside she checked the yard and Emmeline Harris's pen. Not there.

The studio? She burst through the shed doors and found Grace dozing in an old armchair next to Sam's pottery wheel. Anne pulled a blanket up over Grace's knees and Grace stirred.

'Sorry, pet. I didn't mean to disturb you.'

'That's okay.' Grace sat a little straighter.

'Your colour is better today.' Anne was surprised by how well Grace actually looked.

Grace nodded. 'I started to feel better yesterday. Sam set me up in here this morning and tried to show me how to throw on the wheel.' She held up her hands, caked in dry clay. 'Turns out I still haven't found my artistic talent.'

Anne smiled. 'Well, we'll simply have to try something else. Screen printing, perhaps. Or wood turning. I hear collages made of sticks and leaves are making a comeback.'

Grace laughed; a sound so gentle and sweet, it broke Anne's heart. 'Maybe I should add that to my bucket list.'

Addie had told Anne about Grace's journal.

'Good idea.' Anne leaned against Sam's workbench, resting her walking stick on the table top. 'I don't believe I've thanked you, Grace, for bringing my Sam back.'

'I'm the one who should be thanking you, Anne. If you hadn't decided to restart your book club, none of any of this would have happened.'

'It was a rather sterling idea, wasn't it?'

'Most definitely.' Grace closed her eyes.

Anne adjusted the blanket and pulled out the stool Sam kept under the bench. She'd sit with Grace a little while.

Anne had no idea when she first reached out to Grace what would happen. She'd hoped to rekindle book club, of course. Hoped to get Sam involved and bring him back from his darkness. But there was no way she could have imagined a community library being born from the venture. No way she could have predicted the impact Grace would have on her, on Addie, on Sam. But that was the magic of books. They turned strangers into friends and when that happened, there was no limit to the possibilities.

Thirty

Grace woke on Friday morning feeling bright.

'Are you sure?' Sam asked as she got ready to go to the opening.

'I'm not going to miss this. Look at me. I'm fine. Do I look fine?'

'Actually, yes, you do. But, we're not taking any chances.' He brought her the wheelchair that Anne had refused to use. 'Hop in.'

'But—'

He shook his head. 'Remember our promise.'

By 10 am the whole town had gathered outside the library. A thick pink ribbon hung across the door, and Hamish stood beside it with a comically large pair of scissors.

'I think you should do the honours.' He handed the scissors to Grace.

'Anne, will you help me?'

Anne pressed her hand into her chest. 'Of course.'

Together they cut the ribbon and a cheer erupted behind them.

Inside, the library had come to life. There was colour and movement everywhere. Shelves ran the entire perimeter, each one shaped like a wave, creating the illusion the ocean flowed through the library carrying books in its swell. Comfortable armchairs were placed randomly around the open space in the middle of the library, and one of Anne's paintings of the lighthouse hung on the far wall. Above the borrowing counter in navy-and-white perspex lettering were the words 'Wattle Island Community Library'. The kids corner, which Addie had run straight to, was dotted with caterpillar lounges in bright colours of orange, purple and yellow.

Anne reached her right hand out to Grace and they smiled at each other. 'You did it,' she said.

'*We* did it.' Grace nodded.

Hamish pulled out his bagpipes. 'Well, I think there's no better way to open this library—'

'Hamish McKenzie, don't you dare,' Anne protested. 'No one wants to listen to that.'

He ignored her and serenaded the people as they entered the building.

June did a reading for the kids, Robbie and Phil were on canapé duty, and Shellie was showing people how to use the catalogue on the brand new computers in the far corner.

Then, with the jingle of a pink bell, Anne called the fourth meeting of the new Wattle Island Book Club to order. The book club members took their seats in the armchairs which had now been moved into a circle in the middle of the room.

Anne introduced this month's read, *Anne of Green Gables*, a classic to mark the special occasion, and something PG for the kids that were there.

Just behind the group, Grace sat in her wheelchair and watched the book club in full flight. Addie had wandered over and placed herself in Sam's lap, absent-mindedly playing with his beard as he participated with astute observations and funny quips. He was ever so attractive when he smiled.

Even June joined in the discussion.

As the book club conversation continued, Grace wheeled herself away from the crowd and gathered her cardigan from behind the counter.

'Time to go?' Sam asked, stepping up beside her, Addie next to him, book in hand.

She nodded. 'It's been a long week.'

'Why don't we take Grace home?' He looked down at Addie who smiled.

Grace and Sam sat together on the white wicker lounge, a red blanket over Grace's legs.

'You're shivering.' Sam frowned.

'I'm okay.'

'No, you're not. I'll go get Shellie.' He went to stand but she put her hand on his leg.

'Please don't.' Grace didn't need Shellie to tell her this was the beginning of the end. She knew it already. 'You can call her later.'

Sam took Grace's hand.

'Are you sure?'

'Yes. I'd like to enjoy what's left while I can. Once Shellie comes and starts giving me drugs . . .' She drew in a shallow breath.

'How long do we . . .' Sam gulped.

'I don't know. But . . .'

'Right.' He cleared his throat.

'I'm sorry, Sam. I thought . . . I *hoped* we'd have so much more time.'

He shook his head. 'Don't say sorry, Grace. You've given me something far more valuable than time. You've shown me how to forgive. You've reminded me how to love again. And that is for eternity.'

She shifted beside him. 'Sam, if this is too much to ask of you . . . I know this won't be easy . . .'

'Grace, whatever you need, I'm here for you.' He rubbed her hand.

'All I need is you and Addie beside me.'

'Always,' he whispered.

Addie came from inside the cottage, carrying Grace's journal and a tattered copy of *Anne of Green Gables*. She handed the journal to Sam.

'Tick off *build a library*, please, Daddy.' She handed him her unicorn pen and curled up beside him. 'Would you like me to read, Grace? Our very own book club.'

'I'd love that.' Grace's breathing slowed.

'My favourite part. Just for you.'

Grace closed her eyes as Addie started to read.

'Should I stop, Daddy?' Addie asked.

'No. Keep going. Grace is going to have a big rest now.' Sam's voice caught. 'I think she'd like you to read her to sleep.'

'Oh.' She leaned across Sam's lap and kissed Grace's cheek.

Grace could hear Addie's voice as she described the White Way of Delight. It was Grace's favourite part too – Anne Shirley, just arrived on Prince Edward Island, looking on in wonder beside Matthew Cuthbert as they drove the buggy under the white cherry blossoms. She didn't know it yet, of course, but Anne Shirley had found a home in Green Gables.

Addie's voice sounded very far away. Grace could hear Sam breathing, every now and then a sniffle breaking the rhythm.

She could see the loose pages of her journal floating through her mind, like butterflies on a warm spring breeze; bright happy purple crayon ticks beside her bucket list items, mimicking gossamer wings. And somewhere in the distance bagpipes played.

Sam's arms tightened around her.

'I love you, Grace.'

Epilogue

One Year Later

Sam adjusted the pink backpack on Addie's shoulders. 'Are you ready?'

She saluted. 'Yes, sir.'

Standing under the Eiffel Tower, Sam put his hands on his hips. The paved avenue leading to the landmark had been teeming with tourists and Sam had held Addie's hand tightly the whole time. The hot summer sun was beating down and he was glad he'd remembered his sunglasses.

It was winter back home, the air cool, the wattle trees in bloom. All the tourists would have left the island now. Perhaps they were all here.

He made sure Addie's cap was secure.

'It's fine, Dad.'

She hadn't liked it the day before either when he'd smothered sunscreen all over her. He'd been met with a look of disdain he wasn't expecting to have to face for another few years. Somehow in the course of the last twelve months, his baby girl had got herself caught between the child she was and the young lady she would become. He never knew, from day to day, which version he'd get.

They joined the queue to buy their tickets for the climb to the top of the tower. The line moved insufferably slowly as they baked in the heat, but eventually they made it to the front – only to join another queue to actually get up the tower.

When they finally made it to the second floor, having decided to take the stair option, Sam was dripping in sweat.

'Is this it?' Addie frowned.

Sam shook his head and pointed up, the criss-crossing metal-work forming an intricate pattern above their heads.

Addie's eyes grew wide.

'Next part's a lift,' Sam said.

'Phew.'

The lift let them out two hundred and seventy-six metres above the streets of Paris. Sam stared out at the view below.

Addie pulled out her map, and together they tried to match the landmarks below with the cartoon illustrations. The Seine was easy, cutting the city of Paris in two, running right past the tower. They found the Trocadero, its curved arms embracing beautiful gardens; Notre Dame, the fire damage still visible from three months earlier; the Arc de Triomphe, where they'd been yesterday.

Sam pulled out his phone and turned the camera on. 'That's it, Addie. A little to the left.'

Addie shuffled over and held up Grace's journal. The wind was strong and Sam was worried they'd lose it over the edge.

'That's it,' Sam called and took the photo quickly. He returned the journal safely to Addie's backpack as she wiped a tear from her eye.

'Good job, Dad.' She wrapped her arm around his waist. 'Grace would be proud of us.'

So very grown up.

Pushing through the press of the crowd, they did a full circle of the viewing tower before lining up for the inclined elevator that ran down the leg of the tower, back to the grass below.

Their trip up the Eiffel Tower had taken the better part of a day and judging by Addie's dragging feet, she was as tired as Sam was.

Winding their way past the murky Seine, they found a small cafe with sage-green-and-white woven wicker chairs on the footpath, all facing the river. They sat at one of the tables and watched all the people go by. A waitress came to take their order. It was the perfect opportunity for Sam to try out his French.

He'd been learning for the last three months, once they'd decided to come to Paris, but he wasn't sure the app he'd used was any good. Or maybe it was him. With broken sentences he ordered Addie what he hoped were crepes, and a cup of coffee for himself.

The waitress smiled patiently and repeated the order back to him in English.

'Thank you.' Sam grimaced.

She returned soon after with a plate of crepes covered in chocolate syrup and whipped cream for Addie. And a coffee for Sam.

Addie smelled the crepes first, her eyes lighting up, then she took her first bite, smiled, and before Sam had even got halfway through his coffee, she'd devoured the whole plate.

'I can see why this was on Grace's bucket list.' She licked her lips.

With her unicorn pen in hand, Addie opened Grace's journal and placed ticks next to *Climb the Eiffel Tower* and *Eat crepes in a Paris cafe.*

'And tomorrow we can tick off *Visit the Queen's Library,*

Versailles.' She smiled. That was the one Sam knew Addie was the most excited about. The one she couldn't wait to relate back to Anne.

Back home Addie spent most of her free time in the community library. It worried Sam a little that she was so attached to the place, but it made sense, he supposed. It was a place that was so much a part of her mum and of Grace.

The library was now very much a part of the town. The Wattle Island Book Club met there every month, now numbering twenty regulars. Sam went to most meetings. He didn't say much, but certainly enjoyed watching Anne and Ruth go toe to toe over nearly every book they discussed.

The school used the library regularly for lessons and projects, and before he and Addie had left for Paris, Robbie had started up an after-school coding club.

'Coding?' Anne had frowned. 'Sounds like you're turning them into spies.'

Sam smiled at the memory.

Addie closed Grace's journal.

'I have something for you, Addie,' Sam said, putting a paper bag on the table. He'd brought it from home with him, waiting for the right time to give it to her.

She clapped her hands. From inside the bag she pulled out a pink glitter notebook. She smiled, then frowned.

'It's very pretty. But, what's it for?'

'Well, you know how we've been going through Grace's bucket lists?'

She nodded. 'I still think it would be fun to swim with sharks.'

'Not on my watch.' He shook his head. 'Well, it's been fun and we're going to get a lot ticked off on this trip.'

Addie straightened her shoulders. 'Grace would be very happy she's getting to do these things now.' She patted the leather journal.

'She would. But I was wondering if maybe it might also be fun for you to have your own bucket list.'

Her eyes went wide. 'It might be.'

'So I thought you should start your own journal.'

She opened the pink sparkly notebook and with her unicorn pen wrote the words *Addie's Bucket List Journal* on the first page.

She looked up at her dad. 'But what do I put on my list?'

'Well, that's the beauty of it. That's entirely up to you.'

'Swimming with sharks?'

He rolled his eyes.

Tapping the unicorn pen on the table, Addie was deep in thought. Then with a flourish she started writing.

Adrienne Sato's Bucket List, age ten:
- *Have a pink glitter cupcake party*
- *Have a sleepover in the library – no adults allowed*
- *Start a book club for kids*

'What do you think?'

Sam smiled. 'I think that's great.'

Addie handed him the pen. 'Your turn.'

He frowned.

'You have to do one too, Dad. You can use my journal if you like.'

Sam tapped his chin with the unicorn pen. 'Hmm. Let's see.'

Sam Sato's Bucket List, age thirty-one:
- *Learn French properly*
- *Take Addie to Japan*
- *Start a pottery school*

Addie nodded her approval. 'That's brilliant. Especially taking me to Japan.'

Sam laughed. 'Okay. But we do have something pretty important to get done today, don't we?'

'Oh, yes.' She pulled her very best serious face and reached into her backpack. She put the pile of postcards in the middle of the table.

'Let's do Obaachan's first.' She suggested. 'She won't be happy if she doesn't get one soon.'

Sam could picture Anne tapping her white walking stick on the tiled floor of the post office, asking why she hadn't received any mail from abroad yet.

'You're right about that.'

Addie sifted through the postcards they'd collected this past week. 'This one for Obaachan, this one for Hamish, this one for Aunty Shellie, and . . .' She held one up of the Eiffel Tower. 'What about this one for Grandma June?'

'Perfect.'

Sam looked up to the blue sky dotted with fluffy clouds. Thank you, Grace. He smiled and turned his attention back to the very important task of postcard allocation.

Author's Note

While Tadashi's story takes place after the events of the Second World War, it was important for me to understand what happened to people of Japanese origin living in Australia both during as well as after the war. Anti-Japanese sentiment in Australia remained high well into the 1960s, and there were plenty of sources to help me tell Tadashi's story through the late 1940s and early 1950s, including propaganda posters, newspaper articles and government policies.

But researching the details of Tadashi's past was a lot harder, particularly around the internment of Japanese people (and other nationalities) here in Australia. During my research I discovered that nearly all Japanese people living in Australia during the Second World War were interned – more than a thousand of them, including many who were born here. Their assets were frozen, and when the war ended, all but a handful (between 74 and 144, depending on the source) were sent back to Japan.

For Tadashi's story to work, I needed to find out why that small number were allowed to stay. Through Museums Victoria

I was put in touch with Dr Yuriko Nagata, an Honorary Senior Fellow in the School of Languages and Cultures at the University of Queensland, who helped me better understand the largely unknown stories of these Australians. She was instrumental in helping me bring Tadashi's story to life. If you'd like to find out more about this part of Australian history, Dr Nagata's chapter 'A Nikkei Australian Story: Legacy of the Pacific War' in the book *Migrant Nation: Australian Culture, Society and Identity* (ed. Paul L. Arthur, 2017) is a great place to start.

Acknowledgements

During a quiet conversation after an author event, Leanne Wright, a librarian at Port Macquarie Library, started the spark that would become *The Wattle Island Book Club*. While I ended up taking Grace's story in a very different direction from Leanne's journey, she helped me find Grace's heart and without her, *Wattle Island* wouldn't exist. Thank you, Leanne.

Bowral Sweets and Treats became the unofficial sponsor of this book, sending me care packages of chocolates through tough edits and deadlines. Thank you Mishell Currie, for not only the sustenance, but for the calls, messages, moral support and speed reading. Without you— well, that doesn't bear thinking about.

To Nick from Skydive Australia and Angela Helsloot, for painting a picture of what it is like to throw yourself out of a plane, as I'm far too chicken to do it myself (there's only so far I'm willing to go in the name of research); my readers 'brains trust' for their brilliant bucket list ideas; Nicole Elliott, for inspiring Grace's adventurous nature; and Karyn Smedts, for joining me on a kintsugi course (the kind of research I'm far more comfortable with). Thank you also to Cath Healy and Zeinah Keen, for your help with Grace's medical story; to Lyndel Champion, for helping me with the Japanese language and pronunciation; and to Jennifer Johnson, for your eagle eye during the proofread.

In January 2020 the Authors for Fireys auction raised $515,324 that was sent to various charities after the devastating bushfires that summer. I auctioned off the chance to have a character named after the highest bidder. Adrienne Massey, thank you for your generous donation. I hope you love Addie as much as I do.

To the Not So Solitary Scribes and in particular our writing group, the Scribblers' Ink. Emma Babbington, Annie Bucknell, Pam Cook, Jodi Gibson, Sueanne Gregg, Lisa Ireland, Penelope Janu, Maya Linnell, Kaneana May, Vanessa McCausland, Jem McCusker, Petronella McGovern, Chrissie Mios, Carrie Molachino and Kelly Rigby – thanks for the regular book, writing, family and life chats and interventions. Thanks also to other members of Scribblers' Ink I'm looking forward to getting know better over the next little while. I hope you all don't mind that I 'borrowed' the name of our fabulous Friday group to use in this book, but I had to immortalise you.

Special thanks to authors Leonie Kelsall, for being with me every step of this journey; Tabitha Bird, for your insightful and heartfelt feedback, especially around some of the more emotional themes in this novel; Josephine Moon, for your support; and Joanna Nell, for casting your medical eye over Grace's and Anne's stories.

Cassie Hamer, Michelle Parsons, Rosemary Puddy and Claudine Tinellis – the team behind the Northern Beaches Readers' Festival, and my dear friends. You are my squad, my inspiration, my safe place, my loves, the most intelligent wonderful women, and I'm blessed to have you in my life.

To my publisher Ali Watts, editor Genevieve Buzo, publicist Sofia Casanova, marketing executive Jess McKenzie, cover designer Laura Thomas and all the crew at Penguin Random House – thank you for being the best darn team to work with to bring a book baby into the world. I'm so proud of what we've achieved. There is no better team in publishing, of that I'm sure.

As always, to my family for your love and support, but especially to my nephew, James, who has read every one of my books, and whose bucket list includes being mentioned in an author's acknowledgments, so he gets his own exclusive mention this time round ☺. Sorry, rest of the fam, you don't get a mention. Blame James.

And to the readers, book clubs, libraries, booksellers, Bookstagrammers, podcasters and reviewers – thank you for embracing the stories I lovingly, nervously, put out into the world.

Book Club Questions

1. When we first meet Grace, she has a very extensive bucket list of things she hopes to achieve in life. What would be on yours?

2. Grace arrives on Wattle Island with a view to embracing adventure and ends up enriching her own life. In what ways does her presence there also come to enhance the lives of others?

3. Anne believes that 'age doesn't always bring wisdom'. Addie, the youngest character in the book, shows great wisdom. What is it, other than age, that shapes wisdom?

4. Discuss the ways in which the book club on Wattle Island helps the various characters in this story. In what ways is your own book club valuable to you?

5. The Japanese art of kintsugi – translated as 'golden joinery' – celebrates imperfections. How does Grace use this to help Sam understand his own pain and grief? Do you think our scars make us more beautiful?

6. While Grace is determined to uncover the truth about the book club's past, she seems reluctant to share her own personal story. Is it fair to keep Anne and Sam in the dark for so long, or does she owe them the truth earlier?

7. Another person Grace hides the truth from is her mum. Why does she do this? Is this justified?

8. Discuss the role of art in the novel, and in particular the role it plays in Anne's relationship with Tadashi. What other examples can you find in the book of the way art can connect characters and heal them? Have you ever found healing through art or another creative outlet?

9. Racial intolerance was prevalent in Australia after the war. Do you think we have made any real progress in this respect since?

10. Do you have a book that is as precious to you as Anne's copy of *Anne of Green Gables* is to her?

11. The ending to *The Wattle Island Book Club* is bittersweet. Do you feel this is a fitting end to the story? Is the epilogue satisfying?

12. Anne's journey to finding love with Tadashi isn't smooth. In which other novels by Sandie Docker do we find the theme of forbidden love?

The Kookaburra Creek Café

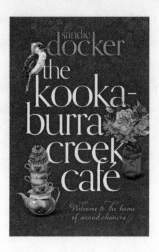

Welcome to the Kookaburra Creek Café.

THE PAST
For Hattie, the café has been her refuge for the last fifty years – her second chance at a happy ending after her dreams of being a star were shattered. But will the ghosts of her past succeed in destroying everything she's worked so hard to build?

THE PRESENT
For Alice, the café is her livelihood. After Hattie took her in as a teenager, Alice has slowly forged a quiet life as the café's manager (and chief cupcake baker). But with so many tragedies behind her, is it too late for Alice's story to have a happy ending?

THE FUTURE
For Becca, a teenager in trouble, the café could be the new start she yearns for. That is, if she can be persuaded to stop running from her secrets. Can Becca find a way to believe in the kindness of strangers, and accept that this small town could be the place where she finally belongs?

One small town. Three lost women. And a lifetime of secrets.

The Cottage at Rosella Cove

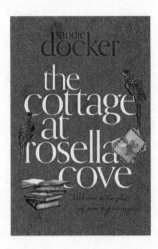

Why had the house stayed empty so long? Why had it never been sold?

LOST
Nicole has left her city life for the sleepy town of Rosella Cove, renting the old cottage by the water. She plans to keep to herself – but when she uncovers a hidden box of wartime love letters, she realises she's not the first person living in this cottage to hide secrets and pain.

FOUND
Ivy's quiet life in Rosella Cove is tainted by the events of World War II, with ramifications felt for many years to come. But one night a drifter appears and changes everything. Perhaps his is the soul she's meant to save.

FORGOTTEN
Charlie is too afraid of his past to form any lasting ties in the cove. He knows he must make amends for his tragic deeds long ago, but he can't do it alone. Maybe the new tenant in the cottage will help him fulfil a promise and find the redemption he isn't sure he deserves.

Welcome to the cottage at Rosella Cove, where three damaged souls meet and have the chance to rewrite their futures.

'The best of the best of heart-wrenching yarns . . .' *Woman's Day*

The Banksia Bay Beach Shack

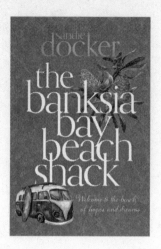

A year is a long time in the memory of a small town. Stories get twisted, truths become warped, history is rewritten.

MYSTERIES

When Laura discovers an old photo of her grandmother, Lillian, with an intriguing inscription on the back, she heads to the sleepy seaside town of Banksia Bay to learn the truth of Lillian's past. But when she arrives, Laura finds a community where everyone seems to be hiding something.

SECRETS

Virginia, owner of the iconic Beach Shack café, has kept her past buried for sixty years. As Laura slowly uncovers the tragic fragments of that summer so long ago, Virginia must decide whether to hold on to her secrets or set the truth free.

LIES

Young Gigi and Lily come from different worlds but forge an unbreakable bond – the 'Sisters of Summer'. But in 1961 a chain of events is set off that reaches far into the future. One lie told. One lie to set someone free. One lie that changes the course of so many lives.

Welcome to the Banksia Bay Beach Shack, where first love is found and last chances are taken.

Discover a
new favourite